'So, so, so great – epic fantasy, epic adventure, epic friendship'

Kate Elliott

'Dynamic storytelling and a fully imagined magical world . . . Dennard's rich descriptions, insightful characterizations and breathtaking action sequences will keep readers on their toes' *Publishers Weekly*

'Two devoted friends dreaming of independence contend with unfathomable magic and the schemes of empires in this action-packed series opener . . . Epic adventure and steamy smooches make for a crowd-pleasing formula' *Kirkus*

'Safi and Iseult share a believable bond, and it's great to read a fantasy book where sisterhood and no-nonsense women take the lead . . . triumphantly fun, *Truthwitch* casts off the current trend for gritty fantasy with a joyous laugh and a cheeky wink' *SFX*

'A fantasy saga for the feminist generation' *Hypable*

'This is a great example of a rollicking, swashbuckling adventure . . . just the thing if you'd like to be swept away from real life for a while' *The Book Bag*

Truthwitch

Before she settled down as a full-time novelist and writing instructor, Susan Dennard travelled the world as a marine biologist. She is the author of the Something Strange and Deadly series as well as the Witchlands novels. When not writing, she can be found hiking with her dogs, exploring tidal pools, or earning bruises at the dojo.

To find out more about *Truthwitch* and the Witchlands novels, please visit **thewitchlands.com**.

Truthwitch

The Witchlands Series: Book One

Susan Dennard

TOR

First published 2016 by Tom Doherty Associates, LLC

This paperback edition published 2017 by Tor
an imprint of Pan Macmillan
20 New Wharf Road, London N1 9RR
Associated companies throughout the world
www.panmacmillan.com

ISBN 978-1-4472-8206-8

1 3 5 7 9 8 6 4 2

A CIP catalogue record for this book is available from the British Library.

Typeset by Ellipsis Digital Limited, Glasgow
Printed and bound by CPI Group (UK) Ltd, Croydon, CR0 4YY

FOR MY THREADSISTER, SARAH

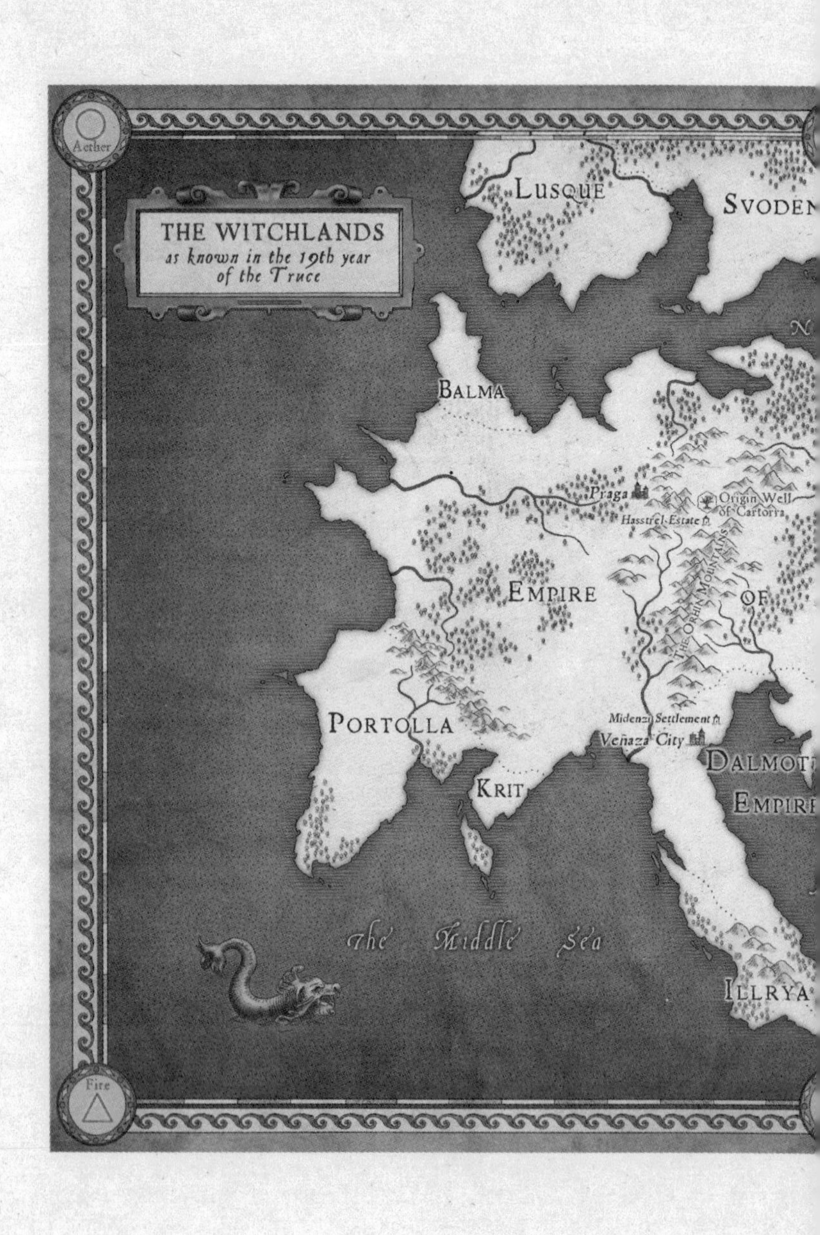
THE WITCHLANDS
as known in the 19th year
of the Truce
Aether
Fire
LUSQUE
SVODEN
BALMA
Praga
Origin Well
of Cartorra
Hasstrel Estate
THE ORHIN MOUNTAINS
EMPIRE
OF
PORTOLLA
Midenzi Settlement
Veñaza City
DALMOT
EMPIR
KRIT
The Middle Sea
ILLRYA

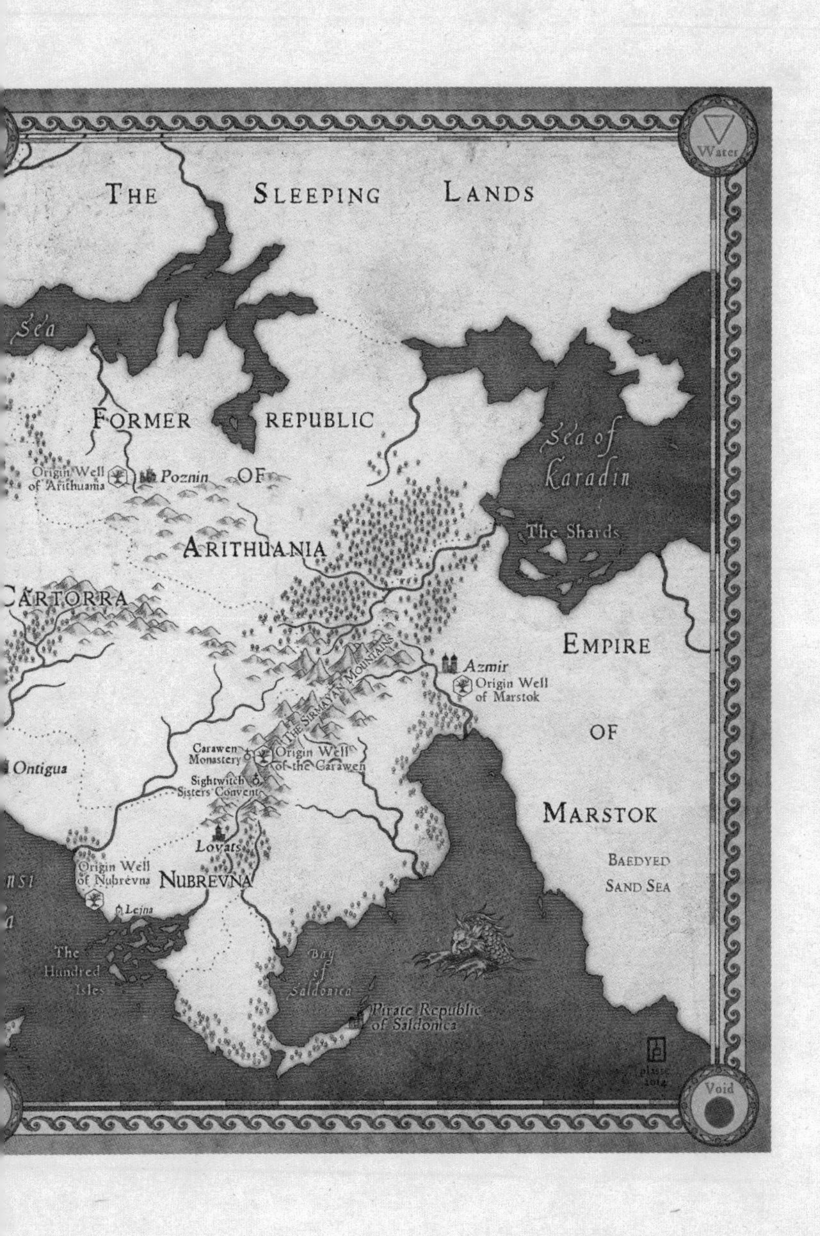

Water
THE SLEEPING LANDS
Sea
FORMER REPUBLIC OF ARITHUANIA
Origin Well of Arithuania
Poznin
Sea of Karadin
The Shards
CARTORRA
EMPIRE OF MARSTOK
Azmir
Origin Well of Marstok
THE SIRMAYAN MOUNTAINS
Carawen Monastery
Origin Well of the Carawen
Ontigua
Sightwitch Sisters Convent
Lovats
Origin Well of Nubrevna
NUBREVNA
Lejna
The Hundred Isles
Bay of Saldonica
Pirate Republic of Saldonica
BAEDYED SAND SEA
Void

Truthwitch

ONE

Everything had gone horribly wrong.

None of Safiya fon Hasstrel's hastily laid plans for this holdup were unfolding as they ought.

First, the black carriage with the gleaming gold standard was *not* the target Safi and Iseult had been waiting for. Worse, this cursed carriage was accompanied by eight rows of city guards blinking midday sun from their eyes.

Second, there was absolutely nowhere for Safi and Iseult to go. Up on their limestone outcropping, the dusty road below was the only path to Veñaza City. And just as this thrust of gray rock overlooked the road, the road overlooked nothing but turquoise sea forever. It was seventy feet of cliff pounded by rough waves and even rougher winds.

And third—the real kick in the kidneys—was that as soon as the guards marched over the girls' buried trap and the firepots within exploded . . . Well, then those guards would be scouring every inch of the cliffside.

"Hell-gates, Iz." Safi snapped down her spyglass. "There are four guards in each row. Eight times four makes . . ." Her face scrunched up. *Fifteen, sixteen, seventeen . . .*

"It's thirty-two," Iseult said blandly.

"Thirty-two thrice-damned guards with thirty-two thrice-damned crossbows."

Iseult only nodded and eased back the hood of her brown cape. The sun lit up her face. She was the perfect contrast to Safi: midnight hair to Safi's wheat, moon skin to Safi's tan, and hazel eyes to Safi's blue.

Hazel eyes that were now sliding to Safi as Iseult plucked away the spyglass. "I hate to say 'I told you so'—"

"Then don't."

"—but," Iseult finished, "everything he said to you last night was a lie. He was most certainly *not* interested in a simple card game." Iseult ticked off two gloved fingers. "He was *not* leaving town this morning by the northern highway. And I bet"—a third finger unfurled—"his name wasn't even Caden."

Caden. If . . . no, *when* Safi found that Chiseled Cheater, she was going to break every bone in his perfect rutting face.

Safi groaned and banged her head against the rock. She'd lost all of her money to him. Not just some, but *all.*

Last night had hardly been the first time Safi had bet all of her—and Iseult's—savings on a card game. It wasn't as if she ever lost, for, as the saying went, *You can't trick a Truthwitch.*

Plus, the winnings off *one round alone* from the highest-stake taro game in Veñaza City would have bought Safi and Iseult a place of their own. No more living in an attic for Iseult, no more stuffy Guildmaster's guest room for Safi.

But as Lady Fate would have it, Iseult hadn't been able to join Safi at the game—her heritage had banned her from the highbrow inn where the game had taken place. And without her Threadsister beside her, Safi was prone to . . . *mistakes.*

Particularly mistakes of the strong-jawed, snide-tongued variety who plied Safi with compliments that somehow slipped right past her Truthwitchery. In fact, she hadn't sensed a lying bone in Chiseled Cheater's body when she'd collected her winnings from the in-house bank . . . Or when Chiseled Cheater had hooked his arm in hers and guided her into the warm night . . . Or when he'd leaned in for a chaste yet *wildly* heady kiss on the cheek.

I will never gamble again, she swore, her heel drumming on the limestone. *And I will never flirt again.*

"If we're going to run for it," Iseult said, interrupting Safi's thoughts, "then we need to do so before the guards reach our trap."

"You don't say." Safi glared at her Threadsister, who watched the incoming guards through the spyglass. Wind kicked at Iseult's dark hair, lifting the wispy bits that had fallen from her braid. A distant gull cried its obnoxious *scree, scr-scree, scr-scree!*

Safi hated gulls; they always shit on her head.

"More guards," Iseult murmured, the waves almost drowning out her words. But then louder, she said, "Twenty more guards coming from the north."

For half a moment, Safi's breath choked off. Now, even if she and Iseult could somehow face the thirty-two guards accompanying the carriage, the other twenty guards would be upon them before they could escape.

Safi's lungs burst back to life with a vengeance. Every curse she'd ever learned rolled off her tongue.

"We're down to two options," Iseult cut in, scooting back to Safi's side. "We either turn ourselves in—"

"Over my grandmother's rotting corpse," Safi spat.

"—or we try to reach the guards before they trigger the trap. Then all we have to do is brazen our way through."

Safi glanced at Iseult. As always, her Threadsister's face was impassive. Blank. The only part of her that showed stress was her long nose—it twitched every few seconds.

"Once we're through," Iseult added, drawing her hood back into place and casting her face in darkness, "we'll follow the usual plan. Now hurry."

Safi didn't need to be told to hurry—*obviously* she would hurry—but she bit back her retort. Iseult was, yet again, saving their hides.

Besides, if Safi had to hear one more *I told you so,* she'd throttle her Threadsister and leave her carcass to the hermit crabs.

Iseult's feet hit the gritty road, and as Safi descended nimbly beside her, dust plumed around her boots—and inspiration struck.

"Wait, Iz." In a flurry of movement, Safi swung off her cape. Then with a quick *slash-rip-slash* of her parrying knife, she cut off the hood. "Skirt and kerchief. We'll be less threatening as peasants."

Iseult's eyes narrowed. Then she dropped to the road. "But then our faces will be more obvious. Rub on as much dirt as you can." As Iseult scrubbed her face, turning it a muddy brown, Safi wound the hood over her hair and wrapped the cape around her waist. Once she'd tucked the brown cloak into her belt, careful to hide her scabbards beneath, she too slathered dirt and mud over her cheeks.

In less than a minute, both girls were ready. Safi ran a quick, scrutinizing eye over Iseult . . . but the disguise was good. Good *enough*. Her Threadsister looked like a peasant in desperate need of a bath.

With Iseult just behind, Safi launched into a quick clip around the limestone corner, her breath held tight . . . Then she exhaled sharply, her pace never slowing. The guards were still thirty paces from the buried firepots.

Safi flashed a bumbling wave at a mustached guard in the front. He lifted his hand, and the other guards came to an abrupt stop. Then, one by one, each guard's crossbow leveled on the girls.

Safi pretended not to notice, and when she reached the pile of gray pebbles that marked the trap, she cleared it with the slightest hop. Behind her, Iseult made the same, almost imperceptible leap.

Then the mustached man—clearly the leader—raised his own crossbow. "Halt."

Safi complied, letting her feet drag to a stop—while also covering as much ground as she could. "*Onga?*" she asked, the Arithuanian word for *yes*. After all, if they were going to be peasants, they might as well be *immigrant* peasants.

"Do you speak Dalmotti?" the leader asked, looking first at Safi. Then at Iseult.

Iseult came to a clumsy stop beside Safiya. "We spwik.

A litttttle." It was easily the worst attempt at an Arithuanian accent that Safiya had ever heard from Iseult's mouth.

"We are . . . in trouble?" Safi lifted her hands in a universally submissive gesture. "We only go to Veñaza City."

Iseult gave a dramatic cough, and Safi wanted to throttle her. No wonder Iz was always the cutpurse and Safi the distraction. Her Threadsister was *awful* at acting.

"We want a city healer," Safi rushed to say before Iseult could muster another unbelievable cough. "In case she has the plague. Our mother died from it, you see, and *ohhhh,* how she coughed in those final days. There was so much blood—"

"Plague?" the guard interrupted.

"Oh, yes." Safi nodded knowingly. "My sister is very ill."

Iseult heaved another cough—but this one was so convincing, Safi actually flinched . . . and then hobbled to her. "Oh, you need a healer. Come, come. Let your sister help you."

The guard turned back to his men, already dismissing the girls, already bellowing orders: "Back in formation! Resume march!"

Gravel crunched; footsteps drummed. The girls trudged onward, passing guards with wrinkled noses. No one wanted Iseult's "plague" it would seem.

Safi was just towing Iseult past the black carriage when its door popped wide. A saggy old man leaned his scarlet-clad torso outside. His wrinkles shook in the wind.

It was the leader of the Gold Guild, a man named Yotiluzzi, whom Safi had seen from afar—at last night's establishment, no less.

The old Guildmaster clearly didn't recognize Safi, though, and after a cursory glance, he lifted his reedy voice. "Aeduan! Get this foreign filth away from me!"

A figure in white stalked around the carriage's back wheel. His cape billowed, and though a hood shaded his face, there was no hiding the knife baldric across his chest or the sword at his waist.

He was a Carawen monk—a mercenary trained to kill since childhood.

Safi froze, and without thinking, she eased her arm away from Iseult, who twisted silently behind her. The guards would reach the girls' trap at any moment, and this was their ready position: *Initiate. Complete.*

"Arithuanians," the monk said. His voice was rough, but not with age—with underuse. "From what village?" He strolled a single step toward Safi.

She had to fight the urge not to cower back. Her Truthwitchery was suddenly bursting with discomfort—a grating sensation, as if skin were being scratched off the back of her neck.

And it wasn't his words that set Safi's magic to flaring. It was his presence. This monk was young, yet there was something *off* about him. Something too ruthless—too dangerous—to ever be trusted.

He pulled back his hood, revealing a pale face and close-cropped brown hair. Then, as the monk sniffed the air near Safi's head, red swirled around his pupils.

Safi's stomach turned to stone.

Bloodwitch.

This monk was a rutting Bloodwitch. A creature from

the myths, a being who could smell a person's blood—smell their very witchery—and track it across entire continents. If he latched on to Safi's or Iseult's scent, then they were in deep, *deep*—

Pop-pop-pop!

Gunpowder burst inside firepots. The guards had hit the trap.

Safi acted instantly—as did the monk. His sword swished from its scabbard; her knife came up. She clipped the edge of his blade, parrying it aside.

He recovered and lunged. Safi lurched back. Her calves hit Iseult, yet in a single fluid movement, Iseult kneeled—and Safi rolled sideways over her back.

Initiate. Complete. It was how the girls fought. How they lived.

Safi unfurled from her flip and withdrew her sword just as Iseult's moon scythes clinked free. Far behind them, more explosions thundered out. Shouts rose up, the horses kicked and whinnied.

Iseult spun for the monk's chest. He jumped backward and skipped onto the carriage wheel. Yet where Safi had expected a moment of distraction, she only got the monk diving at her from above.

He was good. The best fighter she'd ever faced.

But Safi and Iseult were better.

Safi swooped out of reach just as Iseult wheeled into the monk's path. In a blur of spinning steel, her scythes sliced into his arms, his chest, his gut—and then, like a tornado, she was past.

And Safi was waiting. Watching for what couldn't be

real and yet clearly was: every cut on the monk's body was healing before her eyes.

There was no doubt now—this monk was a thrice-damned Bloodwitch straight from Safi's darkest nightmares. So she did the only thing she could conjure: she threw her parrying knife directly at the monk's chest.

It thunked through his rib cage and embedded deep in his heart. He stumbled forward, hitting his knees—and his red eyes locked on Safi's. His lips curled back. With a snarl, he wrenched the knife from his chest. The wound spurted . . .

And began to heal over.

But Safi didn't have time for another strike. The guards were doubling back. The Guildmaster was screaming from within his carriage, and the horses were charging into a frantic gallop.

Iseult darted in front of Safi, scythes flying fast and beating two arrows from the air. Then, for a brief moment, the carriage blocked the girls from the guards. Only the Bloodwitch could see them, and though he reached for his knives, he was too slow. Too drained from the magic of healing.

Yet he was smiling—*smiling*—as if he knew something that Safi didn't. As if he could and *would* hunt her down to make her pay for this.

"Come on!" Iseult yanked at Safi's arm, pulling her into a sprint toward the cliffside.

At least this was part of their plan. At least this they had practiced so often they could do it with their eyes closed.

Just as the first crossbow bolts pounded the road behind

them, the girls reached a waist-high boulder on the ocean side of the road.

They plunked their blades back into scabbards. Then in two leaps, Safi was over the rock—and Iseult too. On the other side, the cliff ran straight down to thundering white waves.

Two ropes waited, affixed to a stake pounded deep into the earth. With far more speed and force than was ever intended for this escape, Safi snatched up her rope, hooked her foot in a loop at the end, gripped a knot at head level . . .

And jumped.

TWO

Air whizzed past Safi's ears and up her nose as she sprang out . . . down toward white waves . . . away from the seventy-foot cliff . . .

Until Safi reached the rope's end. With a sharp yank that shattered through her body and tore into her gripping hands, she flew at the barnacle-covered cliffside.

This was about to hurt.

She hit with a crash, teeth ramming her tongue. Pain sizzled through her body. Limestone cut her arms, her face, her legs. She snapped out her hands to grip the cliff—just as Iseult slammed into the rocks beside her.

"Ignite," Safi grunted. The word that triggered the rope's magic was lost in the roar of ocean waves—but the command hit its mark. In a flash of white flame that shot up faster than eyes could travel, their ropes ignited . . .

And disintegrated. A fine ash kicked away on the wind. A few specks settled on the girls' kerchiefs, their shoulders.

"Arrows!" Iseult roared, flattening herself against the rock as bolts zipped past. Some skittered off the rocks, some sank into waves.

One sliced through Safi's skirt. Then she'd managed to dig her toes in cracks, grab for handholds, and scramble sideways. Her muscles trembled and strained until at last, she and Iseult had ducked beneath a slight overhang. Until at *last,* they could pause and let the arrows fall harmlessly around them.

The rocks were wet, the barnacles vicious, and water swept at the girls' ankles. Salty drops battered over and over. Until eventually the arrows stopped falling.

"Are they coming?" Safi rasped at Iseult.

Iseult shook her head. "They're still there. I can feel their Threads waiting."

Safi blinked, trying to get the salt from her eyes. "We're going to have to swim, aren't we?" She rubbed her face on her shoulder; it didn't help. "Think you can make it to the lighthouse?" Both girls were strong swimmers—but strong didn't matter in waves that could pummel a dolphin.

"We don't have a choice," Iseult said. She glanced at Safi with a fierceness that always made Safi feel stronger. "We can toss our skirts left, and while the guards shoot those, we dive right."

Safi nodded, and with a grimace, she angled her body so she could remove her skirt. Once both girls had their brown skirts free, Iseult's arm reared back.

"Ready?" she asked.

"Ready." Safi heaved. The skirt flew out from beneath the overhang—Iseult's right behind it.

And then both girls stepped away from the rock face and sank beneath the waves.

* * *

As Iseult det Midenzi wriggled free from her sea-soaked tunic, boots, pants, and finally underclothes, everything hurt. Every peeled-off layer revealed ten new slices from the limestone and barnacles, and each burst of spindrift made her aware of ten more.

This ancient, crumbling lighthouse was effective for hiding, but it was inescapable until the tide went out. For now, the water outside was well above Iseult's chest, and hopefully that depth—as well as the crashing waves between here and the marshy shoreline—would deter the Bloodwitch from following.

The interior of the lighthouse was no larger than Iseult's attic bedroom over Mathew's coffee shop. Sunlight beamed in through algae-slimed windows, and wind tugged sea foam through the arched door.

"I'm sorry," Safi said, her voice muffled as she squirmed from her sodden tunic. Then her shirt was completely off, and she tossed it on a windowsill. Safi's usually tanned skin was pale beneath her freckles.

"Don't apologize." Iseult gathered her own discarded clothes. "I'm the one who told you about the card game in the first place."

"This is true," Safi replied, her voice shaking as she hopped on one foot and tried to remove her pants—with her boots still on. She always did that, and it boggled Iseult's mind that an eighteen-year-old could still be too impatient to undress herself properly. "But," Safi added, "*I'm* the one who wanted the nicer rooms. If we'd just bought that place two weeks ago—"

"Then we'd have rats for roommates," Iseult interrupted.

She shuffled to the nearest water-free, sunlit patch of floor. "You were right to want a different place. It costs more, but it would've been worth it."

"*Would've been* being the key words." With a loud grunt, Safi finally wrestled free of her pants. "There'll be no place of our own now, Iz. I bet every guard in Veñaza City is out looking for us. Not to mention the . . ." For a moment, Safi stared at her boots. Then, in a frantic movement, she tore off the right one. "So will the Bloodwitch."

Blood. Witch. Blood. Witch. The words pulsed through Iseult in time to her heart. In time to her blood.

Iseult had never seen a Bloodwitch before . . . or anyone with a magic linked to the Void. Voidwitches were just scary stories after all—they weren't *real*. They didn't guard Guildmasters and try to gut you with swords.

After wringing out her pants and smoothing each fold on a windowsill, Iseult shuffled to a leather satchel at the back of the lighthouse. She and Safi always stowed an emergency kit here before a heist, just in *case* the worst scenario unfolded.

Not that they'd held many heists before. Only every now and then for the lowlifes who deserved it.

Like those two apprentices who'd ruined one of Guildmaster Alix's silk shipments and tried to blame it on Safi.

Or those thugs who'd busted into Mathew's shop while he was away and stolen his silver cutlery.

Then there were those four separate occasions when Safi's taro card games had ended in brawls and missing coins. Justice had been required, of course—not to mention the reclamation of pilfered goods.

Today's encounter, though, was the first time the emergency satchel had actually been needed.

After rummaging past the spare clothes and a water bag, Iseult found two rags and a tub of lanolin. Then she hauled up the girls' discarded weapons and trudged back to Safi. "Let's clean our blades and come up with a plan. We have to get back to the city somehow."

Safi yanked off her second boot before accepting her sword and parrying knife. Both girls settled cross-legged on the rough floor, and Iseult sank into the familiar barnyard scent of the grease. Into the careful scrubbing motion of cleaning her scythes.

"What did the Bloodwitch's Threads look like?" Safi asked quietly.

"I didn't notice," Iseult murmured. "Everything happened so fast." She rubbed all the harder at the steel, protecting her beautiful Marstoki blades—gifts from Mathew's Heart-Thread, Habim—against rust.

A silence stretched through the stone ruins. The only sounds were the squeak of cloth on steel, the eternal crash of Jadansi waves.

Iseult knew she seemed unperturbed as she cleaned, but she was absolutely certain that her Threads twined with the same frightened shades as Safi's.

Iseult was a Threadwitch though, which meant she couldn't see her own Threads—or those of any other Threadwitch.

When her witchery had manifested at nine years old, Iseult's heart had felt like it would pound itself to dust. She was crumbling beneath the weight of a million Threads, none of which were her own. Everywhere she looked, she saw the Threads that build, the Threads that bind, and the Threads that break. Yet she could never see her own Threads or how *she* wove into the world.

So, just as every Nomatsi Threadwitch did, Iseult had learned to keep her body cool when it ought to be hot. To keep her fingers still when they ought to be trembling. To ignore the emotions that drove everyone else.

"I think," Safi said, scattering Iseult's thoughts, "the Bloodwitch knows I'm a Truthwitch."

Iseult's scrubbing paused. "Why," her voice was flat as the steel in her hands, "would you think that?"

"Because of the way he smiled at me." Safi shivered. "He smelled my magic, just like the tales say, and now he can hunt me."

"Which means he could be tracking us right now." Frost ran down Iseult's back. Jolted in her shoulders. She scoured at her blade all the harder.

Normally, the act of cleaning helped her find stasis. Helped her thoughts slow and her practicality rise to the surface. She was the natural tactician, while Safi was the one with the first sparks of an idea.

Initiate, complete.

Except no solutions came to Iseult right now. She and Safi could lie low and avoid city guards for a few weeks, but they couldn't hide from a Bloodwitch.

Especially if that Bloodwitch knew what Safi was—and could sell her to the highest bidder.

When a person stood directly before Safi, she could tell truth from lie, reality from deception. And as far as Iseult had learned in her tutoring sessions with Mathew, the last recorded Truthwitch had died a century ago—beheaded by a Marstoki emperor for allying herself with a Cartorran queen.

If Safi's magic ever became public knowledge, she would be used as a political tool . . .

Or eliminated as a political threat.

Safi's power was *that* valuable and *that* rare. Which was why, for Safi's entire life, she'd kept her magic secret. Like Iseult, she was a heretic: an unregistered witch. The back of Safi's right hand was unadorned, and no Witchmark tattoo proclaimed her powers. Yet one of these days, someone other than one of Safi's closest friends would figure out what she was, and when that day came, soldiers would storm the Silk Guildmaster's guest room and drag away Safi in chains.

Soon, the girls' blades were cleaned and resheathed, and Safi was pinning Iseult with one of her harder, more contemplative stares.

"Out with it," Iseult ordered.

"We may have to flee the city, Iz. Leave the Dalmotti Empire entirely."

Iseult rolled her salty lips together, trying not to frown. Trying not to feel.

The thought of abandoning Veñaza City . . . Iseult couldn't do it. The capital of the Dalmotti Empire was her *home*. The people in the Northern Wharf District had stopped noticing her pale Nomatsi skin or her angled Nomatsi eyes.

And it had taken her six and a half years to carve out that niche.

"For now," Iseult said quietly, "let's worry about getting into the city unseen—and let's pray, too, that the Bloodwitch didn't actually smell your blood." *Or your magic.*

Safi huffed a weary sigh and nestled into a beam of sunlight. It made her skin glow, her hair luminescent. "To whom should I pray?"

Iseult scratched at her nose, grateful to have the subject shift. "We were almost killed by a Carawen monk, so why not pray to the Origin Wells?"

Safi gave a little shudder. "If *that* person prays to the Origin Wells, then I don't want to. How about that Nubrevnan god? What's His name?"

"Noden."

"That's the one." Safi clasped her hands to her chest and stared up at the ceiling. "Noden, God of the Nubrevnan waves—"

"I think it's *all* waves, Safi. And everything else too."

Safi rolled her eyes. "God of *all* waves and everything else too, can you please make sure no one comes after us? Especially . . . *him.* Just keep *him* far away. And if you could keep the Veñaza City guards away too, that would be nice."

"This is easily the worst prayer I have ever heard," Iseult declared.

"Weasels piss on you, Iz. I'm not done yet." Safi heaved a sigh through her nose and then resumed her prayer. "Please return all of our money to me before he or Habim get back from their trip. And . . . that is all. Thank you very much, oh sacred Noden." Then, she hastily added,

"Oh, and please ensure that Chiseled Cheater gets exactly what he deserves."

Iseult almost snorted at that last request—except that a wave crashed into the lighthouse, sudden and rough against the stone. Water splattered Iseult's face. She swiped it away, agitated. Warm instead of cool.

"Please, Noden," she whispered, rubbing sea spray off her forehead. "Please just get us through this alive."

THREE

Reaching Mathew's coffee shop where Iseult lived proved harder than Safi had anticipated. She and Iseult were exhausted, hungry, and bruised to hell-flames, so even the basic act of walking made Safi want to groan. Or sit down. Or at least ease her aches with a hot bath and pastries.

But baths and pastries weren't happening anytime soon. Guards swarmed *everywhere* in Veñaza City, and by the time the girls had straggled into the Northern Wharf District, it was almost dawn. They'd spent half the night hiking blearily from their lighthouse to the capital and then the other half of the night slinking through alleys and clambering over kitchen gardens.

Every flash of white—every dangling piece of laundry, every torn sailcloth or tattered curtain—had punched Safi's stomach into her mouth. But it had never been the Bloodwitch, thank the gods, and right as night began fading into dawn, the sign to Mathew's coffee shop appeared. It poked out of a narrow road branching off the main wharf-side avenue.

REAL MARSTOKI COFFEE

BEST IN VEÑAZA CITY

It was not, in fact, real Marstoki coffee—Mathew wasn't even from the Empire of Marstok. Instead, the coffee was filtered and bland, catering to, as Habim always called it, "dull western palates."

Mathew's coffee was also *not* the best in the city. Even Mathew would admit that the dingy hole-in-the-wall in the Southern Wharf District had much better coffee. But up here on the northern edges of the capital, people didn't wander in for coffee. They came in for business.

The sort of business Wordwitches like Mathew excelled at—the trade of rumors and secrets, the planning of heists and cons. He ran coffee shops all across the Witchlands, and any news about *anything* always reached Mathew first.

It was his Wordwitchery that had made Mathew the best choice for Safi's tutor, since it allowed him to speak all tongues.

More important, though, Mathew's Heart-Thread, Habim, had worked for Safi's uncle her entire life—both as a man-at-arms and as a constantly displeased instructor. So when Safi had been sent south, it had only made sense for Mathew to take over where Habim had left off.

Not that Habim had completely abandoned Safi's training. He visited his Heart-Thread often in Veñaza City—and then proceeded to make Safi's life miserable with extra hours of speed drills or ancient battle strategies.

Safi reached the coffee shop first and after hopping a puddle of sewage that was frighteningly orange, she began tapping out the lock-spell on the front door—a recent installment since the stolen cutlery incident. Habim could complain to Mathew all he wanted about the cost of an Aetherwitched lock-spell, but as far as Safi could see, it was worth the money. Veñaza City had a hefty crime rate—first because it was a port, and second because wealthy Guildmasters were just *so* appealing to piestra-hungry lowlifes.

Of course, it was those same elected Guildmasters who also paid for an extensive, seemingly endless collection of city guards—one of whom was pausing right at the alley-way's mouth. He faced away, scanning the moored ships of the Northern Wharf District.

"Faster," Iseult muttered. She prodded Safi's back. "The guard is turning . . . turning . . ."

The door flew wide, Iseult shoved, and Safi toppled into the dark shop.

"What the rut?" she hissed, rounding on Iseult. "The guards *know* us around here!"

"Exactly," Iseult retorted, shutting the door and bolting the locks. "But from afar, we look like two peasants busting into a locked up coffee shop."

Safi mumbled an unwilling, "Good point," as Iseult stepped forward and whispered, "Alight."

At once twenty-six bewitched wicks guttered to life, revealing bright, curly Marstoki designs on the walls, the ceiling, the floor. It was overdone—too many rugs of clashing patterns leapt at Safi—but, like the coffee, westerners had a certain idea about how a Marstoki shop ought to look.

With the sigh of someone finally able to breathe, Iseult strode toward the spiral staircase in the back corner. Safi followed. Up, up they went, first to the second story, where Mathew and Habim lived. Next, to the slope-ceilinged attic that Iseult called home, its narrow space crowded with two cots and a wardrobe.

For six and a half years now, Iseult had lived and studied and worked here. After she'd fled her tribe, Mathew had been the only employer willing to hire and lodge a Nomatsi.

Iseult hadn't moved away since—though not for a lack of wanting to.

A place of my own.

Safi must've heard her Threadsister say that a thousand times. A hundred thousand times. And maybe if Safi had grown up sharing a bed with her mother in a one-room hut as Iseult had, then she'd want a wider, more private, more *personal* space as well.

Yet . . . Safi had ruined all of Iseult's plans. Every single saved piestra was gone, and all of the Veñaza City guards were actively hunting Safi and Iseult. It was literally the worst-case scenario possible, and no emergency satchel or hiding in a lighthouse was going to get them through this mess.

Gulping back nausea, Safi staggered to a window across the narrow room and shoved it open. Hot, fish-saturated air wafted in, familiar and soothing. With the sun just rising in the east, the clay rooftops of Veñaza City shone like orange flames.

It was beautiful, tranquil, and gods below, Safi *loved* that view. Having grown up in drafty ruins in the middle of the Orhin Mountains—having been locked away in the eastern wing whenever Uncle Eron was in one of his moods, Safi's life in the Hasstrel castle had been filled with broken windows and snow seeping in. With frozen winds and dank, slithering mold. Everywhere she looked, her eyes would land on carvings or paintings or tapestries of the Hasstrel mountain bat. A grotesque, dragon-like creature with the motto "Love and Dread" scrolling through its talons.

But the bridges and canals of Veñaza City were always sunbaked and smelling wonderfully of rotten fish. Mathew's shop was always bright and crowded. The wharves were always filled with sailors' deliciously offensive oaths.

Here, Safi felt warm. Here, she felt welcome, and sometimes, she even felt wanted.

Safi cleared her throat. Her hand fell from the latch, and she turned to find Iseult changing into a gown of olive green.

Iseult dipped her head to the wardrobe. "You can wear my extra day gown."

"That'll show these, though." Safi rolled up a salt-stiffened sleeve to reveal scrapes and bruises peppering her arms—all of which would be visible in the short, capped sleeves that were in style.

"Then it's lucky for you I still have . . ." Iseult swept two cropped black jackets from the wardrobe. "These!"

Safi's lips crooked up. The jackets were standard attire for all Guild apprentices—and these two in particular were trophies from the girls' first holdup.

"I still maintain," Safi declared, "that we should've taken more than just their jackets when we left them tied up in the storeroom."

"Yes, well, next time someone ruins a silk shipment and blames you, Saf, I promise we'll take more than just their jackets." Iseult tossed the black wool to Safi, who swooped it from the air.

As she hastily tore off her clothes, Iseult settled on the edge of her cot, lips pursed to one side. "I've been thinking," she began evenly. "If that Bloodwitch is really after us, then maybe the Silk Guildmaster could protect you. He's your technical guardian after all, and you do live in his guest room."

"I don't think he'll harbor a fugitive." Safi's face tightened with a wince. "It wouldn't be right to drag Guildmaster Alix into this anyway. He's always been so kind to me, and I'd hate to repay him with trouble."

"All right," Iseult said, her expression unchanging. "My next plan involves the Hell-Bards. They're in Veñaza City for the Truce Summit, right? To protect the Cartorran Empire? Maybe you could appeal to them for help since your uncle used to be one—and I doubt even the Dalmotti guards would be stupid enough to cross a Hell-Bard."

Safi's wince only deepened at that idea. "Uncle Eron was a dishonorably *discharged* Hell-Bard, Iz. The entire Hell-Bard Brigade now hates him, and Emperor Henrick hates him even more." She snorted, a disdainful sound that skittered off the walls and rattled in her belly. "To make it worse, the Emperor is looking for any excuse to hand over my title to one of his slimy sycophants. I'm sure that holding up a Guildmaster is sufficient reason to do so."

For most of Safi's childhood, her uncle had trained her like a soldier and treated her like one too—whenever he'd been sober enough to pay attention, at least. But when Safi had turned twelve, Emperor Henrick had decided it was time for Safi to come to the Cartorran capital for her education. *What does she know of leading farmers or organizing a harvest?* Henrick had bellowed at Uncle Eron, while Safi had waited, small and silent, behind him. *What experience does Safiya have running a household or paying tithes?*

It was that last concern—the paying of exorbitant Cartorran taxes—that had Emperor Henrick the most concerned. With all of the nobility wrapped around his ring-clad fingers, he wanted to ensure he had Safi ensnared too.

But Henrick's attempt to nab one more loyal domna had fallen apart, for Uncle Eron hadn't sent Safi to study in Praga with all the other young nobles. Instead, Eron had packed her off to the south, to the Guildmasters and tutors of Veñaza City.

It was the first and *last* time Safi had ever felt anything like gratitude for her uncle.

"In that case," Iseult said, tone final and shoulders sagging, "I think we'll have to leave the city. We can hole up . . . somewhere until all of this blows over."

Safi bit her lip. Iseult made it sound so easy to "hole up somewhere," but the reality was that Iseult's clear Nomatsi ancestry made her a target wherever she went.

The one time the girls had tried leaving Veñaza City, to visit a friend nearby, they'd barely made it back home.

Of course, the three men in the tavern who'd decided to attack Iseult had never made it back home at all. At least not with intact femurs.

Safi stomped to the wardrobe and wrenched it open, pretending the handle was the Chiseled Cheater's nose. If she ever—*ever*—saw that bastard again, she was going to break every bone in his blighted body.

"Our best bet," Iseult went on, "will be the Southern Wharf District. The Dalmotti trade ships are berthed there, and we might be able to get passage in exchange for work. Do you need anything from Guildmaster Alix's?"

At Safi's headshake, Iseult continued. "Good. Then we'll leave notes for Habim and Mathew explaining everything. Then . . . I guess we'll . . . leave."

Safi stayed silent as she towed out a golden gown. Her throat was too tight for words. Her stomach spinning too hard.

It was then, as Safi fastened the ten million wooden buttons and Iseult tied a pale gray scarf around her head, that a knocking burst out through the shop.

"Veñaza City Guard!" came a muffled voice. "Open up! We saw you break in!"

Iseult sighed—a sound of such long, *long* suffering.

"I know," Safi growled, sliding the last button in place. "You told me so."

"Just so long as you're aware."

"Like you'll ever let me forget?"

Iseult's lips twitched with a smile, but it was a false

attempt—and Safi didn't need her Truthwitchery to see that.

As the girls tugged on their scratchy apprentice jackets, the guard started his bellowing again. "Open up! There's only one way in or out of this shop!"

"Not true," Safi inserted.

"We won't hesitate to use force!"

"And nor will *we*." At a nod from her Threadsister, Safi scooted to Iseult's bed. Then they both dragged the cot toward the door. Wooden feet groaned, and soon enough they had it heaved on its side to form a barricade—one they knew worked well, for this was hardly the first time Safi and Iseult had been forced to sneak out.

Although it had always been Mathew and Habim bellowing on the other side. Not armed guards.

Moments later, Safi and Iseult stood at the window, breathing fast and listening as the front door smashed inward. As the entire shop quaked and glass shattered.

Cringing, Safi clambered onto the roof. First she'd lost all her money, and now she'd ruined Mathew's shop. Maybe . . . maybe it was a *good* thing her tutors were out of town on business. At least she wouldn't have to face Mathew or Habim anytime soon.

Iseult scrabbled out beside Safi, the emergency satchel on her back bulging with supplies. Iseult's weapons fit into calf-scabbards beneath her skirt, but Safi could only stow her parrying knife in her boot. Her sword—her *beautiful* folded steel sword—was staying behind.

"Where to?" Safi asked, knowing her Threadsister had a route spinning behind those glittering eyes.

"We'll head inland, as if we're going to Guildmaster Alix's, and then aim south."

"Rooftops?"

"For as long as we can. You lead the way."

Safi nodded curtly before kicking into a run—west, toward the inner heart of Veñaza City—and when she reached the edge of Mathew's roof, she leaped for the next slope of shingles.

She *slammed* down. Pigeons burst upward, wings flapping to get out of the way, and then Iseult bounded down beside her.

But Safi was already moving, already flying for the next roof. And the next roof after that, on and on with Iseult right behind.

Iseult slunk along the cobblestoned street, Safi two steps ahead. The girls had veered inland from the coffee shop, crossing canals and looping back over bridges to avoid city guards. Fortunately, morning traffic had begun—a teeming mass of fruit-laden carts, donkeys, goats, and people of all races and nationalities. Threads with colors as varied as their owners' skins swirled lazily through the heat.

Safi skipped in front of a swine cart, leaving Iseult to chase after her. Then it was around a beggar, past a group of Purists shouting about the sins of magic, and then directly through a herd of unhappy sheep before the girls reached a clogged mass of unmoving traffic. Ahead, Threads swirled with red annoyance at the holdup.

Iseult imagined her own Threads were just as red. The

girls were *so* close to the Southern Wharf District that Iseult could even see the hundreds of white-sailed ships berthed ahead.

But she embraced the frustration. Other emotions—ones she didn't want to name and that no decent Threadwitch would ever allow to the surface—shivered in her chest. *Stasis,* she told herself, just as her mother had taught her years ago. *Stasis in your fingertips and your toes.*

Soon, the Threads of traffic flickered with cyan understanding. The color moved like a snake across a pond, as if the crowds were learning, one by one, the reason for this traffic jam.

Back, back the color moved until at last an old biddy near the girls squawked, "What? A blockade up ahead? But I'll miss the freshest crabs!"

Iseult's gut turned icy—and Safi's Threads flashed with gray fear.

"Hell-gates," she hissed. "Now what, Iz?"

"More brazening, I think." With a grunt and shifting of her weight, Iseult fished out a thick gray tome from her pack. "We'll look like two very studious apprentices if we're carrying books. You can take *A Brief History of Dalmotti Autonomy.*"

"Brief my *behind,*" Safi muttered, though she did accept the enormous book. Next, Iseult hauled out a blue hidebound volume titled *An Illustrated Guide to the Carawen Monastery.*

"Oh, now I see why you have these." Safi lifted her eyebrows, daring Iseult to argue. "They aren't for disguise at all. You just didn't want to leave behind your favorite book."

"And?" Iseult sniffed dismissively. "Does this mean you don't want to carry that?"

"No, no. I'll keep it." Safi popped her chin high. "Just promise that you'll let *me* do all the acting once we reach the guards."

"Act away, Saf." Grinning to herself, Iseult tugged her scarf low. It was soaked through with sweat, but it still shaded her face. Her skin. Then she adjusted her gloves until not an inch of wrist was visible. All the focus would be on Safi and would *stay* on Safi.

For as Mathew always said, *With your right hand, give a person what he expects—and with your left hand, cut his purse.* Safi always played the distracting right hand—and she was good at it—while Iseult lurked in the shadows, ready to claim whatever purse needed cutting.

As Iseult settled into a boiling wait, she creaked back her book's thick cover. Ever since a monk had helped Iseult when she was a little girl, Iseult had been somewhat . . . well, *obsessed* was the word Safi always used. But it wasn't just gratitude that had left Iseult fascinated by the Carawens—it was their pure robes and gleaming opal earrings. Their deadly training and sacred vows.

Life at the Carawen monastery seemed so simple. So contained. No matter one's heritage, one could join and have instant acceptance. Instant respect.

It was a feeling Iseult could scarcely imagine yet her heart beat hungrily every time she thought of it.

The book's pages rustled open to page thirty-seven—to where a bronze piestra shone up at her. She had wedged the coin there to mark her last page, and its winged lion seemed almost to laugh at her.

The first piestra toward our new life, Iseult thought. Then her eyes flickered over the ornate Dalmotti script on the page. Descriptions and images of different Carawen monks scrolled across it, the first of which was *Mercenary Monk,* its illustration all knives and sword and stony expression.

It looked just like the Bloodwitch.

Blood. Witch. Blood. Witch.

Ice pooled in Iseult's belly at the memory of his red eyes, his bared teeth. Ice . . . and something hollower. Heavier.

Disappointment, she finally pinpointed, for it seemed so vastly wrong that a monster such as he should be allowed into the monastery's ranks.

Iseult glanced at the caption beneath the illustration, as if this might offer some explanation. Yet all she read was, *Trained to fight abroad in the name of the Cahr Awen.*

Iseult's breath slid out at that word—*Cahr Awen*—and her chest stretched tight. As a girl, she'd spent hours, climbing trees and pretending *she* was one of the Cahr Awen—that *she* was one of the two witches born from the Origin Wells who could cleanse even the darkest evils.

But just as many of the springs feeding the Wells had been dead for centuries, no new Cahr Awen had been born in almost five hundred years—and Iseult's fantasies had inevitably ended with gangs of village children. They would swarm whatever tree she'd clambered into, shouting up curses and hate that they'd learned from their parents. *A Threadwitch who can't make Threadstones doesn't belong here!*

Iseult had always known in those moments—as she hugged a tree branch tight and *prayed* that her mother would find her soon—that the Cahr Awen was nothing more than a pretty story.

Gulping, Iseult heaved aside those memories. This day was bad enough; no need to dredge up old miseries too. Besides, she and Safi were almost to the guards now, and Habim's oldest lesson was whispering at the back of her mind.

Evaluate your opponents, he always said. *Analyze your terrain. Choose your battlefields when you can.*

"Single-file lines!" the guards called. "Any weapons must be out where we can see them!"

Iseult clapped her book shut in a *whoof!* of musty air. *Ten guards,* she counted. *Spread out across the road with carts stacked behind them to block the crowd. Crossbows. Cutlasses.* If this little interrogation didn't go well, then there was no way the girls could fight their way through.

"All right," Safi muttered. "It's our turn. Keep your face hidden."

Iseult did as ordered and sank into position behind Safi—who marched imperiously up to the first sour-faced guard.

"What is the meaning of this?" Safi's words rang out, clear and clipped over the constant din of traffic. "We are now *late* to our meeting with the Wheat Guildmaster. Do you know what his temper is like?"

The guard's face settled into a bored glower—but his Threads flashed with keen interest. "Names."

"Safiya. And this is my lady-in-waiting, Iseult."

Though the guard's expression remained unimpressed, his Threads flared with more interest. He angled away, motioning for a second guard to loom in close, and Iseult had to bite her tongue to keep from warning Safi.

"I *demand* to know what this holdup is for!" Safi cried at the new guard, a giant of a man.

"We're lookin' for two girls," he rumbled. "They're wanted for highway robbery. I don't suppose you have any weapons on you?"

"Do I look like the sort of girl to carry a weapon?"

"Then you won't mind if we search you."

To Safi's credit, none of the fear in her Threads showed on her face, and she only lifted her chin higher. "I most certainly *do* mind, and if you so much as touch my person, then I will have you fired immediately. All of you!" She thrust out her book, and the first guard flinched. "At this time tomorrow, you'll be on the streets and wishing you hadn't messed with a Guildmaster's apprentice—"

Safi didn't get to finish her threat, for at that moment, a gull screamed overhead . . . and a splattering of white goo landed on her shoulder.

Her Threads flashed to turquoise surprise. "No," she breathed, eyes bulging. "*No.*"

The guards' eyes bulged too, their Threads now shimmering into a giddy pink.

They erupted with laughter. Then they started pointing, and even Iseult had to clap a gloved hand to her mouth. *Don't laugh, don't laugh—*

She started laughing, and Safi's Threads blazed into red fury. "Why?" she squawked at Iseult. Then at the guards,

"Why always *me*? There are a thousand shoulders for a gull to crap on, but they always pick *me*!"

The guards were doubled over now, and the second one lifted a limp hand. "Go. Just . . . go." Tears streamed from his eyes—which only served to make Safi snarl as she stomped past. "Why don't you do something useful with your time? Instead of laughing at girls in distress, go *fight crime* or something!"

Then Safi was through the checkpoint and racing for the nearest fat-hulled trade ships—with Iseult right on her heels and giggling the entire way.

FOUR

Merik Nihar's fingers curled around the butter knife. The Cartorran domna across the wide oak dining table had a hairy chin with chicken grease oozing down it.

As if sensing Merik's gaze, the domna lifted a beige napkin and dabbed at her wrinkled lips and puckered chin.

Merik hated her—just as he hated every other diplomat here. He might've spent years mastering his family's famous temper, yet all it would take at this point was one more grain. One more grain of salt, and the ocean would flood.

Throughout the long dining room, voices hummed in at least ten different languages. The Continental Truce Summit would begin tomorrow to discuss the Great War and the close of the Twenty Year Truce. It had brought hundreds of diplomats from across the Witchlands to Veñaza City.

Dalmotti might have been the smallest of the three empires, but it was the most powerful in trade. And since it was neatly situated between the Empire of Marstok in the east and the Cartorran Empire to the west, it was the perfect place for these international negotiations.

Merik was here to represent Nubrevna, his homeland. He'd actually arrived three weeks earlier, hoping to open new trade—or perhaps reestablish old Guild connections. But it had been a complete waste of time.

Merik's eyes flicked from the old noblewoman to the enormous expanse of glass behind her. The gardens of the Doge's palace shone beyond, suffusing the room in a greenish glow and the scent of hanging jasmine. As elected leader of the Dalmotti Council, the Doge had no family—no Guildmasters in Dalmotti did since families were said to distract them from their devotion to the Guilds—so it wasn't as if he *needed* a garden that could hold twelve of Merik's ships.

"You are admiring the glass wall?" asked the ginger-haired leader of the Silk Guild, seated on Merik's right. "It is quite a feat of our Earthwitches. It's all one pane, you know."

"Quite a feat, indeed," Merik said, though his tone suggested otherwise. "Although I wonder, Guildmaster Alix, if you've ever considered a more *useful* occupation for your Earthwitches."

The Guildmaster coughed lightly. "Our witches are highly specialized individuals. Why insist that an Earthwitch who is good with soil only work on a farm?"

"But there is a difference between a Soilwitch who *can* only work with soil and an Earthwitch who *chooses* to only work with soil. Or with melting sand into glass." Merik leaned back in his chair. "Take yourself, Guildmaster Alix. You are an Earthwitch, I presume? Likely your magic extends to animals, yet certainly it's not exclusive to *only* silkworms."

"Ah, but I am not an Earthwitch at all." Alix flipped his hand slightly, revealing his Witchmark: a circle for Aether and a dashed line that meant he specialized in art. "I am a tailor by trade. My magic lies in bringing a person's spirit to life in clothing."

"Of course," Merik answered flatly. The Silk Guildmaster had just proven Merik's point—not that the man seemed to notice. Why waste a magical skill with art on fashion? On a *single* type of fabric? Merik's own tailor had done a plenty fine job with the linen suit he now wore—no magic necessary.

A long, silver-gray frock coat covered a cream shirt, and though both pieces had more buttons than ought to be legal, Merik liked the suit. His fitted black breeches were tucked into squeaking, new boots, and the wide belt at his hips was more than mere decoration. Once Merik was back on his ship, he would refasten his cutlass and pistols.

Clearly sensing Merik's displeasure, Guildmaster Alix shifted his attention to the noblewoman on his other side. "What say you to Emperor Henrick's pending marriage, my lady?"

Merik's frown deepened. All anyone seemed interested in discussing at this luncheon was gossip and frivolities. There was a man in the former Republic of Arithuania—that wild, anarchical land to the north—who was uniting raider factions and calling himself "king," but did these imperial diplomats care?

Not at all.

There were rumors that the Hell-Bard Brigade was pressing witches into service, yet not one of these doms or domnas seemed to find this news alarming. Then again, Merik supposed it wasn't *their* sons or daughters who would be forced to enlist.

Merik's furious gaze dropped back to his plate. It was scraped clean. Even the bones had been swept into his napkin. Bone broth, after all, was easy to make and could feed sailors for days. Several of the other luncheon guests had noticed—Merik hadn't exactly hidden it when he used the beige silk to pluck the bones off his plate.

Merik was even tempted to ask his nearest neighbors if he could have their chicken bones, most of which were untouched and surrounded by green beans. Sailors didn't waste food—not when they never knew if they would catch another fish or see land again.

And especially not when their homeland was starving.

"Admiral," said a fat nobleman to Merik's left. "How is King Serafin's health? I heard his wasting disease was in its final stages."

"Then you heard wrong," Merik answered, his voice dangerously cool for anyone who knew the Nihar family rage. "My father is improving. Thank you . . . what's your name again?"

The man's cheeks jiggled. "Dom Phillip fon Grieg." He pasted on a fake smile. "Grieg is one of the largest holdings in the Cartorran Empire—surely you know of it. Or . . . do you? I suppose a *Nubrevnan* would have no need for Cartorran geography."

Merik merely smiled at that. Of course he knew where

the Grieg holdings were, but let the dom think him ignorant to Cartorran specifics.

"I have three sons in the Hell-Bard Brigade," the dom continued, his thick, sausage-like fingers reaching for a goblet of wine. "The Emperor has promised them each a holding of their own in the near future."

"You don't say." Merik was careful to keep his face impassive but, in his head, he was *roaring* his fury. The Hell-Bard Brigade—that elite contingent of ruthless fighters tasked with "cleansing" Cartorra of elemental witches and heretics—they were one of the primary reasons that Merik hated Cartorrans.

After all, Merik was an elemental witch, as was almost every person in the Witchlands that he cared about.

As Dom fon Grieg sipped from his goblet, a stream of expensive Dalmotti wine dribbled out the sides of his mouth. It was wasteful. Disgusting. Merik's fury grew . . . and grew . . . and *grew.*

Until it was the final grain of salt, and Merik succumbed to the flood.

With a sharp, rasping inhale, he drew the air in the room to himself. Then he *huffed* it out.

Wind blasted at the dom. The man's goblet tipped up; wine splattered his face, his hair, his clothes. It even flew to the window—splattering red droplets across the glass.

Silence descended. For half a second, Merik considered what he ought to do now. An apology was clearly out of the question, and a threat seemed too dramatic. Then Merik's eyes caught on Guildmaster Alix's uncleared plate. Without a second thought, Merik shoved to his feet and swept a stormy glare over the noble faces now gawking at him. At the wide-eyed servants hovering in the doorways and shadows.

Then, Merik snatched the napkin from the Guildmaster's lap. "You're not going to eat that, are you?" Merik didn't wait for an answer. He merely murmured, "Good, good—because my crew most certainly will," and set to gathering up the bones, the green beans, and even the final bits of stewed cabbage. After wrapping the silk napkin tight, he thrust it into his waistcoat pocket along with his own saved bones.

Then he turned to the blinking Dalmotti Doge, and declared, "Thank you for your hospitality, my lord."

And with nothing more than a mocking salute, Merik Nihar, prince of Nubrevna and admiral to the Nubrevnan navy, marched from the Doge's luncheon, the Doge's dining room, and finally the Doge's palace.

And as he walked, he began to plan.

By the time Merik reached the southernmost point of the Southern Wharf District, distant chimes were ringing in the fifteenth hour and the tide was out. The heat of the day had sunk into the cobblestones, leaving a miserable warmth to curl up from the streets.

When Merik attempted to hop a puddle of only Noden knew what, he failed and his new boots caught the edge of it. Blackened water splashed up, carrying with it the heavy stench of old fish—and Merik fought the urge to punch in the nearest shop window. It wasn't the city's fault that its Guildmasters were buffoons.

In the nineteen years and four months since the Twenty Year Truce had stopped all war in the Witchlands, the three empires—Cartorra, Marstok, and Dalmotti—had successfully crushed Merik's home through diplomacy. Each year, one less trade caravan had passed through his country and one less Nubrevnan export had found a buyer.

Nubrevna wasn't the only small nation to have suffered. Supposedly, the Great War had started, all those centuries ago, as a dispute over who owned the Five Origin Wells. In those days, it was the Wells that chose the rulers—something to do with the Twelve Paladins . . . Although how twelve knights or an inanimate spring could choose a king, Merik had never quite understood.

It was all the stuff of legends now anyway, and over the decades and eventually the centuries, three empires grew from the Great War's mayhem—and each empire wanted the same thing: *more.* More witcheries, more crops, more ports.

So then it was three massive empires against a handful of tiny, fierce nations—tiny fierce nations who slowly got the upper hand, for wars cost money, and even empires can run out.

Peace, the Cartorran emperor had proclaimed. *Peace for twenty years, and then a renegotiation.* It had sounded perfect.

Too perfect.

What people like Merik's mother hadn't realized when they'd penned their names on the Twenty Year Truce was that when Emperor Henrick said *Peace!,* he really meant *Pause.* And when he said *Renegotiation,* he meant *Ensuring these other nations fall beneath us when our armies resume their march.*

So now, as Merik watched the Dalmotti armies roll in from the west, the Marstoki Firewitches gather in the east, and three imperial navies slowly float toward his homeland's coast, it felt like Merik—and all of Nubrevna—were drowning. They were sinking beneath the waves, watching the sunlight vanish, until there would be nothing left but Noden's Hagfishes and a final lungful of water.

But the Nubrevnans weren't crippled yet.

Merik had one more meeting—this one with the Gold Guild. If Merik could just open one line of trade, then he felt certain other Guilds would follow.

When at last Merik reached his warship, a three-masted frigate with the sharp, beak-like bow distinctive to Nubrevnan naval ships, he found her calm upon the low tide. Her sails were furled, her oars stowed, and the Nubrevnan flag, with its black background and bearded iris—a vivid flash of blue at the flag's center—flew languidly on the afternoon breeze.

As Merik marched up the gangway onto the *Jana,* his temper settled slightly—only to be replaced by shoulder-tensing anxiety and the sudden need to check if his shirt was properly tucked in.

This was Merik's father's ship; half the men were King Serafin's crew; and despite three months with Merik in charge, these men weren't keen on having Merik around.

A towering, ash-haired figure loped over the main deck toward Merik. He dodged several swabbing sailors, stretched his long legs over a crate, and then swept a stiff bow before his prince. It was Merik's Threadbrother, Kullen Ikray—who was also first mate on the *Jana*.

"You're back early," Kullen said. When he rose, Merik didn't miss the red spots on Kullen's pale cheeks, or the slight hitch in his breath. It meant the possibility of a breathing attack.

"Are you ill?" Merik asked, careful to keep his voice low.

Kullen pretended not to hear—though the air around them chilled. A sure sign Kullen wanted to drop the subject.

At first glance, nothing about Merik's Threadbrother seemed particularly fit for life at sea: he was too tall to fit comfortably belowdecks, his fair skin burned with shameful ease, and he wasn't fond of swordplay. Not to mention, his thick white eyebrows showed far too much expression for any respectable seaman.

But, by Noden, if Kullen couldn't control a wind.

Unlike Merik, Kullen's elemental magic wasn't exclusive to air currents—he was a full Airwitch, able to control a man's lungs, able to dominate the heat and the storms, and once, he'd even stopped a full-blown hurricane. Witches like Merik were common enough and with varying degrees of mastery over the wind, but as far as Merik knew, Kullen was the only living person with complete control over *all* aspects of the air.

Yet it wasn't Kullen's magic that Merik most valued. It was his mind, sharp as nails, and his steadiness, constant as the tide to the sea.

"How was the lunch?" Kullen asked, the air around him

warming as he bared his usual terrifying smile. He wasn't very *good* at smiling.

"It was a waste of time," Merik replied. He marched over the deck, his boot heels clacking on the oak. Sailors paused to salute, their fists pounding their hearts. Merik nodded absently at each.

Then he remembered something in his pocket. He withdrew the napkins and handed them off to Kullen.

Several breaths passed. Then, "Leftovers?"

"I was making a point," Merik muttered, and his footsteps clipped out harder. "A stupid point that missed its mark. Is there any word from Lovats?"

"Yes—but," Kullen hastened to add, hands lifting, "it had nothing to do with the King's health. All I heard was that he's still confined to bed."

Frustration towed at Merik's shoulders. He hadn't heard any specifics about his father's disease in weeks. "And my aunt? Is she back from the healer's?"

"Hye."

"Good." Merik nodded—at least satisfied with that. "Send Aunt Evrane to my cabin. I want to ask her about the Gold Guild . . ." He trailed off, feet grinding to a halt. "What is it? You only squint at me like that when something's wrong."

"Hye," Kullen acknowledged, scratching at the back of his neck. His eyes flicked toward the massive wind-drum on the quarterdeck. A new recruit—whose name Merik could never remember—was cleaning the drum's two mallets. The magicked mallet, for producing cannon-like bursts of wind. The standard mallet, for messages and shanty-beats.

"We should discuss it in private," Kullen finally finished. "It's about your sister. Something . . . *arrived* for her."

Merik smothered an oath, and his shoulders rose higher. Ever since Serafin had named Merik as the Truce Summit's Nubrevnan envoy—meaning he was also temporarily Admiral of the Royal Navy—Vivia had tried a thousand different ways to seize control from afar.

Merik stomped into his cabin, footsteps echoing off the whitewashed ceiling beams as he aimed for the screwed-down bed in the right corner.

Kullen, meanwhile, moved to the long table for charts and bookkeeping at the center of the room. It was also bolted down, and a three-inch rim kept papers from flying during rough seas.

Sunlight cut through windows all around, reflecting on King Serafin's sword collection, meticulously displayed on the back wall—the perfect place for Merik to accidentally touch one in his sleep and leave permanent fingerprints.

At the moment, this ship might have been Merik's, but Merik had no illusions that it would stay that way. During times of war, the Queen ruled the land and the King ruled the seas. Thus, the *Jana* was Merik's father's ship, named after the dead Queen, and it would be Serafin's ship once more when he healed.

If he healed—and he had to. Otherwise, Vivia was next in line for the throne . . . and that wasn't something Merik wanted to imagine yet. Or deal with. Vivia was not the sort of person content with only ruling land or sea. She wanted control of both—and beyond—and she made no effort to pretend otherwise.

Merik knelt beside his only personal item on the ship: a trunk, roped tightly to the wall. After a quick rummage, he found a clean shirt and his storm-blue admiral's uniform. He wanted to get out of his dress suit as quickly as possible, for there was nothing to deflate a man's ego like a bit of frill around the collar.

As Merik's fingers undid the ten million buttons on his dress shirt, he joined Kullen at the table.

Kullen had opened a map of the Jadansi Sea—the slip of ocean that bisected the Dalmotti Empire. "This is what came for Vivia." He plunked down a miniature ship that looked identical to the Dalmotti Guild ships listing outside. It slid across the map, locking in place over Veñaza City. "Obviously, it's Aetherwitched and will move wherever its corresponding ship sails." Kullen's eyes flicked up to Merik's. "According to the scumbag who delivered it, the corresponding ship is from the Wheat Guild."

"And why," Merik began, giving up on his buttons and just yanking the shirt over his head, "does Vivia care about a trade ship?" He tossed it at his trunk and planted his hands on the table. His faded Witchmark stretched into an unbalanced diamond. "What does she expect us to do with it?"

"Foxes," Kullen said, and the room turned icy.

"Foxes," Merik repeated, the word knocking around without meaning in his skull. Then suddenly, it sifted into place—and he burst into action, spinning for his trunk. "That's the stupidest thing I've ever heard from her—and she's said plenty of stupid things in her life. Tell Hermin to contact Vivia's Voicewitch. *Now.* I want to talk with her at the next ring of the chime."

"Hye." Kullen's boot steps rang out as Merik yanked out the first shirt his fingers touched. He tugged it on as the cabin door swung wide . . . and then clicked shut.

At that sound, Merik gritted his teeth and fought to keep his temper. Locked up tight.

This was so typically Vivia, so why the Hell should Merik be surprised or angry?

Once upon a time, the Foxes had been Nubrevnan pirates. Their tactics had relied on small half-galleys. They were shallower than the *Jana,* with two masts and oars that allowed them to slip between sand bars and barrier islands with ease—and allowed them to ambush larger ships.

But the Fox standard—a serpentine sea fox coiling around the bearded iris—hadn't flown the masts in centuries. It hadn't needed to once Nubrevna had possessed a true navy of its own.

As Merik stood there trying to imagine *any* sort of argument his sister might listen to, something flickered outside the nearest window. Yet other than waves piling against the high-water mark and a merchant ship rocking next door, there was nothing unusual.

Except . . . it wasn't high tide.

Merik darted for the window. This was Veñaza City—a city of marshes—and there were only two things that would bring in an unnatural tide: an earthquake.

Or magic.

And there was only one reason a witch would summon waves to a wharf.

Cleaving.

Merik sprinted for the door. "Kullen!" he roared as his feet hit the main deck. The waves were already licking higher, and the *Jana* had begun to list.

Two ships north, a hulking sailor staggered down a trade ship's gangplank toward the cobblestoned street. He scratched furiously at his forearms, at his neck—and even at this distance, Merik could see the black pustules bubbling on the man's skin. Soon his magic would reach its breaking point, and he would feast on the nearest human life.

The waves swept in higher, rougher—summoned by the cleaving witch. Though several people noticed the man and screeched their terror, most couldn't see the waves, couldn't hear the screams. They were unaware and unprotected.

So Merik did the only thing he could think of. He shouted once more for Kullen, and then he gathered in his magic, so it would lift him high and carry him far.

Moments later, in a gust of air, Merik took flight.

FIVE

Safi's temper was on the verge of exploding, what with the gull crap on her shoulder, the oppressive afternoon heat, and the fact that not *one* of the six ships on this dock needed new workers (especially not ones dressed as Guild apprentices).

Iseult glided ahead, already at the end of the dock and joining the wharfside throngs. Even from this distance, Safi could see Iseult fidgeting with her scarf and gloves as she scrutinized something in the murky water.

Eyebrows high, Safi directed her own gaze to the brackish waves. There was a charge in the air. It pricked at the hair on her arms and sent a chill fingering down her spine . . .

Then her Truthwitchery exploded—a coating, scraping sensation against her neck that heralded wrongness. Huge, vast *wrongness*.

Someone's magic was cleaving.

Safi had felt it once before—felt her power swell as if it might cleave too. Anyone with a witchery could sense it coming. Could feel the world falling out of its magical order.

Of course, if you *didn't* have magic, like most of these people streaming down the dock, then you might as well be dead already.

A shout split Safi's ears like thunder. *Iseult.* Midstride and with a roar for people to *"Stand aside!,"* Safi dove forward, curled her chin to her chest, and rolled. As her body tumbled over the wood, she grabbed for the parrying dagger in her boot. It was for defense against a sword, but it was still sharp.

And it could still gut a man if needed.

As the momentum of the roll drove Safi back to her feet, she dragged the knife down, and in a quick slash, she shredded her skirts. Then she was sprinting once more, her legs free to pump as high as she needed—and her knife in hand.

The waves curled higher. Harder. Gusts of power that grated against Safi's skin like a thousand lies told at once.

The cleaved man's magic must be connected to water, and now the trade ships were heaving, heaving . . . creaking, creaking . . . and then crashing against the pier.

Safi reached the stone quay. In half a breath, she took in the scene: a cleaved Tidewitch, his skin rippling with the oil of festered magic and blood black as pitch dribbling from a cut on his chest.

Only paces away, Iseult was low in her stance—her skirts ripped through as well. *That's my girl,* Safi thought.

And to the left, flying through the air with all the grace of an untested, broken-winged bat, was some sort of Airwitch. His hands were out as he called the wind to carry him.

Safi had only two thoughts: *Who the rut is that Nubrevnan Windwitch?* And: *He should really learn how to button a shirt.*

Then the shirtless man touched down directly in her path.

She shrieked as loud as she could, but all she got was an alarmed glance before she flung her knife aside and slammed into his body. They crashed to the ground—and the young man shoved her off, shouting, "Stay back! I'll handle this!"

Safi ignored him—he was clearly an idiot—and in more time than it ought to take, she disentangled herself from the Nubrevnan and snatched up her dagger.

She spun toward the cleaving Tidewitch—just as Iseult closed in, a swirl of steel meant to attract the eye. But it was having no effect. The Tidewitch didn't lurch out of the way. Iseult's scythes beat into his stomach, and more black blood sprayed.

Blackened organs toppled out too.

Then water erupted onto the street. Ships rammed against the stones in a deafening crunch of wood. A second wave charged in, and right behind it, a third.

"Kullen!" the Nubrevnan bellowed from behind Safi. *"Hold back the water!"*

In an explosion of magic that rushed across Safi's body, air funneled toward the encroaching waves.

The magicked wind hit the water; waves toppled and foamed backward.

But the cleaving Tidewitch didn't care. His blackened

eyes had latched on to Safi now. His bloodstained hands clawed up and he barreled toward her like a squall.

Safi sprang into a flying kick. Her heel crashed into his ribs; he toppled forward right as Iseult spun into a hook-kick. Her boot pummeled the man's chin, shifted the angle of his fall.

He hit the cobblestones. Black pustules burst all over his skin, splattering the street with his blood.

But he was still alive—still conscious. With a roar like a hurricane, he struggled to get upright.

That was when the Nubrevnan man decided to re-appear. He sidled close to the Cleaved—and Safi's panic burned up her throat. "What are you *doing*?"

"I told you I'd handle this!" he bellowed. Then his arms flung back, and in a surge of power that sparked through Safi's lungs, his cupped hands hit the cleaved sailor's ears. Air exploded through the man's brain. His blackened eyes rolled backward.

The Tidewitch crumpled to the street. Dead.

Iseult swept aside her skirts and shoved her moon scythes back into their concealed calf-scabbards. Nearby, Dalmottis made frantic two-fingered swipes across their eyes. It was a sign to ward off evil—to ask their gods to protect their souls. Some aimed their movements at the dead Cleaved, but more than a few aimed the swipe at Iseult.

As if she had any interest in claiming their souls.

She did, however, have an interest in not being mobbed and beaten today, so, twisting toward the dead Tidewitch, she readjusted her headscarf—and thanked the Moon Mother it hadn't been removed in the fight.

She also thanked the goddess that no one else had cleaved. Such a powerful burst in magic could easily send other witches over the brink—a brink from which there was no return.

Though no one knew what made a person cleave, Iseult had read theories that linked the corruption to the five Origin Wells spread across the Witchlands. Each Well was linked to one of the five elements: Aether, Earth, Water, Wind, or Fire. Though people spoke of a Void element—and of Voidwitches like that Bloodwitch—there was no record of an actual Void Well.

Perhaps a Void Well *was* out there, but it had been long forgotten. The springs that had fed it were dried up. The trees that had blossomed year-round were shriveled to desiccated husks. Such stagnation had certainly happened with the Earth, Wind, and Water Wells, and perhaps they too would one day be lost to history.

No matter the Wells' fates, though, scholars didn't think it mere coincidence that the only witcheries to cleave were those linked to Earth, Wind, or Water. And if the Carawen monks were to be believed, then only the return of the Cahr Awen could ever heal the dead Wells or the Cleaved.

Well, Iseult didn't think *that* would be happening anytime soon. No return of the Cahr Awen—and no escaping all these hateful stares, either.

Once Iseult felt certain that her hair was sufficiently covered, her face sufficiently shaded, and her sleeves sufficiently low enough to hide her pale skin, she reached for

Safi's Threads so she could find her Threadsister among the crowds.

But her eyes and her magic caught something off. Threads like she'd never seen before. Directly beside her . . . on the corpse.

Her gaze slid to the cleaved man's body. Blackened blood . . . and perhaps something else oozed from his ears, between the cobblestones. The pustules on his body had erupted—some of that oily spray was on Iseult's slashed skirts and sweaty bodice.

And yet, though the man was undoubtedly dead, there were still three Threads wriggling over his chest. Like maggots, they shimmied and coiled inward. Short Threads. The Threads that *break*.

It shouldn't have been possible—Iseult's mother had always told her that the dead have no Threads, and in all the Nomatsi burning ceremonies Iseult had attended as a child, she had never seen Threads on a corpse.

The longer Iseult gaped, the more the crowds closed in. Spectators curious over the body were everywhere, and Iseult had to squint to see through their Threads. To tamp down on all the emotions around her.

Then one crimson, raging Thread flashed nearby—and with it came a waspish snarl. "Who the *hell-flames* do you think you are? We had that under control."

"Under control?" retorted a male voice with a sharp accent. "I just saved your lives!"

"Are *you* Cleaved?" Safi cried—and Iseult winced at the poor word choice. But of course, Safi was venting her grief. Her terror. Her explosive Threads. She was always like this when something bad—truly bad—happened. She either ran from her emotions as fast as her legs would carry her or she beat them into submission.

When at last Iseult popped out beside her Threadsister, it was just in time to see Safi grab a fistful of the young man's unbuttoned shirt.

"Is this how all Nubrevnans dress?" Safi snatched the other side of his shirt. "These go inside *these*."

To his credit, the Nubrevnan didn't move. His face simply flushed a wild scarlet—as did his Threads—and his lips pressed tight.

"I know," he gritted out, "how a button operates." He knocked Safi's wrists away. "And I don't need advice from a woman with bird shit on her shoulder."

Oh no, Iseult thought, lips parting to warn—

Fingers clamped on Iseult's arm. Before she could flip up her hand and snap the wrist of her grabber, the person flipped up *her* wrist and shoved it against her back.

And a Thread of clayish red pulsed in Iseult's vision. It was a familiar shade of annoyance that spoke of years enduring Safi's tantrums—which meant Habim had arrived.

The Marstoki man shoved Iseult's wrist harder to her back and snarled, "Walk, Iseult. To that cats' alley over there."

"You can let me go," she said, voice toneless. She could just see Habim from the corner of her eyes. He wore the Hasstrel family's gray and blue livery.

"Voidwitch?! *You called me a Voidwitch?!* I speak Nubrevnan, you horse's ass!" The rest of Safi's bloodthirsty screams were in Nubrevnan—and swallowed up by the crowds.

Iseult *hated* when Safi's Threads got so bright they blazed over everything else. When they seared into Iseult's eyes, into her heart. But Habim didn't slow as he guided Iseult around a one-legged beggar singing "Eridysi's Lament." Then they'd reached a narrow slip of space between a dingy tavern and an even dingier secondhand shop. Iseult staggered into it. Her boots kicked through unseen puddles and the stench of cat piss burned in her skull.

She shook out her wrist and spun back to her mentor. This behavior wasn't like the gentle Habim. He was a deadly man, certainly—he had served Eron fon Hasstrel for two decades as a man-at-arms—but Habim was also soft-spoken and careful. Cool and in control of his temper.

At least he was normally.

"What," he began, marching at Iseult, "were you doing? Pulling your weapons out like that? Hell-gates, Iseult, you should have run."

"That cleaving Tidewitch," she began—but Habim only stomped in closer. He was not a tall man, and his eyes had been level with Iseult's for the past three years.

Right now, those line-seamed eyes were rounded with his ire, and his Threads glittered an irate red. "Any Cleaved are the city guards' problem—and the guards are now *your* problem. Highway robbery, Iseult?"

Her breath hitched. "How did you find out?"

"There are blockades everywhere. Mathew and I met one on our way into the city—only to learn that the city guards are looking for two girls, one with a sword and one with moon scythes. How many people do you think fight with moon scythes, Iseult? Those"—Habim pointed at her scabbards—"are obvious. And as a Nomatsi, you have no legal protection in this country, and simply carrying a weapon in public will get you hanged." Habim pivoted on his heel to march away three steps. Then back three steps. "Think, Iseult! *Think!*"

Iseult compressed her lips. *Stasis. Stasis in your fingertips and in your toes.*

In the distance, she could just hear the growing roll of snare drums that meant the Veñaza City guards were on their way. They would behead the Tidewitch's body as required by law for all cleaved corpses.

"A-are you done screaming at me?" she asked at last, her old stammer grabbing her tongue. Distorting her words. "Because I need to get back to Safi, and we n-need to leave the city."

Habim's nostrils fluttered with a deep inhale, and Iseult watched as he pushed aside his emotions. As the lines of his face smoothed out and his Threads turned calm. "You cannot go back to Safi. In fact, you will not leave this alley by the way you came in. Guildmaster Yotiluzzi has a Bloodwitch in his employ, and that creature is straight from the Void with no mercy or fear." Habim shook his head, and the first hints of gray fear twined into his Threads.

Which only made Iseult's throat clog tighter. Habim was *never* scared.

Blood. Witch. Blood. Witch.

"Safi's uncle is in town," Habim went on, "for the Truce Summit, so—"

"Dom fon Hasstrel is *here?*" Iseult's jaw slackened. Habim could have said a thousand things, but none would have surprised her more. She'd met the battle-scarred Eron twice in the past, and his sloppy inebriation had instantly verified all of Safi's stories and complaints.

"All Cartorran nobility are required to be here," Habim explained, falling back into his three-step pace. Left. Right. "Henrick has some grand announcement to make, and in his usual fashion, he's using this summit as his stage."

Iseult was scarcely listening. "Does all the nobility i-include Safi?"

Habim's expression softened. His Threads flickered to a gentle, peach tenderness. "That includes Safi. Which means she currently has her uncle—and an entire court of doms and domnas—to protect her from Yotiluzzi's Bloodwitch. But you . . ."

Habim didn't have to utter the rest. Safi had her title to protect her, and Iseult had her heritage to damn her.

Iseult's hands lifted. Rubbed her cheeks. Her temples. But her fingers were only a distant sensation of pressure on her skin—just as the crowds were a throbbing hum, the rattle of the guards' drums a low hiss.

"So what can I do?" she asked at last. "I can't afford passage on a boat, and even if I could, I have nowhere to go."

Habim waved to the end of the alley. "There's an inn called The Hawthorn Canal a few blocks away. I've hired a room and a horse there. You'll stay overnight, and then tomorrow, at sunset, you can travel to The Hawthorn

Canal's sister inn on the north side. Mathew and I will be waiting for you. In the meantime, we'll deal with the Bloodwitch."

"Why only one night, though? What could possibly h-happen in one night?"

For a long breath, Habim stared so intently it was as if *he* could read Iseult's Threads. As if *he* could search her for truth or lies. "Safi was born a domna. You have to remember that, Iseult. All her training has been toward that one thing. Tonight, she is needed at the Truce Summit. Henrick has openly demanded her presence, which means she cannot refuse—and it means you cannot stand in her way."

With those simple words—*you cannot stand in her way*—Iseult's breath hardened in her lungs. For all that Safi might have lost their savings, and for all that a Bloodwitch might have latched on to their trail, Iseult had still believed that everything would blow over. That this snarl in the loom would somehow untangle, and life would return to normal in a few weeks.

But this . . . this felt like the end. Safi was going to have to be a domna, plain and simple, and there was no room for Iseult in that life.

Loss, she thought vaguely as she tried to identify the feeling in her chest. *This must be loss.*

"I've told you this before," Habim said gruffly. His gaze raked up and down, like a general inspecting a soldier. "A hundred times, I've told you, Iseult, yet you never listen to me. You never believe. Why did Mathew and I encourage your friendship with Safi? Why did we decide to train you alongside her?"

Iseult squeezed the air from her chest, willing the thoughts and the shame to ebb away. "Because," she recited, "no one can protect Safi like her Thread-family."

"Exactly. Thread-family bonds are unbreakable—and you know that better than anyone else. The day that you saved Safi's life six years ago, you and she were bound together as Threadsisters. To this day, you would die for Safi, just as she would die for you. So do this for her, Iseult. Hide away for the night, let Mathew and I deal with the Bloodwitch, and then return to Safi's side tomorrow."

A pause. Then Iseult nodded gravely. *Quit being a fanciful fool,* she chided herself—exactly as her mother had always done. This wasn't the end at all, and Iseult should have been smart enough to see that right away.

"Give me your scythes," Habim ordered. "I'll return them to you tomorrow."

"They're my only weapons."

"Yes, but you're Nomatsi. If you get stopped at another blockade . . . We can't risk it."

Iseult gave a rough scrub at her nose, and then muttered, "Fine," before unstrapping her prized blades. Almost childishly, she thrust them at Habim. His Threads flickered with a sad blue as he moved deeper into the alley and swooped up a waxed canvas bag from the shadows. He withdrew a rough black blanket.

"This is salamander fiber." He draped it over Iseult's head and shoulders and fastened it with a simple pin. "As long as you wear this, the Bloodwitch can't smell you. *Do not remove it* until we're together tomorrow night."

Iseult nodded; the stiff fabric resisted the movement. And Moon Mother save her, it was hot.

Habim then reached into his pocket and plunked out a sack of clanking coins. "This should cover the cost of the inn and a horse."

After accepting the piestras, Iseult turned to a dilapidated door. The sounds of chopping knives and boiling pots drifted through the wood, yet her hand paused on the rusted doorknob.

This felt . . . wrong.

What sort of Threadsister would Iseult be if she left Safi without a good-bye—or at *least* a backup plan for those inevitable worst-case scenarios?

"Can you give Safi a message?" Iseult asked, keeping her words calm. At Habim's nod, she continued. "Tell Safi that I'm sorry I had to go and that she'd better not lose my favorite book. And . . . oh." Iseult raised her eyebrows, feigning an afterthought. "Please tell her not to slit your throat, since I'm sure she'll try to once she finds out you've sent me away."

"I'll tell her," Habim said, voice and Threads solemn. "Now hurry. That Bloodwitch is no doubt on his way right now."

Iseult bowed her head once—a soldier to her general—before yanking open the door and marching into the steamy, crowded kitchen.

SIX

As the snare drums approached, Safi's wrath riled higher and higher. The only reason she didn't chase after that cursed Nubrevnan as he strode toward his ship (with his shirt *still* unbuttoned) was because the tallest, palest man she'd ever seen marched beside him . . . And because Safi had lost sight of Iseult.

But her frantic search for her Threadsister was interrupted when the footsteps and the drumbeats of the approaching guard cut off. When the crowds along the pier fell silent.

A slice, a thunk . . . a splatter.

For a long moment, the only sounds were the pigeons, the breeze, and the calm waves.

Then a strangled sob—someone who'd known the dead man, perhaps—cut the silence like a serrated knife. It echoed in Safi's ears. Shook in her rib cage. A minor chord to fill a hole left behind.

A hand landed on Safi's bicep. Habim. "This way, Safi. There's a carriage—"

"I need to find Iseult," she said, unmoving. Unblinking.

"She's gone somewhere safe." Habim's expression was grim—but that was nothing unusual. "I promise," he added, and Safi's magic whispered, *True*. A warm purr in her chest.

So, stiff as a ship's mast, Safi followed Habim to a nondescript, covered carriage. Once she was seated within, he shut the door and yanked a heavy black curtain over the window. Then, in curt tones, Habim explained how he and Mathew had recognized the girls by their weapons and had shortly thereafter found Mathew's destroyed shop.

Shame crept up Safi's neck as she listened. Mathew was more than just her tutor. He was family, and now Safi's mistakes had ruined his home.

Yet when Habim mentioned sending Iseult to an inn—alone, *unprotected*—all of the afternoon's horror was swallowed up by skull-rattling rage. Safi dove for the door . . .

Habim had her in a stranglehold before she could even twist the knob. "If you open that door," he growled, "the Bloodwitch will smell you. If you keep it shut, however, then the monk can't trace you. That curtain is made of salamander fiber, Safi, and Iseult is wearing a cloak of the same fabric right now."

Safi froze, her vision crossing from lack of air and the scarred back of Habim's right hand blurring. She couldn't believe Iseult had simply walked away without a fight. Without Safi . . .

It made no sense, yet Safi's magic shouted in her rib cage that it was true.

So she nodded, Habim released her, and she straggled into her seat. Habim had always been the more tightly keyed of her mentors. A chime-piece wound faster than the rest of the world, and it left him without patience for Safi's impulsiveness.

"I know this holdup was your doing, Safi." Habim's soft voice somehow filled every space of the carriage. "Only you would be so reckless, and then Iseult followed you as she always does."

Safi didn't argue with that—it was undeniably true. The card game might have been Iseult's idea, yet every single bad decision since could be laid at Safi's doorstep.

"This mistake," Habim continued, "has complicated—possibly ruined—twenty years of planning. Now, with Eron here, we're doing what we can to salvage the situation."

Safi stiffened. "Uncle Eron," she repeated. "*Here?*"

As Habim offered up some story about Henrick summoning all the Cartorran nobility for a grand announcement, Safi forced herself to mimic Habim. To settle back and relax. She needed to think through everything like Iseult always did. She needed to analyze her opponents and her terrain . . .

But analyzing and strategy weren't her strengths. Every time she tried to organize the pieces of her day, they swung apart and were that much harder to reassemble. The only thought she could keep pinned down was *Uncle Eron is here. In Veñaza City.* She hadn't seen him in two years; she'd hoped she would never have to again. Simply *thinking* of Eron reminded her that, for all that she'd built a life in Veñaza City, there was a different one waiting for her back in Hasstrel.

Safi needed Iseult right now. She *relied* on Iseult to keep her mind focused and clear. Acting and running and fighting—those were the only things Safi did well.

Her fingers itched for the door. Her toes curled in anticipation as she reached with aching slowness for the latch.

"Don't touch that," Habim intoned. "What would you do anyway, Safi? Run away?"

"Find Iseult," she said quietly, her fingers still hovering. "And *then* run away."

"Which would allow the Bloodwitch to find you," he retorted. "As long as you stay with your uncle, you'll be safe."

"Because he did such a good job protecting my parents." The words snarled out before Safi could stop them. Yet where she'd expected a swift retaliation from Habim, she got only silence.

Then a stony, "Hell-Bards protect their family, yes, but the empire must come first. In that instance, eighteen years ago, the empire came first."

"Which is why Emperor Henrick dishonorably discharged him, is it? He gave Uncle Eron the shameful task of being my regent and nursemaid out of *gratitude*?"

Habim didn't engage. In fact, his expression didn't waver at all. This was hardly the first time Safi had pressed Habim on her uncle's past, and it wasn't the first time she'd gotten cold silence either.

"You're going home, to Guildmaster Alix's," Habim said eventually, tipping back the edge of the curtain and squinting outside. "You should have gone to him in the first place—he can keep you safe from the Bloodwitch."

"How was I supposed to know that?" Safi finally withdrew her fingers from the latch and sat up to her full height. "I thought I was doing the right thing by not bringing trouble to Alix's door."

"How very considerate of you. Next time, though, try trusting the men charged with your safety."

"Iseult keeps me safe too," Safi said. "Yet notice that you've sent her away."

Again, Habim ignored Safi's bait. Instead, he dipped his chin to watch her from the tops of his eyes. "Speaking of Iseult, she requests that you please not slit my throat. She also apologizes for leaving and asks that you not lose her book."

"Iseult . . . apologized?" That wasn't like Iseult—at least not when this was so clearly Safi's fault.

Which meant there was a hidden message here.

It was a game the girls had played over the years. One Mathew had taught them—*Say one thing, but mean another*—and it had been wildly fun during the more dull hours of Mathew's history lessons.

It wasn't fun now.

Don't slit Habim's throat—that meant to wait. To do as Habim ordered. Fine. Safi would obey for now. But the book . . . She couldn't riddle out that part of the message.

"Iseult's and my things," Safi said slowly, "are in a sack at the harbor."

"I already grabbed it. The driver's holding it." Another furtive glance behind the curtain before Habim pounded the roof.

The carriage clattered to a stop, and Habim offered Safi

an inflectionless, "Stay out of trouble, please." Then he swept through the door and melted into the cacophony of afternoon traffic.

With her fists never feeling as if they were squeezed tightly enough, Safi stepped into the city. Horses' hooves, carriage wheels, and fancy boot heels drowned out her frustrated teeth grinding. Alix's home was a many-columned mansion surrounded by a jungle of roses and jasmine. Like all the Dalmotti Guildmasters, he lived in the wealthiest corner of the city: the Eastern Canal District.

Safi had a bedroom inside, and the young, fair-haired Alix had always been kind to her. But this luxe, labyrinthine estate had never felt like home—not in the way that Iseult's attic room always had.

Not in the way the girl's new rooms were *going* to.

For several long moments, Safi stood at the iron gate and considered making a run for it. Her throat burned with a hunger for speed. But she knew she couldn't find Iseult—not without risking the Bloodwitch.

Gods below, everything was falling apart, and it was all Safi's fault. *Safi* had fallen for Chiseled Cheater's charms. Then *Safi* had suggested the holdup.

It was always this way: Safi would initiate something over her head, and someone else would clean up the mess. That someone had been Iseult for six years now . . . but how many messes would Safi have to make before Iseult had had enough? One of these days, Iseult would give up on her like everyone else had. Safi just prayed—desperately, violently *prayed*—that it wasn't today.

It isn't though, her logic pointed out. *Or Iseult wouldn't have left a message with Habim or told you to find the book.* Well, Safi would only be able to puzzle through Iseult's coded message if she went inside Alix's mansion as ordered.

So with her knuckles cracking against her thighs, she marched up to the gate and rang the bell.

Despite the flowers and incense jars in the Silk Guildmaster's home, the smell wafting off the nearby canal always dominated Safi's nose. There was no escaping it, and as Safi gazed from the window of her second-story bedroom, she tapped her toes on the sky blue rug. A frantic counterbeat to her heart.

Fine silk gowns were draped on the large four-poster bed that she rarely slept in. This wasn't the first time Guildmaster Alix had crafted dresses for Safi—although these were far finer than anything she'd ever received before.

Footsteps clacked behind her. *Mathew.* Safi knew that loping stride, and when she turned to her tutor, she found his thin, freckled face was a mask of hard lines, his red hair aglow in the afternoon light.

Mathew and Habim could not have been more different—in looks or in personality—and of the two, Safi had always preferred Mathew. Perhaps because she knew Mathew regarded her more highly than Habim ever had. They were kindred spirits, she and Mathew. More inclined to act than to think, to laugh than to frown.

Even without his Wordwitchery, Mathew was a master criminal—a con man of the highest caliber. Habim had taught Safi to use her body as a weapon, yet it was Mathew who'd taught her to use her mind. Her words. And though Safi had never understood why Mathew insisted she learn his confidence skills, she'd always been too afraid to ask—just in case he then decided to stop.

Like Habim, Mathew currently wore the gray and blue livery of the Hasstrels, but *unlike* Habim, Mathew wasn't a servant for Safi's uncle.

"Your things." Mathew flung a familiar bag onto the bed, and Safi made no move to retrieve it—though she did glance at it, checking for the shape of Iseult's books . . .

There they were; a blue corner poked from the top.

"My shop is destroyed." Mathew's lanky form closed in on Safi, blocking her view of the book—or of anything but his green, flashing eyes. "A broken door, broken windows. What the *hell-flames* possessed you to hold up a Guild-master?"

Safi wet her lips. "It . . . was an accident. The wrong mark hit our trap."

"Ah." Mathew's shoulders relaxed. Then he suddenly stepped in close and gripped Safi's chin, like he'd done a thousand times over the past six years. He twisted her head left, right, looking for cuts or bruises or any sign that she might start to cry. But she was unharmed and tears were far, *far* away.

Mathew's hand fell. He rocked back a single step. "I'm glad you're unhurt."

With that single phrase, Safi's breath whooshed out and she flung her arms around his neck. "I'm sorry," she murmured into his lapel—a lapel with the wretched

Hasstrel mountain bat embroidered on it. "I'm so sorry about your shop."

"At least you're alive and safe."

Safi pulled free, wishing Habim would see it that way too.

"Your uncle needs you tonight," Mathew went on, striding to the bed. He yanked one of the gowns off the coverlet, its pistachio silk shimmering in the afternoon sun.

Safi glared at the dress. It was, to her annoyance, quite beautiful and exactly the sort of thing she'd choose for herself. "Does he need me or my witchery?"

"He needs *you*," Mathew said. "There is a ball tonight, to kick off the Truce Summit. Henrick has specifically requested your attendance."

Safi's gut flipped. "But why? I'm not ready to be a full domna or lead the Hasstrel lands—"

"It's not that," Mathew interrupted, turning his attention back to the dress in his hand . . . then shaking his head dismissively and draping it on the bed once more. "You're not needed in that capacity."

True.

"The fact is that we don't know why Henrick wants you here, but Eron could hardly refuse."

Magic shivered over Safi's skin. *False.* "Don't lie to me," she said quietly. Lethally.

Mathew didn't answer but hoisted up a second dress instead—this one thicker and in pale pink. Safi bared her teeth. "You can't send my Threadsister away and not explain *why*, Mathew."

Mathew held Safi's gaze for several long breaths, for

once seeming as unyielding as his Heart-Thread. Then his posture loosened—and an apology slid into the line of his shoulders. He dropped the gown in a heap. "There are big wheels in motion, Safi. Wheels your uncle and many others have spent twenty years rolling into position. The Truce ends in eight months, and the Great War will resume. We . . . cannot let that happen."

Safi's head coiled back—this was *not* what she'd expected. "How could you or my uncle possibly affect the Great War?"

"You'll know soon enough," Mathew replied. "Now get cleaned up, and wear this gown tonight." The faintest dusting of power coated Mathew's words, and as he held out a silvery white dress, the Witchmark on the back of his hand—a hollow circle for Aether and a scripted *W* for Wordwitchery—almost seemed to glow.

Safi's nostrils flared. She snatched away the filmy gown, the fabric slipping through her fingers like sea foam. "Don't waste your magic on me." Something about her Truthwitchery cancelled out Mathew's persuasiveness.

But all Mathew said in return was "Hmmm," as if he knew more than she could ever imagine. Then he twirled elegantly toward the door. "A maid will arrive shortly to help you with your bath. Don't forget behind the ears and under the fingernails."

Safi bit her thumb at Mathew's back . . . but the act of defiance felt empty. Ashy. Her wrath from the carriage was already seeping out and oozing into the floorboards like the blackened oil of the cleaved man's blood.

Safi tossed the gown on the bed, and her eyes settled

on the corner of the Carawen book. She would fix this mess she'd made. Once she understood Iseult's message, Safi would pick through her opponents—her uncle, the Bloodwitch, the city guards—and she would estimate her terrain—Veñaza City, the Truce Summit ball.

Then Safi would fix this.

SEVEN

Iseult ducked into the street behind the wharf as ordered by Habim. Hunching deep beneath the scratchy hood, she wefted her way through horses and carts, merchants and Guild lackeys, and Threads of every imaginable shade and strength. At last, she caught sight of a stamped wooden sign that declared The Hawthorn Canal.

Iseult recognized it now—Safi had played taro here a few months before. Yet unlike last night, she'd actually *won*.

A splash of white beneath the sign caught Iseult's eyes, glaring and conspicuous against the smear of colors that was a Veñaza City thoroughfare.

It was a Carawen monk with no Threads. None.

Iseult's insides iced over. She froze midstep, watching the monk stride down the street—away from her. He was clearly on the hunt. Every few steps, he would pause and the back of his hood would tilt as if he sniffed the air.

It was his lack of Threads, though, that kept Iseult immobile. She'd thought she'd simply missed the Bloodwitch's Threads in the wildness of the fight yesterday, but no—he *still* bore no Threads.

Which was impossible.

Everyone had Threads. End of story.

"You want a rug?" asked a carpet salesman, pushing in close to Iseult, all sweat-stained robes and heavy breathing. "Mine are straight from Azmir, but I'll give you a good deal."

Iseult flicked up a flat palm. "Back away or I will cut off your ears and feed them to the rats."

Normally, this threat served Iseult well. Normally, though, she was in the Northern Wharf District, where her Nomatsi skin went mostly ignored. And *normally*, she had Safi at her side to show teeth and look suitably terrifying.

Today, Iseult had none of those things, and unlike Safi—who would have reacted instantly, who would have run at the first sight of the monk—Iseult only wasted more time evaluating her terrain.

It was in that two-breath pause that the carpet vendor shoved in closer and squinted beneath her hood.

His Threads blazed into gray fear, black hate. "'Matsi *shit*," he hissed, swiping fingers across his eyes. Then he lunged, voice lifting as he tore back Iseult's hood. "Get away, 'Matsi shit! *Get away!*"

Iseult hardly needed that second command—she was finally doing what Safi would've done from the start: she got away.

Or she tried to, but traffic was stopping to ogle her. To close in. Everywhere she turned or jerked, she met eyes locked on her face, her skin, her hair. She jolted back from Threads of gray fear and steely violence.

The commotion attracted the Carawen's attention. He

stopped his forward trek. Swiveled toward the rising shouts of the crowd . . .

And looked directly at Iseult.

Time stretched out and the crowd shrank back, blurring into a quilt of Threads and sound. For a fraction of a heartbeat that felt like eternity, all Iseult saw were the young monk's eyes. Red eddied across the palest blue she'd ever seen. Like blood melting through ice. Like a Heart-Thread twining through blue Threads of understanding. Vaguely, Iseult wondered how she'd missed that flawless blue color at the holdup.

As all of these thoughts careened through her brain at a thousand leagues a second, she wondered if this monk would *really* hurt her like everyone feared . . .

Then the monk's lips rippled back. He bared his teeth, and the pause in the world fractured. Time flooded forward, resumed its normal speed.

And Iseult finally ran, bolting behind a gray horse. She chucked her elbow—*hard*—into its lower rump. It reared. The young woman on its back screamed, and with that burst of high-pitched vocals and the sudden violent, whinnying from the horse, the entire street surged out of the way.

Orange, frantic Threads flared around Iseult—but she barely registered them. She was already shoving and sprinting for an intersection one block back. There was a bridge over the nearest canal there. Maybe if she could cross the canal, she could lose the Bloodwitch.

Her feet thrashed through mud, hopped over beggars, skidded around carts, but then halfway to the bridge, she glanced back—and wished she hadn't. The Bloodwitch was definitely pursuing and he was definitely fast. The same people who'd been intent on slowing Iseult now cleared out of his path.

"Move!" Iseult shrieked at a Purist with his *Repent!* sign. He didn't move, so she clipped him on the shoulder.

He and his sign went spinning like a windmill. But it worked in Iseult's favor, for even though she lost speed—even though she was forced to dive beneath a passing litter carried by four men—it looked as if she aimed left, for the bridge. And she heard the Purist bellowing to go after her *across the canal.*

So she didn't go left as planned. Instead, she slung right on her heel and aimed straight back into traffic, praying the monk listened to the Purist and went left. Praying—desperately praying—that he couldn't smell her blood-scent through these salamander fibers.

She foisted her hood in place and hurtled onward. There was another intersection coming up—a thick flow of traffic east to west toward a second bridge. She'd have to barrel through, continue straight.

Or not. Just as she pelted behind a woodcutter's cart and popped around a cheesemonger's stall, she hit empty air.

Iseult tossed her arms wide, teetering toward an unexpected canal of green, sludgy waters almost as packed with people as the streets.

Then a long flat-hulled pram slid beneath Iseult, and in half a breath, she absorbed the scene below: *Shallow deck covered in nets. Fisherman gaping up at me.*

Iseult stopped fighting her fall. Instead, she leaned into it.

Air rushed against her. White lacey nets closed in fast. Then she was on the deck, knees bending, hands catching herself.

Something sliced through her palm. A rusted hook, she realized before she scrabbled upright. The pram listed wildly. The fisherman roared, but Iseult was already pumping toward the next passing boat—a low ferry with a frilly red awning.

"Look out!" Iseult shouted, lunging high and grabbing hold of the balustrade. She hauled herself up as wide-eyed passengers reared back. Blood smeared on the railing's pickets. Faintly, she hoped this burning slash didn't make her that much easier to follow for the Bloodwitch.

She scooted across the ferry in four bounds—it would seem everyone wanted Iseult off the boat as badly as she did. She topped the railing, sucked in a breath while another pram coasted by—this one covered in the day's mackerel.

She jumped. Her feet squished and suddenly she was sprawling on silver scales with a face full of gooey eyes. The fisherman shrieked at her—more displeased than surprised—and Iseult hefted herself up to find his black beard bearing down.

She pushed past—elbowing him in the gut, right as they cruised by a low staircase clumped with pole fishermen.

A rough jump later and Iseult latched on to the flagstone stairs. None of the fishermen offered to help—they only shuddered back. One even stabbed at her with his fishing pole, his Threads a terrified gray.

Iseult grabbed the end of the pole. The man's Threads

blazed brighter, and he tried to yank the pole back—but proceeded to yank up Iseult instead. *Thank you,* she thought, straggling up the stairs. She glanced back once and saw blood streaked on the stones. Her palm was gushing a lot more than the distant pain warranted.

She reached the street. Traffic swarmed past, and she scrambled for some strategy. All of her plans were falling through the hell-gates, but surely Iseult could take a moment to think. She was crap at running pell-mell—it was why Safi was the leader in these situations. Without time to strategize, Iseult always ran herself into corners.

But as she stood there, slinking alongside the canal and clutching her bleeding hand in her cloak, she got the moment she needed.

Wide road, she thought. *A main artery from town, likely alongside this canal the whole way. Traffic organized in two directions, and a man leading a saddled brindle mare. No sweat darkening the mare's shoulders. If I take her, I can flee the city entirely and hide overnight with the tribe.*

Though returning to the home she'd spent most of her life avoiding was hardly Iseult's ideal solution, the Midenzi settlement was the only place she knew of that wouldn't kick her out at first sight of her skin.

It was also the *only* place she felt certain the Bloodwitch—even if he hunted her by sight and by blood—couldn't follow. The lands around the settlement were riddled with traps that no non-Midenzi could navigate.

So in a flurry of speed, Iseult shrugged off her cloak, tossed it over the man's head, and then vaulted into the mare's saddle—praying all the while that the mare's flattening ears were a sign she was ready to ride.

"I'm so sorry," she shouted as the man flailed beneath the salamander cloak. "I'll send her back!" Then she dug in her heels and left the man behind.

As the mare launched into a fast trot through traffic, Iseult flung her gaze across the canal. And found the Bloodwitch watching her. There were gaps in the boats now; he couldn't cross the water as she had.

But he *could* smirk at her—and wave too. A flicker of his right fingers and then a tapping of his right palm.

He knew her hand was bleeding, and he was telling her he could follow. That he *would* follow, and likely be smiling that terrifying smile all the way.

Iseult tore her gaze from his face, forcing her attention ahead. As she pressed low onto the mare's back and kicked the horse even faster, she prayed that the Moon Mother—or Noden or any other god that might be watching—would help her get out of this city alive.

Merik stared at the miniature Dalmotti ship gliding over the chart of the Jadansi Sea. It showed that the corresponding trade ship was just hauling wind from the Veñaza City harbors—and Merik wanted to fling the cursed miniature out the window.

The *Jana*'s Voicewitch, Hermin, sat at the head of the table. Though by no means common, Voicewitches were the most common Aetherwitch, and since they could find and communicate with fellow Voicewitches over vast distances, every ship in the Nubrevnan Royal Navy had one onboard—including Vivia, with whom Voicewitch Hermin was now connected.

Hermin's eyes glowed pink—a sign he was tapped into the Voicewitch Threads—and afternoon light flickered over his wrinkled face. Distant voices, rattling carts, and clopping hooves drifted in through open windows.

Merik knew he should shut them, but it was too sticky and too hot without the breeze. Plus, the tallow in the lanterns smoked and stank—an even fouler stench than the sewage on the Veñaza City canals.

But Merik thought it was worth saving money with smelly animal fat rather than paying heaps for smokeless Firewitch lanterns. And of course, that was a point upon which he and Vivia disagreed.

One of many.

"I don't think you understand, *Merry*." Though Hermin spoke with his own gravelly voice, he spoke in Vivia's exact style—all drawled words and condescending emphasis. "The Foxes strike instant fear in foreign navies. Hoisting that flag *now* will give us a strong advantage when the Great War resumes."

"Except," Merik said with no inflection, "we're here to negotiate peace. And though I agree Fox flags were once effective for intimidation, that was centuries ago. Before the empires had navies to crush ours."

It seemed so gallant on the surface—attacking trade ships to feed the poor—and tales of the old Fox navies were still favorites back home. But Merik knew better. Stealing from the more fortunate was still stealing, and promising to avoid violence was easier than actually refraining.

"I have one more meeting," Merik insisted. "With the Gold Guild."

"Which will fail as all your other meetings have. I thought you wanted to feed your people, Merry."

Sparks ignited in his chest. "Never," he growled, "question my desire to feed Nubrevna."

"You *claim* you want it, yet when I give you a way to gather food—a way to teach the empires a lesson—you don't jump at the chance."

"Because what you propose is piracy." Merik found it hard to look at Hermin as the Voicewitch continued to croon Vivia's words.

"What I propose is evening the odds. And may I remind you, Merry, that unlike you, I've attended summit meetings before. I've seen how the empires crush us beneath their heels. This Aetherwitched miniature is a means of fighting back. All you have to do is tell me when the trade ship reaches the Nubrevnan coast, and then I'll do all the dirty work."

All the killing, you mean. It took every piece of Merik's fragile self-control not to shout that at Vivia... But there was no point. Not when two Voicewitches and a hundred leagues stood between them.

He rolled his shoulders once. Twice. "What," he finally continued, "does Father say about this?"

"Nothing." Hermin drawled that word exactly as Vivia would. "Father is on the verge of death, and he stays as

silent as when you left. Why he roused himself to name *you* as envoy and admiral, I'll never understand . . . Yet it seems to be working in our favor, for we have an opportunity here, Merry."

"One that fits very neatly into your strategy for an empire of your own, you mean."

A pause. "Justice must be served, *little brother*." An edge coated Vivia's words now. "Or have you forgotten what the empires did to our home? The Great War ended for them, but not for *us*. The least we can do is pay back the empires in kind—starting with a bit of noble piracy."

At those words, the heat in Merik's chest lanced outward. Coiled into his fists. Were he with Vivia, he would let this storm loose—after all, she had the same rage simmering in her veins.

When Merik was a boy, his father had been certain that Merik was a powerful witch like his sister, that Merik's tantrums had been manifestations of a great power within. So at seven years old, King Serafin had forced Merik into the Witchery Examination.

Yet Merik's tantrums hadn't been a sign of power at all. Merik had barely been deemed strong enough for a Witchmark, and King Serafin had barely been able to hide his disgust in front of the Examination Board.

That same morning, on the carriage ride back to the royal palace and with Merik's new diamond tattoo burning on the back of his hand, Merik had learned in sharp, unyielding detail how deep his father's distaste ran. How a weak prince served no purpose to his family. Merik would be joining his aunt, the Nihar outcast, on the family lands in the southwest.

"You forget," Hermin said, still articulating Vivia, "who will lead when Father dies. You may have authority right now, but you are only a temporary admiral. *I* will be queen and admiral when the watery sleep finally claims Father."

"I know what you will be," Merik said softly, his anger falling back in the face of cold fear.

Vivia as queen. Vivia as admiral. Vivia sending Nubrevnans like lambs to the slaughter. The farmers and the soldiers, the merchants and the miners, the shepherds and the bakers—*they* would die on Cartorran swords or in Marstoki flames. All while Vivia watched on.

And Merik's one solution—rebuilding trade and proving to Vivia that there were peaceful ways to keep Nubrevnans fed . . . That plan had failed.

The worst of it, though, was that even if he refused to help Vivia in this piracy endeavor, Merik knew she would find another way. Somehow, she would hoist the Fox flag—and somehow, she would condemn all of their homeland to Noden's Hell.

In the momentary pause while Merik struggled for some solution out of this nightmare, a knock sounded at the cabin door.

Ryber, the ship's girl and Kullen's Heart-Thread, poked her head in. "Admiral? I'm sorry to interrupt, sir, but it's urgent. There's a man here to see you. He says his name is fon . . ." Her dark face scrunched up. "Fon *Hasstrel*—that was it. From Cartorra. And he wants to discuss possible trade with you."

Merik felt his jaw drop. Trade . . . with *Cartorra*. It seemed impossible, yet Ryber's earnest expression wasn't changing.

Noden Himself was interfering on Merik's behalf—and He did so right when Merik needed it most.

Merik wouldn't ignore a gift like that, so he rounded back to Hermin. "Vivia," he barked, "I'll help you, but on one condition."

"I'm listening."

"If I can negotiate a single line of trade for Nubrevna, then you'll stop your piracy. Immediately."

A pause. Then a slow, "Perhaps, Merry. If you *do* somehow establish trade, I'll . . . consider lowering the Fox flag. Now tell me: Where is the Dalmotti miniature right now?"

Merik couldn't keep from smiling—a sly thing—as he glanced at the map. The miniature was just leaving the marshy edge of the Veñaza City bay.

"It hasn't set sail," he declared, something buoyant and hopeful rising in his chest. "But I'll inform you the instant that it does. Hermin"—Merik clapped his hands on the Voicewitch's shoulder. The old sailor flinched—"You can end the call now. And Ryber?" Merik flung his gaze at the door, smiling all the wider. "Bring in this fon Hasstrel man right away."

After washing, Safi followed an unfamiliar coffee-haired maid back to her room, where the woman dressed her in the silvery white gown that Mathew had chosen. Then the maid coaxed Safi's hair into a series of hanging curls that draped and bounced and glistened in the sunset.

It was strange being dressed and doted upon—Safi hadn't experienced it in over seven years. Uncle Eron could never afford more than a handful of servants on the Hasstrel estate, so the only time a maid had served Safi had been during the annual trips to Praga.

Uncle Eron might have been a disgraced Hell-Bard, stripped of rank for only the gods knew why—and then appointed as a temporary dom until Safi was deemed fit to take over—but he still paid his tithes *exactly* as Henrick demanded. Every year, Eron and Safi had gone to the Cartorran capital to hand over their meager funds and swear fealty to Emperor Henrick.

And every year, it had been *awful*.

Safi had always been taller than the boys, always stronger, while the other girls had always whispered about Safi's sloshed uncle and snickered at her ancient gowns.

Yet it wasn't the shame that made the trips miserable. It was the fear.

Fear of the Hell-Bards. Fear that they would see Safi for the heretic she was—for the *Truthwitch* she was.

In fact, were it not for Prince Leopold—or Polly, as Safi had always called him—taking her under his wing each time she visited, she felt certain the Hell-Bards would have caught her by now. It was the job of the Hell-Bard Brigade, after all, to sniff out unmarked heretics.

And by order of the crown, they were allowed to behead

those heretics if they seemed dangerous or unwilling to cooperate.

Polly will probably be there tonight, Safi thought as she scrutinized herself in a narrow mirror beside the bed. It had been eight years since she'd last snuck off with him to explore the sprawling imperial library. She couldn't imagine how his long pale lashes and flopping golden curls would translate into a twenty-one-year-old man.

Safi certainly looked different, and this pale gown accentuated it. The tight bodice emphasized the strength of her waist and abdomen. The fitted long sleeves showed off her corded arms, the tight bodice emphasized what few curves she possessed, and the flowing skirts softened her hips into a feminine roundness. The dangling braids brought out the curves of her jaw. The brightness of her eyes.

Guildmaster Alix and his staff had truly outdone themselves this time.

Once the maid had left—after laying a stunning white cape across the bed—Safi darted for her satchel and yanked out Iseult's Carawen book. Then she strode to the window, where the canals glowed like flames beneath a setting sun.

Gauzy pink light filtered across the book's blue cover, and when Safi creaked it back, the pages whispered open to page thirty-seven. A bronze winged lion glimmered up at her, marking the last page Iseult had been reading.

Safi quickly scanned the text—a listing of Carawen monk divisions.

The bedroom door burst wide. Safi had just enough time to stuff the book back into the satchel before her uncle marched into the room.

Dom Eron fon Hasstrel was a tall man—muscled and hard-boned like Safi. Yet unlike Safi, his wheat hair blended into silvery gray and he wore purple bags beneath bloodshot eyes. For all that he'd been a soldier, he was nothing but a drunk now.

Eron stopped several paces away and scrubbed at the top of his head. It left his hair at all angles. "By the Twelve," he drawled, "why are you so pale? You look like the Void got you." Eron lifted his chin—and Safi noticed just the slightest wavering in his posture. "You must be nervous about the ball tonight."

"As are you," she said. "Why else would you be this drunk before dinner?"

Eron's lips eased into a smile—a surprisingly alert smile. "There's the niece I remember." He crossed to the window, fixed his gaze outside, and set to toying with a thin gold necklace he always wore.

Safi bit her lip, hating that—as usual—a hole was opening in her chest at the sight of Uncle Eron. Though her blood ran with the same Hasstrel blue as his, she and her uncle were strangers.

And when Eron was drunk—which he was more often than he was not—then Safi's witchery sensed nothing. No truth, no lies, no reaction whatsoever—as if whatever person he might be was washed away once the wine started flowing.

There had been, and always would be, a wall of stone and silence between them.

Leveling her shoulders, Safi strode to Eron's side. "So why am I here, Uncle? Mathew said you plan to interfere with the Great War. How exactly do you intend to do that?"

A gruff laugh from Eron. "So Mathew let that slip, did he?"

"Do you need to use my witchery?" Safi pressed. "Is *that* what this is about? Some drunken scheme to reclaim your Hell-Bard honor—"

"*No.*" The word snapped out—strong. Unyielding. "This is not a drunken scheme, Safiya. Far from it." Eron splayed his hands on the glass, and the old burn scars on his fingers and knuckles stretched taut.

Safi hated those scars. She'd stared at the white pocks a million times growing up. Wrapped around a wine jug or pinching a whore's bottom. Those scars were all Safi really knew of her uncle—the only glimpse she'd had into his past—and whenever she saw them, she couldn't help but fear that *this* was the future awaiting her; an insatiable thirst for what could never be.

Eron wanted his honor.

Safi wanted her freedom.

Freedom from her title and her uncle and the frozen, frozen Hasstrel halls. Freedom from the fear of Hell-Bards and beheadings. Freedom from her witchery and the entire Empire of Cartorra.

"You have no idea what war is like," Eron said, his tone hazy as if his mind also drifted across the old scars. "Armies razing villages, fleets sinking ships, witches igniting you with a single thought. Everything you love gets taken away, Safiya . . . and slaughtered. But you will learn soon enough. In all too vivid a detail, you will learn—unless you do as I ask. After tonight, you can leave forever."

A pause filled the room—then Safi's jaw slackened. "Wait—I can *leave?*"

"Yes." Eron offered an almost sad grin, fidgeting once more with his necklace. When he spoke again, the first sparks of truth—of happy warmth—awakened in Safi's chest.

"After you play the role of the dancing, drinking domna," he began, "and you do it for all of the empires to see . . . Well, after that, you'll be entirely free to go."

Free to go. The words reverberated through the air like the final note in an explosive symphony.

Safi swayed back. This was more than her mind could swallow—more than her witchery could swallow. Eron's words quavered and *burned* with truth.

"Why," Safi began carefully, afraid the wrong word would erase everything her uncle had said, "would you let me leave? I'm supposed to be domna of the Hasstrel lands."

"Not quite." He raised a single arm over his head and leaned against the glass. Everything about his posture was strangely indulgent, and his necklace, now removed, hung between his fingers. "Titles won't matter soon, Safiya, and, let's face it, neither you nor I ever expected you to actually lead the estate. You aren't exactly cut out for leadership."

"And you *are?*" She bristled. "Why did I study my whole life if this was your plan all along? I could have just left—"

"It wasn't my plan," he cut in, shoulders tensing. "But things change when war is on the horizon. Besides, do you regret all the tutoring and training you received?"

His head tipped to one side. "Your encounter with the Gold Guildmaster almost ruined everything I have planned, but I've managed to salvage the evening. Now all you have to do is act like a frivolous domna for a single night, and then your duties will be done. Forever."

Safi sputtered a laugh. "That's it? That's all you want from me? All you've *ever* wanted from me? Forgive me if I don't believe you."

He shrugged dismissively. "You don't have to believe me, but what does your magic say?"

Safi's witchery hummed with truth, warm behind her ribs. Yet still she found it impossible to swallow this story. Everything she'd ever wanted was suddenly being handed to her. It seemed far, *far* too good to be true.

Eron arched a pale eyebrow, clearly amused by Safi's bewilderment. "When the chimes toll midnight, Safiya, the Bloodwitch will no longer be a problem. Then you can do whatever you please and live out the same unambitious existence you've always enjoyed. Although . . ." He paused, gaze sharpening. There was no sign of drunkenness now. "If you wanted to, Safiya, you could bend and shape the world. You have the training for it—I've seen to that. Unfortunately," he spread his scarred hands, stretching the chain taut, "you seem to lack the initiative."

"If I lack the initiative," Safi whispered, the words tumbling out before she could stop them, "then it's because you made me this way."

"Too true." Eron smiled down at her, a rueful thing that frizzed with honesty. "But don't hate me for that, Safiya. Love me . . ." His arms opened idly. "And *dread* me. It's the

Hasstrel way, after all. Now finish getting dressed. We leave at the next chime."

Without another word, Eron stalked past Safi and left the room. Safi watched him go. She *made* herself watch his brisk gait and broad back.

Safi sank into the injustice for several *blistering* seconds. Unambitious? Lacking initiative? Perhaps that was true when it came to living in a frozen castle amidst a world of power-hungry nobility and ever-watchful Hell-Bards, but not when it came to a life with Iseult.

Safi pulled out the Carawen book once more and flipped it open. The piestra shone up at her, blooming like a rose at sunset. This page in particular was important, and Safi simply had to sort out why . . .

She dragged her finger down the ranks and divisions of monks. *Mercenary Monk, Teacher Monk, Guardian Monk, Artisanal Monk* . . . Her fingers paused on *Healer Monk*. It was one such monk who'd found Iseult when she'd fled her tribe. Iseult had gotten lost at a crossroads north of Veñaza City, and a kind Healer Monk had helped her find her way.

And that old crossroads was beside the lighthouse that the girls now used. Iseult must be planning to leave Veñaza City altogether and return to the usual hideout.

Safi dropped the book. Her head lolled back. She couldn't go there yet—she had to get through tonight first. She had to get this Bloodwitch off her trail and her uncle firmly taken care of. Then, with no worry of pursuit *ever* again, she could head north of the city and find her Threadsister.

Safi exhaled sharply, head lowering and body shifting toward the mirror. Eron wanted a dutiful domna, did he? Well, Safi could give him that. Throughout her childhood, the Cartorran nobility had seen her as a quiet, embarrassed thing, cowering behind her uncle while her toes tapped and her legs bounced.

But Safi wasn't that girl anymore, and the Hell-Bards had no power in *this* empire. So Safi puffed out her chest, pleased at how the gown emphasized her shoulders. How the sleeves stopped high enough to reveal her palms, striped with as many calluses as any soldier.

Safi was proud of her hands, and she couldn't wait for the doms and domnas to stare at them with revulsion. For the nobility to feel her fingers, rough as sandstone, when she danced with them.

For one night, Safi could be Domna of Cartorra. Hell, she would be a rutting *empress* if it got her back to Iseult, and away from the Bloodwitch.

After tonight, Safiya fon Hasstrel would be free.

EIGHT

Iseult stared at the dark mane of her brindle mare, one hand on the reins and the other held high in a poor attempt to stem her wound's bleeding.

The canal beside her glowed orange with the setting sun, and the stench of Veñaza City was finally starting to fade from her nostrils—as was the day's heat. Soon, Iseult would leave this damp marshland entirely and enter the wild meadows that surrounded her Nomatsi home. Mosquitoes would swarm her, and the horseflies would feast.

The traffic flooding from the guard's eastern checkpoint had been thick enough for Iseult to slink out of the capital unseen. Then, once the roads had emptied of people, she'd hopped onto her new steed and urged the mare into a full gallop.

The bleeding from the cut on her palm hadn't staunched, so she'd torn off the olive trim of her skirt and wrapped her hand. Each time the blood soaked through, she'd ripped off more cloth. Bandaged the wound more tightly—and then held her hand even higher.

Only one night, she told herself over and over, a refrain

thundering in time to the horse's four-beat gallop, then the three-beat canter. Finally, two leagues from the city limits, when the mare was dark with sweat, Iseult had dropped to a two-beat trot. *One night, one night.*

Beneath that percussive reminder pulsed a desperate hope that Iseult hadn't somehow endangered Safi by pointing her to the old lighthouse. Split-second plans weren't her strong point—and that's what the message to Habim had been. Haphazard. Rushed.

Eventually, Iseult reached a telltale copse of alders and slowed the mare to a walk before sliding off the saddle. Her upper thighs seared, her lower back groaned. She hadn't ridden in weeks—and not at such a speed in months. She could still feel her teeth rattling from the gallop. Or maybe that was the buzz of the cicadas in the whitethorns.

Though it looked like Iseult followed nothing more than a game trail winding through the grass, she knew it for what it was: a Nomatsi road.

She moved more slowly now, careful to read the Nomatsi markers as they came. A stick hammered into the dirt that looked *almost* accidental—it meant a claw-toothed bear trap at the next bend in the path. A cluster of "wild" morning glories on the left side of the path meant a fork in the road ahead—east would lead to a Poisonwitch mist, west to the settlement.

Following this path would get the Bloodwitch off of Iseult's tail for good. Then, after a few hours within the settlement's thick walls, Iseult could set out once more to meet Safi.

Although the Dalmotti Empire technically allowed

Nomatsis to live as they pleased—so long as their caravans stayed at least twenty miles outside of any city—they were also declared "animals." They had no legal protection yet *plenty* of Dalmotti hatred to contend with. So to say the Midenzis did not take kindly to outsiders was a vast understatement. As one of the only Nomatsi tribes to have settled down and stopped nomadic traveling, the Midenzis had found a safe niche here and clung to it.

The walls were thick, the archers keen, and if the Bloodwitch could somehow navigate this far, he would find a chest full of barbed arrows awaited him.

Yet, just as the Midenzis fought to keep outsiders away, they also fought to keep their own people in. If you left the settlement, you were deemed *other,* and *other* was the one thing a Nomatsi never wanted to be—not even Iseult.

When the telltale oaks masking the edge of the settlement's walls finally appeared, black and menacing in the night's darkness, Iseult stopped. This was her last chance to run. She could turn around and spend the rest of her life without ever seeing the tribe again—though a short life that might be with the Bloodwitch hunting her.

The moon was rising east of Iseult, illuminating her for all to see. She'd wound up her braid and tied it beneath her headscarf. Nomatsi women kept their hair chin length; Iseult's fell halfway down her back. She needed to keep that hidden.

"Name," a voice called out in the guttural Nomatsi tongue. A hostile steel Thread flickered at Iseult's left along with the faint shape of archers in the trees.

She lifted her hands submissively, hoping the bindings on her palm weren't too obvious. "Iseult," she shouted. "Iseult det Midenzi."

Oak leaves rustled; branches creaked. More Threads shimmered and moved as guards scooted over their trees to confer, to decide. The moments slid past with aching slowness. Iseult's heart beat against her lungs and echoed in her ears while the mare tossed her head. Then stamped. She needed to be rubbed down.

A shout split the night sky.

Two sparrows took flight.

Then came another shout from a throat Iseult knew—and she felt like she was falling. Plummeting off some mountain peak, losing her stomach as the earth closed in fast.

Stasis, she screamed inwardly. *Stasis in your fingertips and in your toes!*

She didn't find stasis, though. Not before the scrape of the huge gate hit her ears. Then footsteps hammered on the ground and a figure in Threadwitch black came sprinting toward her.

"Iseult!" her mother shouted with tears streaking down a face almost identical to Iseult's. False tears, of course, since true Threadwitches didn't cry—and Gretchya was nothing if not a true Threadwitch.

Iseult had just enough time to consider how small her mother seemed—only up to Iseult's nose—before her mother yanked her into a rib-snapping embrace and Iseult's mind filled with only one thought. A prayer, really, that the Bloodwitch stayed far, *far* away.

* * *

Iseult found that walking through the moonlit Midenzi settlement was both easier and harder than she'd expected.

It was easier because although little had changed in the three years since her last visit to the tribe, it all seemed smaller than she recalled. The timber walls surrounding the village were as weathered to gray as she remembered, but now they didn't seem so insurmountable. Just . . . tall. If not for the Nomatsi trail and the archers in the trees, the wall would be a mere inconvenience for that Bloodwitch.

The round homes built from stones as brown as the mud on which they stood looked like miniatures. Toy homes with narrow, low doors and shuttered windows.

Even the oaks that grew halfheartedly throughout the fifteen-acre settlement seemed scrawnier than Iseult remembered. Not large or strong enough for her to scale into the branches like she'd once done.

What made trekking through the tribe *harder* than Iseult expected was the people—or rather their Threads. As she followed her mother to her home at the center of the tribe, shutters popped wide, revealing curious faces. Their Threads were strangely dampened, wrung out like old towels.

Iseult flinched every time a figure rounded a corner or a door banged wide. Yet, every time, Iseult would also find she didn't recognize the moonlit face scrutinizing her.

It made no sense. New people in the tribe? Threads that were faded to near invisibility?

When Iseult finally reached her mother's round home, she found it as strangely tiny as everywhere else. Though Gretchya's hut wore the same orange rugs over the same wide plank floors from Iseult's childhood, it was all so *small.*

The worktable that had once come up to Iseult's waist, now only reached her mid-thigh—as did the dining table beneath the window on the eastern side. Behind the stove was a hatch that led to a dug-out basement. It looked so compact that Iseult wasn't sure she could even brave it down there.

The two times she'd come back—for only one night each visit—the cellar had felt terrifying and enclosed compared to Mathew's open-aired attic. And, after having had a bed of her own, the single pallet Iseult had always shared with her mother had seemed cramped. Inescapable.

"Come." Gretchya gripped Iseult's wrist and towed her to the four low stools around the stove that were customary in a Threadwitch's home. Iseult had to quash the need to wrench free of her mother's fingers. Gretchya's touch was even colder than she remembered.

And of course, her mother didn't notice the bloodied wrapping on her daughter's palm—or maybe she noticed but didn't care. Iseult couldn't gauge her mother's emotions because Threadwitches could neither see their own Threads nor those of other Threadwitches. And Gretchya was far more skilled at masking her feelings than Iseult had ever been.

In the guttering lantern light, though, Iseult could at least see that her mother's face had changed very little in three years. Perhaps a bit thinner and perhaps a few more lines around her frequently frowning mouth, but that was all that was different.

Gretchya finally released Iseult's wrist, snatched up a nearby stool, and set it before the hearth. "Sit while I'll spoon out borgsha. The meat is goat today—I hope that is still to your taste. Scruffs! Come! *Scruffs!*"

Iseult's breath hitched. *Scruffs*. Her old dog.

A *thump-thump-thump* sounded on the stairs into the house, and then there he was—old and saggy and with a listing canter.

Iseult slid off the stool. Her knees hit the rug, happy heat chuckling through her. She opened her arms, and the ancient red hound galloped toward her . . . until he was there, wagging his tail and nosing his grayed muzzle into Iseult's hair.

Scruffs, Iseult thought, afraid to speak his name. Afraid the stammer would be there from this unexpected surge of emotions. *Contradictory* emotions that she didn't want to wade through or interpret. If Safi were here, she'd know what it was that Iseult felt.

Iseult scratched at Scruffs's long ears. The tips were crusted with flecks of what looked like parsley. "Have you b-been eating borgsha?" Iseult backed onto the stool, still rubbing Scruff's face and trying to ignore how foggy his eyes were. How much gray had taken over his snout.

A melodic voice broke out. "Oh. You *are* home!"

Iseult's fingers froze on Scruffs's neck. Her vision throbbed inward, smearing the room and the dog's face. Perhaps if she pretended not to notice Alma, the other girl would simply fade into the Void.

No such luck. Alma skipped from the door to Iseult. Like Gretchya, she wore the traditional Threadwitch black dress that fit tightly through the chest but was loose over the arms, waist, and legs. "Moon Mother save me, Iseult!" Alma gaped down, her long-lashed green eyes shuttering with surprise. "You look just like Gretchya now!"

Iseult didn't answer. Her throat was hard with . . . with something. Anger, she supposed. She didn't want to look like Gretchya—a *true* Threadwitch like Iseult could never be. Plus, Iseult hated that Scruffs wagged his tail. Butted his head on *Alma's* knee. Turned to *Alma* and away from Iseult.

"You are a woman now," Alma added, plopping onto a stool.

Iseult gave a curt nod, skimming a quick eye over the other Threadwitch. Alma was a woman now too. A beautiful one—no surprise. Her chin-length coal-black hair was thick, glossy . . . perfect. Her waist was small, her hips curved, and her shape all that was feminine and . . . *perfect.*

Alma was, as she'd always been, the perfect Threadwitch. The perfect Nomatsi woman. Except when Iseult's gaze settled on Alma's hands, she saw thick calluses.

Iseult flipped up Alma's palm. "You've trained with a sword."

Alma flung a furtive glance at Gretchya, who nodded slowly. "A cutlass," Alma admitted. "I've been practicing with one for the past few years."

Iseult dropped Alma's wrist. Of course Alma had learned to fight. Of course she would be perfect at that too. There could never be anything that Iseult performed better—it was as if the Moon Mother made sure that any skill Iseult tried to hone, Alma acquired it too . . . and perfected it.

When it had become clear that Iseult would never be able to make Threadstones or keep her emotions distant enough, Alma had moved from being an extra Threadwitch in a passing Nomatsi tribe to being *the* Threadwitch apprentice of the Midenzi settlement. When Gretchya became too old to guide the tribe, Alma would take over.

In Nomatsi caravans, it was the job of the Threadwitch to unite Thread-families, to arrange marriages and friendships, and to unsnarl the looms of people's lives. One day, just as Gretchya did now, Alma would use her magic to lead the Midenzis.

"Your hand," Alma said. "You're hurt!"

"It's fine," Iseult lied, hiding her palm in her skirt. "It stopped bleeding."

"Clean it anyway," Gretchya said, tone unreadable.

Iseult's nose twitched. Here were two women whose Threads she couldn't see. Yet before Iseult could request a moment alone to sort through everything—coming home, the Bloodwitch hunting her, Alma's *perfection*—a man poked his black-haired head through the door. "Welcome home, Iseult."

Spiders walked down Iseult's spine. Alma's fingers squeezed on Scruffs's neck—and Gretchya blanched.

"Corlant," she began, but the man cut her off, sliding the rest of his long body inside.

Corlant det Midenzi had changed almost none since Iseult had last seen him. His hair was perhaps thinner, and gray swept the sides, but the creases above his eyebrows were as deep as Iseult remembered—parallel trenches from a tendency to always look mildly shocked.

He looked mildly shocked now, brows high and eyes glittering as they scrutinized Iseult's face. He approached her, and Gretchya made no move to stop him. Instead, Alma shot to her feet and hissed at Iseult, "*Stand.*"

Iseult stood—though she didn't see why she had to. Gretchya was the leader of the tribe, not this syrup-tongued Purist who had sowed discord throughout Iseult's childhood. Corlant ought to be the one sitting.

He stopped before her, his Threads shimmering with a green curiosity and tan suspicion. "Do you remember me?"

"Of course," Iseult said, folding her hands in her skirts and tipping her head back to meet his gaze. Unlike the rest of the tribe, *he* was just as tall as she remembered, and he even wore the same murky brown robe and the same smudged gold chain around his neck.

It was a bad attempt to look like a Purist priest. By now Iseult had seen enough *real* priests trained in *real* Purist compounds to know how badly Corlant missed his mark.

Yet it didn't seem to change the fact that Alma and Gretchya were showing Corlant deference. Were sharing panicked glances behind his back while he examined Iseult.

He strutted around her, gaze roving. It sent the hairs on her arms spiking upward. "You have the taint of the outside on you, Iseult. Why are you back?"

"She plans to stay this time," Gretchya inserted. "She will resume her position as my apprentice."

"So you have been expecting her?" Corlant's Threads

turned darkly hostile. "You made no mention of this to me, *Gretchya*."

"It wasn't certain," Alma piped up, beaming gloriously. "You know how Gretchya hates to snag the settlement's weave if she doesn't have to."

Corlant offered a grunt, his attention settling on Alma. His Threads twisting with more tan suspicion, and deep beneath that, a lusty lilac. Then his gaze speared Gretchya, and the lust flared outward.

Iseult's stomach curdled. This was not the dynamic she'd left behind. Corlant had been a nuisance when she was a child—always spouting the dangers and the sins of witcheries. Always claiming that true devotion to the Moon Mother was in the denial of one's magic. The eradication of it.

But Iseult had ignored him along with the rest of the tribe. Yes, Corlant had hung around her home and begged Gretchya for attention. He had even asked her to become his wife—not that Gretchya could marry. Only Heart-Threads could marry in a Nomatsi tribe, and Threadwitches didn't have Heart-Threads.

At first, Gretchya had ignored Corlant's advances. Then she'd used reason, pointing to the Nomatsi tribal laws and the Moon Mother's rules as well. By the time Iseult had fled the tribe, though, Gretchya had resorted to latching the doors at night with iron padlocks and paying two local men in silver to keep the serpentine Corlant away.

When Iseult had visited last, though, Corlant had been gone—and Iseult had assumed the man had left for good. Clearly, though, that wasn't the case—and clearly things had changed. Somehow Corlant had gotten the upper hand here.

"I have alerted the tribe to Iseult's arrival," Corlant said, spine unfurling to its fullest length. His head almost reached the ceiling. "The Greeting should begin soon."

"How smart of you," Gretchya said—but Iseult didn't miss the muscle twitch in her mother's jaw.

Gretchya was scared. Truly *scared*.

"I was so distracted by Iseult's return," Gretchya continued, "that I completely forgot a Greeting. We will have to get her changed—"

"No." Corlant's voice slashed out. He spindled back toward Iseult, eyes cruel and Threads hostile once more. "Let the tribe see her exactly as she is, tainted by the outside." He plucked at Iseult's apprentice sleeve, and Iseult forced her head to bow.

She might not be able to read her mother or Alma, but she could read Corlant. He wanted control; he wanted Iseult's submission, so as her knees creaked into an unpracticed curtsy, Iseult rumbled a groan. Pulled it up from her stomach and clutched her hands to her gut.

It sounded horribly overdone, and for a brief flicker of a heartbeat, Iseult desperately wished *again* that Safi were with her. Safi could brazen through this no problem.

But if Alma heard the falseness in Iseult's moan, she made no sign of it. She simply lurched toward Iseult. "Are you ill?"

"It's my moon cycle," Iseult gritted out. She met Corlant's eyes, pleased to see his Threads already paling with revulsion. "I need new blood wrappings."

"Oh you poor thing!" Alma cried. "I have a raspberry leaf tincture for that."

"We must burn your current wrappings and get you unspoiled clothing," Gretchya inserted, twisting toward Corlant, who—to Iseult's surprise and satisfaction—was retreating. "If you could please shut the door on your way out, Priest Corlant, we will begin the Greeting very soon. Thank you again for informing the tribe of Iseult's return."

Corlant's eyebrows bounced high, but he offered no argument—nor spoke another word as he slipped outside and heaved shut the door. A door *without* padlocks but with faded, chipped wood where the iron had once been.

"Good thinking," Alma hissed at Iseult, none of her happy glow remaining. "You aren't really on your cycle are you?"

Iseult shook her head, but then Gretchya grabbed her bicep tight. "We must work quickly," she whispered. "Alma, get Iseult one of your gowns and find the Earthwitch healer salve for her hand. Iseult, take off your kerchief. We must deal with your hair."

"What's going on?" Iseult was careful to keep her voice flat despite the growing thump beneath her ribs. "Why is Corlant in charge? And why did you call him *Priest* Corlant?"

"Shhh," Alma said. "You must not let anyone hear." Then she scampered to the basement hatch and descended below the floorboards.

Gretchya towed Iseult to her worktable. "Everything has changed. Corlant runs this tribe now. He uses his witchery to—"

"Witchery?" Iseult cut in. "He's a Purist."

"Not entirely." Her mother turned to the desk, sweeping stones and spools of multicolored thread aside—looking for only the gods knew what. "The rules have become much stricter since you left," Gretchya went on. "Ever since the rumors of the Puppeteer began and cleaving became more frequent, Corlant has been able to wedge himself deeper and deeper into the tribe. He feeds off their fear and fans it to flames."

Iseult blinked in bewilderment. "What is the Puppeteer?"

Her mother didn't answer, her eyes finally lighting on what she needed: shears. She snatched them up. "We must cut your hair. It's just . . . you look too much like an outsider—and, if Corlant is to be believed, then too much like the Puppeteer. Thank the Moon Mother you were smart enough to hide your head—we can pretend it was short all along." Gretchya motioned for Iseult to sit. "We must convince the tribe that you are harmless. That you are *not* other." Gretchya held Iseult's gaze; a silence grew.

Then Iseult nodded, telling herself she didn't care. It was just hair and she could always grow it again. It didn't *mean* anything. Her life in Veñaza City was gone; she had to let go of that past.

Then she sat, the sheers grated into the first chunk of hair, and it was done. There was no going back.

"For all that Corlant pretends to be a Purist," Gretchya began, slipping into the same inflectionless voice Iseult had grown up hearing, "he is also a Voidwitch. A *Cursewitch*. I figured it out shortly after your last visit. I noticed that when he was near me, the Threads of the world were dimmer. Perhaps you noticed too?"

Iseult nodded her acknowledgment—and ice trickled down her neck. All the dulled Threads of the tribe were Corlant's doing. She hadn't even known such a thing was possible.

"Once I realized what he was," Gretchya continued, "and once I saw how his power drained away mine, I thought I could use it as leverage against him. I threatened to tell the tribe what he was . . . But in turn, he threatened to take my witchery completely.

"I ended up putting the noose around my own neck, Iseult, for after that conversation, Corlant threatened to erase my magic whenever he wanted something from me."

Gretchya spoke so matter-of-factly—as if the *something* that Corlant wanted was as simple as a bowl of borgsha or borrowing Scruffs for the day. But Iseult knew better. She remembered the way Corlant had lingered in the shadows near the chicken coop and watched Gretchya through the window. How his throbbing purple Threads had made Iseult learn all too young what "lust" meant.

Goddess save her, what would have happened to Iseult if she hadn't gotten out of the settlement when she had? How close had she been to wearing the same noose as her mother?

Despite the six and a half years of loathing Iseult had so carefully and intentionally honed, she felt like a knife was digging into her breastbone. *Guilt,* her brain declared. *And pity for your mother.*

To think that Corlant had been a Cursewitch all along.

Able to kill a person's magic as easily as Iseult saw a person's Threads. It was another witchery linked to the Void—and another myth proven to be all too real.

Iseult loosed a breath, careful to keep her head still as Gretchya snip-snip-snipped. "Wh-what . . ." she began, appalled by the shake in her voice. She could practically feel the frown her mother turned on her—could practically hear the inevitable reprimand: *Control your tongue. Control your mind. A Threadwitch never stammers.* "What," Iseult gnashed out at last, "is this Puppeteer?"

"She is a young Threadwitch." The shears ground against Iseult's hair—harder, faster. Hair scattered across the floor like sand. "Each passing Nomatsi caravan has had a slightly different tale, but the general story is unchanged. She cannot make Threadstones, she cannot control her emotions, and . . . and she abandoned her tribe."

Iseult swallowed tightly. This Puppeteer *did* sound similar.

"They say that unlike *our* Aetherial connection to the Threads," Gretchya continued, "this girl's power comes from the Void. They say she can control the Cleaved. That she keeps vast armies of them under her command—and in the darkest version of the tale, she even brings the dead back to life."

Cold latched on to Iseult's shoulders. "How?"

"The Severed Threads," Gretchya answered softly. "She claims she can control the *Threads* of the Cleaved. Bend them to her will, even when they are dead."

"The three black Threads of the Cleaved," Iseult whispered, and the snap of the shears abruptly stopped. At the same moment, Alma scurried up from the basement, a black gown in one hand and white blood-wrappings in the other. She hurried to the stove and heaved open the iron door.

Gretchya twisted around to face Iseult. "You know Severed Threads?"

"I have seen them."

Gretchya's eyes went wide, her face bloodless. "You must tell no one of this, Iseult. *No one*. Alma and I thought they were a lie. A way for this Puppeteer—and Corlant too—to scare people."

Iseult's mouth went dry. "You can't see these Threads?"

"No. And we have seen Cleaved before."

"I-I can't m-make Threadstones," Iseult spat, "so why sh-should *I* be the one who sees these Severed Threads?"

Gretchya was silent, but then she tugged at Iseult's hair and the snipping of the shears resumed. Moments later, smoke began to curl from the stove. Alma returned to the work table and offered Iseult the traditional black gown of a Threadwitch. Black was the color of all Threads combined, and along the collar, the narrow wrist cuffs, and the skirt's hem, there were three lines of color: a straight magenta line for the Threads that bind. A swirling sage line for the Threads that build. A dashed gray line for the Threads that break.

"How long do you intend to stay?" Alma's question was a rough whisper, no louder than the fire.

"Only a single night," Iseult said, forcing her mind to *avoid* considering the Bloodwitch. She had enough to worry about in the tribe.

Absently, she picked up a strip of uncut red stone from the worktable. A ruby, Iseult thought, and around it was a strand of sunset pink thread expertly wrapped with loops and knots.

Several stones away was its twin. And Iseult didn't miss the sapphires along the back of the table or the smattering of opals.

Only in a Threadwitch's home could one find such valuable jewels left unprotected. But a Threadwitch knew her own stones—she could follow them, even—and no Nomatsi would ever be stupid enough to risk stealing from a Threadwitch.

"Do you like the Threadstone?" Alma asked. She leaned against the table—though she kept rubbing her palms against her thighs as if they sweated.

Yet not once did Gretchya say to Alma, *Keep your hands still. A Threadwitch never fidgets.*

"Alma made it," Gretchya said.

Of course you did. Iseult had never been able to get a Threadstone to work, and here was Alma, with a piece to outshine any other.

"I did," Alma said—though the words almost came out as a question: *I did?*

Iseult's gaze snapped to her. "Why would you make a Threadstone for me?" She felt her forehead bunch up, felt her lips curl back. It was such a disgusted face—such an uncontrolled and un-Threadwitch expression—she instantly wished she hadn't made it.

Alma flinched—yet quickly schooled her face blank and plucked up the second ruby wrapped in pink thread.

"It's a . . ." She trailed off, glancing at Gretchya as if unsure what to say.

"It's a gift," Gretchya prompted. "Do not be shy—Iseult only frowns at you because she is confused and cannot control her expressions."

Heat licked up Iseult's face. Irate heat. Or perhaps shamed heat. "But how did you make it?" she ground out. "I'm a Threadwitch—you can't see my Threads, so you can't attach them to a stone."

"Your . . . your mother," Alma started.

"I showed her how," Gretchya finished. She dropped the scissors on the worktable and marched toward the stove. "The cloths will finish burning soon and Corlant will be back. Hurry."

Iseult pressed her lips thin. Her mother's response was no answer at all.

"You should be grateful," Gretchya continued as she poked at the stove's flames. "Those rubies in your hand will glow when Safiya is in danger—and when you are too. It will even allow you to track each other. Such a gift should not be taken lightly."

She *wasn't* taking the gift lightly—yet nor would she feel gratitude toward Alma. Ever. Alma had made this out of guilt. She was, after all, the reason Iseult had been denied a place as a Threadwitch apprentice—and also rejected as Gretchya's heir.

"Get dressed," Gretchya ordered Iseult. "And quickly, while Alma sweeps up this cut hair. We must tell Corlant and the tribe that you changed your mind and wish to return to the tribe as a Threadwitch."

Iseult opened her mouth—to point out that her mother could not have *two* apprentices and that the tribe was well aware of Iseult's magical failings—but then she let her lips fall shut. Alma was grabbing for the broom and following orders just as a Threadwitch ought to. Because Threadwitches did not argue; they followed the cool course of logic where it led.

Logic had led Iseult here, so she would ignore her hurt and fear, and she would follow logic as she'd been trained. As she'd managed throughout her time in Veñaza City, with Safi at her side.

NINE

Never—not in ten million lifetimes—would Safi have expected to slip into her role as a domna this easily. Not with so many people around her, their body heat filling the vaulted ballroom and their constant lies scraping over her skin. But the children from her past had angled into adulthood while their parents had seamed into old age.

And with all the sparkling wine and the shine of chandeliers, with the wall of glittering glass that overlooked the Jadansi's marshy shore, it was hard for Safi *not* to enjoy herself.

In fact, she found it no different from pulling a con with Iseult. She was playing the right hand while her uncle cut some unknown purse. If this was all that Uncle Eron wanted from her, then Safi could—almost happily—comply. Especially with Prince Leopold fon Cartorra at her side.

He had grown into a fine specimen of a man—though still much too pretty to be taken seriously. In fact, he was undoubtedly the most beautiful person, male or female, in the room. His curls were a glossy strawberry, his skin had a golden red-cheeked glow, and those long blond lashes that Safi so vividly remembered were still draped over his sea green eyes.

Yet for all his external changes, he was the same sharp-tongued, playful boy she remembered.

He tipped back a gulp of wine. It set his curls to flopping—and several nearby domnas to sighing.

"You know," he drawled, "the blue velvet on my suit lacks the depth I'd hoped for. I specifically requested imperial sapphire." His voice was a rich baritone, and the way he balanced his words with pauses was almost musical. "But I'd call this more of a dull navy, wouldn't you?"

Safi snorted. "I'm glad to see you haven't changed, Polly. For all your wit, you remain as infatuated with your looks as ever."

He flushed at the name *Polly*—as he had every other time she'd uttered it this evening, which had only made her want to say it more.

"Of course I haven't changed." Leopold shrugged gracefully. "My perfect face is all I have, and studying hard will only get you so far in Cartorra." He flipped his un-Witchmarked hand at her. "But *you*, Safiya"—pause—"have changed quite a bit, haven't you? That was a dramatic entrance you made."

She looked away, her own cheeks heating up—but not with shame. With fury.

She'd arrived at the ball a full hour late. Twilight had already melted into moonlight because Uncle Eron had insisted on finishing an entire jug of wine before departure.

Upon arrival at the Doge's palace, though, Safi understood why: Eron's former Hell-Bard brothers were on duty.

Four of the armored knights stood sentry in the Doge's garden, where cypress branches whispered in the breeze and tree frogs harmonized. Two more Hell-Bards guarded the palace entrance, and the final six waited stonily behind Emperor Henrick.

Every time Safi spotted another one of the enormous, axe-wielding knights, her stomach dropped to her toes. Her fists balled up tight. Yet every time, she kept her chin high and her shoulders back.

Not that any of the Hell-Bards noticed Safi or her uncle. In fact, only one showed any reaction as they strode past—and as far as Safi could tell from beneath the steel helm that all Hell-Bards wore, he'd been young. Too young to have served with Uncle Eron.

Actually, now that Safi considered it, maybe that Hell-Bard's bold wink in the gardens hadn't been directed at Uncle Eron but at *her*.

She did look rutting gorgeous tonight.

By the time Safi and Uncle Eron had reached the entrance hall, the other doms and domnas had long since moved to the ballroom. The Emperor, however, had insisted that he and Prince Leopold wait until the final dom arrived.

When Polly spotted Safi striding toward him, he rushed in front of his uncle's throne—as if buffering her from the Hell-Bards' stares like he'd always done in childhood—and swept a charming bow. He even cut in when Henrick held Safi's hand a bit too long after she knelt in fealty (gods below, she had forgotten how very toad-like the Cartorran emperor looked—and how very sweaty his grip was).

And Leopold even went so far as to escort Safi personally into the ball, and, oh, if that hadn't caught the gossip tongues in a mousetrap. She had almost laughed at the first slack-jawed domna. It was as if everyone had forgotten how she and Leopold had conspired as children.

After the prince had directed Safi to a servant with sparkling wines, he'd pushed a flute into her hand, and then snagged one for himself before guiding her to the food.

The *food*!

Table after table was set up beside the window and laden with a thousand delicacies from across the three empires. Safi was determined to try every single item before the ball ended.

"A chocolate volcano," Leopold said, pointing to a silver basin in which there appeared to be chocolate bubbles. "The one disadvantage of forbidding Firewitches in Cartorra is that"—pause—"we miss out on tricks like this." He motioned to a servant in beige satin. The man quickly ladled out the chocolate and poured it over a bowl filled with fresh strawberries.

Safi's eyes bugged, yet as she grabbed for the bowl, Leopold deftly snatched it away, smiling. "Allow *me* to serve you, Safiya. We have spent too many years apart."

"And I have spent too many hours between meals." A glare. "Give it to me now, Polly, or I shall castrate you with a fork."

Now *his* eyes bugged. "By the Twelve, have you heard the

things you say?" But he did relinquish the bowl of strawberries, and after biting into the first, Safi moaned her delight.

"These are divine," she gushed from beneath a mouthful of chocolate. "They remind me of the ones from—" She broke off, her chest suddenly too large.

She had been about to say the strawberries reminded her of the ones from home. *Home!* As if the mountains and valleys around the Hasstrel estate had ever been home—or the strawberries ever this divine.

Leopold did not seem to notice Safi's sudden silence, though. His eyes ran over the colorful diplomats. The domnas in their fitted black skirts and frilly, high-necked bodices of a thousand rich, earthy tones. The doms in their black waistcoats and velvet puffy shorts that only served to make their legs look knobby and ridiculous.

In fact, Leopold seemed to be the only male capable of making the shorts and tights look appealing—and didn't he know it, judging by the way he strutted about. The tights revealed strong legs—surprisingly well-muscled—and the blue velvet brought out flecks of the same shade in his eyes.

Safi was pleased to note that her own gown was garnering envious looks, and the only gown Safi thought better than her own was that of Vaness, the Marstoki Empress. White strips of cloth draped a thousand ways over the woman's bronze skin, and her dark hair tumbled over the bold exposure of her right shoulder. Gold studs were pasted over her Witchmark—a square for Earth and a single, vertical line for Iron—while two shackle-like bracelets adorned her wrists (said to represent her servitude to her people). She wore no crown, and was—in Safi's opinion—utter simplicity and elegance.

Though Safi had only seen Vaness from a distance, she had immediately appreciated the bored dip in the young woman's shoulder. The flat expression of a person who had better places to be and more meaningful things to do.

Safi had promptly tried to copy that pose—though she'd also promptly forgotten after spotting the first cream-filled pastry.

As if reading her mind, Leopold asked, "Have you seen the Empress's daring gown? Every man has his jaw on the floor."

"But not you?" Safi asked, eyes narrowing.

"No. Not me."

The lie of the statement crawled over her skin, but she didn't care enough to press. If Leopold wished to hide his interest in the Empress's perfect shoulders, why should Safi care?

"Do you wish to meet the Empress?" he asked abruptly.

Safi gasped. "Really?"

"Of course."

"Then *yes*, please." She thrust her unfinished strawberries at a waiting attendant while Leopold stepped lightly into the throngs of people. She followed him toward a low stage at the back corner where a small orchestra tuned their instruments.

But it was strange, for as Safi and Leopold moved amongst the curious nobility of all ages and nationalities, there was a single bright question on everyone's lips. Safi could no more hear what they murmured than she could read their thoughts, but whatever it was they considered, their question burned with the sharp light of truth. It flickered down the back of Safi's neck and in her throat—and it made her *enormously* curious to know of what they spoke.

Leopold reached a swarm of colorfully clad women—their gowns also made from the same striped, draping cloth as the Empress's—and a clump of men. *Nubrevnan men,* Safi thought when her eyes settled on their loose black hair and salt-roughened skin. Their coats fell to their knees, most of them the color of stormy blue, though one man wore silver gray and cut into her path.

"Excuse *you,*" she muttered, trying to sidestep him.

But the man stopped, blocking Safi entirely, before glancing back.

Safi choked. It was the Nubrevnan from the pier, cleaned up and practically glowing beneath the candlelight.

"Why it's *you,*" she said in Nubrevnan, her voice overly dulcet. "Whatever are you doing here?"

"I might ask you the same." He didn't look impressed as he shifted his body toward her.

"I am a Domna of Cartorra."

"Somehow that doesn't surprise me."

"I see," she drawled, "that you have learned how to work a button. Congratulations on this no doubt life-altering feat."

He laughed—a surprised sound—and bowed his head. "And I see you have cleaned the bird crap off your shoulder."

Her nostrils flared. "Excuse me, but Prince Leopold fon Cartorra is expecting me—and surely your prince needs you as well." She spoke flippantly, barely aware of what she said.

Yet the result was extreme, for the young man *smiled*. A true, beautiful smile that made everything in the room fall away. All Safi saw for a single, stuttering heartbeat was how his dark eyes almost crinkled shut and his forehead smoothed out. How his chin tipped up slightly to reveal the muscles in his neck.

"I have absolutely nowhere to be," he said softly. "Nowhere but here." Then, as if she was not stunned enough, the man swooped her a half-bow and said, "Would you honor me with a dance?"

And just like that, all of Safi's shields crumbled. She forgot how to be a domna. She lost control of her cavalier cool. Even the Nubrevnan language seemed impossible to wield.

For this man seemed to be mocking her—just like the doms and domnas from her childhood, just like Uncle Eron. He intended to embarrass her. "There is no music," she rushed to say, launching past the man.

But he caught her arm with the ease of a fighter. "There will be music," he promised before calling, "Kullen?"

The enormous man from the pier materialized beside them.

"Will you tell the orchestra to play a four-step?" The Nubrevnan's gaze never left Safi's face, but his smile eased into mischief. "If you don't know the Nubrevnan four-step, Domna, then I can choose something else, of course."

Safi held a strategic silence. She *did* know the four-step, and if this man thought to embarrass her on the dance floor, then he was about to be very surprised.

"I know the dance," she murmured. "Lead the way."

"Actually," he answered, voice rippling with satisfaction, "I don't move, Domna. People move for *me*." He flourished a single hand, and suddenly all the Nubrevnans cleared away.

Then Safi caught the words of nearby viewers: "Do you see with whom Prince Merik dances?"

"Prince Merik Nihar is dancing with that fon Hasstrel girl."

"Is that Prince Merik?"

Prince Merik. The name swirled and licked across the floor and into Safi's ears, glowing with the pureness that only a true statement could.

Well, hell-gates, no wonder the man looked so smug. He was the rutting prince of Nubrevna.

The dance began, and it did not take long before Merik realized he'd made a mistake.

Where he'd hoped to teach the girl some manners—she was supposed to be a domna, after all, not some street urchin—and perhaps to relieve some of the ever-present rage in his chest, Merik was only serving to humiliate himself.

Because this foul-mouthed domna was a far better dancer than he could have ever anticipated. Not only did she know the four-step—a Nubrevnan dance popular between lovers or performed as a feat of athletic prowess—but she was good at it.

Each triple stamp of Merik's heel and toe, she repeated right on beat. Each double twirl and flip of his wrist, she managed to throw back as well.

And this was only the first quarter of the Nubrevnan four-step. Once they actually moved body-to-body, he had no doubt he'd be sweating and gasping for air.

Of course, if Merik had paused to consider this offer of a dance before making it, he would have seen the humiliation coming. He'd watched the girl fight, after all, and he'd been impressed by her use of speed and wiles to best a man bigger and stronger than she.

The music stopped its simple four-beat plucking and shifted into the full sliding sound of bows on violins. With a silent prayer to Noden upon His coral throne, Merik strode forward. The March of the Dominant Sea, it was called. Then he paused with one hand up, palm out.

The young domna swept forward. She winked at Merik two steps in and added an almost effortless twirl before meeting him with an upright palm of her own. The Waltz of the Fickle River, indeed.

Their other hands flipped up, palm to palm, and Merik's only consolation as he and the domna slid into the next movement of the dance was that her chest heaved as much as his did.

Merik's right hand gripped the girl's, and with no small amount of ferocity, he twisted her around to face the same direction as he before wrenching her to his chest. His hand slipped over her stomach, fingers splayed. Her left hand snapped up—and he caught it.

Then the real difficulty of the dance began. The skipping of feet in a tide of alternating hops and directions.

The writhing of hips countered the movement of their feet like a ship upon stormy seas.

The trickling tap of Merik's fingers down the girl's arms, her ribs, her waist—like the rain against a ship's sail.

On and on, they moved to the music until they were both sweating. Until they hit the third movement.

Merik flipped the girl around to face him once more. Her chest slammed against his—and by the Wells, she was tall. He hadn't realized just *how* tall until this precise moment when her eyes stared evenly into his and her panting breaths fought against his own.

Then the music swelled once more, her legs twined into his, and he forgot all about who she was or what she was or why he had begun the dance in the first place.

Because those eyes of hers were the color of the sky after a storm.

Without realizing what he did, his Windwitchery flickered to life. Something in this moment awoke the wilder parts of his power. Each heave of his lungs sent a breeze swirling in. It lifted the girl's hair. Kicked at her wild skirts.

She showed no reaction at all. In fact, she didn't break her gaze from Merik, and there was a fierceness there—a challenge that sent Merik further beneath the waves of the dance. Of the music. Of those eyes.

Each leap backward of her body—a movement like the tidal tug of the sea against the river—led to a violent *slam* as Merik snatched her back against him. For each leap and slam, the girl added in an extra flourishing beat with her heels. Another challenge that Merik had never seen, yet rose to, rose *above*. Wind crashed around them like a growing hurricane, and he and this girl were at its eye.

And the girl never looked away. Never backed down.

Not even when the final measures of the song began—that abrupt shift from the sliding cyclone of strings to the simple plucking bass that follows every storm—did Merik soften how hard he pushed himself against this girl. Figuratively. Literally.

Their bodies were flush, their hearts hammering against each other's rib cages. He walked his fingers down her back, over her shoulders, and out to her hands. The last drops of a harsh rain.

The music slowed. She pulled away first, slinking back the required four steps. Merik didn't look away from her face, and he only distantly noticed that, as she pulled away, his Windwitchery seemed to settle. Her skirts stopped swishing, her hair fluttered back to her shoulders.

Then he slid backward four steps and folded his arms over his chest. The music came to a close.

And Merik returned to his brain with a sickening certainty that Noden and His Hagfishes laughed at him from the bottom of the sea.

TEN

One by one, the settlers of the Midenzi tribe came to welcome Iseult. To scrutinize the one girl who'd left the commune and now wanted to return.

Iseult's head felt too light, and snipped hairs scratched at the back of her neck, but like the good Threadwitch she was meant to be, she did not scratch. Nor did she fidget on her stool by the hearth or show any expression beyond the required smile.

The Threads of the Nomatsi were frighteningly pale. Only Corlant's Threads, pulsing behind Iseult as he stood beside the stove and watched the Greeting, burned at full brightness. Perhaps too bright, even.

By the thirtieth visitor, Iseult was exhausted from pretending that Corlant wasn't right there, observing like a raptor. Alma's face remained serene throughout—of course—and the smile she offered visitors seemed genuine. Not to mention tireless.

By the sixtieth visitor, Iseult had petted Scruffs so thoroughly, he actually looked uncomfortable. By the eightieth visitor, he got up and moved.

Stasis. Stasis in your fingertips and in your toes.

"That was only one hundred and ninety-one," Corlant declared once the final visitor was gone. "Where is the rest of the tribe, I wonder?" Nothing about Corlant's tone was wondering, and as he coasted toward the door, his Threads were pink with excitement. "I will make sure the whole tribe knows about the Greeting." He latched a penetrating stare on Gretchya, and in a voice made of mudslides, added, "Do. Not. Leave."

"Of course not," Gretchya said, lowering to a stool beside Iseult . . .

Then Corlant left, and Gretchya was instantly back on her feet. She towed up Iseult while Alma darted for the basement hatch.

"We must hurry," Gretchya whispered. "Corlant clearly knows what Alma and I have planned. He will try to stop us."

"Planned?" Iseult asked, but at that moment, there was a sudden *slash* like the shears through Iseult's hair. In an explosive spiral, everything that bound the three witches to the village *slammed* into their chests.

The Threads that bound had broken.

Iseult could not see it, but she felt it. A sudden lurch in her heart that almost knocked her off her feet.

Alma shoved Iseult toward the door. "Run," she hissed. "To the gate—*run!*"

Something about Alma's panicked, green eyes pierced Iseult's brain. She bolted through the door . . . only to stumble, arms windmilling to keep her upright.

For a mob waited outside. With lanterns and torches and

crossbows. The four hundred Nomatsis who had missed the Greeting had gathered on silent feet, their Threads hidden by Corlant's magic.

And there was Corlant himself, slithering through the crowd, a head taller than everyone else and Threads writhing with purple hunger.

People scattered from his path. Faces leered in the shadows—faces Iseult recognized, hateful faces from her childhood that made her knees buckle and chest hollow out.

She flung a glance behind her—but the house was empty. Only Scruffs remained, growling with raised hackles.

Iseult waited, breath held, as Corlant raked her with a ravenous gaze that sent purple across his Threads. Then, with deliberate slowness, he crossed his thumbs at Iseult. It was the sign to ward off evil.

"Other," he said softly, almost inaudible over the evening crickets and the breaths of the crowd. "Hang the other." Then again, louder. "Other, other. *Hang* the other."

The tribe took up the chant. *Other. Other. Hang the other.* The words slid off tongues, venomous and building. The people packed in. Iseult didn't move. She tried to thrust herself deep into the logic of a Threadwitch. There was a solution out of this—there *had* to be. But she couldn't see it. Not without Safi beside her. Not without time to pause and plan.

The people swarmed her. Their Threads erupted with life, as if suddenly set free—a thousand shades of terror-stricken white, and bloodthirsty purple bore down on Iseult. Then hands crushed against her. Fingers grabbed and poked. Her head snapped as her hair was yanked. Tears sprang from her eyes.

Other, other, hang the other.

No one even spoke the words anymore—they were too busy whooping their war cries to the night and screeching for Iseult to die. But their Threads hummed with that same rhythm as they shoved and kicked and groped. As they forced her to shamble one agonizing step after another toward the largest oak in the settlement.

And beneath that four-beat rhythm—*Other, other, hang the other*—was a rapid three-beat vibration. *Puppeteer. Puppeteer.* A frightened bass beneath an already violent descant.

Corlant had truly convinced the tribe that Iseult was the Puppeteer, and now she would die for it.

Then the oak loomed before Iseult, a mass of jagged lines against a bright moonlit sky. A man grabbed at Iseult's breast, his Threads erratically shaking. A woman raked her nails down Iseult's cheek, her Threads starved for violence.

As spots of pain flecked Iseult's vision, her heart finally hardened into the stone it was meant to be. Her pulse slowed; her body temperature plummeted; and all the sights, sounds, and pain of the moment vanished behind a wall of objective thought.

This attack was fueled by Corlant. By fear. The people were afraid of the Cleaved and the unknown Puppeteer . . . and therefore afraid of Iseult.

With your right hand, give a person what he expects—and with your left hand, cut his purse.

"Sever." The word boiled up in Iseult's throat, hissed out

with spittle. "Sever," she repeated again, the same hiss. The same thoroughly blank expression on her face. "Twist and sever."

Then again. "Sever, sever. Twist and sever." It was the same rhythm as the crowds' strumming Threads, their pulsing fear. Iseult latched on to that four-beat song and three-beat bass . . .

Then she gave them what they wanted to see.

She gave them a Puppeteer.

"Sever, sever. Twist and sever. Threads that break. Threads that *die*." The words she screamed were gibberish. Iseult couldn't touch these people's Threads and she certainly couldn't control them. But the Nomatsis didn't know that, so on she chanted: "Sever, sever. Twist and sever. Threads that break. Threads that *die*."

Louder, Iseult shrieked until there was enough space for her to straighten. For her to inhale and yell all the more. Until at last the bloodthirsty Threads began to drown beneath the blinding white Threads of fear. Corlant was nowhere to be seen.

Then a new distraction arrived: a firepot flew through the air and Gretchya's voice lashed out, "Ignite!"

The pot exploded. Iseult dropped to the ground as flaming shards whistled down. Her mother hadn't abandoned her.

People ran; Iseult ran too. Toward her mother's voice—toward her mother's house. Yet as her feet pounded the dirt and exploding pots flashed on other houses, ignited thatch rooftops, and sent the Nomatsi into panicked flight, Iseult felt the Threads around her shift once more.

It always happened—that moment when a mark realized he'd been cheated—and it was happening now. The people were noticing they'd lost their Puppeteer, yet their taste for blood had not been sated; it had only grown.

Iseult reached the edge of her mother's house—but Gretchya was nowhere in sight.

"Iseult!"

Her gaze snapped left. Alma bolted toward her on an unsaddled mare. Its brown coat and black legs were almost invisible in the darkness—as was Alma's black gown.

Alma reined the horse to a stop and heaved Iseult onto the bay in front of her. A traditional Nomatsi shield was strapped to Alma's back—a wooden square meant to protect a Nomatsi on the run.

Alma set the bay into a gallop toward the gate. The keen of the peoples' Threads stretched tighter. Pulsed faster. They knew they had been duped.

Which was why stones began to zip toward the girls, why the unmistakable *thwang!* of loosed bows filled the air along with Corlant's roars, "Stop them! *Kill them!*"

But Iseult and Alma were to the oaks by the wall now. The stones pounded into tree trunks; arrows clattered through branches—and thunked into Alma's shield.

"Where's my mother?" Iseult shouted. The gate was closing in fast—and it was shut.

No . . . not shut. Cracked. Swinging ajar.

Alma aimed the horse for that widening gap. The bay changed the trajectory of her gallop, briefly exposing the girls' right sides. Something punched into Iseult's right bicep.

The force of it knocked her sideways, into the cage of Alma's arms. She didn't know what had hit her—a stone, perhaps . . . But the pain throbbed. She looked down, alarmed, and saw the tip of a needle arrowhead poking through the skin above her elbow. A long cedar shaft with black and white cock feathers came out the other end.

She threw back a single glance and saw Corlant, lowering a bow and wearing a satisfied smile on his moonlit face. Then Alma's voice was shrieking in her ear, "Hold on!"

So Iseult turned away and held on as they galloped into the moonlit meadow—the cries of the villagers briefly blocked out by the gate. Iseult's legs squeezed tight and her toes pointed up like her mother had taught her.

Mother.

Iseult squinted, and she thought she saw a figure on horseback bouncing over the grass with a smaller figure right behind. Scruffs. Gretchya must have opened the gate and made a run for it, trusting Alma to get Iseult out.

Corlant clearly knows what Alma and I have planned. That was what Gretchya had said . . . A plan. A plan against Corlant, who clearly wanted Iseult dead—even if Iseult couldn't possibly fathom why.

For half a breath, Iseult wished she'd faced the Bloodwitch instead of Corlant. Instead of the tribe. Yet that idea vanished almost instantly, for at least now she *lived*. Had the Bloodwitch tried to shoot her, she didn't think he would've missed.

Corlant had almost succeeded, though. If his arrow had gone three inches to the left, Iseult's chest would have been pierced. A single inch to the right would have ruptured a vital artery.

So Iseult sent a silent thanks to the moon they now galloped beneath—along with a prayer that Safi was still out there waiting for her . . .

And that the Bloodwitch was not.

ELEVEN

The Bloodwitch named Aeduan was bored. There was only so much wrist-rolling, finger-flexing, and ankle-wiggling he could do to keep his muscles primed for fighting—or keep his temper at bay.

Four chimes had passed since he'd first stretched out on this rafter in the Doge's palace ceiling, and he had long ago pulled back his hood, and even undone the buckles along the top of his cloak. Since the only people to see him were the sixteen other hired guards in the rafters—and a family of pigeons who hadn't stopped *cooing* since Aeduan had sprawled out beside their nest—he wasn't particularly worried about this breach in Carawen protocol reaching the Monastery.

Even if it did, the old monks cared more about mercenary missions than they did about respecting the Cahr Awen. After all, the Cahr Awen was just a myth, but bronze piestras were quite real.

Yet always just out of Aeduan's reach. Yotiluzzi had declared a bounty on the two girls who'd held up his carriage, and Aeduan wanted that bounty. Badly. So he'd tracked the Truthwitch to the Southern Wharf District . . . only to lose her scent.

Shortly after, by sheer luck, he'd run into that Nomatsi girl along the canals—except that she'd eluded him too. Worse, Aeduan hadn't been able to follow her, for she'd possessed no blood-scent.

Never in Aeduan's twenty years of living had he encountered someone whose blood he could not smell.

Never.

This surprise had . . . unsettled him. Had made his molars grind even more than losing the valuable Truthwitch had. Now here Aeduan was, trapped in a ceiling instead of hunting those two girls.

Aeduan pressed his thin, bronze spyglass to his eye and peered through a spy hole carved into the ceiling. People streamed over marble floors. Vibrant shades of orange, green, and blue velvet sprinkled with pastel silks. It was such a waste of time. Nothing was going to happen at the diplomatic ball, for as Aeduan's father always said: the Twenty Year Truce made people lazy and unambitious.

When the first throbbing strands of a Nubrevnan four-step hit Aeduan's ears and heels began to stamp, he opted for a change of scenery. After a crocodilian scrabble through the tiny space, Aeduan reached a ladder. He passed two other mercenaries, who eyed him nervously.

"A demon from the Void," they whispered, and Aeduan pretended not to hear. He liked those rumors. After all, there were perks to having people fear him, such as the best choice of stakeout spots. Even the Cartorran Hell-Bards and the Marstoki Adders, Empress Vaness's personal bodyguards, had let Aeduan enter the palace walls first.

When Aeduan hit the edge of the ceiling, a hole opened up—more spying space behind the ballroom wall. A rope ladder of absolutely no quality or defensive use spanned the fifty feet to the floor. It was just another example of how lax the Dalmottis (and everyone else) had become. Should there be any actual need for the guards in the ceiling, it would take them much too long to descend.

Just as the four-step shifted into its second movement, Aeduan's boots hit the floor. The violins sang into the shadowy wall space, shaking the dust and the wood with their vibrato. Over them was the light tapping of heels that Aeduan recognized as a vine-like dance.

Aeduan actually knew the Nubrevnan four-step. Not well, and he would rather gut himself on a roasting spit than ever engage in it. But he did know the moves. His mentor had forced him to learn it during those first few years at the Monastery.

Aeduan was just aiming left when a familiar blood-scent hit his nose. *Venom-laced secrets and endless lies.* Aeduan didn't know if the rumors were true—if a Marstoki Adder's blood was truly made of acid—but he did know that the Poisonwitch bodyguards were best avoided, if for no other reason than how their scents hurt his nose.

So Aeduan abandoned his leftward trek and moved right instead. When at last he found a spy hole, even smaller than those in the ceiling, and pressed his eye to it, the third movement of the four-step had begun.

And Aeduan's eyebrows shot high.

It was only two dancers, their heels and toes clattering against the marble at a speed Aeduan had never seen—and, even more impressive, a wind had begun to swirl around them. One of the dancers clearly had some form of air magic.

Observers pulled back like a tide as the dancers spun, their feet moving stormily onward though their faces remained still, their eyes thinned and focused. The wind continued to sweep up, twirling in time to the music. In time to the steps. It tossed the girl's skirts, her hair, and it tugged at the gaping viewers as the couple spun past.

Yet the longer Aeduan watched, mildly entertained by the skill needed to dance with such speed and grace, the more an itch began to tickle Aeduan's nose.

Instinctively, he scanned the nearest faces and sniffed. He smelled . . . a sharp blood. A wild one.

One that reminded him of mountain ranges and cliff-sides; of meadows laced with dandelions and of a truth hidden beneath the snow.

A thrill rose in his gut. The Truthwitch was *here*—at this very party.

The final bouncing notes of the four-step rang out, drawing Aeduan's eyes back to the dancers. The wind was dying down; they were marching apart for the final pose of the dance. The Nubrevnan man was clearly someone of importance, judging by the way people gazed upon him with fear or respect. But he held little interest for Aeduan, for his blood-scent was unfamiliar.

It was the girl that drew Aeduan's eye—drew his witchery. Aeduan's smile widened, and his fingers reached for a stiletto strapped over his heart. A heart she had impaled only yesterday.

Yet, as he wondered who such a woman might be—surely Aeduan would have heard of a Truthwitch domna—a loud clapping took over the ballroom. It was from a single source, and though all the other spectators joined in with the applause, this clap remained the loudest.

Aeduan's limited gaze finally latched on to the pale-haired imperial heir, Leopold. He stood near Empress Vaness and waited for people to clear a pathway before he lifted his foot to approach the dancers.

"Well done," Leopold finally called, still clapping. But there was an overdone layer to his applause. "Such magnificent dancers."

The Nubrevnan rounded a shining, flushed face toward the imperial prince. He bowed low. "Prince Leopold."

Leopold only gave him a nod. "Prince Merik—you have stolen Safiya from us." There was no missing the blackness in his tone, nor the intentional way he dismissed the other prince to look pointedly at his uncle, the squat Cartorran emperor who stood nearby.

Safiya's expression shifted from its dance-drunk intensity to simple, pink-faced embarrassment. "Polly," she murmured, almost inaudible over the crowds. "I'm sorry—I lost you in all the people."

"No need to apologize." Leopold spoke in a far louder voice than her proximity required and spread his arms wide. "Another dance! Let's make this a Pragan waltz." Then he swept the Truthwitch a regal bow and clasped her arms.

Aeduan's fingers tapped out an excited rhythm on his

stiletto. This night had just become very interesting. The Truthwitch who had tried to rob Guildmaster Yotiluzzi was now dancing with not one, but two princes.

Oh, the Bloodwitch named Aeduan was no longer bored. No longer bored at all.

And now he had work to do.

Safi was sick of dancing. Literally, she felt ill from all the spinning, and her breath—she'd not had a single moment to catch it since . . . Merik.

Prince Merik.

The man who couldn't dress himself properly had turned out to be royalty. The man who'd thrown himself against a Cleaved was a *prince*. It was almost impossible to conceive, yet it explained his high-chinned bearing, his lack of fear when Safi pushed him—and his willingness to push right back.

Something had happened between Safi and Merik during their dance. Something as powerful as the wind and the music that had gusted around them. A shift in the air that preceded a storm.

Hell-flames, Safi needed Iseult now. She needed her Threadsister to help her sort through this wildness in her chest.

As the room and the faces spun past her in another stomach-tilting waltz, as lies and truths crashed over Safi from all directions, she knew she needed to stop. To leave.

Yet, just as something had shifted within Safi after the

dance—after *Merik*—something had shifted within the room. A tension coiling inward like a waiting serpent.

And the dancing—it never stopped. Six times, Safi was swept over the floor in Leopold's arms. Then six *more* times the Emperor himself insisted on partnering with her. Her hands were clammy and gripped too tightly. Sweat seemed to gather in his pocked skin, and Safi wished Leopold would step back in.

Until the music abruptly stopped and the dancing halted with it.

Until Henrick called for silence in the room and beckoned for Safi to join him at a low dais.

Until a heavy, impossible sentence fell from Henrick's mouth: "Behold Safiya fon Hasstrel. My betrothed and the future Empress of Cartorra."

Safi's knees gave way. She fell against Leopold, who—thank the gods—was nearby. Somehow he managed to sweep her upright and twirl her toward a room filled with stilted applause—as if everyone were as shocked by the announcement as she.

"Polly," she rasped, gaze fixing on his face. "Polly, please . . . tell me . . . Polly—"

"It's true," he murmured, squeezing her hand.

She tried to draw back, her heart threatening to punch its way from her chest. She'd trusted Leopold. She'd trusted Uncle Eron too. Yet this . . . She was not acting as a domna, but as a *bride*.

Leopold wouldn't release her, though. His sea green eyes had become steely. The gentle slope to his jaw had tensed with an unexpected determination.

Safi gasped. "You knew this was coming. Why didn't you tell me?"

His only response was to tow her—forcefully, yet not unkindly—toward his uncle. The Emperor.

Safi's future husband.

"To many happy years together!" Leopold shouted, thrusting Safi forward. She staggered into Henrick's grasp. His sweating hands closed over hers.

Safi almost jerked back at his touch and his crooked-toothed smile. Almost shrieked that this was *not* the freedom she'd been promised. Marrying an emperor was as far from freedom as Safi could imagine, so what was that *horse-shit* of a story her uncle had fed her?

As far as Safi could see, this was it. This was the end of everything.

She scanned every face in the crowd, her arm quaking in Henrick's. She searched for Uncle Eron's blue eyes. For Mathew's red head. *Anyone,* for rut's sake. She just needed someone to hold her gaze and reflect back that it was all right to be furious. To be bone-deep *scared.*

But no one in the crowd was familiar. She even looked for Prince Merik, in his silver gray coat, but he and the rest of the Nubrevnans had vanished from the ball as well.

Safi was alone with her shaking knees. With the sickness in her throat. With Henrick's clammy palms crushing her fingers.

Then Safi's frantic gaze landed on a wrinkled face and stout body that she vaguely remembered from her childhood: Domna fon Brusk. The woman's hairy chin moved like a cow chewing cud, and she bobbed a curt, reassuring nod at Safi.

As the twenty-fourth chimes began to ring and the applause subsided, Domna fon Brusk navigated toward Safi. Her eyes never left Safi's face, her pace never slowed. Four steps in time to each tolling bell.

Then the final chime rang out. It reverberated through the room.

Every flame in the ballroom, in the gardens, and on the harbor hissed out. The party descended into black.

Aeduan was still in the wall when the lights went out.

He had slunk along from spy hole to spy hole, never losing sight of the Truthwitch—or her blood-scent—since she'd followed the summons of Emperor Henrick.

The girl clearly hadn't known what was coming. Never had Aeduan seen the blood drain from a person's face so quickly—and for the briefest fraction of a moment, Aeduan had felt pity.

Yet as Aeduan watched the girl tumble toward Emperor Henrick, the hairs on his arms pricked up. Then the hairs on the back of his neck.

He had just enough time to think, *Magic*—and then feel his power specify, *Firewitch*—before every flame wuffed out.

In two lung-stretching inhales, Aeduan's Bloodwitchery roared to the height of its power—and he made a blood-recognition for every shrieking person in the ballroom—and every guard in the walls, the ceilings. It was just a cursory recording of different scents so he could move without sight.

And so he could follow who *else* moved without sight.

For someone had just orchestrated this blackout, and Aeduan knew immediately that it was linked to the girl, Safiya—because her scent was leaving.

As was a second someone with the acrid scent of battlefields and burning bodies. And a *third* someone who smelled of mountain peaks . . . and vengeance.

Aeduan set off toward the nearest of two wall exits when the lamps flared back to life in a second rush of hair-raising magic. Relieved whimpers and sighs drifted through the walls—and pinpricks of yellow light shot through spy holes.

Aeduan darted for the nearest, and his gaze flew to where his Bloodwitchery told him the girl would be . . .

The space was empty. Completely empty. Where the girl had been standing . . . she still stood. Somehow, she had not moved from Henrick's side. Aeduan honed in on her scent.

It was *not* the scent of the girl named Safiya. This was someone else entirely. Someone with an older blood—much older, in fact.

Aetherwitch, he thought. Then he specified it to *Glamourwitch.*

Aeduan scanned the limited field of people he could see, could smell. But there was no sign of someone working powerful magic. Yet Aeduan had no doubt a Glamourwitch was in that room, manipulating what people saw.

Aeduan also had no doubt he was the only person anywhere in this building—possibly the entire Witchlands—who could wade through what was going on. It was not arrogance that made him think so but simple truth.

A truth that kept him well paid, and that might, after this evening, lead to employers of greater wealth than Guildmaster Yotiluzzi. This girl was a Truthwitch *and* the future bride of the Cartorran emperor. Someone would want to know who had taken her—and that someone would no doubt pay very well.

Aeduan launched into a quick, light-footed stride once more. The girl was reaching the edge of his range. Though he could track her over long distances, it was easier work if he kept her within a hundred paces.

Yet as he ran, the person with acrid battlefield blood stepped into his path, and with the man came the smoking stench of actual flames.

The Firewitch was burning the entrance to the walls.

Aeduan allowed just the slightest fear to spike through him. Flames . . . bothered him.

But then he pushed aside the instinct to stop, to descend into *that place*, and with a great mental wrench, he brought his mind back to the forefront and shoved more power into his lungs.

He also made sure to snap his cloak's fire-flap across his nose. The saying that a Carawen monk was prepared for everything was not an understatement—and Aeduan took that phrase to a completely different level. His white Carawen cloak was made of salamander fibers, so no fire could burn it. Though the flap would block his ability to track blood-scents, he only needed to wear it long enough to get through these flames.

Aeduan reached the exit, dropped directly into the fire, and dispatched his first knife. Then, as he rolled through the flames and flipped back to his feet, he dispatched a second.

The Firewitch dove aside, ducking behind a potted plant in the long entrance hall of the palace. The second knife cracked into the clay, shook the azalea bush within.

Aeduan yanked down his fire-flap, and the smell of blood rushed over him. His first knife must have hit the Firewitch. *Good.* Aeduan threw his gaze down the hall. He saw nothing, yet he sensed the girl was almost to the large doors at the end.

The Firewitch spun around the other side of the pot. Flames roared from his mouth, his eyes—even as blood gushed from a knife in his knee.

Aeduan had never seen anything like it—never known a Firewitch could possess such power.

Yet he could ponder that later. Leaping aside, he propelled himself into a sprint that was impossible to follow. Aeduan could control his own blood, which meant that for spurts of exhausting intensity, he could push his body to an extreme level of speed, of power.

Yet as he raced over the marble floor, more figures materialized before him—from around pots and even dropped on ropes from the ceiling.

Aeduan jolted; his footsteps faltered as he instinctively grabbed for more throwing knives.

But no. As these shadowy shapes ran toward Aeduan, he realized he smelled nothing. No scent, no blood.

The Glamourwitch was still at work here, so Aeduan

thrust himself back into his blood-fueled sprint. His toes barely skimmed the marble; the shadows approached; flames thundered—hot and desperate—behind him.

Then Aeduan was close enough to the entrance doors to slow his speed. Gulping in air and throwing all of his Bloodwitchery back into tracking the Truthwitch, he almost forgot to keep an eye out for *real* people.

A fatal mistake for anyone but a Bloodwitch, and as a gold-hilted knife thunked into Aeduan's shoulder, a temper he rarely released rumbled to life—then erupted.

With a battle cry, Aeduan ripped his sword from its scabbard and attacked the person ahead—the person whose knife was now scraping against his shoulder bone. A man with fair hair.

The Silk Guildmaster, Alix. The tiny, effeminate man was unarmed. He was waiting to die. Willing to die.

But Aeduan never fought the undefended. He barely had time to redirect his aim; his sword whisked past the man's shoulder, skimmed over his silk robe.

The Guildmaster only spread his arms as if to say, *Take me,* and his eyes never opened—which meant that the concentrated crease on the man's brow was one of attention. Of a witchery focused elsewhere.

And Aeduan smelled a blood-scent of tornadoes and silk, of glamors and woven illusions.

This man was the Glamourwitch. A man Aeduan's own master, Yotiluzzi, had dined with on a thousand occasions. The man who led the Silk Guild wasn't magically tied to silk at all.

As this realization washed over Aeduan, he also realized

he'd lost Safiya's scent. She had left his hundred-pace range, and he would have to track her like a dog on the hunt. Aeduan launched into a sprint—a natural one—out the door . . . where twenty city guards waited beneath a glaring white moon.

It was nothing Aeduan couldn't handle. In fact, it was almost laughable. Twenty men couldn't stop him. All they could do was slow him, at best. Yet as Aeduan's sword arced up and his magic reached for the nearest soldier, and as four crossbow bolts chunked into Aeduan's chest, he realized these men moved with the concerted effort of an army. By the time Aeduan waded through all of these swords and arrows and knives, he might actually be too drained to keep following the girl Safiya.

So he did something he rarely ever did—if only because he hated acquiring life-debts. He pinched the blue opal pierced in his left ear and whispered, "Come."

Blue light flashed in the corner of his eye; magic shivered down the side of his body. The Threadstone was now active.

Which meant every Carawen monk in the area would come to Aeduan's aid.

TWELVE

As Safi hurtled through the Doge's marble entrance hall, Uncle Eron towing her along at a speed she had *never* seen him run, she had absolutely no idea what was happening.

The lights had blacked out, and then Habim's hand had slid around Safi's. She hadn't known how she'd recognized him—years of grasping those same hilt-roughened palms was all she could figure—but she *had* known and she'd followed without question.

But the lights had flared into being before she or Habim or Uncle Eron were out of the ballroom. Most gazes were locked on where Safi had just stood, and the few gazes that scanned toward her simply skimmed over.

She risked a peek back—and saw *herself.* Standing exactly as she had stood. *False!* her magic frizzed against her spine.

Then Habim towed Safi into the dark hall, and all she could do was try to keep her silver skirts out of the way as she and Eron hurtled through the hall. Habim hung back.

"Faster," Eron hissed, never looking at his niece. Never

offering an explanation for what in the rutting hell was going on. Uncle Eron had hidden things and bent the truth, but he hadn't outright lied. It *was* midnight; Safi *was* leaving.

Safi's and Eron's heels echoed through the hall like the city guards' snare drums—until a boom ripped out. Flames.

But Safi kept her gaze locked on Eron's graying head and her mind focused on pumping every ounce of speed into her legs. She wouldn't look back. She would trip if she did.

They were almost to the doors outside when Safi caught sight of Guildmaster Alix, sweating and concentrated. Yet what he was doing or why, Safi had no time to ponder. She simply leaped over the threshold—and into an army.

A cry writhed up her throat, but Eron cut directly through the men—who one by one saluted him.

Safi had never—*never*—seen people give her uncle respect. She almost lost control of her feet, of her lungs. But then Eron glanced back, and the sharpness in his gaze—the precursor to a temper she recognized and understood—sent her into a frenzied race once more.

Over the stone paths, beneath the hanging jasmine, Safi's feet didn't slow. She had finally reached that strange aloofness Iseult latched on to so easily—the place Habim had tried to teach Safi for years.

Just as he had taught her to defend herself.

Just as he had taught her to fight and to maim.

And to sprint like the Void was at her heels.

As Eron guided her down a narrow gardener's path and

toward a nondescript workers' gate in the iron fence around the palace, Safi realized that Uncle Eron had *never* intended for her to be a domna. Every piece of her training—every lesson Mathew and Habim had ever hammered into her brain, had been leading up to this moment.

The moment when she would be declared the future Empress of Cartorra and would run away from it at breakneck speed.

Eron reached the gate; it swung wide and Mathew appeared. But Eron did not slow—in fact, now in the open street, he picked up his pace. So did Safi and Mathew.

Three sets of rasping breaths soon filled every space in Safi's ears. Louder than the night wind or the rising clash of steel on steel—a battle that now raged within the palace walls.

They reached an intersection, and Eron darted into the shadow of an overhang. Safi followed, blinking at the sudden loss of moonlight. Then, as her eyes adjusted, a cart and donkey coalesced before her. A wiry peasant sat disinterestedly at the cart's front, sunflower stalks as his cargo.

Eron snatched a clump of sunflowers and flipped them back. They were attached to a blanket of salamander fibers.

"Get under," Eron ordered, his voice raw with exertion. "We'll deal with the Bloodwitch, but until then, you need to hide."

Safi didn't get under. Instead she grabbed her uncle's arm. "What's going on?" Her words were split by gasps. "Where am I going?"

"You have to escape," he said. "Not just the city, but all

of Dalmotti. If we're caught, we'll be hung as traitors." Eron dropped the edge of the blanket and yanked a flask from his waistcoat. A swig, a swish, and he spat it to the cobblestones. Three more times he did this while Safi gaped on.

Then Eron mussed his hair and shot Safi a rigid stare. "Do not fail us," he said quietly before staggering around and shuffling off.

It was like watching summer turn to winter. Eron fon Hasstrel transformed before Safi's eyes. The cold, soldier-like uncle she'd seen seconds before became a grinning, sloppy-faced drunk—and *nothing* in Safi's magic reacted. It was as if both versions of her uncle were true.

Or false, for she could sense nothing at all.

In that moment, a sickening horror scalded through her. Her uncle had *never* been a drunk. As inconceivable as it was—as unwieldy and too oddly shaped for her mind to grab on to—there was no denying what Safi could plainly see. Uncle Eron had convinced Safi, Safi's magic, and all of Cartorra that he was nothing more than a wasted old fool.

And then he'd used that lie to help her escape tonight.

Before Safi could call out to him and *beg* for answers, his figure shimmered once—and then vanished. Where he'd walked, Safi saw only cobblestones and moonbeams.

She jerked toward Mathew. "Where did he go? Did the Glamourwitch do that?"

Mathew nodded. "I told you your uncle's plan was big. We fear . . . no, we *know* that the Truce will dissolve any day now and with no hope for a continuation."

At Safi's confused headshake, Mathew sighed. "I know it's impossible for you to understand right now, but trust me: we're working for peace, Safi. Yet a union to Emperor Henrick would have ruined everything."

"But *why*," Safi stammered, "does Henrick want to marry me in the first place? The Hasstrel lands are worthless. *I'm* worthless!"

Mathew hesitated, eyes flicking away before he finally said, "We think the Emperor might have learned about your witchery."

Safi's throat squeezed shut. *How?* she wanted to croak. She'd hidden it for eighteen years and no Hell-Bard had caught her yet.

"A marriage to Henrick," Mathew went on, "would have been the same thing as enslavement for you, Safi. There would have been no escape. Yet since neither Eron nor you can openly oppose such a union, we're faking this kidnapping. *That* was why Eron gave you no warning. If you had known what was to come, then you wouldn't have shown nearly enough surprise. Henrick and his Hell-Bards would have suspected immediately."

Safi swallowed—or tried to. Her throat was too clogged. Not only did that Bloodwitch know what she was, but the Emperor of Cartorra did too. Who else had found out? Who else would come hunting for her?

"Don't worry," Mathew said, clearly sensing her panic. "Everything is prepared, Safi, and we'll get you to safety." He pushed her toward the black blanket, but she dug in her heels.

"What about Iseult? I'm not leaving her."

"Habim and I will find her—"

"*No.*" Safi ripped from his grasp, not caring that smoke

plumed over rooftops now. That the roar of a nearby battle grew louder each second she stood her ground. "I'm not leaving without Iseult. Tell me where I'm supposed to go, and I'll get there on my own."

"Even after all of this, you still don't trust us?" In the darkness, Mathew's face was hidden, yet there was no missing the hurt in his voice. "We risked everything to get you from that party."

"I don't trust Uncle Eron," Safi said. "Not after what I've seen tonight."

"You *should* trust him. He built a life of shadows and lies, yet he never dragged you into it. Do you know how much that cost him? Cost all of us?" Mathew motioned vaguely toward the cart. "Believe me when I say that Dom Eron wants nothing more than to keep you safe. That's what we all want. Now come. We're out of time."

Mathew gripped Safi's elbow, and his shaded eyes bored into hers. "You will ride this cart north, Safi, to meet a boat. You will not move until you get there. The boat will carry you across the sea to a city called Lejna in the Hundred Isles, where you will wait at a coffee shop—one of *my* coffee shops. Someone will come for you in four days and take you the rest of the way. To freedom, Safi, so you won't have to marry Henrick. And I promise—on my life and Habim's—I promise to bring Iseult with us."

The words trilled over Safi. They buzzed through her arm where Mathew's skin touched her. He was bewitching her. She knew he was doing it—her own Truthwitchery *screeched* at her that this was deception. Yet Mathew's magic was stronger than Safi's. She could no more fight it than the pull of a riptide.

Her feet carried her to the cart, her body crawled beneath the blanket, and her mouth said, "I will see you across the sea, Mathew."

Her tutor's face tightened—a wince of pain or regret, Safi couldn't say. She was drowning beneath the power of his witchery.

But when he leaned in to brush a kiss over her forehead, she had no doubt the emotion was one of love. Of family.

Then he dropped the blanket over her head, the world turned black, and the cart rattled to a start beneath her.

It felt like years that Safi was beneath the awful salamander blanket with sunflower leaves scratching overhead. She heard little beyond the donkey's hooves and the creaking wheels; she smelled nothing but her own hot breath; and she saw only black.

Yet Mathew's Wordwitchery held its sway, the words so deep in her brain that she had to obey—had to lie there, silent and still, while the cart rolled north.

Never—*never*—had Mathew done that to her. Perhaps a coercive phrase or two, but her Truthwitchery had always canceled it out. This was so much power that she was still bound to it a ring of the chimes later.

A silent cry simmered in Safi's chest. Eron had used her. He had kept this enormous secret so she would be "genuinely surprised" at the party, and that was *goat crap*. Safi wasn't some puppet to be flicked around on a stage or a taro card to be tossed out at her uncle's whim.

And how did Safi even know Uncle Eron was *actually* shipping her off to freedom? Clearly her witchery failed her when faced with his lies and promises. If Eron had so effortlessly twisted the truth about tonight's events, then he could do so again.

Sickened heat rushed into Safi's mouth. Coated her tongue. Iseult was the only person Safi could trust, and the girls had a life in Veñaza City—a simple life, perhaps, but one that was all their own. Safi couldn't give up on that.

Yet for how long would Iseult wait at the lighthouse? For that matter, if Iseult was at the lighthouse now, wouldn't that mean Mathew and Habim wouldn't know where to find her? How could they bring Iseult with them if she wasn't where she was supposed to be?

They couldn't, which meant it was time for Safi to take control of her own strings. To play her own cards once more.

Time passed; Safi's determination strengthened and at last Mathew's magic relinquished its hold. In frantic, jerky movements, Safi shimmied to the edge of the cart to lift up the blanket . . .

Fresh air washed over her—as did moonlight. She gulped it in, blinking and squinting and so grateful to be moving again. Thatch-roofed inns and taverns bounced by. Stable yards too.

This was the edge of Veñaza City, where inns clustered and empty roads began. If Safi traveled much farther, she'd have no chance of finding a steed—of bounding farther north to the lighthouse. Plus, Safi needed a weapon. A girl dressed in fine silk and traveling alone was clearly asking for trouble.

As Safi's eyes ran over a stable yard, she glimpsed a tired stable boy leading a mottled gray gelding, the horse's head upright. He was alert and ready to ride.

Even better, there was a pitchfork beside the entrance to the yard. It wasn't a sword and it was certainly heavier than Safi usually wielded, but she had no doubt she could use it against anyone who got in her way.

She peeled back the blanket a few more inches and peeked at the peasant driving the cart. He didn't look back, so with a swing of her legs and a thrust of her arms, she rolled off the cart. She froze on the dried mud, while her body reoriented. There was no sound of the ocean, though the rhythm in the wind suggested the coast was near—as did the faint stench of fish.

Though she didn't recognize the suburb, Safi could guess that the lighthouse was near—a few miles north at most.

She darted toward the inn's yard as fast as her feet could carry her. A glance at the cart showed it ambling onward, and then a glance at the gray gelding showed it almost to the stable door.

Safi slowed only once, beneath the inn's arched gate, to heft up the pitchfork. It was definitely heavier than her sword, but the iron wasn't rusted and the fork points were sharp.

She raised it high, pleased when the scrawny stable boy caught sight of her charging his way. He blanched, dropped the horse's reins, and cowered against the stable door.

"Thank you for making that easy," Safi declared, grabbing the reins. The horse eyed her curiously, but made no move to run.

Yet before Safi could get her foot in the stirrup, her eyes landed on a small leather scabbard on the stable boy's belt. She stomped her foot back down and heaved the pitchfork back up. "Give me your knife."

"B-but it was a present," the boy began.

"Do I look like I care? If you give me that knife, I'll give you enough silk to buy twenty-five knives just like it."

He hesitated, clearly trying to figure out how *that* deal would work, and Safi bared her teeth. He fumbled the knife from his belt.

She took it, stabbed the pitchfork in the mud, and snatched up her skirts. But the knife was dull and the silk strong. It took too many heartbeats to rip the blade through . . .

A cry of alarm went up in the inn. Whoever this gray belonged to had decided he wanted to keep him.

Safi threw the layers of silk in the boy's face. Then with a great deal *less* grace than she normally exhibited when mounting a horse, she clambered into the gelding's saddle, gripped her new knife tight, laid the pitchfork over the pommel, and kicked into a canter.

The horse's owner reached the doorway just in time to see Safi wave good-bye—and to hear her shout "Thank you!" She gave the man one of her very brightest smiles. Then she veered the horse south and away from the northbound cart. She would circle around to a different street ahead.

But she didn't get far. In fact, the gray had barely galloped to the next inn when she realized something was wrong.

There were five men in the street before her. They jogged in a perfect row, their white cloaks streaming behind them and their scabbards and weapons clanking.

Carawen monks, and the one in the middle was covered in blood. He even had arrow shafts poking out from his chest, his legs, his arms.

Bloodwitch.

Safi's stomach punched into her lungs. Eron had tried—and failed—to stop the monk. With movements that felt impossibly slow, Safi yanked at the reins and wrenched the gelding north. Thank the gods, the horse was well trained. His hooves kicked up dried mud and he galloped in this new direction.

Safi didn't look back; she knew the monks would follow. The last inn blurred past and a world of marshy coastline spread before her. Far in the distance the road inclined into cliffsides and limestone.

In moments, the cart and driver she'd just escaped came into view—and there was no missing the man's Witchmark. Its shape was familiar enough to recognize, even with her speed. The man was not a peasant at all, but a Voicewitch.

Safi had just enough time to scream at him, "The Bloodwitch hunts me! Tell my uncle!" before barreling past him down the empty, moonlit road.

THIRTEEN

Iseult and Alma caught up to Gretchya in moments.

Shouts pursued for a time—as did the writhing gray Threads of the violent—but only two more arrows thunked into Alma's shield. And somehow, though Alma did not follow the Nomatsi trails, her mare's footing was sure.

After what felt like an hour, Alma directed the horses to a wide willow on a lazy brook. Gretchya hopped down first, a firepot in hand and Scruffs at her side. She circled the tree before motioning that all was clear.

Iseult slid off the horse—and almost toppled into her mother. Her legs were rubber and her arm . . .

"You've lost too much blood," Gretchya said. "Come." She took Iseult's hand and guided her into a world of drooping branches and whispering leaves. The bay mare followed willingly, as if she knew this place. The stolen brindle, however, took some convincing from Alma.

"You planned this," Iseult croaked, following her mother to a tree trunk dappled in moonlight.

"Yes, but not for tonight." Gretchya lifted a long stick

from against the tree and motioned up, to where two lumps sat on branches just out of reach—and just out of notice. Gretchya batted off both sacks.

Thump, thump! The bulging satchels hit the earth and dust plumed. A green apple rolled out.

Iseult dragged herself onto the willow's roots, her back against the wide trunk. Scruffs settled beside her, and with her left hand, she scratched at his ears while Alma continued to coax the pony beneath the branches, the now arrow-filled Nomatsi shield still affixed to her back.

Though Iseult couldn't see the blood on her right sleeve—not in this darkness—she couldn't miss the pain. *At least,* she thought dimly, *the cut on my right hand doesn't hurt anymore.*

After rummaging in the bags, Gretchya bustled to Iseult's side with the dusty apple and a leather healer kit in tow. She wiped the apple on her bodice. "Eat this."

Iseult took it but barely got it to her mouth before her mother offered her a pendant. A small rose quartz hung from the end of a braided string. "Wear it," Gretchya ordered, crouching on the earth beside Iseult.

But Iseult made no move to take the necklace. An apple was one thing, but Painstones were rare and cost hundreds of piestras.

Gretchya tossed the stone impatiently; it landed on Iseult's lap, the quartz glowing a dim pink. Instantly, the pain reared back. Iseult's breaths deepened. She felt capable of thinking again.

No wonder these things were addictive.

Iseult's gaze settled on Alma once more, who now stood

at the edge of the hanging branches with her back to Iseult and Gretchya. She kept watch while the horses munched at small patches of grass.

"Corlant," Iseult began as Gretchya scooted to her side, a lancet in one hand and linen cloths in the other, "wanted to kill me. Why?"

"I don't know." Gretchya hesitated. "I . . . can only guess that he thought your arrival was a sign that Alma and I were leaving. He figured out our plans, I think, and hoped to keep us in the settlement by hanging y—" She broke off, wet her lips, and did not finish the sentence.

Before Iseult could point out that Corlant's measures seemed much too extreme if all he wanted was to keep Gretchya in the tribe, Gretchya was slicing through the arrow shaft poking from Iseult's bicep. Then she grasped the arrowhead on the left side . . . and yanked it through.

Blood gushed. It pulsed out in time to Iseult's heartbeat—not that she could feel it. In fact, she simply munched on her apple, occasionally patted Scruffs's head, and watched her mother work.

Next came healer witch salves to ward off infection and creams to speed healing. They were all pricey items, yet before Iseult could protest, Gretchya began to speak, and Iseult found herself falling into the familiar, inflectionless voice of her childhood.

"Alma and I began making preparations to flee shortly before you left six and a half years ago," Gretchya explained. "We gathered piestras and gemstones one by one. Then one by one we sewed them into our gowns. It was slow work. Corlant was often there, forcing himself into the house. Yet he also left often, vanishing from the settlement entirely for days at a time.

"During those times, Alma would take the mare here and drop off supplies. She brought the last of our things only yesterday. Our plan was to flee four days from now. I owe the Moon Mother a thousand thank-yous that we did not leave before you came."

Somehow, amongst all those words, the ones that shone the brightest for Iseult were the ones unspoken. "You planned all this . . . before I was even gone from the tribe? Why did you send me away then? Why not just go with me? Or at least tell me w-when I v-visited?"

"Control your tongue, Iseult." Gretchya flashed her an intolerant look. "You may not realize it, but it took me years of planning to get you out. I had to find you lodging in Veñaza City. I had to find you a job—and I had to do it all without Corlant noticing. So when Alma and I decided to leave as well, it took years more to plan. We would have come for you, Iseult. In Veñaza City. Why did you leave?" she demanded.

"I . . . got in trouble." Iseult sensed the stammer, ready to pounce, so she chomped into her apple to hide it. "The settlement was the only place I could think to hide—"

"You should have stayed in the city like I told you to. I ordered you never to return."

"You 'ordered' that three years ago," Iseult countered. "F-f-*forgive* me if I tangled your careful weave."

Her mother's bandaging grew rougher—tenser. But there was no pain . . . and thankfully, there was no more reference to her stutter.

"We will go to Saldonica now," Gretchya said at last. "You can come with us."

Iseult's eyebrows shot up. Saldonica was at the opposite end of the Jadansi Sea—a wild city-state, seething with illegal trade and crime of every imaginable sort. "But why there?"

Alma cleared her throat and angled away from her vigil beside the branches. "I have aunts and cousins that live in the Sirmayan Mountains. Their tribe travels to Saldonica each year."

"In the meantime," Gretchya added, "we will sell Threadstones. Apparently there is a growing market for them in Saldonica."

"Pirates need love too." Alma's lips fell into that easy smile of hers and she glanced at Gretchya as if this was a shared joke between them.

And the brewing ache in Iseult's throat grew larger. She could barely swallow the apple.

Gretchya closed her healer kit. "We have enough money saved for a third ticket to Saldonica, Iseult. We planned to invite you."

Iseult found that hard to believe, yet she had no idea what her mother—or Alma—felt right now. No idea what colors shimmered in their Threads or what emotions held sway.

It didn't matter anyway, though, for Iseult had plans of her own. A *life* of her own to build with Safi.

"I can't go with you," Iseult said.

"If not with us, then where?" Gretchya pushed to her feet, matter-of-fact and almost . . . relieved. This was what she had wanted all along: a daughter like Alma. A true Threadwitch.

"Safi's waiting for me nearby."

"But she isn't," Alma blurted, and with her hand outstretched, she hurried toward Iseult.

On her palm was a glowing ruby. The second Threadstone.

Iseult choked and dropped the apple. She wrenched out her own Threadstone—it also shone with a red light. Safi was in trouble.

Iseult jumped to her feet. The Painstone fell from her lap. Agony crashed over her.

First it was pain, in a great downward rush. Then exhaustion that turned her body to limp straw. She staggered forward, into Gretchya's arms. Yet before she could tumble too far, before she could fall onto her mother's shoulder and faint, Alma swooped the necklace off the earth and draped it over Iseult's neck.

Instant relief. Shocking, terrifying relief.

And as Iseult withdrew from her mother, Gretchya turned to Alma. "Can you sense Safi's location?"

Alma nodded, her grip on the stone turning white-knuckled. Then she pointed southeast. "That way. But she's moving north fast. She must be in great danger."

"We'll go," Gretchya declared, moving toward the bay mare. "We have two cutlasses and the bow—"

"*No.*" Iseult straightened to her full height. A breeze surged into the willow, shaking branches and pulling at her cut hair. Somehow, with that burst of cool, fresh wind, Iseult finally regained control of her tongue. Of her heart.

"Please, do as you had planned and travel to Saldonica." Iseult's fingers wrapped around the Painstone, ready to return it.

"Keep it." Gretchya laid a hand on Iseult's wrist. "You'll never make it to Safiya otherwise."

"And take Alichi," Alma said, motioning to the gray mare. "She knows the terrain."

"The brindle will be fine."

"The brindle won't be fine," Gretchya snapped—and Iseult flinched. There was actual emotion in her mother's voice. "Alichi is rested and knows the trail. So you will take her, the Painstone, and some money. A cutlass too." Gretchya tugged Iseult toward the mare. "Or would you rather have a bow? You can also take the shield."

"I'll be fine."

"How do I know that?" Gretchya rounded back on Iseult, her eyes hard. "I never knew if I would see you again. Do you think it was easy for me to let you go? Do you think it is easy now? I loved you too much to keep you in those walls." Her mother drew closer, her words urgent and fast. "You will take Alichi, and you will go to Safiya's rescue as you always do. You will leave me again because you were meant for bigger things than I can give. And as always, I will pray to the Moon Mother for your safety."

She pushed the reins into Iseult's left palm, but Iseult found her fingers had stopped working. Her voice too, for there was a hole, deep and exposed, where her heart had just been.

"Here." Alma appeared beside Iseult and offered her a

cutlass—the kind used to hack through grass and undergrowth—in a simple scabbard on a worn belt.

But Iseult could not reply. She was still felled by her mother's words. Alma wound the belt around Iseult's hips and hung the second Threadstone over Iseult's neck. Two bright red lights throbbing over a dull pink. Then she gripped Iseult's left bicep. "My family's tribe is called Korelli," Alma said. "They come to Saldonica in late autumn. Ask for them—if you ever come. I hope you do."

Iseult didn't answer—and she had no time to wallow in her confusion, for in moments, she was seated forward against the mare's neck, her cutlass set back and out of the way.

"Find me again," Gretchya said. "Please, Iseult. There is so much I haven't told you about . . . *everything*. Find me again one day."

"I will," Iseult murmured. Then without another word or another glance, she dug her heels into Alichi's sides, and she and the mare set off after Safi.

Iseult and Alichi found the road easily enough. As Alma had promised, Alichi knew the route and her canter was sure. Scruffs chased after her for several minutes, but he soon gave up.

Iseult's heart clenched with each step that the hound lagged, and she couldn't keep from waving when he finally shambled to a stop.

After a quarter hour, the silver meadows ahead shifted into moonlit marshes and sandbars. The breeze began to smell of salt and sulfur, then a wide dirt road appeared before her.

Yet rather than kick the mare into full speed, Iseult pulled the horse to a stop. She was just north of the weedy crossroads at which she'd met the silver-haired monk—a woman as different from that Bloodwitch as the Aether was from the Void.

Then the mare's ears twisted south. Alichi sensed company. Iseult swung her gaze down the road, to where a horse and rider approached at full gallop. Iseult could see the unmistakable halo of Safi's blond hair. She could also see the unmistakable white cloaks of four mercenary Carawens less than a quarter mile behind.

What the hell-flames had Safi gotten into? And how the hell-flames was Iseult going to get them out?

Iseult closed her eyes, gave herself three inhales to find that place she never could hang on to when her mother or Alma were around. Alichi shifted uneasily, clearly ready to get away from whatever was coming—and Iseult was inclined to agree. The horses couldn't gallop forever, and Iseult was pretty sure that four Carawen monks would be hard to stop without some defense.

A defense like the lighthouse.

Iseult pushed the mare into a canter. She needed to be at the perfect speed to fall in with Safi—

"Move!" Safi's voice shrieked out. *"Get off the road, you idiot!"*

Iseult only looked back once to scream, *"It's me, Safi!"* Then she kicked the mare into a gallop—just as Safi hurtled into position beside her.

They galloped side by side.

"Sorry to make you wait!" Safi roared over the rapid four-beat race. Her legs were bared, her silk gown shredded, and she clutched a pitchfork to her stomach. "And sorry for the trouble on my ass!"

"Good thing I have a plan, then!" Iseult shouted back. She couldn't hear the pursuing monks, but she could sense their Threads—calm, ready. "The lighthouse is close enough for us to make a stand."

"Is the tide out?"

"Should be!"

Safi's white Threads flickered with icy blue relief. She shifted her gaze briefly to Iseult—then back to the road. "Where's your hair?" she shouted. "And what happened to your arm?"

"Cut my hair and got shot with an arrow!"

"Gods below, Iseult! A few hours away and your whole life tumbles through the hell-gates!"

"I might say the same to you," Iseult shouted back—though it was getting hard to scream and ride. "Four opponents on your tail and a ruined dress!"

Safi's Threads flickered to an almost giddy pink and then *flared* with panicked orange. "Wait—there are only four Carawens?"

"Yeah!"

"There should be a fifth." Safi's Threads glowed even more brilliantly. "And it's him. The Bloodwitch."

Iseult swore, and a great downward sweep of cold knocked away her calm. If a soldier like Habim had failed to stop the Bloodwitch, then she and Safi stood no chance.

But at least the lighthouse was starting to take shape now—its stout walls separated from the road by a long strip of beach and receding tide. The horses pounded off the shore and into the waves. Saltwater blasted upward. The old tower with its barnacles and gull crap was thirty paces away . . . twenty . . . five . . .

"Dismount!" Iseult screamed, pulling the reins with far more force than was fair. She scrabbled off the horse and with hands that were almost shaking, she unstrapped the cutlass. Beside her, Safi splashed into the ankle-deep waves with her pitchfork gripped tight.

Then without another word, the girls settled into defensive stances, their backs to the tower, and waited for the four monks to gallop across the beach toward them.

FOURTEEN

The *Jana* slipped through coastal waters with barely a peep from her usually groaning wood. Merik stood at the weatherworn tiller, gripping it tight and steering the warship, while beside him on the quarterdeck were Kullen and three Tidewitch officers.

As one, Kullen and the officers chanted below their breaths, their eyes wide behind wind-spectacles. The lenses protected them from the bewitched air while the sea shanty on their tongues kept them focused. Normally Ryber would pound the wind-drum—with the unbewitched mallet—to give the men a beat to sing by. And normally, the entire crew would bellow a shanty.

But tonight, quiet and stealth were required, so the four men sang alone while the wind and tides they summoned hauled the ship onward. The remainder of Merik's crew sat across the main deck, nothing to do when magic did all the work for them.

Merik glanced at Kullen every few moments, though he knew his Threadbrother hated it. Yet Merik hated seeing Kullen's lungs seize up and his mouth bob like a fish—and the attacks always seemed to happen when Kullen summoned more magic than he ought.

Right now, the way the *Jana* skimmed across the sea's surface, Merik had no doubt Kullen was calling on heaps of power.

Merik and his men had left the Doge's palace earlier than planned. After the disastrous Nubrevnan four-step, Merik had wanted to be anywhere but the party. His magic had been out of control, his temper exploding in his veins—and it was all because of that stormy-eyed Cartorran.

Not that he would ever admit that, of course. Instead, he'd blamed the early departure on his new job for Dom Eron fon Hasstrel.

That man had arrived at the perfect moment, and the conversation that had followed had been more fruitful than Merik could have dared hope.

Dom Eron was a soldier—everything in his bearing and gruff voice had indicated that, and Merik had instantly liked him.

What Eron was *not* was a keen businessman, and for all that Merik might've warmed to the man, he was hardly going to point out that Dom Eron's proposal was heavily in Merik's favor.

All Merik had to do was carry a single passenger—Dom Eron's niece or daughter or something like that—to an abandoned port city at the westernmost tip of the Hundred Isles. As long as the woman reached Lejna unharmed (he'd been especially emphatic about the "unharmed" part), then the bewitched document now sitting on Merik's table would be considered fulfilled. Negotiations for trade could begin with the Hasstrel farmers.

It was a miracle. Trade would change everything for his nation—from how many people died of starvation to how negotiations at the Truce Summit went. Merik didn't even mind that he would have to sail right back to Veñaza City after dropping this Hasstrel girl off on the Lejna pier. What were Tide and Windwitches for, if not crossing the Jadansi in days?

So Merik had signed the contract alongside Dom Eron, and then the instant the man was gone, Merik had summoned Hermin back to his cabin. "Inform Vivia that the piracy endeavor is no more—and also mention that the Dalmotti trade ship is only just leaving the Veñazan harbor. Just in case she decides she won't back down."

As Merik had anticipated, Vivia wasn't ready to give up her scheme—but that was fine. Merik could continue to lie. Soon enough he would have trade with *someone,* and that was all that mattered.

"Admiral!" Ryber's high-pitched voice cut through Merik's thoughts.

Kullen and the other witches flinched—and Merik swore. He had ordered silence, and his crew knew how he punished disobedience.

"Don't stop," Merik muttered to Kullen, and with his fingers fidgeting with his shirttails, he marched around the steering wheel and off the quarterdeck. Wide-eyed sailors gawked as he stomped past. Several men ogled up at the crow's nest, where Ryber was waving her arms frantically—

as if Merik didn't know exactly where the ship's girl was stationed.

Oh, Merik would most certainly put Ryber in the leg irons tomorrow. He didn't care if she and Kullen were Heart-Threads so long as Ryber remained a reliable sailor. This, however, was direct disobedience, and it would earn her six hours strapped in the irons with no water, food, or shade.

"Admiral!" A new voice rattled over the deck. It was a salt-wasted sound—Hermin. "Admiral!" he bellowed again.

And Merik almost lost control of his own voice. Two of his best sailors breaking the rules? Ten hours in the leg irons. For each of them.

Ryber's bare feet hit the deck. "There's a battle going on, sir! At an old lighthouse nearby."

Merik didn't care about old lighthouses. Whatever battle Ryber had seen was not his problem.

"Sir," Hermin huffed as he hobbled toward Merik. The Voicewitch's lame foot could barely keep up with his good one, yet he pushed himself as fast as he could. "Sir, we got a message from Eron fon Hasstrel's Voicewitch." He gulped in air. "Our passenger is on the run. Last seen on horseback north of the city and aiming for an old lighthouse. The Hasstrel's men can't get to the domna in time. So it's up to us."

"Carawen monks?" Ryber asked Hermin. Then she turned back to Merik. "Because that's what I saw through the spyglass, Admiral. Two people standing off against four monks."

"Hye, it's the Carawens," Hermin admitted with a nod.

"And if we don't get this passenger away, then whatever binding agreement you've got is considered null."

For half a breath, Merik merely stared at Hermin. At Ryber. Then the Nihar rage got the best of him. He tipped back his head and gave a fist-clenching *roar.*

It would seem the old lighthouse battle *was* his problem, and there was absolutely no reason for stealth now. He needed this Hasstrel document untainted. It was Word-witched, so if Merik didn't meet the contracted requirements, his signature would simply vanish from the page.

An unsigned trade agreement was useless.

Bellowing for his oarsmen to get in position, Merik spun on his heel and strode back toward his officers and first mate. They hadn't paused their concentrated magic—though they had changed course. The *Jana* now sailed west, toward shore. Toward the lighthouse.

"Stop," Merik ordered.

Four mouths broke off mid-shanty. The wind gusted down . . . and vanished. The *Jana* drifted onward, but her pace slowed instantly.

Merik eyed Kullen. Sweat shone above the first mate's lip, but he showed no signs of exhaustion. "I'm going ashore," Merik said. "The ship falls under your command. I want you to bring the *Jana* as close to the lighthouse as the depths will allow."

Kullen bowed his head, fist over heart. "Have Ryber keep her eye to the spyglass," Merik went on. "Once I get the passenger away from these monks, I'll give the wind-flourish. Then I want you to carry the passenger here. As soon as her feet hit the deck, you'll order the oarsmen and the Tidewitches to make sail."

Merik didn't wait for confirmation before marching to the bulwark. Behind him, the Tidewitches and Kullen resumed the sea shanty. The wind and currents picked up once more.

Merik leaned against the waist-high railing, chest puffing full. Then came a sharp exhale and a second lung-expanding inhale.

Air spiraled around his legs, and his magic focused inward. The air streams picked up speed and power.

Merik took off.

His eyes teared up. Salty wind was forced into his nose and down his throat. His heart soared straight into his skull.

For that brief second when all of his Windwitchery was focused into a single funnel below him—when he shot through the air as easily as a petrel on a wave—he was invincible. A creature of joy and strength and power.

And then his height would plummet. He would drop low to the water and conserve his energy by feeding off the natural skip of air—for his powers were limited and his magic quickly tapped. He couldn't maintain flight for long.

The lighthouse zoomed closer. Closer. The water turned shallow, the waves white-tipped.

Then he was close enough to the tower to see two girls burst around the side. They hopped up steps Merik hadn't seen were there.

One was a girl in black with a short blade.

And the other was a girl in silvery white . . .

A girl Merik recognized instantly, even from this distance. Even with half her gown slashed off. He had just enough time to curse Noden—and His coral throne too—before all his attention went into slowing his descent . . .

And crushing any blighted monk who *dared* get near his passenger.

FIFTEEN

As Lady Fate would have it, Aeduan was the only Carawen who couldn't find a horse. His magic had led him and the other Carawens to the outskirts of Veñaza City. Then, at a cluster of inns, the Truthwitch had ridden into the street ahead. With a simple point of Aeduan's finger, the four monks moved into formation and the real pursuit had begun—or it had for the other Carawens who'd easily found "borrowed" steeds at the first two inns.

By the time Aeduan finally found a piebald mare outside a tavern, he was at least five minutes behind the others. Fortunately, Aeduan was a good rider, and the piebald trusted him. Horses always did.

Soon enough, he was galloping down the long coastal highway, the arrows in his chest bouncing uncomfortably. They were barbed, and if he removed them, he would only shred his flesh further—and then his body would automatically heal. A waste of energy better used in this chase.

Aeduan caught up to a cart barreling north at wheel-shattering speed. It smelled faintly of the Truthwitch, and Aeduan glimpsed a blanket beneath sunflower stalks.

A satisfied smirk pulled at his lips. It was a blanket made of salamander fiber, and if the girl had only remained beneath the blanket, Aeduan might never have caught her scent again.

Her mistake.

Soon Aeduan was past the cart and the panicked driver, and it was only he and the piebald for several minutes of maximum, exhilarating speed.

Then a tower appeared, a dark blotch against a night sky. Aeduan would have missed it were it not for the four white figures beside the stone ruins—or the riderless horses galloping toward him.

Just as Aeduan aimed into the waves, his mare decided the other horses had the right idea. Aeduan gave up on her. With a splash, his boots hit the water and he kicked into a jog.

Yet he only made it halfway to the tower before the four Carawens wheeled around it and out of sight. Moments later, a figure plummeted from the sky. *Windwitch.*

Aeduan rounded the tower . . . and a gale slammed into him. He barely managed to grab hold of the lighthouse stones before two monks hurled past in a tornado of air and water. Twenty paces, fifty . . . They crashed limply to the beach—and they probably wouldn't rise for a long while.

As the wind died down, swirling over the shallow waves, Aeduan clawed himself back to his feet and sprinted onward, to a set of steps. The Truthwitch's scent had ascended, so Aeduan would as well.

But he'd only circled one set of barnacle-laden stairs

when two monks staggered into his path. Aeduan grabbed at the first man's cloak. "What is it?"

The monk jolted, as if woken from a daze. "Cahr Awen," he rasped. "I saw them. We must stand down."

"What?" Aeduan reared back. "That's impossible—"

"Cahr Awen," the monk insisted. Then in a bellow that blasted over Aeduan, over the sounds of winds and waves, *"Stand down, men!"* The monk wrenched his cloak from Aeduan's grasp and pushed down the remaining steps.

Aeduan watched in horror as the second monk followed.

"Fools," Aeduan growled. *"Fools!"* He leaped up the last few steps, reached the top floor . . . and skittered to a stop.

The Nomatsi girl was there, dressed in black and sunk low in her stance. She held a cutlass, arced up in a stream of silver steel, while her black Threadwitch gown swept in the same direction . . . And beside her, standing tall, was the white-gowned Safiya with a pitchfork swooping in a blur of dark iron, her white, shorn skirts swinging downward.

It was the circle of perfect motion. Of the light-bringer and dark-giver, the world-starter and shadow-ender. Of initiation and completion.

It was the symbol of the Cahr Awen.

Cahr Awen.

In that tenth of a frozen heartbeat as all the images clamored for space in Aeduan's brain, he allowed himself to wonder if it was possible—if these two girls of moonlight and sunshine *could* be the mythical pair that his Monastery had once protected.

But then the girls moved apart—and a Windwitch

appeared behind them. The man, wearing a Nubrevnan naval uniform, was hunched over as if too exhausted to fight. His face was hidden in shadows, his fingers flexed, and wind gathered slowly toward him.

Aeduan cursed himself. Of course these girls would look like the Cahr Awen with air currents spiraling around them.

"Stay back!" the Truthwitch shouted. "Don't move!"

"Or what?" Aeduan muttered. He lifted his foot to move forward—

But the Nomatsi girl actually answered. "Or we will decapitate you, Bloodwitch."

"Good luck with that." He stepped forward, and Safiya darted at him, pitchfork out. "Get away from us—"

Her voice ripped off as Aeduan took control of her blood.

It was his secret weapon. A blood-manipulation he only used in the most *dire* of situations. He had to isolate the components of Safiya's blood—the mountain ranges and the dandelions, the cliffsides and the snowdrifts—and then he had to pin them down. It was exhausting work, and took even more energy and focus than the high-intensity sprint. Aeduan couldn't maintain this control for long.

Safiya's body was stiff, her pitchfork extended like a glaive. She looked trapped in time. Not even her eyes moved.

In a rush of speed, Aeduan darted toward Safiya. Yet just as he reached her—just as he crouched down to heave her onto his shoulders—the Windwitch burst into action.

The man's arms flung upward, and both he and Safiya

rocketed off the tower in a roar of wind. It kicked Aeduan backward—propelled him toward the tower's edge.

Aeduan lost control of Safiya's blood.

He launched into a sprint. Safiya was ten feet high now and flying backward, her body a frantic spin of limbs and skirts. She was screaming over the wind: *"Iseult! Iseult!"*

If Aeduan ran, he could leap into the Windwitch's airfunnel—

A body hurled into him. He toppled sideways, barely transferring into a roll before the Nomatsi girl thrashed him to the ground.

Yet Aeduan was already spinning, fingers clawing for any wrists or elbows he could break, his Bloodwitchery grabbing for any blood to lock down.

But just as Aeduan's fingers caught empty air, his Bloodwitchery found nothing—the girl was already flipping off him, already charging toward the edge of the tower.

She would jump. Aeduan knew she would jump.

So he leaped to his feet too and bolted after the girl named Iseult.

She hit the edge of the lighthouse; she jumped.

Aeduan hit the edge too; he jumped.

And they fell. Together. So close Aeduan could grab her if he wanted to.

But it was like she knew it. Like she'd planned it that way.

Midair in a fall that would last barely a second, she swiveled around. Her legs writhed through his and flipped their bodies—

His back hit the sand. So hard the world went black.

Distantly, he felt the girl crash against him. Arrowheads dug even deeper. They smashed his ribs, his lungs. There was pain everywhere. His organs—they were all destroyed.

And he was pretty certain his spine was broken too.

That was a first.

Then waves washed over his skin. A breath passed. Aeduan thought he might make it out alive . . .

Until he felt a black explosion in his chest.

It cleared through all the other pains, and his eyes snapped wide. The hilt of his stiletto poked from his heart. His cloak and tunic were too stained to show the blood flowing out—but he knew it was there. Pulsing faster than his power could keep up with.

Yet he couldn't withdraw the knife. He couldn't do anything because he couldn't move. His spine was definitely broken.

Aeduan lifted his gaze, the world streaming and blurry . . . and then morphing into a face.

A face of shadows and moonlight only a foot away from his. The girl's lips shuddered with each gasping breath. Her hair flew on the breeze—a natural breeze, Aeduan realized—and her thighs trembled against his broken ribs.

He saw no one else, heard no one else. For all he knew, they were the only people left alive in this battle.

In the entire world.

Then his gaze fell on a Painstone hanging from her neck. Its rosy glow was fading, almost gone, and he could see from the strain on her face that she was hurt. Badly.

Yet she still managed to unstrap a cleaving knife from

Aeduan's baldric. She still managed to drag it to his neck and hold it there.

The blade trembled against his skin.

She had stabbed him in the heart with his stiletto, and now she was going to decapitate him.

But the cleaver stopped; the girl called Iseult cringed and her Painstone flared a soft pink . . . before winking out completely.

A groan erupted from her lips. She almost toppled forward—and Aeduan glimpsed the wound on her right bicep. Bloodstained linens. Blood he should be able to smell.

"You . . . have no . . . scent," he ground out. He could feel his own hot blood gushing over his teeth, dribbling from the sides of his mouth. "I can't smell . . . your blood."

She didn't answer. All of her concentration was on holding the cleaver steady.

"Why . . . can't I smell you? Tell . . . me." Aeduan wasn't sure why he wanted to know. If she cut off his head, he would die. It was the only wound from which a Bloodwitch couldn't recover.

Yet still, he couldn't seem to stop asking. "Why . . ." Blood sprayed with that word, splattered the flat steel of the cleaver. A fleck hit her cheek. "Why can't . . . I . . ."

She eased the blade away from his throat. Not gently—it cut through skin and dragged onward, as if she was too tired to even lift it.

Aeduan's impaled heart fluttered. It was a strange feeling of relief and confusion that lifted with the blood in his mouth. She wasn't going to kill him. He had no idea why.

"Do it," he rasped.

"No." She shook her head, a jerky movement. Then wind—of the charged, unnatural variety—gusted over them. It sprayed her hair from her face, and Aeduan forced himself to note every detail.

He might not have been able to smell her blood, but he would remember her. He would remember her round jaw that didn't quite fit with her pointed chin. He would remember her snub nose and pale freckles. Her angled, cat-like eyes. Her short lashes. And her narrow mouth.

"I will hunt you," he croaked.

"I know." The girl dropped the cleaver on the sand and used Aeduan's chest to push herself upright. His ribs crunched, and his stomach squished. She was not light, and his organs were pulp.

"I will kill you," he went on.

"No." The girl's eyes thinned; she pushed herself further upright and the moon streamed over her. "I d-d-d . . ." She coughed. Then wiped her mouth. "I don't think you will."

It seemed to take all her concentration to get those words out, and it was with an edge of frustration that her fingers laced around the stiletto once more.

She shoved the blade deeper into Aeduan's heart.

Against his most desperate, frantic desire—against every instinct that screamed at him to stay alert—his eyelids fell shut for half an agonizing breath. A moan slipped over his tongue.

In that moment, the weight on his body vanished. Footsteps slapped through the water away from him.

When his eyes finally opened again, he saw no sign of the girl—not that he could have turned his head to look.

Then a wave washed over him, and Aeduan sank beneath the sea foam.

SIXTEEN

The wind roared in Safi's ears as she flew. Her eyes streamed, her skirts tossed, and she quickly gave up shouting at Prince Merik to go back. He couldn't hear her.

The ocean blurred beneath Safi, lucent and trembling, and Safi thought vaguely that she should enjoy this—she was *flying* after all.

But she didn't enjoy it. All she cared about was Iseult, left behind. With the Bloodwitch.

In the back of her mind, other urgent thoughts snarled—like why Prince Merik was stealing Safi from the lighthouse. How he'd gotten there at such a perfect time.

Then Safi was hurtling much too fast toward a sharp-bowed Nubrevnan warship—and *that* engulfed all her other concerns.

Oars spun, sailors in blue scurried about, and a booming drumbeat hit Safi's ears. Right as she thought she would crash onto the main deck and break all her bones, her pace slackened. She drifted gently down.

In two breaths, Safi had her balance and was on her feet. One more breath, and she had a lock on Prince Merik. He was almost to the quarterdeck by the time she grabbed his shirt and ripped him about. *"Take me back!"*

He didn't resist but rather pointed toward shore. "My first mate has your friend."

Safi followed his finger. Sure enough, she found the tall blond man with his attention on a figure flying this way.

Iseult.

But Safi's Threadsister was limp. As Safi bolted for the first mate, she roared for a healer or surgeon or *someone* to help.

The first mate eased Iseult onto the quarterdeck with his magic, and Safi was instantly beside her. She tugged Iseult's head onto her lap and pressed fingers to her throat, praying for a pulse . . . Yes, yes. Faint, but there.

Although, in the glaring moonlight, there was no missing the growing smear of red on Iseult's arm or the dead Painstone around her neck.

Movement flickered in the corners of Safi's vision. The prince, the first mate, other sailors closing in. Then came a flash of white and a woman's voice. "Get my kit!"

Safi yanked around to find a Carawen monk striding toward her from the ladder belowdecks.

"Get away from that girl," the woman ordered.

But Safi didn't move. After being hunted by Carawens, she wasn't *about* to let another one get close. If those four monks had been working with the Bloodwitch, then this one probably was too.

The woman had silver white hair, yet the way the moon glided over her skin, she couldn't have been any older than

Mathew or Habim—and she was freeing her blade with the poise of an equally skilled swordswoman. "Step back, girl."

"So you can finish what the other monks started? No thank you." In a rush of movement, Safi yanked a cutlass from the first mate's scabbard, and spiraled at the Carawen monk . . . who deftly ducked beneath Safi's next attack—and then slapped the flat of her blade against Safi's knee.

"Someone stop her," the monk yelled.

And just like that, Safi's air choked off.

She tried to billow her lungs, to clench her stomach, to do *anything* that would draw in breath, but there was nothing.

With an easy swat, the monk knocked away Safi's blade. The cutlass clattered across the wood, and Safi clutched at her throat. Stars blinked across her vision. The first mate was a full-blown Airwitch—and he was collapsing Safi's lungs.

It was at that moment, as Safi's knees buckled and the world swirled into darkness, that Merik stepped over her, his expression hard but not cruel. "Evrane means your friend no harm. She's a healer monk, Domna. A *Waterwitch* healer."

Safi clutched at her throat, unable to speak. To *breathe*.

"If you promise to behave," he continued, "then Kullen will return your air. Can you promise that?"

Safi nodded desperately, but she was too late. Her body was too starved of breath, and darkness overtook her.

* * *

Safi awoke with her tongue fat and sticky. Footsteps thumped above, water sloshed against creaking wood, and the smell of salt and tar was thick in her nostrils. For several moments, all she could make out was a dark room with a weak beam of sunlight filtering through a window at her left. Then the room oriented, and Safi saw Iseult sprawled across a single, bolted-down pallet in the opposite corner. Iseult's eyes were closed, her breath rasping.

Safi lurched to her feet, stumbling off a second pallet and almost sprawling flat from the blood roaring across her vision.

"Iseult?" She dropped to the floor beside her Threadsister. Sweat dripped down Iseult's face, her skin even more ashen than usual, and when Safi pressed a gentle hand to Iseult's brow, the skin was boiling.

Only once had Safi seen Iseult this badly hurt—after she'd broken her shinbone—but this injury was worse. There was no Mathew or Habim to help them now. Safi and Iseult were alone. Completely *alone* on a foreign ship with no one on their side.

And with none of it making any sense. Iseult had mentioned getting shot, but the how, the where, the *why*—Safi had absolutely no idea.

The iron latch on the door spun up. Safi stilled—the whole world stilled. Then the white-robed monk slipped in. Slowly, as if facing a wild animal, she flipped her hand in Safi's direction. The sun-browned skin was marked with an upside-down triangle for Water witchery and a circle for her specialization with the fluids of the body. Safi fixed her gaze and her magic on the woman, and the longer she stared, the more she saw the healer's heart was true.

Nonetheless, Safi couldn't bring herself to fully trust . . . what had the prince called her? *Evrane*. Safi had been tricked too often lately. For now, she would watch the monk work and use the moment to gain any information she could.

Safi rolled to her feet and backed away from Iseult, hands up submissively. "I won't interfere. Just make sure you heal her."

"She'll do the best she can," said a new voice. Merik appeared in the doorway as the monk crossed lightly to Iseult.

Safi smiled at the prince, a bored, *unthreatening* flash of teeth. "I was wondering when you'd come along, Prince. Care to tell me where we are?"

"The western Jadansi. You've been onboard for four hours." He stepped warily to the center of the room, as if he wasn't stupid enough to trust Safi's demeanor. He wore a simple navy frock coat over a fresh shirt and breeches, and Safi was suddenly struck by her own filth. Her gown was shredded and stained, and far too much of her dirt-streaked calves and thighs were exposed.

Then, faster—and more quietly—than Safi could have ever expected, Merik shot in close, hooked Safi's arms behind her back, and pressed something cool against her throat. The smell of sandalwood and lemons pierced her nose.

Safi didn't cower back, though. She simply cocked her

head sideways and drawled, "You do realize your blade is still sheathed?"

"And you do realize that I can still kill you with it?" Merik's breath tickled against her ear. "Now tell me, Domna: Are you wanted by the authorities? Any authorities of any nation?"

Her eyes narrowed. Merik had been at the ball. He had heard the betrothal announcement . . . Or had he? Safi hadn't seen him in the crowd, so perhaps he'd abandoned the ball before Henrick's declaration.

Safi prodded her magic for some indication of Merik's true nature. Power instantly charged through her, both clawing *and* warm. A contradiction of falsehoods and truth, as if Merik might return Safi to Emperor Henrick if he were given the chance . . . Or he might not.

Safi couldn't risk it. Yet before she could speak, Merik pressed the dagger harder to her flesh. "I have a crew to protect, as well as an entire nation. Your life is nothing compared to that. So do not lie to me. Are you wanted?"

Safi hesitated, considering if she *was* endangering Merik's fleet. Uncle Eron had staged her flight to look like a kidnapping—that much Mathew had told her. Yet as far as she could tell, there was no way that Emperor Henrick could find out where Safi had been taken.

So she tipped up her chin—exposing her throat all the more.

"Your strategy is a poor one, Prince, for if there *are* people following me, I have no incentive to tell you."

"Then I guess I'll kill you."

"Do it," she taunted. "Slit my throat with your still-sheathed dagger. I'd love to see how you manage that."

Merik's expression didn't waver. Nor did the dagger. "First tell me why the Carawens were after you."

The monk's shoulders stiffened, drawing Safi's eyes to her white-cloaked back. "I have no idea, but you could ask that Carawen over there. She seems to know."

"She doesn't." Merik's voice was sharp with impatience. "And you would do well to address her properly. She is Monk Evrane, sister to King Serafin of Nubrevna."

Now, *there* was some useful information. "So if Monk Evrane is the king's sister," Safi mused, "and the king is *your* father . . . Why, Monk Evrane must be your aunt! How nice."

"I'm surprised," Merik said, "it took you so long to figure this out. Even a Domna of Cartorra should be well-educated."

"I never cared much for my studies," she volleyed back—and Merik snorted.

It was a laughing snort that seemed to catch him by surprise—and seemed to annoy him too, for he abruptly schooled his face and withdrew the sheathed blade.

Safi cracked her jaw. Stretched her shoulders. "Now *that* was a fun standoff. Shall we do it again tomorrow?"

Merik ignored her, and with a free hand, he yanked a cloth from his coat and wiped down his engraved scabbard. "On this ship, my word is law, Domna. Do you understand? Your title means nothing here."

Safi nodded and fought the overwhelming urge to roll her eyes.

"But I am willing to offer you a deal. I won't lock you in chains if you promise to stop behaving like a feral dog and instead behave like the domna you're supposed to be."

"But Prince"—she lowered her eyelids in an indolent blink—"my title means nothing here."

"I will take that as a 'no' then." Merik turned as if to leave.

"Deal," Safi spat, seeing it was time to fold. "We have a *deal*, Prince. But just so you know, it's a cat."

The prince frowned. "What's a cat?"

"If I'm going to be anything feral, it'll be a cat." Safi bared her teeth. "A *mountain lion*, of the Nubrevnan fish-eating variety."

"Hmm." Merik tapped his chin. "I can't say I've ever heard of such a beast."

"Then I suppose I am the first." Safi waved dismissively at him before dropping back to Iseult's side.

But Evrane lifted a halting hand. "You are too dirty to be here, Domna." Her voice was husky, yet not unkind. "If you really want to help your friend, then you will get cleaned. Merik, will you see that she is taken care of?" She glanced at her nephew—who was already aiming for the doorway.

"It's Admiral Nihar," the prince corrected. "At least while we're at sea, Aunt Evrane."

"Is that so?" the monk asked calmly. "In that case, it is *Monk Evrane*. At least while we are at sea."

Safi had just enough time to see Merik's expression turn sour before the prince was out the door—and Safi was scrambling after him.

* * *

Climbing the ladder topside proved harder than Safi anticipated—what with her body sore and the relentless onslaught of an early morning sun. Hissing and rubbing her eyes, she stumbled across the stone-scoured deck. Her legs were numb from disuse, and as soon as she got a solid grip on the wood, the ship would groan and heave the other way.

The prince walked just ahead, deep in conversation with his first mate, Kullen, so Safi angled a hand over her eyes. *Learn your terrain.* There was little to see beyond rolling waves—only the eastern horizon had a craggy spit of land separating the sea from a cloudless sky.

Safi scooted around sailors. They scrubbed the wood, scurried up the riggings, heaved and towed—all to the hoarse bellows of a limping older man. Though some stopped to salute their prince, not *all* of them paused. One man in particular caught Safi's attention, her witchery curdling at the sight of him—as if to say he was untrustworthy. Corrupt.

"'Matsi-loving smut," the man snarled as Safi passed.

She grinned at him in return, making absolutely certain to memorize his square-jawed face.

Soon she had stumbled to the ship's stern (she counted thirty paces) and stepped into the welcome shadow of the quarterdeck. Merik opened a door, murmuring something to Kullen. Then the first mate saluted and marched back the way he'd come—his voice rising with surprising ferocity. "Did I *say* you could take a caulk, Leeri? No naps until you're dead!"

With her ears ringing from Kullen's roar and her vision

blanketed by the loss of sunlight, Safi paused at the doorway until the room took shape.

It was an elegant cabin and not at all the sort of space she would've imagined for a rugged man like Merik. In fact, he seemed rigid and uncomfortable as he waited beside an intricately carved table with high-backed chairs.

"Shut the door," he ordered. Safi did, but tensed her muscles. She might have danced and fought with this man, but that didn't mean she trusted him in a room alone.

False, countered her power, a sense of calm winding through her chest. *Merik is safe.*

Safi relaxed . . . but only slightly. Perhaps he meant her no physical harm, but she still didn't know if he was ally or opponent.

Merik pointed vaguely to the back of the room. "There is water for cleaning and a uniform for you."

Safi followed his finger to a collection of shiny swords on the back wall. *Beneath* the swords sat a small barrel and some white towels upon a low bed.

She didn't care about the water or the towels—it was the swords she found intriguing. They were strapped down, yet clearly easy to snap free. Though only if she found she needed one, of course.

Merik seemed to misinterpret Safi's stare, for his expression softened. "My aunt is a good healer. She will help your Threadsister."

True. "What about you, though, Prince? Will you kill Iseult for being Nomatsi?"

Merik's lips bounced open—with shock. With revulsion.

"If I hated Nomatsis, Domna, then I would have killed her on sight."

"What of your men?" Safi pressed. "Will *they* hurt Iseult?"

"They follow my orders," he answered.

But Safi didn't like how her magic winced at that statement. As if it were not *quite* true. Her foot started tapping. Her *bare* foot. "Do I get new shoes?"

"I haven't found any that will fit you." Merik smoothed at his shirt, pulling cotton against the lines of his chest. "For the time being, you will go barefoot. Will you survive?"

"Yes." Habim had insisted Safi toughen her feet against the elements. *You never know in what condition you'll find yourself,* he always said. *Shoes should be a luxury, not a requirement.* At least once a month he'd insisted that Safi and Iseult go barefoot for a whole day, and both girls had enough callouses to walk across hot coals. Or . . . at least *very* hot sand.

Merik grunted, almost gratefully, and gestured for Safi to join him at the table. She did, though she made sure to stay on the opposite side. Within bolting distance for the swords—just in *case* the world suddenly went to goat tits (as it had been inclined to do lately) and Safi had to fight her way through the entire ship.

"The *Jana* is here." Merik plunked a coin-size replica of the *Jana* on the map. Like a magnet to a lodestone, the boat slithered over the paper and locked in place near the eastern coast of the narrow Jadansi Sea.

"We are going here." Merik twirled his fingers—graceful

fingers, despite their roughness—and a soft breeze puffed into the miniature *Jana*'s sails. It slipped over the map, scooting past another tiny vessel before stopping beside a series of islands. "There is a town in the Hundred Isles called Lejna, and I am charged with leaving you there. We should arrive tomorrow."

"Hundred Isles," Safi repeated softly. "And what do you expect me to do once I'm there?"

"I was simply told to leave you. I have no idea why, since it's a ghost town, but the compensation is too good for me to ignore: a trade agreement with the Hasstrels."

Safi's eyebrows bounced high. "You do realize that our estate is practically crown-owned, our farmers are half-starved, and we have no money left."

"Any contract," Merik said, jaw clenching, "is better than what Nubrevna currently has. If I can open trade with a single Cartorran estate, then I'll take it."

Safi nodded absently, no longer listening. When Merik had said *contract*, his eyes had slid to a rolled-up scroll at the edge of the table. Yet before Safi could ask about it, her stomach growled. "What of food, Prince?"

"You didn't eat enough at the ball?" Merik offered a grin.

But Safi couldn't smile back. The ball and the Nubrevnan four-step were a lifetime ago.

As if reading her mind, Merik's smile faltered. He fiddled with his collar. "I didn't realize it would be you, Domna. Had I known at the ball that you were my passenger—" He shrugged, his mind clearly turning inward. His thoughts tumbling aloud. "I suppose I would have taken you to the *Jana* and saved us both a lot of time and trouble. But your name wasn't on my Wordwitched contract until after I left the party. Even then, I didn't realize *you* were the Domna of Hasstrel."

Safi nodded, unsurprised. Eron had needed her at the party as his distracting right hand, and his plan would never have worked if Merik had carried her away too soon.

More important, Merik would never have agreed to carry Safi at all had he known to whom she would end up betrothed.

A silence spread, broken only by the groaning wood and shouting sailors. Merik turned his attention to the charts—and Safi couldn't resist studying him.

Although she knew Merik must be the same age as Leopold, he seemed so much older. His shoulders were broad and high, the muscles oft-used, while his skin was sun-darkened and rough. At the moment, a triangular crease burrowed between his eyebrows, as if he frowned often.

Merik took his duties as prince and admiral seriously. Safi didn't need her magic to know that—and an unexpected dread cinched in her chest. She didn't want Merik hurt by her uncle's schemes. As far as she could tell, she and Merik were *both* just puppets. Both just cards being played against their will.

The Queen of Bats and the King of Foxes, she thought fancifully . . . Then more savagely: *Or perhaps we have no taro suit at all, and we're both just Fools.*

Merik adjusted his collar and glanced at the door. "Food is on the way, Domna, so clean up. And for both our sakes, please scrub well." Again, he offered a slight smile before marching briskly from the cabin. Safi watched him go, waiting until he was firmly outside the cabin . . .

The door clicked shut, and in less than a heartbeat, she had dived to the scroll and unfurled it.

Written in a familiar script was exactly what Merik had described.

> *This agreement is between Eron fon Hasstrel and Merik Nihar of Nubrevna. Merik Nihar will provide passage for Safiya fon Hasstrel, from Veñaza City in the Dalmotti Empire to Lejna in Nubrevna. Upon the passenger's safe delivery to the seventh pier in Lejna, negotiations for a trade agreement will begin.*
>
> *All negotiations on page two of this contract will terminate should Merik Nihar fail to bring the passenger to Lejna, should the passenger spill any blood, or should the passenger die.*

Safi flipped to the second page, which was filled with dull language like "imports" and "market value." She rubbed the pages between her fingers. They were light and filmy.

Wordwitchery. And since the handwriting was clearly Mathew's, Safi knew *whose* magic it was.

It was the same sort of document as the Twenty Year Truce. Once the bargain was fulfilled, Merik and Uncle Eron could alter the contract's language and negotiate over great distances.

Safi flipped to the end of the document. It bore the usual language—identical, in fact, to the final page of the Truce.

If all parties are in agreement, then they must sign below. Should any party fail to meet the terms agreed upon, his or her name will vanish from this document.

A knock sounded at the door.

Safi jumped—then she shoved the contract pages back together. "Just a moment!"

"I have food for you," a muffled voice answered.

Kullen. The brutish first mate. She tossed the contract onto the table before shooting to the back of the room. After dunking a cloth into the barrel, she called, "Come in!"

Then Safi hardened her face. She would cooperate with her new allies, but at any sign of trouble—at any *hint* that Kullen might take her breath again—Safi was claiming control. There were swords within easy reach and a contract that said she couldn't spill any blood.

SEVENTEEN

Merik strode across the *Jana*'s main deck, scowling into the hot sun. Getting Safiya fon Hasstrel to Lejna without incident might prove harder than he'd planned. She behaved like she fought, like she danced—pushing people to the edge and testing their limits.

It hardly helped that Safiya's legs had been on display since he'd rescued her, distractingly paler than her arms and face. It was that pallor that unnerved Merik. The undeniable fact that he was seeing skin meant only for a lover's eyes.

Merik expelled a rough breath. Thinking of Safiya fon Hasstrel in an intimate capacity was not wise. Whenever he considered her—or was *near* her—the Nihar rage kindled. Boiled up hot and fast.

Since Merik's temper had snapped in the Doge's dining room, there had been a charge in his veins that made his breath gust. Made him want to summon vast, angry winds. It was the same wild anger that he'd released too easily as a child. He *couldn't* give into it now, if for no other reason than it was too much like Vivia. Unbridled and violent.

Merik didn't like unbridled. He didn't like rough seas. He liked order and control and perfectly tucked-in shirt-tails. He liked calm waves, clear skies, and knowing his fury was leagues away.

Therefore, Merik would have to avoid Safiya as much as possible—no matter how easily she startled laughs and smiles from him. And no matter how distracting her bare legs might be.

The closest of Merik's sailors—men from his previous ship—paused their mopping to salute. Crisp, earnest movements from sailors Merik could trust to their watery graves.

Merik nodded curtly before his gaze drifted to the Tide-witch helmsman. *That* man was a holdover from King Serafin's crew, and like most of the King's old men, the Tide-witch was thoroughly unimpressed by Merik. Still, at least he steered the *Jana* true.

For now.

Merik ran a thorough eye up each mast, across the rigging, over the sails. Everything appeared to be orderly, so he set off for the ladder belowdecks.

Once he was under and firmly ensconced within the passenger cabin, he found his aunt fidgeting with her opal earring. "I just spoke with Voicewitch Hermin," she said quietly. "He has managed to contact the Voicewitch at the Carawen Monastery. It turns out that the monks at the lighthouse were ordered to capture the domna alive, yet once the monks saw her, most of them backed off."

"Why?" Merik asked, glancing at the sleeping Iseult. How anyone could fear her was beyond him. Then again, he'd seen many Nomatsi caravans as a boy, so he was used to their deathly pallor and pitch-black hair.

When his aunt didn't answer his question, Merik turned back to her. She was shaking her head. "All I know for certain is that there is one Carawen monk still hunting the domna. His name is Aeduan, and he works for the highest bidder." With a loud exhale, Evrane moved to the window and squinted into the sun. "So long as he lives, these girls are in danger—for Aeduan is a Bloodwitch, Merik."

Merik's head reared back. "Such a thing exists?" At his aunt's grim nod, he thought back to the fight at the lighthouse. In the insanity of the moment, he'd thought he had imagined the red in the young monk's eyes. The way the monk had locked Safiya in place.

But no. It had all been real. A *Bloodwitch* had been real.

"Surely, though," Merik said slowly, "this Bloodwitch cannot reach us before Lejna. And once we drop off the domna, the monk is no longer our problem."

Evrane's eyebrows shot up. "You would abandon these girls to a wolf so easily?"

"To protect my crew I would. To protect Nubrevna."

"Yet an entire crew could face a single man. Even a Bloodwitch."

"Not without casualties, and I can't risk my sailors for two girls—no matter how badly we need that contract. Once we drop off the domna, then she and her friend are no longer my problem."

"Has so much time passed since I saw you last?" Color rose on Evrane's cheeks. "If you think that your father will respect you more because you act like Vivia—because you abandon helpless girls—then perhaps you do not want your father's respect."

For a long moment, the only sounds were the groan of the ship planks and the slosh of the waves. "You have no right," Merik clipped out at last, "to compare me to Vivia. She regards her crew as fish fodder; I see them as family. *She* resorts to piracy in order to feed Nubrevna; I look for permanent solutions." Merik's voice lifted as he spoke, his anger burning brighter. Hotter. "Domna fon Hasstrel offers one of those solutions, and she is *anything* but helpless. So I will protect my men—*tooth and talon*—and leave the domna to fend for herself."

On the mattress, Iseult stirred in her sleep, and Merik's breath loosed out. He willed his temper below the surface. His aunt meant well, and she had every reason to prevent Merik from acting like his sister.

"Please," Merik finished gruffly, "remember that the Nubrevnan navy doesn't normally ferry monks—or outcast nobility—across the ocean, and should Father learn I've taken you onboard . . . well, you can guess his reaction. Don't make me regret my decision to carry you. I'll protect Domna Safiya for as long as the Hasstrel contract remains unfulfilled, and I'll get her to Lejna by any means I have. But at first sign of the Bloodwitch, my men must come first."

For several long moments, Evrane stood still and silent, her eyes locked on Merik's. But then she released a sharp breath and turned away. "Yes, Admiral Nihar. As you wish."

Merik watched the back of her silver head as she shuffled

to the pallet and once more knelt by Iseult. An urge to apologize tickled the back of his throat—a need to ensure Evrane understood why he made these choices.

But Evrane had made up her mind about the Nihar family long ago. Her relationship to King Serafin was no better than Merik's was to Vivia. Worse, even.

As Merik left the cabin and made his way above, he considered the best way to handle the Bloodwitch if indeed the man was alive. It would seem the only strategy would be to reach Lejna in the shortest time possible. So, though Merik was loath to do it, he would have to call on his Tidewitches once more. Of course, that would leave his sailors with little to do.

Fortunately, Merik knew exactly how to handle downtime. "Drill positions!" he bellowed, cupping his hands. "I want all sailors in drill positions *now!*"

Iseult drifted in sleep. She'd been stuck in that awful place between dreams and waking—that hole where you knew if you could only open your eyes, you'd be *alive*. This half-dreaming had always struck her during illness. When she'd wanted nothing more than to wake up and beg for a tincture to ease her swollen throat or itchy pox.

The worst, though, was when the half-dreams grabbed hold of Iseult amidst a nightmare. When she knew that she could flee a shadow's grasp if she could just . . .

Wake.

Up.

A loud creak sounded above her, and with great effort, she

lifted her eyelids. The shadows reared back . . . only to be replaced by pain. Every inch of her was drowning in the agony.

A woman materialized, her hair silver and face familiar. *I am still dreaming,* Iseult thought hazily.

But then the woman touched Iseult's bicep and it was like a firepot going off. The here and the now kicked into Iseult's body.

"You," Iseult croaked out. "Why . . . are you here?"

"I'm healing you," the monk said calmly, her Threads a glittering, concentrated green. "You have an arrow wound on your arm—"

"No." Iseult fumbled for the monk's beautifully white cloak. "I mean . . . *you.*" Her words spun . . . no, the room spun and Iseult's words swirled with it. She wasn't even sure she spoke in Dalmotti. It might've been Nomatsi falling from her tongue.

"You," she tried again—almost certain that she was, indeed, using the Dalmotti word for *you,* "rescued me." As she squeezed the words past the pain and the spinning, she noticed dirt smudges on the monk's cloak. She instantly released her grip, ashamed. Then she sucked in a thin breath. So much pain. Boiling like hot tar. *Stasis. Stasis in your fingertips and in your toes.*

"Six and a half years ago, you f-found me at a crossroads. North of Veñaza City. I was a little girl, and I'd lost my way. I had a ragdoll."

Air hissed between the woman's teeth. She rocked back, Threads shining with confused tan. Then her head shook faster, her Threads now turquoise with disbelief . . .

Until suddenly, she was leaning in close, blinking and blinking and blinking. "Your name is Iseult?"

Iseult nodded, briefly distracted from her pain. The monk's eyes gleamed strangely, as if tears welled. But perhaps that was the darkness of the room. The angle of the sun. The monk's Threads showed no blue grief—only plum eagerness and giddy pink.

"That was you," the monk continued, "on the coast six and a half years ago?"

"I was twelve," Iseult said. "M-my doll's name was . . . Eridysi."

Again, a sharp exhale from the monk. A swaying backward as if felled by what she heard. "And did you learn *my* name? Did I tell it to you?"

"I don't think so." Iseult's voice was weak and distant, but she couldn't tell if it was because her ears or her throat had stopped working. The fire in her arm was kicking upward now, like a rising tide.

The monk drew back, quickly becoming the capable healer once more. She laid a warm hand on Iseult's shoulder, just above the arrow wound. Iseult flinched, then relaxed as sleep tugged at her.

But Iseult didn't want sleep. She couldn't face the dreams again. Wasn't it bad enough that she'd been beaten and mobbed in real life? To have to relive it in her sleep . . .

"Please," she said thickly, reaching for the monk's cloak once more—not caring about the dirt. "No more dreams."

"There will be no dreams," the woman murmured. "I promise, Iseult."

"And . . . Safi?" The pull of slumber rippled down Iseult's spine. "She's here?"

"She is here," the monk confirmed. "She should return at any moment. Now sleep, Iseult, and heal."

So Iseult did as she was told—not that she could have resisted even if she'd wanted to—and sank beneath the tide of a healing sleep.

EIGHTEEN

Far north of the *Jana* and yet in the same waters, Aeduan the Bloodwitch awoke. He was roused by the annoying sensation of fingers poking his ribs.

As the clouds of unconsciousness receded, Aeduan's senses expanded. Sunlight warmed his face and water caressed his arms. He smelled brine.

"Is he dead?" asked a high voice. A child.

"'Course he's dead," said a second child whom Aeduan suspected was the one fidgeting with his baldric. "He washed ashore last night and ain't moved since. How much you think his knives'll sell for?"

A snap sounded—as if Aeduan's baldric had been unbuckled.

The final dregs of sleep fell away. His eyes popped wide, he grabbed the child's wrist—and the scrawny boy picking his pockets yelped. A few paces away, a second boy gawped on. Then they both started shrieking—and Aeduan's eardrums almost split.

He released the first boy, who scuttled away in a flurry of kicked-up sand. It sprayed Aeduan, and a groan rattled over his tongue. He punched his fists into the beach—they sank into the soupy, wet sand—and shoved himself upright.

The world shook and smeared: beige beach, blue sky, brown marshlands, running boys, and a scampering sandpiper several feet away. Aeduan gave up trying to sort out where he was—this landscape could have been anywhere around Veñaza City. Instead, he turned his attention to his body.

Though it strained his muscles, he reached down to start with his toes. His boots were intact, though completely soaked—the leather would shrink as soon as they dried—but nothing in his feet was broken.

His legs were fully healed too, though his right pant leg had ripped all the way to the knee and there were long strands of marsh reed wrapped around his calf.

Next he inspected his thighs, his hips and waist, his ribs (still a bit tender), his arms . . . Ah, the scars on his chest were bleeding—which meant the ones on his back would be bleeding too. But those tiny slices were old wounds. Ancient, even. The cursed things opened and seeped whenever Aeduan was hurt to the brink of death.

At least nothing *new* bled, nothing was broken, and nothing was missing that he couldn't replace. He still had his salamander cloak and his Carawen opal. As for what the Nomatsi girl had taken—his stiletto and his cleaving knife—he could easily get more.

Yet thinking of the Nomatsi girl with no blood-scent made Aeduan want to gut something. His hand moved to his baldric, and as the sandpiper pranced closer, his fingers twitched over a throwing knife.

But no. Scaring the bird would do nothing to sate his fury. Only finding the Threadwitch would.

Not that he knew what he would do to the Threadwitch once he found her. Killing her definitely wasn't it—he owed her a life-debt now. She'd spared him (sort of) and he would have to repay that.

Yet if there was one thing Aeduan hated, it was saving lives he wasn't supposed to care about. There was only one other person to whom he owed such a debt, and at least she fully deserved it.

Aeduan's fingers fell from the knife. With a final snarl at the eastern sun, he hauled himself to his feet. His vision spun even more and his muscles tremored, telling him he needed water and food.

A distant clanging sounded. Nine chimes, which meant the day was still young.

Aeduan swung his head toward the sound. Far to the south, he could just discern a village. Probably where the boys lived. Probably not too far from Veñaza City. So, rolling his wrists and flexing his fingers, Aeduan set off through the waves of an incoming tide.

The quarter-to-twelve chimes were tolling when Aeduan finally reached Guildmaster Yotiluzzi's home. The guard there gave him a single once-over, balked, and then heaved open the gate.

To say Aeduan looked like he'd been dragged through the hell-gates and back was an understatement. He'd glimpsed himself in a window on the way through town, and he looked even worse than he felt. His short hair was crusted with blood, his skin and clothes streaked in sand, and despite having walked for three hours, his boots and cloak still hadn't dried.

Nor had his chest or back stopped seeping blood.

Every street and bridge, every garden or alley, people had cleared from his path—and they'd recoiled just like Yotiluzzi's guard was doing now. Though at least the people of Veñaza City hadn't uttered "Voidwitch," or swiped two fingers over their eyes to ask for the Aether's protection as this guard did now.

Aeduan hissed at the man as he stalked past. The guard jolted, and then stumbled out of sight behind the door. As Aeduan strode into the garden, a saying flittered through his mind: *Don't pet the cat that's had a bath.* It had been something his mother always said when he was young—and something Aeduan hadn't thought of in years.

Which only made his scowl deepen, and it took all his self-control not to slash at the flowers and leaves dangling over the paths. He hated these Dalmotti gardens, with their jungle-like vegetation and unchecked growth. This sort of garden wasn't defendable—it was just a tripping hazard for old Guildmasters and one more example of laxness in the Dalmotti Empire.

When at last Aeduan came to the long patio on the western side of Yotiluzzi's house, he found the servants clearing away the table where Yotiluzzi usually spent his mornings.

A maid spotted Aeduan trudging over the path. She screamed; the glass in her hands fell—and shattered.

Aeduan would have simply strolled on if the woman hadn't then shrieked, *"Demon!"*

"Yes," he growled, his wet boots slapping onto the patio. He locked eyes with her; she trembled. "I am a demon, and if you scream again, I will make sure the Void claims your soul."

She clutched her hands to her mouth, shaking, and Aeduan smiled. Let her tell *that* story to everyone she met.

"Where have you been?" Yotiluzzi's reedy voice bounced out from the open library doors. He snatched up his robes and stomped outside, his wrinkly jowls shaking. In the bright sunlight, there was no missing the fury in the Guildmaster's eyes. "And what has *happened* to you?"

"I was away," Aeduan answered.

"I know damned well you were away." Yotiluzzi wagged a finger in Aeduan's face.

Aeduan hated when the old man did that. It made him want to break the finger in half.

"What I want to know is where and why?" Yotiluzzi's finger kept waving. "Have you been drinking? Because you look like filth, and no one has seen you since last night. If you keep this up, I will have to terminate your contract."

Aeduan didn't respond. He let his lips press into a line, and he waited for the Guildmaster to get to the point. In the background, servants continued to gather breakfast plates—but they moved slowly, their eyes latched on Aeduan and dishes rattling in their hands.

"I have great need of you," Yotiluzzi finally said. "There is money to be made, and every second you waste is less money in my pocket. The betrothed of Henrick fon Cartorra was kidnapped, and the Emperor wants you to find her."

"Oh?" Aeduan lifted his chin at that. "And the Emperor is willing to pay for it?"

"Quite well." Yotiluzzi's finger jabbed back into Aeduan's face. "And I will reward *you* well if you can track her—"

In blur of speed, Aeduan gripped Yotiluzzi's finger and wrenched the old man close. "I will go straight to the Emperor myself, thank you."

Yotiluzzi's anger vanished. His mouth bounced open. "You work for me."

"Not anymore." Aeduan dropped the old man's finger—it still had grease on it from breakfast. Aeduan was hardly clean at present, yet that slimy bit of butter made him feel truly dirty.

"You can't do that!" Yotiluzzi cried. "I own you!"

Aeduan pushed into the house. Yotiluzzi shouted after him, but Aeduan was soon out of earshot, jogging through the opulent hallways, up the two flights of stairs, and then finally into his tiny servant's room.

All of his belongings were in a single bag—for he was a Carawen monk, prepared for everything and always ready to go.

He rifled through the sack, searching for two items: an extra stiletto and a paper with a long list of names. After stowing the stiletto in his squeaking and still-damp baldric, Aeduan examined the list. There were only a few names not struck through.

One at the bottom read, *14 Ridensa Street.*

Though Aeduan already knew what his father would

want—for Aeduan to join the Emperor, find the Truthwitch, and then *keep* the girl for his father's growing army—it had been several weeks since Aeduan had last updated his father. Much had unfolded as of late, so Aeduan would visit this Voicewitch at 14 Ridensa Street when he found a spare moment.

Aeduan wouldn't mention the Nomatsi girl, though. He'd been careful to keep his first life-debt hidden from his father, and he was even more determined to keep this new one a secret too. A girl with no blood-scent would only open questions.

Aeduan didn't like questions.

Ignoring the way his wet salamander cloak rubbed, he hefted his bag onto his shoulder and without another look, he left the room he'd called home for the past two years. Then he wound his way back through Yotiluzzi's mansion. Servants reared out of his path as he descended, and Yotiluzzi still bellowed from his library.

As Aeduan walked onward, he was pleased to find he'd left a trail of muddy boot-prints throughout the house.

Sometimes justice was all about the small victories.

When Aeduan arrived at the Doge's palace some half-chime after leaving Yotiluzzi's home and bathing in a public bathhouse (thank the Wells his old scars had stopped bleeding by then), he was shocked to find that the gardens in which he'd faced the unexpected battalion were now nothing but charred plants and wind-carried ash.

He shouldn't have been surprised; there *had* been a raging fire when he'd left.

Dalmotti guards and soldiers crawled everywhere, and none paid attention to Aeduan. When he reached the entrance hall he'd fought through the night before—which was now exposed wall beams and smoldering embers—one guard did step into Aeduan's path, though.

"Stop," the man ordered. He bared his teeth, stained with soot. "No one in or out, Voidwitch."

Clearly this man recognized Aeduan. Good. He would be all the more easily frightened.

Aeduan sniffed the air, knowing his eyes swirled red as he did so, and latched on to the man's blood-scent. *Salty kitchens and baby's breath.* A family man—too bad. That made him off-limits for violence.

"You will let me in." Aeduan lifted a single eyebrow. "Then you will escort me to the Doge's office."

"Oh, will I?" the man scoffed, but there was an undeniable wobble in his throat.

"Yes, for I am the only person on this continent who can find the girl named Safiya. And because I know who kidnapped her. Now, move." Aeduan jerked his chin toward the hall. "Tell your superiors I am here."

As Aeduan knew would happen, the guard hurried off. After several minutes of waiting (and staying occupied with a running count of the men around him), the guard returned with the message that yes, Aeduan could be escorted in immediately.

Aeduan followed the family-man/guard, his attention on the damage from the night before. At least half the palace was completely burned through. The gardens were even worse. Any plants that still lived were coated in ash.

When Aeduan finally reached the Doge's private chamber, after being scrutinized by twelve sets of guards—one for each nation present in the room, it would seem—he found a safe-haven upheaved. The room of lush red carpets, ceiling-high shelves, and glittering crystal lamps was clearly the Doge's personal space, yet now it was invaded by people of all ages, classes, and colors—while soldiers in all manner of uniform marched about.

The nut-skinned Illryans cowered beside the door, clearly wishing they could get back to their mountains in the south. The wispy Svodes clumped near the window, their gazes aimed north, and the Balmans passed around what looked to be a wine jug. Lusquans, Kritians, Portollans—each nation clung together.

Yet notably absent were the Marstoks. In Aeduan's quick scan, he saw no sign of Empress Vaness or her Sultanate.

Nor did he see the Nubrevnans.

Soon Aeduan had found the Emperor of Cartorra, pacing beside a long desk, his arms flying in all directions and his shouts rattling the crystal. The Dalmotti Doge, stuck on the receiving end of Henrick's bellows, sat stiff and twitchy behind his desk.

"Aha!" called a tenor voice to Aeduan's left. "There you are." Leopold fon Cartorra hopped gracefully from a shadow—leaving Aeduan to wonder how he'd missed the fair-haired, green-clad prince lurking beside the bookcase.

Or for that matter, how he'd missed *smelling* the prince.

Aeduan had recorded the imperial heir's blood-scent at the ball: *new leather and smoky hearths.* Aeduan should have sensed it here.

His confusion was quickly swallowed up by a second voice and a second figure materializing from the shadows. Somehow Aeduan had missed this man too—which only irritated him more. Especially since this second man was at least a hand taller than anyone else in the room.

"You know about my niece," the man slurred. He looked as though he hadn't slept in days. His eyes were red as embers, and his breath . . .

Aeduan's nose wrinkled up. The man smelled stronger of wine than wine itself. It even dominated his blood-scent.

"Come, Monk," Leopold urged, motioning toward his still-bellowing uncle. "We were told you have information on my uncle's betrothed. You must tell us everything, and . . . oh, hey now." Leopold had caught sight of his sleeve, which was dusted in soot. With a dejected sigh, he brushed halfheartedly at it. "I suppose this is what I get for wearing pale velvet into a world of ash. I imagine my hair is just as bad."

It was—the reddish blond was almost gray—yet Aeduan did not utter a word about it. "The Emperor," he reminded tersely.

"Right. Of course." Leopold shoved unapologetically around soldiers and servants. Aeduan followed, and the drunkard—who Aeduan had deduced was Dom Eron fon Hasstrel—dragged behind.

"You know who has my niece," the man said. "Tell me—

tell me everything you know." He grabbed for Aeduan's cloak.

Aeduan easily sidestepped. Which left Dom Eron staggering toward the Emperor. Then *into* the Emperor. Henrick shoved Eron back with a snarl before his eyes landed on Aeduan. His lips curled up.

So this is the Emperor of Cartorra, Aeduan thought. He'd seen the man from afar last night, yet he'd never stood close enough to distinguish all the pockmarks on Henrick's cheeks. Nor to see the single tooth that thrust out farther than all the rest. It jutted over his upper lip when his mouth was closed, much like a dog.

A very pissed off dog.

"Who has the domna?" Henrick asked. Despite being at least six inches shorter than Aeduan, the Emperor's voice was full and deep. It was the sort of voice for yelling over cannons, and Aeduan smelled a hint of the battlefield on the Emperor's blood. "Tell us what you know," Henrick went on. "Was it the thrice-damned Marstoks?"

"No," Aeduan answered carefully. Slowly. He needed to make sure no one knew that Safiya was a Truthwitch. Likely the uncle knew . . . though perhaps not. Aeduan suspected a man like Eron would shamelessly use a Truthwitch given the chance.

"See?" breathed the Doge. "I told you it wasn't Vaness!" He tapped frantically at something on his desk. "The Empress's signature would have vanished if it was they who had committed this!"

Aeduan's lips pressed tight as he realized he stared upon the Twenty Year Truce. Or rather, the final page of it, where all the continental leaders had signed. He found Vaness's childlike scrawl—she'd only been a girl when she'd penned her signature—was still firmly scripted at the bottom of the page. Either the Truce's magic was broken, or the Nubrevnans hadn't taken this domna against her will.

Aeduan turned back to Emperor Henrick. "The Nubrevnans have the domna. I saw them carry her to sea."

A collective jaw-slackening settled around the room. Even Henrick looked as if he'd swallowed something foul.

"But," Prince Leopold began, rubbing his lower lip with his thumb, "it was a Marstoki Firewitch who burned the palace to a crisp. And"—he glanced at Henrick, as if for support—"the Marstoks have left Veñaza City. The Empress and her entire Sultanate vanished shortly after the party. That suggests guilt to me."

"Yes," the Doge said with a nervous steepling of his hands, "but so did the Nubrevnans. They left right after the first dance between . . ."

"Between the prince and my niece," Eron finished, standing a bit straighter than before. "Sodding Nubrevnans! I will crush them—"

"There will be no crushing," Henrick grumbled with a disgusted glare. He angled toward Aeduan. "Tell us what you saw, Monk. All of it."

Aeduan did nothing of the sort. In fact, he glossed over almost every detail and skipped ahead to the only thing that mattered: the fight between a Nubrevnan Windwitch and Carawen monks at the lighthouse. "He took the domna to sea with his winds," Aeduan finished. "I could not follow."

Henrick nodded thoughtfully, the Doge blinked furiously behind his spectacles, Dom Eron seemed to have no idea what Aeduan was talking about, and Leopold simply eyed Aeduan with sleepy disinterest.

"How did you follow the girl to the lighthouse?" Henrick asked. "With your witchery?"

"Yes."

Henrick grunted, and a tiny smirk thrust out his fang. "And can you use your power again? Even across the Jadansi?"

"Yes." Aeduan tapped out a vague beat on his sword pommel. "I will follow her for a price."

Henrick's nostrils fluttered. "What sort of price?"

"Who cares?" Dom Eron cried, rounding on Aeduan. "I'll pay you whatever you want, Bloodwitch. Name your price and I'll pay it—"

"With what money?" Henrick cut in. He laughed, a scathing sound. "You borrowed from the crown to attend this summit, Eron, so if you have any money hiding in your purse, it is owed to me first." With another laugh, Henrick swiveled back to Aeduan. "We will cover your fees, Voidwitch, but it will come from the coffers of whomever has kidnapped Domna Safiya. If it is the Nubrevnans who have her, then it is the Nubrevnans who will pay."

"No." Aeduan's fingers tapped faster. "I require five thousand piestras up front."

"Five thousand?" Henrick reared back. Then lurched forward—close enough to make most men flinch.

Aeduan didn't flinch.

"Do you realize to whom you speak, Voidwitch? I am

the Emperor of Cartorra. You get paid when I say you get paid."

Aeduan stopped tapping. "And I am a Bloodwitch. I know the girl's scent and I can track her. But I will not do so without five thousand piestras."

Henrick's chest heaved, a full bellow clearly on the way, but Leopold stepped in. "You shall have the money, Monk." The prince lifted his hands submissively toward his uncle. "She is your *betrothed*, Uncle Henrick, so we must pay whatever price is needed to get her back, no?" He turned from the Emperor to the Doge and then to Dom Eron, somehow managing to get a nod from each man.

Aeduan was impressed. And he was all the more impressed when Prince Leopold fon Cartorra turned to him, stared him in the eye, and said, "You may come with me to my chambers. I should have at least half the money there. Will that suffice?"

"Yes."

"Good." Leopold smiled an empty smile. "Now, I believe we can all agree"—he looked back to his uncle—"that we have wasted enough time here. If you will give me permission, Your Majesty, I will join the monk on his search for your betrothed. I know Safiya well, and I think my insight could aid the monk."

Any esteem Aeduan had felt fled instantly at those words. The prince would slow him. Distract him. Yet before he could protest, Henrick nodded curtly. "Yes, join the Voidwitch. And keep his leash tight." The Emperor sneered at Aeduan, clearly hoping to illicit a response.

So Aeduan gave none.

Moments later, Leopold motioned for Aeduan to follow and he set off through the room. Aeduan stalked after him, wrists rolling and frustration brewing in his blood.

At least no one had mentioned that Safiya was a Truthwitch. Once Aeduan was well compensated for all the hassle of hunting the girl, he could still hand her off to his father.

For although these Cartorrans were paying Aeduan to find Safiya fon Hasstrel, no one had said anything about *returning* her.

NINETEEN

In the two hours since Merik had led Safi back to her room and ordered her to stay belowdecks for safety purposes, Safi had run through the same thoughts over and over again.

And questions—so many questions. From her uncle's plans to her betrothal with Henrick, it all played out atop an unwavering terror for Iseult.

There were footsteps too—hammering and relentless. They shook through Safi's skull until she wanted to scream. Until she wound up pacing in the tiny cabin while Evrane tended Iseult's wound.

"Stop," Evrane eventually snapped. "Or leave the room. You distract me."

Safi opted to leave—especially now that she had someone's permission to do so. Here was her chance to examine the main hold. To sort out how she would get Iseult to their hard-earned *freedom*. She could hear Habim's lessons as clearly as if he were beside her, harping about strategy and battlegrounds.

The hold turned out to be a shadowy space crammed

full of trunks and nets, sacks and barrels. Every nook she inspected had *something* squeezed in—including sailors—and there was no light save a square burst above the topside ladder.

It all stank of sweat and unwashed bodies, while the caustic stench of chicken crap wafted up from a livestock deck below. Safi was just grateful she couldn't hear the chickens—or any other animals. There was already too much noise for her temper to endure.

Though most sailors seemed to be overhead, Safi counted twenty-seven men curled up against crates or nestled beside casks. There seemed to be no crew quarters, and Safi filed that away for later consideration.

Of the twenty-seven sailors Safi passed, nineteen bit their thumbs or hissed "'Matsi-lovin' smut" at her. She pretended not to understand and even went so far as to offer an amiable nod. Yet in the dim light, she memorized their sun-seamed faces. Their vile voices.

When a lanky, black-skinned boy with shoulder-length braids hopped down the ladder belowdecks, Safi's witchery purred that *he* was safe. So Safi snagged him by the shoulder as he stumbled by. "Would the crew ever turn on a Nomatsi?"

The boy blinked, all his braids shaking before he answered in a decidedly *female* voice, "Not if the Admiral isn't behind it—and I don't think he would be. He doesn't mind the 'Matsis like the rest of us."

"Us?"

"Not me!" The girl's hands shot up. "I swear, I swear. I don't have a problem with 'Matsis. I just meant the crew."

True. Safi dug her knuckles in her eyes. Overhead, toes dragged, swords clanked, and voices barked. Whatever drill was running, Safi wished it would stop.

She launched back into her pacing. A double beat to the drum's slow rhythm. A triple beat. Why couldn't she come up with a plan? Iseult made it look so easy, yet every time Safi tried to organize her thoughts, they swirled apart like silt in a stream.

"You shouldn't walk so much," the girl said, still following Safi's steps. "The crew will complain, and then the Admiral might lock you up."

That gave Safi pause. Being locked up would severely limit her chances of defense or escape should it become necessary.

"I have a good spot topside," the girl offered. She pointed to the ladder. "You can't pace, but you can watch the drills."

Safi's nostrils twitched. She marched to the lowest rungs and glared into the bright sunlight overhead. Merik was up there. And Kullen too, who could incapacitate Safi at even the slightest disobedience.

But going topside *would* give Safi a better handle on the ship, the crew, and the layout. Maybe she could assemble a strategy if she learned more.

"No one will see us?" she asked the girl, thinking of Merik's orders to stay below.

"I swear it."

"Then show me."

The girl bared another grin and scrabbled up the ladder. Safi scaled behind and soon found herself surrounded by sailors, their cutlasses high and feet moving in vine-like steps across the heaving deck. Though many men ogled Safi as she sneaked past, she heard no jeers, felt no aggression. The prejudiced men, it would seem, were mostly below.

Which meant she wouldn't stay here long. She'd get the information she needed and return to Iseult's side.

Safi followed the girl, counting fifteen steps from the ladder to the forecastle's shade. The girl slunk behind four barrels that stank of dead fish and hunkered down. Safi crouched beside her, pleased to find that she was indeed hidden. The spot also gave her a clear view of the practicing sailors—of which, she realized with a sickening twist, there were *many*.

With all the crew displayed in rows instead of clambering in the rigging or scouring the decks, Safi estimated at least fifty men. Probably twice that, since she was gull crap when it came to math.

Safi craned her neck until she glimpsed Merik, Kullen, and three other men beside the tiller. They all wore wind-spectacles and their mouths moved in unison.

Behind them, Safi found the source of the endless thundering. A young man—with braids like the girl's—pounded an enormous horizontal drum.

Safi wished she could break his mallet in half.

Though more than that, she wished she could get a breath of fresh air. "Gods below," she swore, turning back to the girl. "What is that stench?"

"It's chum. We save our offal." The girl flicked a gleaming scale off the closest barrel, and now that Safi examined the planks around her, she found *many* scales. Leaking from the barrels, clinging to the sides. "It's for the sea foxes," the girl added. "We have to feed them when we pass by or they'll attack."

"The . . . sea foxes," Safi repeated flatly. "As in the mythical serpents that feast on human flesh?"

"Hye." The girl's ready smile flashed again.

"But surely you don't *believe* in them. They're just stories to scare children—like mountain bats. Or the Twelve Paladins."

"Which are *also* real," the girl argued. As if to prove her point, she pried a worn pile of gold-backed taro cards from her pocket and flipped over the top card.

It was the Paladin of Foxes, and a furry teal serpent coiled around a sword. Its fox-like face stared at Safi.

"Nice trick," Safi murmured, fingers itching for the deck. She'd seen many taro cards in her life, but she'd never seen ones with sea foxes instead of normal *red* foxes. It made her wonder what was painted on the other five suits.

"Not a trick," the girl countered. "I'm just showing you what a sea fox looks like. They're these huge serpents in water, see? But every few decades, they shed their skins and come to shore as beautiful women who seduce men—"

"And drag them to their graves," Safi finished. "The mountain bat legend is the same. But what I want to know is if you've actually *seen* a sea fox."

"No. Although," the girl rushed to add, "some of the older crew claim they fought foxes during the War."

"I see," Safi drawled—and she *did* see. Merik and his captains must keep the chum onboard to appease the more superstitious in their ranks—just like Uncle Eron sent sheep to the Hasstrel caves each year for the "mountain bats."

Throughout her childhood, Safi had scoured the alpine forests around the Hasstrel estate for any sign of a bat-like dragon. She'd combed the nearby caves, where the bats supposedly lived, and she'd spent hours beside the dead Earth Origin Well, waiting for a beautiful woman to suddenly appear.

But after ten years with nary a glimpse, Safi had finally accepted that mountain bats—if they'd ever existed—were as dead as the Well they lived beside.

Sea foxes, Safi decided, were no different.

"My name's Ryber, by the way." The girl bobbed her head. "Ryber Fortsa."

"Safiya fon Hasstrel."

Ryber bit her lip as if trying to stifle a grin. But then she gave up. "You're a domna, right?" She flipped up another taro card.

The Witch. It showed a woman, face hidden, staring at an Origin Well—the Earth Origin Well, actually. Except that unlike the Well Safi had grown up exploring, the illustrated version was still alive. The six beech trees around it were burgeoning, the flagstone walkway intact, and the waters swirling.

As with the Paladin of Foxes, the image was nothing like any Witch card Safi had seen.

Ryber tapped the card back into her deck, and Safi returned her gaze to the sailors. One young man had caught her eye, his face sweaty and painfully red—and his skill with a cutlass nonexistent.

In the time it took Safi to crack *all* of her knuckles, he was disarmed twice by his opponent. The worst of it was that his opponent was not only nearing the age of retirement, but had a crippled leg too.

If Safi needed a cutlass any time soon, then this boy's was the one to nab. "Your crew," Safi said, tilting back to catch a fresh scampering of wind, "seems divided. Some can fight, but most can't."

Ryber sighed, an acknowledging sound. "We haven't had much experience. The good ones"—she pointed to the old man with the limp—"fought in the War."

"Isn't it your first mate's duty to make sure you improve?" Safi squinted at the tiller. Wind sent Kullen's pale hair flying, and he still muttered alongside the other witches. Merik, however, was no longer there. "The mate isn't even watching the drills."

"'Cause he's sailing us. Normally he *does* push us."

Something about the defensive way Ryber spoke made Safi inspect the girl more closely. Despite her boyish figure and decidedly unflattering braids, Ryber wasn't a homely girl. In fact, now that Safi was looking closely, she realized Ryber's eyes were a brilliant silver. Not gray, but true, shimmery *silver.*

The First Mate would have to be blind not to fall in love with those eyes.

"So you're together," Safi prodded.

"No," Ryber said quickly—much too quickly. "He's a good first mate is all. Fair and smart."

The lie fretted down Safi's skin, and she had to bite back a smile as she slid her attention to Kullen. All she saw was an enormous man with a powerful witchery—a man who could all too easily take Safi down. Yet perhaps there was more behind his icy exterior.

Ryber heaved a long sigh and plied another card from her deck. *The Paladin of Hounds.* She stared at the hound-like serpent, also wrapped around a sword, and there was an emptiness in her eyes that spoke of things best forgotten. But then her gaze settled on Kullen; the lines on her face relaxed.

Ryber and the first mate *were* together, and it was more than just a dalliance. It was serious and it ran deep.

True.

Safi's lips pursed. She and Ryber seemed to be around the same age, yet here was something Safi knew little about. She'd had romances in Veñaza City. Flirtations with young men like the Chiseled Cheater, but those encounters had always ended in quick kisses and even quicker goodbyes.

"Does the prince," she asked absently, "have relations with anyone?" Safi tensed, instantly wishing she could snatch back those words. She didn't know where they'd come from. "I *mean,* is it allowed for Prince Merik's crew to have relations?"

"Not with each other," Ryber answered. "Also, we're off Nubrevnan soil, Domna. That makes the prince Admiral Nihar."

That caught Safi's attention, and she embraced the distraction wholeheartedly. "The prince's title changes according to where he is?"

"Sure it does. Doesn't yours?"

"No." Safi bit her lip as a fresh burst of salty wind lashed behind the barrels. Rather than cool her, though, it seemed to scald—to make fresh sweat bead on her brow. But this was different heat from before—an angry heat. A *frightened* heat.

And she only got hotter as Ryber went on to describe how Merik's rationing of meals had upset a lot of men and only widened the gap between those who supported Merik and those in favor of Princess Vivia. How dirty and overcrowded the capital city had become since the Great War.

The potent truth behind these stories made Safi's ankles bounce and her fingers curl. The world that Ryber described was nothing like the one Safi had left behind. There was poverty in the Dalmotti Empire—of course there was—but there wasn't starvation.

Perhaps . . . perhaps Merik did need trade—even with a cursed estate like the Hasstrels.

Just as Safi towed in her leg to stand—to return to the cabin and check on Iseult—Evrane's voice hit her ears.

"So you will let the girl *die?*" Evrane's shouts swept up from the nearby ladder. Louder than the drilling sailors. Louder than the pounding drum. "You *must* take us ashore!"

Ice slid down Safi's spine. Splintered through every piece of her. She rolled onto her knees, onto her feet. Then she stood, ignoring Ryber's whispers to stay hidden. Just as she lifted above the barrels, Merik's dark head appeared on the ladder. He climbed deftly onto the deck, his aunt's cloaked figure behind.

Merik strode several paces forward, head swiveling as if he searched for someone, and sailors cleared aside.

Evrane stalked to his side. "That girl needs a Firewitch healer, Merik! She will die without one!"

Merik didn't answer—even when Evrane's voice lifted with fury and she demanded that Merik take them ashore.

Safi's fingers flexed. Her toes, her calves, her gut—everything tensed for action.

If Merik wasn't willing to save Iseult's life, then that simply confirmed he wasn't Safi's ally. So, contract or not, enemy sailors or not, Admiral Nihar was now Safi's *opponent* and this ship was her battleground.

TWENTY

Merik had gone belowdecks to check on the domna. He didn't like how he'd left her in the cabin. Her Threadsister was ill, and Merik understood how that could wrinkle a person's disposition.

Whenever there were wrinkles, Merik had to smooth them out.

Besides, this was basically the only wrinkle he *could* fix at the moment. Vivia's Voicewitch was hounding Hermin, demanding that Merik tell her where the Dalmotti trade ship was and refusing to back off until she had seen this new Hasstrel contract for herself.

Merik had lied—again—and claimed the trade ship was only half the distance it actually was, but he had a feeling Vivia was starting to catch on.

Before he could reach the passenger cabin, his aunt intercepted him at the bottom of the ladder. "We need to stop," she declared, her face dark in the shadows but her silver hair glowing. "Iseult is too ill to survive much longer. What ports are near?"

"None that we can visit. We're still in Dalmotti territory." Merik tried to step onward.

Evrane cut him off, bristling. "What do you not understand about 'too ill to survive'? This is nonnegotiable, Merik."

"And this is not your ship to command." Merik didn't have the patience for this right now. "We stop when I say we stop, Aunt. Now stand aside so I can visit the domna."

"She is not in the cabin."

And just like that, the familiar pressure ignited beneath Merik's skin. "Where," he asked softly, "is she?"

"Topside, I assume." Evrane flicked her wrists disinterestedly at the cargo space, as if to say, *You do not see her here, do you?*

"Yet," Merik continued, his voice still dangerously low, "she was supposed to stay belowdecks. Why didn't you keep her in the cabin?"

"Because that is not my responsibility."

At those words, Merik's temper fanned into flames. Evrane knew what was in the Hasstrel contract. She *knew* that Safiya had to stay belowdecks for safety reasons. A single drop of her blood could mark the end of the contract entirely.

And the thought of Safiya spilling blood . . . of her getting hurt . . .

He sprang up the ladder, his aunt's words following him. "So you will let the girl *die?* You *must* take us ashore!"

Merik ignored his aunt. He would find Safiya and explain to her—gently, of course, and not with this fire controlling him—that she absolutely could not leave her cabin.

She would listen, obey, and then Merik could relax again. No more wrinkles in sight.

Merik barked at his men to stand aside as he aimed for the quarterdeck. His magic wanted release, and try as he might, he was helpless to smooth it away.

"Admiral!"

Merik ground to a halt. That was Safiya's voice. Behind him.

He twisted back slowly, his chest heaving now. His winds throbbing inside, worse than before. Worse than they'd been in years. His control was slipping away.

It shattered completely when he saw her standing at the center of the deck, a cutlass in hand.

"You will take us ashore." Her tone was cold and exact. "You will take us *now*."

"You disobeyed orders," Merik said, inwardly cursing. What happened to a gentle explanation? "I told you my word is law, I told you to stay belowdecks."

Her only response was to raise the cutlass high. "If Iseult needs a Firewitch healer, then we will go ashore."

Distantly, Merik realized that the wind-drum had stopped pounding. That the ship had started to rock without the Tidewitches to keep it calm.

Merik swept out his own cutlass. "Go belowdecks, Domna. Now."

That made Safiya smile—a vicious thing—and she stepped calmly up to Merik's blade. Then she rolled back her shoulders and pushed her chest against the tip. Her shirt dimpled in. "Get a Firewitch healer, Admiral, or I will make sure your contract is ruined."

Heat pounded behind Merik's eyeballs. Safiya would open her own skin. She would spill blood, and Merik would lose everything he'd worked for. Somehow, she knew what the contract said, and she was testing him.

So Merik lowered his blade.

Then he gave into his rage. The winds swept free, blasted over his sailors. "Kullen! Take her air!"

Safiya's face drained of blood. "*Coward!*" she snarled. "Selfish coward!" She attacked.

Merik barely had enough time to launch himself backward toward his cabin before her blade slashed the air where his head had been.

He flew toward the quarterdeck, the word "coward" hitting his ears from all directions. It writhed from his sailors' lips, and as he lowered to the deck, he found Kullen's eyes in the crowd. The first mate shook his head—a sign that he would not help this time.

Then Merik understood why: his father's sailors only saw a woman—a *Cartorran* woman at that—who'd called their new admiral a "coward." If Vivia or Serafin were leading this ship, then justice would be swift, thorough, and violent. These men expected that. Demanded it.

And it wasn't as if they knew about the Hasstrel contract.

Which meant Merik was going to have to fight Safiya fon Hasstrel, and he would have to do it without spilling her blood.

Merik's feet touched down, and there was the girl, hurtling toward him with her braid flying behind. Sailors dispersed from her path, their attention on what would come next.

Then Safiya was before him, cutlass arching out. Merik met it with his own. Sparks blazed along the steel—this girl was strong. He needed to get the blades out of this fight as soon as possible. Even the slightest nick could be too much for the contract.

Another hacking blow from the girl. Merik parried, but his back was against his cabin. Worse, the world was angling sharply left, and the ship was in that pausing stillness between heaves.

The girl used that inertia, and by the Wells, she was fast. One slash became two. Three. Four—

But there. The ship lurched the other way, and her knees wobbled. She had to widen her stance before unfurling her next attack.

Merik was ready. When her blade swung high, he ducked low. Her sword thunked into the wall, and Merik tackled her. Yet the instant she was over his shoulder, her fists hammered into his kidneys. Into his spine.

His grip loosened, and the ship rocked. He felt his balance go. She'd hit the deck headfirst.

So he tapped into his Windwitchery. Air gusted beneath the girl, flinging her torso high and returning Merik's balance . . . until she wrestled fully upright onto his shoulder and kneed him in the ribs.

He doubled over—he couldn't help it. Planks zoomed toward his face.

His magic exploded. In a cyclone of power, he and the domna blasted off the deck. They spun. They tumbled. The world blurred until they were above the masts. Wind whipped around them, under them. Safiya hardly seemed to notice how high they were.

Merik tried to control the power beneath his skin. In his lungs. But there was no denying that the girl awakened this rage inside him. His witchery no longer responded to him but to *her*.

Her fist launched at Merik's face. He had just enough time to block it before her foot hooked behind his ankle. She whipped him backward—her body spinning with his until they were upside down. Until all he saw was sailcloth and rigging and Safiya's fists thrashing in.

Merik countered, but he pushed too hard—or maybe his witchery did. Either way, she went twirling out and away from the sails. Then she left Merik's winds entirely and plummeted, headfirst, toward a hundred gaping sailors.

Merik *thrust* a magicked wind beneath her, propelling her back his way. Flipping her—and himself—right side up. The ocean and the rigging streamed through his vision.

Then Safiya kicked him. Right in the gut.

His breath thundered out. His magic choked off.

He and the domna fell.

Merik had just enough time to angle his body beneath her and think, *This will hurt,* when his back hit the deck.

No . . . that wasn't the deck. That was a swirl of wind. Kullen was slowing their speed, before—

Merik slammed onto the wood with a brain-rattling *crack!* The girl toppled onto him, crushing his lungs and ribs.

Despite the pain and the shock, Merik took his chance while he had it. He hooked his knees into hers and flipped her beneath him. Then he planted his hands on either side of her head and glared down. "Are you finished?"

Her chest heaved. Her cheeks were sunset red, but her eyes were gleaming and sharp. "Never," she panted. "Not until you go ashore."

"Then I will put you in chains." Merik shifted as if to rise, but she clutched his shirt and yanked. His elbows caved; he fell flat against her, noses almost touching.

"You don't . . . fight fair." Her ribs bowed into his with each gasping breath. "Fight me . . . again. Without magic."

"Did I hurt your pride?" He chuckled roughly and dipped his mouth toward her ear. His nose grazed down her cheek. "Even without my winds," he whispered, "you would lose."

Before she could respond, Merik rolled off her and shoved to his feet. "Take her below and chain her!"

Safiya tried to scramble up, but two sailors—men from Merik's original, loyal crew—were already upon her. She wrestled and roared, but when Kullen stepped stonily to her side, she stopped fighting—although she didn't stop shouting. "I hope you burn in hell! Your first mate and your crew—I hope you all *burn*!"

Merik turned away, pretending not to hear. Not to care. But the truth was, he did hear and he did care.

TWENTY-ONE

It took Aeduan mere minutes to get Emperor Henrick to hire him, but any time saved was lost while getting his new companion, the foppish Prince Leopold—as well as eight Hell-Bard escorts—out of the palace.

Two hours after leaving the Doge's personal office, Aeduan finally found himself jogging beside Leopold's carriage and heading to the Southern Wharf District. Traffic was dense. People had come from all corners of Veñaza City to see "the Doge's burned-down palace." Or to see, as most people referred to it, "what the thrice-damned fire-eating Marstoks had done."

Aeduan had no idea how that rumor had started, but he suspected it *had* been started. Perhaps a loudmouthed palace guard had blabbed or some war-hungry diplomat had intentionally let the rumor slip. Either way, animosities for the Marstoks were high as Aeduan jogged the streets and bridges of Veñaza City—a bad sign for the Twenty Year Truce renewal—and everything about the situation felt guided. Strategized. Someone wanted Marstok as the enemy.

Aeduan filed that away to tell his father.

He also filed away the fact that, of the eight Hell-Bards in Leopold's employ, only the commander was still breathing normally inside his helm after two blocks of jogging.

So much for an elite fighting force.

Then again, Aeduan was shamefully exhausted himself by the time Leopold's carriage clattered into the Southern Wharf District, where the Cartorran warships creaked.

It was almost evening—and Aeduan's newly healed muscles burned from the exertion, his fresh skin was overheated from the crowded streets, and his old scars wept blood once more—which meant his only clean shirt was now stained through.

Oh, Aeduan couldn't wait to exact revenge—somehow—when he saw that Threadwitch again.

Leopold staggered out of his carriage into the hot sunset. He wore a teal velvet suit that was far too fine for sailing, and at his hip was a cutting-rapier with a gold cage-hilt—more for flash than use.

But money was money, and Aeduan's new lockbox of silver talers inside the carriage was easily worth baking in the sun and listening to this foppish prince's endless stream of complaints.

"What," the prince called out, a gloved hand over his mouth, "is that stench?"

When none of the Hell-Bards stepped forward to answer—when in fact they all stepped just out of earshot, as if intentionally avoiding conversation with their prince—the duty of a response fell to Aeduan.

"That stench," he said flatly, "is fish."

"And the feces of filthy Dalmottis," hollered a bearded

man striding down the pier. He wore the emerald green coat of the Cartorran navy and, judging by his high chin and the three men scurrying at his heels, he was the admiral that Leopold was supposed to meet.

The four officers formed a line before Leopold and popped curt bows along with four rounds of "Your Imperial Highness."

Leopold smirked like a boy with a new toy, and as he adjusted his sword, he declared in Cartorran, "Board your ships, men. The fleet sets out with the tide and, according to this monk, it is a Nubrevnan that we hunt."

The admiral shifted his weight, the captains traded glances, and somehow, the Hell-Bards slunk even farther away. For of course, there would be no sailing with the tide. A single ship sailing to Nubrevna was risky at best. An entire fleet was a suicide mission. Everyone here knew that except the one man who ought to: the imperial heir to Cartorra.

Yet none of the officers seemed inclined to speak up—not even the admiral. Inwardly, Aeduan groaned. Surely these people did not fear this vapid prince. Aeduan could understand fearing Emperor Henrick, but the Emperor was not here to loose his waggle-toothed ire.

Aeduan turned sharply to the prince and said in Dalmotti, "You cannot bring a fleet to Nubrevna."

"Oh?" Leopold blinked. "Why not?"

"Because it would be useless."

Leopold flinched, and his cheeks flared red—the first sign of a temper. So, though it killed Aeduan to do it, he tacked on a brusque, "Your Imperial Highness."

"Useless, is it?" Leopold thumbed the edge of his lips. "Am I missing something then?" He twisted to the admiral, and in clipped Cartorran, he asked, "Isn't this what navies are for? Reclaiming things that warmongering Nubrevnans take from you?" Leopold's cheeks twitched as he spoke, and Aeduan amended his earlier thought.

Leopold might indeed possess a terrifying temper—particularly if one's admiralty depended on his ignorant princely whim.

So with a harsh exhale, Aeduan spoke up once more. *He* had no admiralty to lose, after all. "Navies are for sea battles, Your Imperial Highness. Meaning *at sea*. Yet we do not go to Nubrevna for battles, because the domna will likely be in Lovats by the time your warships can even reach the Nubrevnan coast. Were I this Nubrevnan Windwitch, that is where I would take her."

Leopold's cheeks ticked again, and when he spoke, it was in Dalmotti and addressed to Aeduan. "Why does the girl's arrival in Lovats make a difference? A Nubrevnan kidnapped my uncle's betrothed. We claim her."

"The Twenty Year Truce," Aeduan said, "does not allow foreign vessels to touch down on a nation's soil without permission—"

"I know what the cursed Truce says. But I repeat, they have my uncle's betrothed. That is already a violation of the Truce."

Except that it isn't, Aeduan thought. But he didn't feel like arguing, so he only gave a sharp nod. "The only way to access Lovats is to sail past the Sentries of Noden—and those stone monuments are heavily guarded by Nubrevnan soldiers. Assuming your fleet could get by—which they couldn't—they would still have to contend with the bewitched Water-Bridges of Stefin-Ekart."

"So," Leopold's voice was lethally devoid of inflection, "what am I supposed to do, then?"

The admiral, his captains, and the distant Hell-Bards collectively flinched—and Aeduan no longer blamed them. At least Henrick understood war and costs and strategy.

Not to mention basic history.

Yet, this was an opportunity for Aeduan. A good one, the likes of which he might never have again. It was a chance to gain the trust of a prince.

"A single ship," Aeduan said slowly, twisting his wrists—inward three times, outward three times. "We need the fastest frigate in the fleet as well as every Tide- or Windwitch available. If we can intercept the Nubrevnans before they reach their homeland, we can claim the domna without affecting the Truce . . . Your Imperial Highness."

Leopold eyed Aeduan, the Veñazan breeze lifting his pale curls in all directions. Then, as if coming to some internal decision, he tapped his rapier hilt and nodded at Aeduan. "Make it happen, Monk. Immediately."

So Aeduan did just that, smugly pleased to have four officers and eight Hell-Bards—all of them eyeing Aeduan's bloodied chest warily—now forced to take orders from him.

The experience was also . . . disconcerting. People rarely stared at Aeduan directly, much less stood in such close proximity. So when the planning finally ended and the men returned to ignoring him once more, Aeduan found himself relieved.

It was as he returned to Leopold's carriage after overseeing the transport of his lockbox onto a Cartorran cutter that a familiar scent wafted into his nose.

He paused, two steps from the carriage, and sniffed the air.

Clear lake water and frozen winters.

Aeduan knew that smell, yet he couldn't pin down the corresponding blood. Leopold smelled of new leather and smoky hearths; the Hell-Bards stank of the noose and cold iron; and the officers all bore distinctly oceanic blood-scents.

Whoever had recently passed this pier, Aeduan had met them but had not bothered to record their scent.

Which meant they were not important.

So, shrugging aside the smell, Aeduan tugged his hood low. The seventeenth chimes were tolling, which meant Aeduan had *just* enough time to find 14 Ridensa Street—and to finally update his father on this latest, most lucrative employer.

TWENTY-TWO

Manacles rubbed against Safi's wrists as she watched Iseult's sleeping face.

There was an unmistakable line of drool lingering on Iseult's lips, but Evrane was gone and Safi was chained too far away to do anything.

She could do *nothing* that mattered, it seemed. She'd acted like a child by letting her temper explode at Merik—and she didn't care. What she cared about was that her attack had failed. That she'd only made things worse in the end.

The room was dim, clouds rolling over the afternoon sun, and water sloshed behind her. The ship was gaining speed, the rocking all but stopped, and the giant drum booming once more. The stomp of sailors' feet had also resumed.

Safi drew her knees to her chest. Her chains rattled, a mocking sound.

"That was quite a display."

Safi lurched upright—and found Evrane in the doorway. Light as a mouse, the monk crossed the room to Iseult.

"How is she?" Safi asked. "What can I do?"

"You can do nothing chained up." Evrane dropped to the floor and draped a hand over Iseult's arm. "She is stable. For now."

Safi's breath burst out.

For now wasn't long enough. What if Safi had initiated something she couldn't complete? What if Iseult never woke up—*could* never wake up?

Evrane twisted toward Safi. "I should have kept you in the room. I am sorry for that."

"I would have attacked Merik belowdecks or above."

Evrane sniffed dryly. "Are you injured from your . . . sparring?"

Safi ignored the question. "Tell me what's wrong with Iseult. Why does she need a Firewitch healer?"

"Because there is something wrong with Iseult's muscle, and that is a Firewitch healer's domain." Evrane plucked a glass jar from within her cloak. "I am a Waterwitch healer, so I specialize in the fluids of the body. My salves"—she flourished the jar at Safi—"are from Earthwitch healers, so they can only heal skin and bone." Evrane set the salve on the pallet. "There is inflammation in Iseult's muscle that is bewitched. Either the cut on her hand or the arrow wound in her arm was cursed. I . . . cannot tell which, but it is undoubtedly the work of a Cursewitch."

"A Cursewitch?" Safi repeated. Then again, "A *Cursewitch?*"

"I've seen spells like this before," Evrane continued. "I can keep the curse clear of her blood, but I fear it will still spread through her muscle. As we speak, it moves for her shoulder.

If it gets much closer, then I will have to amputate—but that is risky to do on my own. It is best done with an Earthwitch healer and a Firewitch healer to help. Of course, even if we had such witches available, most Earthwitch healers are Cartorran. Most Firewitch healers are Marstoki. Merik would never allow such enemies onboard."

"They are not enemies now," Safi muttered, her mind still reeling from the idea of amputation. That word seemed so strange. So impossible. "The War ended twenty years ago."

"Tell that to the men who fought in it." Evrane gestured toward the main hold. "Tell that to the sailors who lost their families to Marstoki flames."

"But healers can't hurt." Safi pushed her fingers against the wood until her knuckles cracked. "Isn't that part of your magic?"

"Oh, we can hurt," Evrane answered. "Just not with our power."

Safi said nothing. There was nothing to say. Every breath that passed, the deeper into hell she tumbled and the less likely Iseult was to survive.

Yet even though Safi was chained, she wouldn't give up. Merik's treaty, her uncle's plan, and even her own future could be damned and thrice-damned again. Safi *would* find a way to get off this ship and she *would* get Iseult to a Firewitch healer.

"So you are a noblewoman," Evrane said, "yet you clearly know your way around a blade. I wonder how that happened." She carefully reached for her healer kit at the foot of the pallet. Then, with precise movements, she untied the bandage on Iseult's arm. The drum pounded and pounded and pounded.

"In Nubrevna," Evrane continued, "we call our doms and domnas 'vizers,' and my family's land—the Nihar holding—was southeast of the capital. A crap holding, to tell you the truth." Evrane threw Safi a wry smile as she ever-so-carefully peeled back the bandage. "But crap holdings tend to breed the most power-hungry vizers, and my brother was no exception. He eventually won the hand of Queen Jana, and the Nihars were inducted into the royal snakes."

The Cartorran nobility is the same, Safi thought. Vicious, cut-throat, lying. While a man like Merik might feel duty-bound to his land and his people, Safi had never suffered that loyalty. The Hasstrel people had never wanted her, nor had her fellow doms and domnas. And as Uncle Eron had so succinctly put it, Safi wasn't exactly cut out for leadership.

Evrane set aside the dirty bandages and reached for her jar of salve. "Politics is a world of lies, and the Nubrevnan court is no different. Yet, when my brother became King . . ." She frowned and opened the jar. "When Serafin became King and Admiral of the Royal Navy, he became the worst snake of them all. He puts vizer against vizer, son against daughter—even his own.

"I stayed a few years after the family moved to Lovats," Evrane went on, "but eventually I gave up. I wanted to help people, and I could not do so in the capital." Evrane replaced the tub in her kit and then waved her Witchmark in Safi's direction. "It is part of being blessed with Waterwitch healing, I suppose. I need to help and when I am idle, I am unhappy. So years before the Truce began, I gave up my title and traveled to the Sirmayan Mountains to take my Carawen vows. The Wells have always called to me, and I knew that I could help others with a white robe upon my back. Where do you come from, Domna?"

Safi sucked in tiredly; her chains shook with the movement. "I'm from the Orhin Mountains—in central Cartorra. It was cold and wet and I hated it."

"And Iseult is from the Midenzi settlement?" Evrane laid the new linen over Iseult's arm and, with almost painful slowness, eased it around her bicep. "I remember it now."

Safi's lungs compressed. *Silver hair. A healer monk.* "You," Safi exhaled. "*You* were the monk who found her."

"Hye," Evrane answered simply, "and that is a very significant thing." Evrane angled a grim look Safi's way. "Do you know why it is significant?"

Safi wagged her head slowly. "It's . . . an incredible coincidence?"

"Not coincidence, Domna, but Lady Fate at work. Do you know 'Eridysi's Lament'?"

"You mean the song that drunken sailors sing?"

Evrane chuckled softly. "That is the one, though it is actually part of a much longer poem. An epic, really, that the Carawen monks believe to be . . ." She paused, her gaze unfocusing as if she searched for the right word. "A *foretelling,*" she finally said with a nod, "for Eridysi was a Sightwitch, you see, and many of her visions eventually came to pass.

"Ever since I joined the Monastery, I have felt, Domna, that I was part of that Lament."

Safi turned a skeptical eye on Evrane. From what she knew of the song's lyrics, it was all about betrayal, death, and eternal loss. Hardly the sort of thing one would *want* to be real—much less a prophecy of one's own personal path.

Yet when Evrane spoke again, it was not of Lady Fate or foretellings, and her attention had returned to Iseult's delicate face. "Iseult is very sick," she murmured, "but I swear by the Origin Wells that she will not die. *I* will die before I let that happen."

Those words shook through Safi, resonating with such intense truth that Safi could only nod in return. For she would do the same for Iseult, just as she knew Iseult would always do for her.

Merik stared at the table of charts before him—at the Aetherwitched miniature Vivia had procured. Kullen leaned against the wall nearby, stiff and expressionless. The cold in the air was the only sign of his anxiety.

Sunlight peeked through the clouds, and the *Jana* dipped and rose with the ocean's roll. On the map, the miniature *Jana* cruised smoothly onward . . . But not the Dalmotti trade ship. It had slowed significantly and would soon reach the exact place Merik had told Vivia it would be—and it would arrive at the exact moment he'd told her as well.

Merik's lies were becoming truth right before his eyes.

He supposed he could try to stop his sister with some

new tale about the trade ship abruptly changing course . . . But he doubted she would believe him. In all likelihood, she was already in position, waiting for her unsuspecting prey to sail past.

"I have dug us a deep grave," Merik said, voice rough.

"But you'll dig us back out again." Kullen spread his hands. "You always do."

Merik tugged at his collar. "I was careless. Blinded by my excitement over a thrice-damned contract, and now . . ." He exhaled sharply and turned to Kullen. "Now I need to know if you can do what needs doing."

"If you mean," Kullen said impatiently, "how are my lungs? Then they are perfectly fine." The temperature dropped further; snow flickered around Kullen's head. "I've had no issues in weeks. So I promise"—Kullen placed a fist over his heart—"that I can fly to Vivia's ship and keep her from piracy. At least until you arrive."

"Thank you."

"Don't thank me." Kullen shook his head. "It is sheer luck that we are here and not in Veñaza City. If we were still on the other side of the sea, then we wouldn't be able to intervene at all." A pause. Then the air warmed slightly. "There is something else we should discuss before I go."

Merik didn't like the sound of that.

"The 'Matsi girl belowdecks," Kullen went on. "Do you have a plan for her?"

Merik inhaled wearily and checked his shirt—still tucked in. "I'm working on it, Kullen. I won't let her die, all right? But the *Jana* and our people must come first."

Kullen nodded, seemingly satisfied. "Then I will do what needs doing."

"As will I," Merik said. "Now gather the crew and summon the Tidewitches. It's time to haul wind."

TWENTY-THREE

It was nearing sunset, and Evrane had departed to find food, leaving Safi to contemplate Iseult and Lady Fate all alone. Surely the odds of Iseult encountering the same monk who'd helped her were high—after all, how many Carawen monks could there possibly be on the continent?

And *surely* this reunion was more akin to chance and probability—like Ryber drawing the Paladin of Foxes from the taro deck—than it was to some ancient poem steering the monk's life.

At the sound of approaching footsteps, Safi's thoughts scattered. The cabin door creaked open to reveal Merik, a wooden bowl in hand.

Her lips curled back. "Come to fight me again?" It was a churlish comment, but Safi couldn't bring herself to care.

"Should I?" He strode into the cabin and toed the door shut. "You don't seem to be misbehaving."

"I'm not," she grumbled—and it was true. Despite wanting to snarl and shout and make him regret *ever* putting iron against her skin, she wasn't stupid enough to waste the energy. Now, more than ever, she needed a plan.

"Good." Merik marched over and set the bowl within grabbing distance—though *he* wisely stayed back.

Chains jangling, Safi peeked into the bowl. Pale soup with a dry roll floating on top. "What is it?"

"What we always have." Merik sank into a crouch. Their eyes met. His were a rich, dark brown. Yet he seemed distracted, the triangle on his forehead sunk to a frown. "It's mostly bone broth, and whatever else we can find for the pot."

"Sounds . . . delicious."

"It isn't." He shrugged. "But look, I'll even break your bread." He plucked the roll from the bowl and, with an almost apologetic smile, he ripped it apart and dropped each bite-size chunk into the broth.

Safi watched him through half-lowered lashes. "Is this some trick? Why are you being nice to me?"

"No trick." More bread plopped into the bowl. "I want you to know that I understand why you . . . attacked me." Slowly, he pulled his gaze back to Safi's. It was somber now. Bleak even. "I would have done the same thing in your position."

"Then why don't you stop? If you understand, why don't you take Iseult ashore?"

Merik's only response was to grunt noncommittally and drop the last of the bread into the bowl. Safi stared at it, bobbing in the broth, and frustration boiled up her shoulders.

"If," she said quietly, "you expect me to be *grateful* for soup—"

"I do," he interrupted. "We don't have much food on this

ship, Domna, and you're eating my dinner ration. So yes, a bit of gratitude would be nice."

Safi had no retort for that. In fact, she had absolutely no words at all—and her wariness suddenly doubled. What did Merik want from her? Her magic sensed no deception.

Merik nudged the bowl. "Eat, Domna . . . oh, wait! I almost forgot!" He withdrew a spoon from his coat. "How is that for service? Do you know how many men onboard would kill for the use of a spoon?"

"And do you know," she retorted, "how many men I can *kill* with a spoon?"

That earned her a lazy smile, but when she reached for the spoon, Merik didn't release it. Their fingers touched . . .

And heat coiled up Safi's arm. She flinched, her hand and the spoon shooting back.

"We'll be stopping soon," Merik said, seemingly unaware of her reaction. "There might be fighting, and . . . I wanted to warn you."

"Who will be fighting?" Safi's voice was oddly high-pitched, her fingers still humming as she gripped the spoon. "Are Iseult and I in danger?"

"No." Merik's head shook once, but the word—and the movement—frizzed against Safi's power. *False*. "I will keep you safe," he added, almost as an afterthought. Safi's magic purred, *True*.

Frowning, she sipped the soup. It was disgusting—even as hungry as she was. Bland to the point of tasteless and cold to the point of congealed.

"Don't watch me eat," she huffed. "I won't *actually* kill anyone with the spoon."

"Thank Noden." His lips twitched up. "I was worried for the entire crew." A pause, then a curt wag of his head, as if he shook off some dark cloud that plagued him.

When Merik met Safi's gaze, his eyes were sharp—the sharpest she'd ever seen them—and she had the uncomfortable sense that he *saw* her. Not just the surface of her, but all her secrets too.

"In all honesty," he said at last, "you *are* a threat, Domna. That's why I have to keep you in chains. You would do anything for your Threadsister, and I would do the same for Kullen."

True.

When Safi stayed silent except for her soup-sipping, Merik went on. "Kullen and I have known each other since we were boys—since I went to the Nihar estate, where his mother works. When did you meet Iseult?"

Safi swallowed her current mouthful, almost choked on the bread, and then croaked, "Why do you want to know?"

Merik sighed. "Good-natured curiosity."

True.

Safi's mouth pursed to one side. Merik was being strangely open with her—which he certainly didn't *have* to be—and Safi supposed there was no tactical advantage if he found out how she and Iseult had become friends.

"We met six years ago," she finally answered. "She works . . . or *worked*, I suppose, for my tutor in Veñaza City. Whenever I visited him for a lesson, Iseult was there. I . . . didn't like her at first."

Merik nodded. "I didn't like Kullen either. He was so tense and hulking."

"He still is."

Merik laughed—a full, rich sound that sent warmth cinching around Safi's stomach. With his eyes crinkled and his face relaxed, Merik was handsome. Disarmingly so, and against her better judgment and *strongest* wish, Safi found herself relaxing.

"I thought Iseult was tense too," she said slowly. "I didn't understand Threadwitches back then—or Nomatsis. I just thought Iseult was strange. And cold."

Merik scratched his chin, rough with stubble. "What changed?"

"She saved my life from a Cleaved." Safi looked at Iseult, stiff upon the pallet. And much too pale. "We were only twelve years old, and Iseult saved me without any thought for herself."

There had been an Earthwitch near Mathew's shop. The woman had started to cleave with Safi only paces away, and when the Earthwitch had lunged, Safi'd thought it was all over for her. Hell-flames or Hagfishes, she hadn't known, but she'd been certain they were coming for her.

Until Iseult was suddenly there, jumping on the woman's back and fighting like it was *her* life trapped in the balance.

Of course, Iseult hadn't been strong enough to stop the Earthwitch, so thank the gods Habim had arrived only moments later.

That was the first day Habim had begun training Iseult to defend herself alongside Safi. More important, it was the first day Safi had seen Iseult as a friend.

And now this was how Safi repaid her—by sending their lives up in smoke.

Safi stirred her soup, watching the bread swirl. "How did you and Kullen become friends?"

"A similar story." Merik wet his lips and, with a bit too much nonchalance, said, "Kullen has bad lungs. I . . . don't know if you've noticed. It's ironic, really—he's an Airwitch and can control someone else's lungs, yet not his own." Merik gave a dry laugh. "Kullen had his first truly bad breathing attack when he was eight, and I used my winds to revive him. Rather straightforward." Merik nodded to the soup. "How's the dinner?"

"I've had worse."

He bowed his head. "I'll take that as a compliment. We do what we can here, with what little we have." He lifted his eyebrows as if he intended a double meaning.

It was lost on Safi. "What's your point?"

"That I think you do the same—make do with what you have. I will help Iseult when I can."

"I can't wait that long. Iseult can't wait."

Merik shrugged one shoulder. "You have no choice, though. You're the one in chains."

Safi flinched as if he'd hit her. She dropped the spoon and thrust away the bowl. Broth sloshed out the sides.

Let Merik mock her helplessness. Let him laugh at her chains. She had lit this pyre; she would put it out—and she didn't need his or anyone else's permission to do that.

"It tastes like crap," she said.

"It does." Merik gave a knowing nod—which only incensed her more. "But at least I get some dinner now."

He swooped up the bowl and then marched from the room as smoothly as he'd come in.

Iseult was stuck in the half-dreaming again. Voices lingered outside of her awareness, and dreams hovered just beyond. Someone was *here*.

It wasn't the people in the ship's cabin, of which Iseult could hazily hear. This presence was a different shadow—someone who wriggled and writhed in the back of her mind.

Wake up, Iseult told herself.

"Stay asleep," the shadow murmured. It had a voice she knew: Iseult's own voice. "Stay asleep but open your eyes . . ."

The voice was stronger than Iseult. It coated her mind with a sticky, inescapable syrup, and though Iseult *screamed* at herself to awaken, all she managed was exactly what the voice wanted.

She cracked open her eyes, and saw the cabin's oiled bulkhead.

"A boat," the shadow murmured. "Now tell me, Threadwitch, what is your name?" The shadow still spoke in Iseult's voice, though there was a giddy layer over her words, as if she constantly smiled. "And do you travel with another girl? A Truthwitch? You must, for there are only so many Threadwitches at sea right now—three, to be exact, of which only one is the appropriate age."

"Who," Iseult began, though she had to fight to get the single word over her lips. Her voice sounded a million miles away, and she wondered if perhaps she actually spoke in the real world—if that was why her throat seemed to burn with the effort. "Who are you?"

The shadow's glee solidified, and an icy trickle slid down Iseult's spine. "You are the first person to sense me! No one has ever heard what I say or what I command. They simply follow orders. How is it that *you* know I'm here?"

Iseult didn't answer. Just voicing the one question had sent white-hot pain through her body.

"My, my," the shadow declared, "you are very ill, and if you die, I won't learn *anything*." The shadow pressed in more closely, and its fingers rummaged through Iseult's thoughts. "It's hard to read you anyway—you're quite closed off. Has anyone ever told you that before?" The shadow didn't wait for a reply. Instead, a question thundered through Iseult's mind. "DO YOU TRAVEL WITH A TRUTHWITCH NAMED SAFIYA?"

Iseult's gut went tight. The ice along her spine slashed outward. With every bit of strength and training Iseult could muster, she *slammed* down on her emotions, her thoughts, and every fragment of knowledge that threatened to rise to the surface.

But she was too slow. The shadow sensed her fear and lunged for it.

"You do! You do! You *must* to have such a wild response. Oh, Lady Fate favors me today. This was all so much easier than I expected." Happiness rippled off the shadow. Iseult imagined it was clapping its delight. "Now, you must stay alive, little Threadwitch, yes? Can you manage that? I will need you again when the time comes."

Time? Iseult thought, unable to speak. "Until we meet again!" the shadow trilled. Then the dark presence swept away.

And Iseult awoke to the real world.

The next several minutes were a blur of the monk helping Iseult sit up, of Safi's Threads flaring from across the room, of the world spinning and swaying.

"Safi?"

"I'm here, Iz."

Iseult relaxed slightly—until the monk inspected her bandage. Then it took all of Iseult's self-control not to shriek at her to *get the hell away!* Oh, Moon Mother save her, how could there be so much pain?

You are very ill indeed—that was what the shadow voice had said and, watching the frightened gray Threads that flickered over both the monk and Safi, Iseult had no doubt the voice was right.

What she didn't know, though, was whether the voice was *real*.

Iseult grabbed for the monk's wrist. "Will I die?"

The monk went very still. "You . . . could die. The muscle is cursed, but I am doing all I can to keep the blood clean."

Iseult almost laughed at that. Corlant must have cursed his arrow. *No wonder he looked so smug after shooting me.* He'd known the wound would kill her in the end.

Though . . . why? The reason *why* Corlant wanted Iseult dead was still lost to her. If he'd truly only craved revenge against Gretchya and Alma, then he wouldn't have so blatantly aimed his arrow at Iseult.

It was more than Iseult could sort through right now. Too many thoughts, confusing and contradictory. No mental strength to carry it all.

"Water will help." The monk dipped her head to a water bag. "Please try to drink while I find food." She rolled to her feet and glided from the room.

Iseult swiveled her head toward Safi. For a flicker of a heartbeat, Iseult almost wished she could cry—could squeeze out a few teardrops as easily as the rest of the world. Just so Safi would know how relieved Iseult was to have her there. "You're chained up."

A wince pulled at Safi's eyes. "I upset the Admiral."

"Of course you did."

"It's not funny." Safi sank against the wall, her Threads pulsing between the same gray and concerned green. "Things are bad, Iz, but I'll fix them, all right? I swear, I'll fix them. Evrane has promised to help us."

Evrane. So that was the monk's name. *Evrane*. So plain and unassuming.

"What happened to you, Iz? How did you get hurt?"

Iseult loosed a ragged breath. "Later," she murmured. "I'll explain . . . later. Tell me how we got here."

Safi threw a cautious glance at the door before lowering her voice. "It all started in Veñaza City, right after Habim sent you away."

As Safi described what had passed, Iseult found it harder and harder to stay tethered to the real world—to pick out the details that mattered.

Chocolate strawberries . . . *Not important,* she decided hazily. But dancing with Prince Merik of Nubrevna? *Import-*

ant. And being named the betrothed of Henrick fon Cartorra—all because the Emperor might know about Safi's magic . . .

"Wait," Iseult cut in, blinking against the pain in her arm. "You're the Emperor's betrothed? Does that make you the Empress of Cartorra—"

"No!" Safi blurted. Then more calmly, "Uncle Eron said I wouldn't have to marry Henrick."

"But if Henrick knows about your magic, then what does that mean? Who else knows?"

"I don't know." Safi's forehead pinched up. Then, in an even faster rush of words, she finished her tale.

But the second half of the story was more confusing than the first, and Iseult couldn't seem to move past the betrothal. If Safi became Empress, then Iseult would have nowhere to go.

The door clicked open. Evrane slipped in with a bowl.

"Why," Evrane hissed at Safi, "does my patient look twice as pale as when I left? You have exhausted her, Domna!"

"I'm always pale as death," Iseult said, winning a taut smile from Safi.

When at last Evrane had deemed Iseult sufficiently fed, she eased Iseult onto her back. Then Safi lifted her voice, chains rattling. "I'll find a Firewitch healer, Iz, all right? I swear to you I will, and I swear that you *will* get better."

"Oath accepted," Iseult breathed. Her eyes were too heavy to keep open, so she let them flutter shut. "If you don't find a healer, Saf, and I die, I promise to haunt you for the rest . . . of your miserable . . . life."

Safi's laugh burst out, overloud, and Iseult's eyelids briefly popped wide. Safi's Threads were hysterically white.

But, ah, Evrane was smiling. That was nice. It warmed Iseult's heart ever so slightly.

Iseult felt the woman's hand rest upon her brow. A heartbeat passed, and despite the squeaking of the ship's wood, Evrane's magic quickly towed Iseult beneath sleeping waves.

TWENTY-FOUR

When Merik stepped onto the main deck to send Kullen after Vivia—and to send the *Jana* surging behind—he found a haze of purple clouds bruising the evening sky.

Rain would come eventually, but for now, the air was thick and still. The sort of breezeless calm that left witchless ships stranded.

As Merik's crew had done the night before, the sailors of the *Jana* were organized in rows across the deck—all except Ryber, who stood beside the wind-drum, her gaze anchored on Kullen at the ship's bow.

Merik stifled a sigh at seeing Ryber like that. He'd have to remind her to keep such open regard masked. He knew what she and Kullen shared, but the rest of the men didn't—and couldn't. Not if Ryber wanted to stay stationed on this ship and in Merik's crew.

Merik marched to the quarterdeck to gaze over his men. Unlike the night before, there was no need for silence. So Merik forced a grin—one like he used to flash when it was just he and his tiny crew sailing the soil-bound waters of

Nubrevna. "Give us a song to sail by," he roared. "How about the 'Ol' *Ailen*' to start?"

The 'Ol' *Ailen*' was a favorite, and several of the sailors matched Merik's smile as he strode to the wind-drum and accepted the unmagicked mallet from Ryber. Neither she nor any of the crew knew what they sailed toward, and as much as Merik would like to think they would oppose Vivia's piracy, he wasn't entirely sure.

Merik hammered the drum four times and, on the fifth beat, the men of the *Jana* began to sing.

"Fourteen days did they fight the sto-orm,
Fourteen days did they brave the wind!
Fourteen days without oceans calm,
Saw the men of the ol' Ailen.
Hey!
Thirteen days did they pitch and ya-aw,
Thirteen days did they pray for end!
Thirteen days of sailing on,
Saw the men of the ol' Ailen."

As the crew's salt-rusted voices blended into the third verse, Merik handed the mallet to Ryber and moved into position beside the three Tidewitches. Kullen chose that moment to launch himself off the deck, wind roaring in his wake. He was soon nothing but a speck on the horizon.

The youngest of the Tidewitches offered Merik wind-spectacles, and once Merik had them strapped on—and once the world had become a bubbled, warped place—he barked, "Gather your waters, men!"

As one, the Tidewitches' chests expanded. Merik's too, and with his inhale came the familiar power. No rage sparked beneath it. Merik felt as calm as a tidepool. Then Merik and the Tidewitches exhaled. Wind swirled around Merik's legs. Waves rippled inward toward the ship.

"Prepare Tides!" Merik bellowed, and the elemental charge inside him eased out, ignited the air around him. *"Make way!"*

In a great suction of power, the magic left Merik's body. A boiling, dry wind gusted over the ship. Snapped into the sails.

At the same moment, the Tidewitches' waters thrust against the *Jana*'s waterline and the ship lurched forward. Merik's knees wobbled, and he was struck by how much more smoothly these launches went with Kullen in control.

"Nine days of a sea fox chasin',
Nine days of tooth and fin!
Nine days of jaws a-snappin',
Saw the men of the ol' Ailen.
Hey!"

Merik fell into the rhythm of the shanty and the beat of the wind-drum. The power pulsed through him, strangely smooth—uncommonly vast. For once in his life, he felt as if he had more magic than he knew what to do with, and as the Tidewitches sang softly, Merik's winds filled the *Jana*'s sails. Soon, he lifted his voice in song.

Four days without fresh water,
Four days with none to drink!
Four days of salt and hot air,
Saw the men of the ol' Ailen."

The shanty soon ended, but Ryber kept pounding the drum and hollered, "'The Maidens North of Lovats!'"—which Merik knew was her favorite song, since *she* was a maiden from north of Lovats.

Four beats later, the chorus of sailors resumed, and onward the *Jana* moved, cutting the seas like a needle through sailcloth and never losing sight of Kullen's small shape.

Until Kullen wasn't small anymore—until he was zooming in so fast that Merik thought they would collide.

Kullen slowed, slowed and then *toppled* onto the deck, sailors scattering from his path.

"It isn't a Dalmotti ship!" he roared, straggling to his feet. Then he was racing to the tiller to Merik, his face violently red. "Vivia has already attacked and it's not a trade ship at all."

Merik blinked stupidly at those words. They were incomprehensible—gibberish beneath the blood now rushing into his skull. "Not a trade ship?"

"No," Kullen panted. "It's a Marstoki naval galleon, and it's carrying weapons and Firewitches."

Safi stared out the window at lavender skies and peaceful seas. Ever since Evrane had stormed into the cabin, snarling about "Vivia, that bitch," Safi had stretched her chains and moored her attention to the glass. The terrain was changing shape before her eyes—possibly her opponents too. Merik had mentioned fighting, and Safi could only assume they sailed straight for it.

All the while, Evrane paced—unleashing her worry to no one in particular, yet doing it in time to the pounding drum. Iseult simply slept on.

At last, Safi's vigil was rewarded: a smear of dark shapes formed on the horizon, eventually solidifying into a Nubrevnan warship like Merik's and a second ship with a hull so dark it was almost black.

Safi tugged against her chains, her arms bending back until she was close enough to the window to fully inspect the black ship. Three masts—snapped in half. A flag, falling over the bulwark.

She caught her breath. There was no mistaking the gold crescent moon on that flag. It was the symbol of the Empire of Marstok, and the green background made it the standard of the Marstoki *navy*.

"Oh bat shit," Safi whispered.

"Does Vivia think," Evrane said to no one in particular, "that there will be no retaliation from Dalmotti? Piracy does not go ignored—especially not from a naval empire."

"I don't think Dalmotti will retaliate," Safi said. Evrane paused midstride, and Safi pointed to the window, chains clattering. "The ship she attacked is from the Marstoki navy."

"Wells preserve us," the monk breathed. Then she

lurched to the window and her face paled. "What have you done, Vivia?"

Safi pressed her face to the glass beside Evrane. Nubrevnan sailors marched men in Marstoki green across a gangway. The Marstoks' wrists were bound, and they were near enough for Safi to see solid triangles on more than a few hands.

Witchmarks. *Fire*witch marks. "Why are none of the Firewitches fighting back?" Safi would never *not* use her magic to save herself or her friends. Her leg started bouncing, more questions flying through her mind. "And why are the Marstoks being led off their ship?"

"I assume," Evrane said, resuming her frantic pacing, "that Vivia intends to claim the Marstoki vessel and all its contents—then abandon her own ship. Because of the Truce, she cannot kill the Marstoks outright."

Nodding slowly, Safi thought back to Uncle Eron and his enormous plan to stop the Great War. Was *this* the sort of act that would dissolve the Truce early? Was *this* what he'd hoped to prevent?

Safi had no idea and no way of knowing, so she shifted her attention back to the Marstoks shambling onto Vivia's ship. There weren't many Firewitches, but enough to easily fight back against the princess's crew.

In fact, one bearded man seemed vicious enough to save his whole ship. He snarled and snapped at every Nubrevnan prodding him over the gangway. Then Safi caught sight of his triangular Witchmark—there was a hollow circle at the center.

"They have a Firewitch healer," she said, voice husky with shock.

"Perhaps," Evrane murmured.

"Not perhaps," Safi insisted. "I see the mark on his hand. He just crossed the gangway onto the other ship."

Evrane rounded on Safi, eyes wide. "You are sure of what you saw?"

"Hye." Safi slouched back from the window, her chains slackening. She suddenly saw what she needed to do. The plan was all there before her. She knew where to walk belowdecks, how to sneak about topside, and which sailors to avoid. "We can get to the Firewitch," she said. "While everyone is distracted, we can bring him here."

"No." Evrane's lips puckered into a grim line. "We cannot bring an enemy sailor onto this ship. That goes too far—even for me. Yet we can reverse your plan and bring Iseult to the healer." The monk withdrew a key from her cloak and held it up.

Safi gasped. "How did you get that?"

"I stole it from Merik." She flashed a humorless grin and pushed to her feet. "Unlock yourself, and then wake up Iseult. While I ensure the coast is clear, you need to get her standing. We will have only one chance to make a run for it."

Safi nodded, release winding through her shoulders. Through her legs. She was finally acting—and even better, she was *running*. That was something she knew how to do well.

In the back of her mind, though, something poked and scratched: Merik would be furious over this. After all, she was putting his contract at risk, and he'd already chained her up for that.

But the consequences were worth it—Iseult was worth it.

So, with a bolstering breath, Safi plucked the key from Evrane's hand. Then, as the monk darted from the cabin, Safi slipped the key into her first manacle. It opened with a satisfying *clink*.

Merik flew to the Marstoki war galley, moving so fast that he left his stomach behind. Kullen soared beside him, almost invisible in the wildness of their winds. Yet through it all, Merik still managed to pick out Vivia.

Stocky and dark-haired like Merik, she roared orders beside a gangway connecting the Marstoki galleon to her ship. Nubrevnan sailors led submissive Marstoks across and then organized them in seated rows across the main deck.

Merik's feet touched down, yet he didn't tow in his magic. Instead, he spun once and *lashed* it across the deck.

It spun around his sister, yanking her to Merik. But she only grinned, landing gracefully beside her brother.

"You lied," he growled, tearing off his wind-spectacles, "about what the miniature was."

"And you lied about *where* it was."

Dimly, Merik was aware of sailors fleeing—as if a giant wave might be spiraling toward him. But Vivia's magic was slow and Merik's rage all-consuming. He freed his pistol and pressed it to her head.

"You wouldn't dare," she snarled. Water splashed as she abandoned her wave. "I am your sister and your future *queen.*"

"You aren't queen yet. Return these men to their ship."

"*No.*" The word was almost lost to the wind, the voices. "Nubrevna needs weapons, Merry."

"Nubrevna needs food."

Vivia only laughed—a crowing sound that had mocked Merik his entire life. "There is a war coming. Stop being so naïve and start caring about your countryme—" Her words broke off as Merik cocked his pistol, readying the Firewitch spell within.

"Never," he hissed, "say that I don't care for my countrymen. I fight to keep them alive. But you . . . You'll bring the fires of Marstok upon their heads. What you have done here violates the Twenty Year Truce. I will present you to the vizers and King Serafin for punishment—"

"Except that it doesn't violate it," Vivia snapped, lips curling back, "so don't get all formal on me, Merry. No one is *hurt.* My crew has peacefully escorted the Marstoks onto my ship—which I will give up to ensure the Truce stays intact."

"Your crew will escort the Marstoks right back. We leave this vessel, Vivia, and we leave its contents." With a final thrust of muscle and magic, Merik spun on his heel, ready to end this "peaceful escort."

"So will you tell Father, then?" Vivia shouted. "Will you tell him that you lost the ship he sought?"

Merik's feet stopped, and he angled back toward his sister. Her eyes—dark and identical to Merik's—blazed.

"What did you say?"

She bared her teeth in a full smile. "Who do you think ordered that miniature, Merry? This was all Father's idea and Father's orders—"

"Lies." Merik burst forward, pistol rising—

A wall of wind blasted him. He stumbled, almost fell, and then hazily thought, *Kullen.*

A second wind returned his balance—and his sanity too. His Threadbrother—wherever the Hell he was—was finally putting a stop to something Merik never should've begun. Never *would've* begun if there weren't so much at stake. This was his sister, for Noden's sake.

Kullen reeled into Merik's path, eyes huge and face red. "We have a situation," Kullen panted. "It's bad." He gestured weakly toward the galleon's mizzen mast and kicked into a jog.

Merik sprinted after him, all thoughts of Vivia or his father gone, swallowed by a new tide of fear.

"I thought it . . . odd," Kullen yelled between gulps for air, "that there was only a skeleton crew here. There's no way . . . this ship could have crossed the Jadansi . . . with so few men. So I checked belowdecks." He skirted the ladder, pointing as he passed. "There *were* more men."

"I don't understand," Merik shouted over his pounding feet. "You think what? That some of the crew left?"

"Exactly." Kullen slowed to a stop beside the broken mizzen mast. His chest trembled much too fast as he added, "I think . . . most of this crew boarded . . . other ships. And then these men . . . Well, look for yourself." He pointed to the mast, which was broken at Merik's chest-level. Then Kullen waved to something else—something resting against the balustrade only a few feet away.

Two axes.

Merik's stomach turned to iron. "They cut the mast themselves. Shit. *Shit.* Vivia was ambushed, Kull—"

"Admiral!" Ryber's voice carried over the still air. *"Admiral!"* she shouted again, and Merik found he was getting awfully tired of that title. Of the weight that crashed onto him each time someone uttered the word. *"We have four warships on the horizon! Hulls up and coming this way!"*

Merik exchanged a single, wide-eyed look with Kullen. Then he launched back to the main deck, back to his sister—who continued to march Marstoks onto her ship.

But Merik had no time for fury or new orders, for at that moment, Hermin stumbled to the edge of the *Jana* and roared through cupped hands, "It's the Marstoks, Admiral! They're calling for the immediate surrender of Emperor Henrick's betrothed. Else they'll sink us!"

Merik rushed to the railing. "They want *who?*"

"They want the Emperor's betrothed!" Hermin paused, eyes burning pink with his magic. Then he added, "Safiya fon Hasstrel!"

It was as if the whole world slowed down. As if it sucked in a breath and held tight. The waves rolled sluggishly as mud, the ship rocked at half-speed.

Safiya fon Hasstrel. Emperor Henrick's betrothed.

It made such sudden, clear sense—why she had fled Veñaza City, why her safety was worth a treaty with the Hasstrels, and why a Bloodwitch might be after her.

Yet Merik couldn't wrap his mind around it. If she was

betrothed to Henrick, then that made her the future Empress of Cartorra. It made her Henrick's property too.

And why were Merik's lungs dropping low at that thought?

Footsteps hammered on the wood. Kullen appeared, cheeks flushed so red, a breathing attack had to be imminent. With that terrifying realization, the world surged back to its usual speed. Merik grabbed Kullen's arm. "Are you all right?"

"Fine," Kullen snapped. "What do you need?"

"I need you on the *Jana*, so we can . . ." Merik hesitated, the words for his next command suddenly vanishing in a surge of doubt.

"So we can . . . ?" Kullen prompted.

"Hand over the domna," Merik finally said. He didn't like it, but it was one life versus many. "Escort Safiya topside and give her up to the Marstoks."

Kullen set his jaw, gaze darkening but no argument coming forth. He may have disagreed but he was still saluting and following orders. He rocketed off the Marstoki deck.

Merik spun around, summoning commands for Vivia and her crew, but his words died on his tongue. Nubrevnan sailors were streaming below the Marstoki galleon's deck, and six witches stood in a row, eyes trained on Vivia.

That row included Merik's Tidewitches.

"Gather your winds and waters!" Vivia bellowed.

Merik lunged, using his wind to cross the ship in mere breaths. He slammed down beside his sister. "What the Hell are you doing? As your admiral, I *ordered* you to release the Marstoks and return to your ship!"

Vivia sneered. "And we all know that *I* should have been named admiral. Look around you, Merry." She waved to the Tidewitches. "You have lost Father's men, and *I* have gained an arsenal."

Merik's breath choked off at those words—at the reality of what faced him. His ship, his command, and everything he'd worked for were dissolving before his eyes. Taken by the same sister who'd always crushed him beneath her boot heel. "There will be consequences," he said, voice low but words desperate. Pleading, even. "Someone, somewhere will demand blood for what you're doing."

"Perhaps." She shrugged, a movement so casual it showed her true feelings more than words ever could. "At least, I will have protected our people, though, just as *I* will be the one to bring the empires to their knees." Vivia turned her back on Merik. "Prepare Tides, men! We sail to the Sentries of Noden to deliver our new weapons!"

A distant boom rang out. Merik jerked toward the horizon—to where the four Marstoki war galleons now sailed. And to where cannonballs sped for the *Jana*. Merik had just enough time to *thrust* his winds frantically out.

The cannonballs dropped into the sea.

Merik leaped off the Marstoki ship and flew to the *Jana*'s main deck. His knees crunched; he transferred the power into a roll, then he was on his feet and screaming for Hermin. "Tell the Marstoks we surrender! Tell them to cease their fire and we'll hand over the domna!"

The Voicewitch limped onto the main deck, eyes glowing pink and lips moving furiously.

Merik scanned his ship and his crew, heart rising as he counted the gaps. Not all of his father's sailors had abandoned him. Merik's original crew had remained.

A second boom thundered. Merik pitched around, grabbing ineffectually for enough magic to stop the cannon fire.

Wind cycloned out—but not from Merik . . . from Kullen. The first mate was dragging to Merik's side and *heaving* his witchery outward.

Merik had no time to thank Kullen, or to fret over Kullen's lungs. "Why aren't the Marstoks stopping?" he roared at Hermin. "Tell them they can have the girl!"

Hermin's head was wagging. "They say the girl isn't enough now. They want their ship back, Admiral." With a shaking hand, Hermin pointed to the Marstoki galleon.

Despite its broken masts, it was sailing toward Nubrevna on Tidewitched waves—and with no witches of his own, it was Merik who would be left behind to pay the price.

TWENTY-FIVE

Iseult came hazily into consciousness wondering why the world stank of dead fish, why the ceiling had turned to cloudy, purple skies, and why her arm was on fire.

A whimper crawled from her throat. She opened her eyes—and instantly screamed.

A man bowed over her, his curly beard so massive it fell on her stomach. His hands rested on her wounded arm, and whatever he did, it hurt like the hell-gates.

Iseult yelped again and tried to wriggle free.

"Hush," Safi whispered, her hands firmly gripping Iseult's shoulder. "He's healing you."

"The muscle is repairing," murmured Evrane from Iseult's other side. "And it will only get worse before it gets better."

With a tight swallow—her throat was so dry—Iseult looked back at the bearded healer. His Threads were a concentrated green, though they shivered with annoyed shades of red.

He *was* healing her, but he wasn't pleased about it.

That was when Iseult noticed the ropes around his wrists—they were almost hidden beneath his voluminous sleeves. He was a prisoner. And yes, now that she focused beyond the healer, she saw other Threads spinning with annoyance and the occasional furious crimson. Beneath the Threads were men in rows, their uniforms the same as the healer's.

She angled back to Safi. "Is this the Prince's ship?"

"No. It's his sister's ship, actually—"

A boom exploded in the distance.

"What was *that?*" Iseult croaked.

Safi's Threads flashed with guilty rust. "We're, uh, under attack by a Marstoki naval fleet."

"Apparently," Evrane said in a steely tone, "your friend is betrothed to the Emperor of Cartorra, so now the Marstoks are after her."

Another thunderous boom echoed into Iseult's ears. Safi threw a frantic glance toward the ocean. "They're approaching fast." She switched to Marstoki, angling back to the healer. "Hurry, or you will taste a Carawen sword—"

"He most certainly will not," Evrane inserted.

"—and a Carawen stiletto."

"He will not feel that either, *but*"—Evrane shifted into the Marstoki language too—"we will all drown if you do not finish quickly."

The man sneered. "I can only work so fast. This wretched Nomatsi has the flesh of demon-spawn."

In a move too quick to prevent, Safi ripped a knife from Evrane's baldric and thrust it against the man's neck. "Say that again, and you die."

The man's glare deepened—but he also put new effort into his work. More cannon fire sounded, but it seemed a thousand miles away. As did the stink of dead fish and the tickling of the healer's beard.

At last, Safi's voice cut through Iseult's pain: "You're finished? The wound is healed?"

"Yes, though she will need time to recover."

"But she will not die?"

"No. Unfortunately. 'Matsi filth—" The man's voice choked off, replaced by a howl, and the feel of his beard vanished from Iseult's stomach.

Just as Iseult's vision started to sharpen and clear, Safi shoved the healer toward the other sailors. "Damn you," she spat after him. "Son of a Voidwitch. May you tumble through the hell-gates forever—"

"That's enough," Iseult said.

She tried to stand. Evrane crouched low, offering her a hand—no, offering her something *in* her hand. A short cord with a tiny Painstone.

"This will numb you until the healer's magic is finished." She slipped the cord over Iseult's right wrist. The stone flared to life—and the pain washed back. Fresh energy coursed through her, and she even managed a smile for Evrane as she stood.

The instant Iseult reached her feet, though, a sharp light filled her eyes.

She couldn't see a thing for the silver radiance of it, vibrating and swirling. Flashing with lines of purple hunger and black death . . .

Threads, Iseult realized, fear and awe mingling together. The largest Threads she had ever seen—at least half the length of the boat. And oddest of all, they seemed to come from beneath the hull. Underwater.

"Something's coming," she whispered. "Something massive and . . . hungry."

Evrane stiffened. Then she grabbed Iseult's shoulder. "Can you see animal Threads?"

"No." The silver and black were so bright, so fast. "But what else would be under the boat?

"Noden save us," Evrane breathed. "The sea foxes are he—"

The last of Evrane's words were lost in an explosion of water and sound. The warship tipped back as something huge—something *monstrous*—crashed up from the sea.

Water rained down, and the bound Marstoks shouted their terror.

But Iseult barely noticed the sailors—all she saw was the creature before her. A serpent as wide as the ship's mast snaked from the waves toward the starboard prow. Rather than scales, it wore thick silver fur, and its head was shaped like a fox's—though ten times . . . *twenty* times larger than any normal fox.

As it snapped its jaw and swiveled toward the warship, Iseult saw more teeth than any natural creature should possess.

And fangs. The thing most definitely had fangs.

But what scared Iseult the most was how the creature blazed with the Threads of the bloodthirsty—and how its mouth was opening wide . . .

The creature screamed.

* * *

When Ryber had described a sea fox, this was *not* what Safi had imagined.

And she definitely hadn't imagined that it would scream like the souls of the damned. A thousand layers screeched from the monster's mouth—and then screeched from a *second* monster now towering over the *Jana* nearby.

Safi's eardrums split, and she was vaguely aware of her pulse ramping up. She flung a glance toward the *Jana,* searching for Merik across the foaming sea—but her search was short-lived when the nearest fox's shriek broke off.

It had found a target: one of the Marstoks closest to the ship's rail. The man's hands sparked and sputtered as he reached for his witchery, but with his wrists bound, he was too clumsy to fight back.

Safi scrambled to her feet, thrust out her knife, and roared, *"Leave him alone!"*

The sea fox whipped its long neck Safi's way.

Shit. Safi had just enough time to admire the icy blue of the monster's eyes—zooming in fast—before she flung out her throwing knife. It stabbed an inky pupil, and the sea fox flipped down, screaming, to splash beneath the water. The boat tipped dangerously, but the sea fox didn't resurface.

Safi flung a desperate glance at the *Jana* and found the second sea fox had left as well.

"Nice job," called Iseult. She stepped carefully across the main deck, clearly not in possession of her sea legs. A cleaver gleamed in her left hand.

Safi's heart soared into her skull. Seeing Iseult, standing

tall—no matter if her energy was from the Painstone—made Safi want to laugh in relief. Or cry. Probably both.

But it was Iseult's eyes that really got her. They were bright and they were *open*.

"New weapon?" Safi asked, her voice embarrassingly pinched and thick.

Iseult's lips quirked up. "I have to save your hide somehow."

Safi's throat squeezed tighter. "Carawen steel is the best, you know."

"It is," Evrane growled, stalking toward the girls—sea legs strong against the boat's trembling. "And you, Domna"—she glared at Safi—"just wasted that steel on making the monster angrier."

"I got rid of it." Safi motioned to the now-empty waves.

"No! That is how they hunt." Evrane unsheathed a second throwing knife. "They test the ship—see how we fight. Then they dive. As we speak, both foxes are swimming for the surface, building momentum as they go. They will try to unbalance the boats and grab any men who fall."

Safi's mouth dropped open; salty air swept in. "You mean it's coming back?"

"Yes." She shoved the knife at Safi. "So take this knife and *widen your stances, fools!*"

Safi snatched up the knife just as Iseult cried, "Here it comes!"

Wood exploded in a deafening crunch. The boat tipped sharply left . . . left . . . Safi angled her body into the deck, against the ship's rise.

Screams ripped out behind her. Marstoki sailors tumbled

for the water, and with their hands bound, they would fall right in.

Safi and Iseult locked eyes—and Safi knew her Threadsister thought the same thing. As one, they stopped fighting the rise of the ship, and instead they fell into it.

The wood grabbed at Safi's bare soles. Locked her down and forced her into tiny, bouncing hops behind Iseult, whose boots slid more easily over the wet planks.

Iseult reached the other side first, and with a roar, she grabbed at a green tunic right before its owner toppled overboard. It was the bearded Firewitch healer.

"Not so filthy now, huh?" Safi shouted.

But then a cry burst up. A second Marstok—just a boy—fell toward the railing. Safi dove for him. He flipped over the edge. Safi flipped after. She snagged his ankle—and then Iseult snagged hers.

"I've . . . got you," Iseult gritted, hugging the railing with her bad arm. "Not for long, though—oh *shit*."

The boat stopped tipping. Gravity took hold, and the ship fell the other way in a howl of water and resisting wood.

Safi and the boy swung onto the boat, Iseult shrieking from the pain of holding on . . . until Evrane was there, somehow still on her feet, and towing Safi upright.

The sea fox burst from the waves—way too close to where Iseult was scrabbling back.

Safi threw her knife. It punched into the fox's eye, inches away from the first knife.

The monster shrieked and dove once more. Saltwater rained down, the ship pitching all the more wildly.

Safi pulled Iseult to her feet. Iseult's right arm hung limp, her face creased with pain—though she still managed to yell, "Nice aim."

"Except I was going for the other eye."

"Stop doing that!" Evrane shouted, several paces away and with the young Marstok beside her. "You're wasting my knives!" Her sword arced out. She slashed the boy's bindings. "And stop standing there! We need to free these men while we can."

Iseult nodded tiredly and staggered for the nearest set of sailors. But Safi was—yet again—weaponless.

Evrane unbuckled her last throwing knife. "Don't lose this, Domna."

"Yes, yes." Safi seized it and twisted for the nearest sailor. With three quick hacks, she had him unbound. She moved to the next man, then the next. One after another, she freed them from their ropes. The unbound men went on to help their comrades, while a handful of free Firewitches moved into a defensive square formation at the center of the deck. Safi spared a glance toward the water—still empty—and toward the *Jana*.

The sea fox that had terrorized it was also nowhere to be seen.

For half a moment, Safi thought maybe the monsters had given up the hunt . . . but then Iseult shrieked out, "Here it comes! Southern side!"

Southern side. The exact side on which Safi now sawed through a sailor's ropes. *Shit, shit, shit* . . . She cut through the last of the fibers and the man scrabbled away.

The sea fox erupted from the waves, flinging its head

over the railing. Teeth hurtled in—teeth and swirling eyes and a scream to crush her skull.

It was going to eat her. It would snap her body in half and swallow her—

Wind slammed into Safi's chest. Into her legs. She spun wildly back, away from the monster's maw. As sea and sky and ship blurred together with Firewitch flames, she spotted Merik flying at her.

Gratitude—*relief*—surged through her.

Safi hit the deck—as did he. On top of her. Then, as the boat hitched the other way, he rolled off and thundered, "*What the hell are you doing here?*"

Safi blinked, briefly stunned. Then she scrabbled up and shouted, "You're giving me to the Marstoks!"

"Not anymore, I'm not!" He unsheathed his cutlass and, in a blur of steel, he sliced through Marstoki bindings. One after the other. And as he moved, he yelled, "Noden has favored me, Domna, and only a fool ignores such gifts."

"Gifts?" she squawked, sawing at an old man's ropes and eyeing the waters. "How is a thrice-damned sea fox a *gift?*"

"Stop talking!" Merik pointed to the ship's ladder. "Go below and stay out of the way!"

"Don't do that!" Iseult cried, stumbling toward Safi with Evrane on her heels. Her breath was ragged, her face pinched. "The fox is going for the back. We need to reach the men at the front."

Without another word, they all bolted for the ship's fore. Safi and Iseult yanked man after man from the railing and shoved them at Evrane and Merik, who sliced rope after rope. The Firewitches stayed in their tight formation, ready to fight.

But the fox was much, *much* too fast for the Firewitches—or anyone else. It crashed into the ship's aft. Wood cracked, and as the ship tipped violently up, Safi tried to keep from plummeting into the sea.

Water exploded from the front of the ship. The second sea fox reared up, shrieking and hurtling close, ready to pluck man after man off the exposed deck—flaming flesh or no.

Safi looked at Iseult. Her Threadsister nodded. As before, the girls stopped fighting the vertical rise, and together, they barreled down the deck. Right for the sea fox's mouth.

Safi hit the railing—it was almost parallel to the waves now—and straightened to her fullest height. Her knife slashed through furry jaw. Blood rained down.

Then Iseult was there, whirling low along the bulwark. Her cleaver bit deep into the monster's neck. The sea fox jolted, head dropping.

More blood spurted as Iseult turned her cleaver high while Safi twirled in low, pushing all her strength into the perfect thrust of her knife.

The creature's mouth fell wide. Safi let the knife loose. It flew straight and true, into the fox's throat.

And Iseult's cleaver thrust out. It sliced through the monster's forehead.

The sea fox screamed—a raw, final sound—before it sank beneath the waves.

The first sea fox released its hold on the ship. Safi and

Iseult had just enough time to latch on to the railing and *not* get catapulted into the sea when the warship dropped. Waves sprayed, men rolled and tumbled, but Safi and Iseult clung tight.

Until at last the ship's heaving settled down. Until at last Safi could scrabble to Iseult and drag her Threadsister upright. "How are you? Where does it hurt?"

"Everywhere." Iseult cracked a smile. "It's not a strong Painstone."

Before Safi could yell for Evrane's help, Merik bellowed, "Don't celebrate yet!" His feet pounded over the deck and a wind spiraled faster and faster around him. Evrane raced just behind.

"The thing's still not dead." Merik reached Safi. His wind grabbed her clothes, her hair. "It'll be back."

"And," Evrane inserted, motioning at the horizon, "we still have a fleet of Marstoks coming our way."

"Not to mention the second sea fox." Iseult grabbed Safi by the sleeve and tugged her away from the rail. "It's coming, fast. And for the front this time."

"Brace yourselves," Merik roared. "I'll use the power to carry us—"

The sea fox hit. The ship rocketed skyward, and as Safi's feet left the deck—as the world became glowing clouds and purple haze—Merik's wind engulfed them. In a tumble of air, Merik flew the four of them to the *Jana*. They crashed to the forecastle with no grace and copious pain. But Safi didn't have time to check for injury. When she searched for Iseult—and found her clutching her arm several paces away—Safi also caught sight of a fire.

No, *four* fires. The barrels of chum were aloft and aflame. Heat rolled off them—as did the stench of roasting fish, and nearby was Kullen. His breath came in punctuated gasps and his eyes bulged from his head. But he kept his hands out, the barrels aloft, and his magic true.

"Kullen," Merik yelled, already on his feet and sprinting for the drum. "Get the first barrel in position!" He yanked up a mallet and then waited while the closest flaming barrel flipped and floated before the drum.

Merik pounded the mallet. Air punched out and grabbed hold of the barrel. It sped over the water, still burning bright. Then it splashed down, before the nearest Marstoki galleon.

"Next barrel!" Merik called, and moments later, the second one launched out. Then the third and the fourth. Each one splashed in front of the Marstoks.

"It's leaving," Iseult said. Her gaze followed under the ship and then beyond—toward the now-sunken chum. "It's chasing the barrels."

"They are creatures of carnage," Evrane said, and Safi jumped. She'd forgotten all about the monk, who slouched wearily nearby. "They like the taste of charred flesh."

Safi kept her eyes on the water, watching as two black shadows sped away from the boat, then erupted from the waves in the distance. They attacked the flaming barrels; tangled and fought for the chum.

All the while, the Marstoki galleons sailed closer—right for the sea foxes. For a brief second, Safi *almost* pitied the Marstoks, whom she doubted had chum to catapult away for distraction.

But the moment passed when she caught sight of Iseult, sweating and wincing. As Safi turned her attention to helping Iseult, a wind—a magicked wind—swept over the *Jana* and hauled into her sails.

With a resistant groan, the warship set off to the east.

TWENTY-SIX

Despite the tiny Painstone and Firewitch healer's work, Iseult's arm pulsed with a low, insistent pain, and she found it hard to remain stoic as the gray Jadansi and distant shore melted past. A magicked wind from the admiral and his first mate practically lifted the *Jana* off the sea in a race to carry her from the Marstoks.

Iseult and Safi sat on the forecastle, their lungs billowing for air, and Iseult kept glancing at Evrane beside them. She couldn't help it. This woman had guided her—*saved* her, really—six and a half years ago. She was both everything Iseult remembered and nothing at all.

The Memory-Evrane had been so angelic. And taller. But Real-Evrane was scarred and toughened and textured—not to mention, a whole half a head shorter than Iseult.

But the monk's hair—that was as glossy and radiant as Iseult recalled. A halo fit for the Moon Mother.

Iseult broke her curious gawk—it was hard to stare for long. Evrane and Safi and everyone else wore Threads of a thousand brilliant shades. They pressed down on Iseult no matter where her eyes landed. On sailors who were terrified or triumphant, who were giddy off violence or ready to collapse with exhaustion.

And then a few nearby Threads shivered with revulsion. Their owners had spotted Iseult's skin and eyes. None seemed hostile, though, so Iseult blocked them out.

After what might have been hours or minutes, the *Jana* began to slow. The magical wind stopped entirely, leaving a hole in Iseult's ears where it had roared. A tenderness on her skin where it had kicked. Only a natural breeze carried the ship now, and a full moon shone overhead.

"Welcome to Nubrevna," Evrane murmured.

Iseult pushed to her feet, the Painstone briefly flaming bright, and shuffled to the bulwark. Safi and Evrane followed.

The land was not so different from the coast north of Veñaza City—rocky, jagged, pounded by wild waves. But in place of forests, large, white boulders dotted the cliff tops.

"Where are all the trees?" Iseult asked.

"The trees are there," Evrane answered tiredly. "But they do not look like trees anymore." With a snap, she unbuckled her cleaver's sheath. Then she plucked an oily cloth from her cloak.

Safi's breath hitched. "Those aren't boulders, are they?" She turned to Evrane. "They're tree stumps."

"Hye," the monk answered. "Dead trees do not stand for long when a storm blows through."

"Why . . . why are they dead?" Iseult asked.

Evrane seemed briefly surprised, and she glanced from Safi to Iseult, as if to verify the question was genuine.

Upon seeing it was, Evrane frowned. "All of this coast was

razed in the Great War. Cartorran Earthwitches poisoned the soils from the western border to the mouth of the River Timetz."

Cold sank into Iseult's lungs. She glanced at Safi, whose horrified Threads were shrinking inward.

"Why," Safi asked Evrane, "have we never heard that before? We've studied Nubrevna, but . . . our history books always described this land as vibrant and alive."

"Because," Evrane said, "those who win wars are those who write history."

"Still," Safi said, voice rising, Threads scattering outward, "if it was all a lie, I should've known it." She grabbed hold of Iseult's hand, clenching so tight that it hurt through Iseult's Painstone. Throbbed into Iseult's wound.

But the pain was refreshing. Iseult embraced it, glad that it made her spine straighten and her throat open. Her gaze settled on Evrane's saintly, concentrated face as the monk cleaned her cleaving knife—the one Iseult had used. Sea fox blood still crusted the swirling steel.

As Evrane scrubbed, her movements practiced and sure, Iseult was suddenly struck by how many knives Evrane must have wiped clean in her lifetime. She was a healer monk, but she was a fighter too—and she'd lived at least half of her life during the Great War.

When Iseult and Safi oiled their blades, they wiped away fingerprints and sweat—protected the steel against everyday handling.

But when Evrane—and when Habim and Mathew . . . and even Gretchya too—polished their swords, they scraped away blood and death and a past Iseult couldn't imagine.

"Tell us," she said softly, "what happened to Nubrevna."

"It started with the Cartorrans," Evrane said simply, her words dancing away on the breeze. "Their Earthwitches tainted the soil. A week later, the Dalmotti Empire sent its Waterwitches to poison the coast and the rivers. Last, but hardly least, the Marstoki Firewitches burned our entire eastern border to the ground.

"It was clearly a concerted effort, for you must understand: Lovats has never fallen. In all the centuries of war, the Sentries of Noden and the Water-Bridges of Stefin-Ekart have kept us safe. So I suppose the empires thought that if they briefly allied, they might topple us once and for all."

"But it didn't work," Iseult said.

"Not right away, no." Evrane's cleaning paused, and she stared into the middle distance. "The empires focused their final attacks during the months leading up to the Truce. Then, when their armies and navies were forced to withdraw, their magic was left behind to finish us off. The poison spread through the soil, moved upstream, while the Marstoki flames burned whole forests to the ground.

"Peasants and farmers were forced inland. As close as they could get to Lovats. But the city was already too crowded. Many died, and many more have died since. Our people are starving, girls, and the empires are very close to toppling us once and for all."

Iseult blinked. There was finality in Evrane's voice, a rose-colored acceptance in her Threads.

Beside her, Safi's breath slithered out. "Merik truly needs this contract," she whispered, her voice devoid of emotion. Her Threads muted and frozen—as if she were too shocked to feel. "Yet my uncle has made it impossible for him to claim. It's too specific—no spilled blood . . ."

A pause hung in the air. The wind and the shouts of the sailors dulled. Then suddenly, it all snapped forward—too fast. Too bright.

Safi lurched away from the bulwark, her Threads avalanching outward with more colors than Iseult could follow. Red guilt, orange panic, gray fear, and blue regret. These weren't the frayed Threads that break but rather the tough, reaching Threads that build. Each emotion, no matter the color, surged out of her, reaching across the deck as if trying to connect with someone—anyone—who might feel as wildly as she.

Then Safi turned to Iseult and said in a voice made of stone and winter, "I'm so sorry, Iseult." Her gaze slid to Merik, and she said it again, "I'm so sorry I dragged you into this."

Before Iseult could assuage—could argue that none of this was Safi's fault—a white Thread flared in the corner of her eyes. *Terror.* She jerked around right as Kullen, standing on the main deck, started to cough. Then doubled over.

Then fell.

Iseult ran for him, Safi and Evrane on her heels. They reached Kullen as a girl with braids did too, her skin a stark contrast to Kullen's deathly pallor. Yet Merik was already there. Already pulling Kullen into a sitting position and massaging the man's back.

Massaging his *lungs*, Iseult realized as she skidded to a

stop several paces away. Safi paused beside her. Evrane, however, pushed all the way to Kullen and dropped to a crouch.

"I'm here, Kullen," Merik said, voice ragged. His Threads burned with the same white terror as Kullen's. "I'm here. Relax your lungs and the air will come."

The first mate's mouth worked like a fish, gulping at nothing. Though air seemed to squeak out, he could get no breath in. And each cough that shattered through him was weaker than the last.

Then, eyes huge and cheeks pale, Kullen turned to Merik and shook his head.

Safi dropped to the deck beside them. "How can I help?" She looked first at Merik, then to the girl, and finally to Kullen—who stared back at her.

But the first mate could only wag his head at Safi before his eyes rolled back and he fell forward into Merik's arms.

Instantly, Merik and the younger girl flipped him onto his back, and Merik tipped Kullen's mouth wide. He lowered his lips to Kullen's, and then exhaled full gusts of magicked air into his Threadbrother's throat.

Over and over, he did this. An eternity of puffing and heaving, of urgent, terrified Threads. Sailors gathered around, though they seemed smart enough to hang back. Safi threw a panicked look at Iseult, but Iseult could offer no solutions. She had never seen anything like this before.

Then a tremble moved through Kullen's chest. He was breathing.

Merik gaped for several long seconds at Kullen's ribs

before doubling over in relief. His Threads blazed with the pink light of Threadbrothers—pure and dazzling.

"Thank you, Noden," he mumbled into Kullen's chest. "Oh, Noden, *thank you.*"

The same sentiment shimmered through the Threads of every sailor—through Safi's and Evrane's as well.

Yet none were so bright as Merik's or the girl's—and the girl's shone with the pure red of a Heart-Thread.

"Let me check him," Evrane said with a gentle hand on Merik's back. "To be sure he did not damage something."

Merik shot up, his face contorted with fury. And his Threads . . .

Iseult flinched from the force. "You disobeyed my orders!" he shouted at his aunt. "You jeopardized my ship and my men! *The domna was my only bargaining card!*"

Evrane stood still, Threads calm. "We needed a Firewitch healer for Iseult. She would have died without one."

"We *all* would have died!" Merik pushed Evrane again. She didn't resist. "You abandoned your post with no thought for others!"

Safi's Threads blazed into a defensive fury. She sprang to her feet. "It wasn't her fault—she was only doing what I ordered."

Merik swiveled toward Safi. "Is that so, Domna? So you weren't fleeing your betrothed? You weren't avoiding capture, *Truthwitch?*"

Cold tunneled through Iseult's stomach. Down her muscles. But how did he know?

Doesn't matter, Iseult told herself, already bending her knees to lunge for Safi. To protect her . . .

Until Safi's Threads flared with beige uncertainty—as if she might try to hide this truth from Merik. So Iseult schooled her face into absolute Threadwitch calm. She would not betray Safi's secret.

"Where did you hear that rumor?" Safi finally asked, her words careful and even.

"The Marstoks know." Merik leaned toward her. "Their Voicewitch kindly told mine. Do you deny it?"

The world dragged, as if Safi's inner debate spread around her. The breeze became soft and distant. *Don't admit it. Please don't admit it.* It was one thing for Emperor Henrick to possibly know of Safi's witchery, but there was no reason for the whole world to learn too. What if Merik decided to use her—or to marry her, as Henrick had? Or what if Merik decided to *kill* Safi instead, before an enemy could lay claim to her?

Yet as Safi's Threads melted from gray fear to a lush, determined green, Iseult's breath rolled out with defeat.

"So what?" Safi squared her shoulders. "So what if I am a Truthwitch, Admiral? What difference does it make?"

In a burst of speed, Merik grabbed Safi's wrists, flipped her around, and wrenched her arms behind her. "It makes all the difference," he snarled. "You told me no one sought you. You told me you were not important, and yet you're a Truthwitch betrothed to Emperor Henrick." He pushed her arms further back.

Safi's face tightened, but when Iseult tipped forward to defend—to *fight* for her Threadsister—Safi shook her head in warning.

When Safi spoke again, her tone and Threads were

shockingly controlled. "I thought that if you knew who I was, you would turn me over to the Cartorrans."

"Lie." Merik leaned in close, his face inches from Safi's. "Your magic knows when I speak the truth, Domna, and I told you I never intended harm. All I want is to get food to my people. Why is that so hard for anyone . . . ?" His voice cracked. He paused, his Threads melting from crimson rage to deep blue sadness. "I've lost my Tidewitches now, Domna, and the Marstoks hunt me. All I have left are my ship, my loyal sailors, and my first mate. But you almost took them away from me too." Safi's mouth opened as if to argue, but Merik wasn't finished. "We could have escaped as soon as the sea foxes arrived. Instead, we almost died because you were not in your cabin like you should've been. I had to find you, and that left us as *bait* for the foxes. Your recklessness almost killed my crew."

"But Iseult—"

"Would have been fine." Merik dipped her back—and Safi's posture wilted. "I planned to get your friend a Firewitch healer as soon as we hit Nubrevnan soil. You know this is true, don't you? Your witchery must tell you so."

Safi met Merik's gaze. Then, Threads burning with brilliant blue regret and guilty red, she nodded. "I see it."

Merik's temper erupted once more. He seized Safi and ordered, "Move."

To Iseult's complete shock, Safi *did* move, her Threads melting into Merik's and shimmering with hints of a brighter red.

Iseult's lips parted, her foot rising to charge after Safi. To stop Merik from doing whatever it was he'd planned.

A hand clasped her wrist. "Don't."

She jerked her head around and found the girl with the braids shaking her head. "Don't interfere," she said in a hollow voice. "A few hours in the irons won't kill her."

"In the what?" Iseult whipped around—and nausea swelled in her stomach at the sight of Merik pushing Safi down, yanking out her legs . . .

And locking her ankles in straps of iron.

The enormous fetters groaned shut, locks clicked, and Safi could do nothing but stare across the ship at Iseult.

Again, Iseult lurched forward, but this time an older sailor sidestepped her. "Leave 'er there, girl. Or you'll be locked in 'em too."

As if to prove the point, Evrane shot forward, roaring, "You cannot do this to her, Merik! She is a Domna of Cartorra! Not a Nubrevnan!"

Merik straightened and motioned vaguely at his sailors—though his eyes stayed on his aunt. "You *are* a Nubrevnan, though, and your disobedience will not go unpunished either."

Evrane's Threads turned turquoise with surprise as two sailors jostled her to a second set of leg irons. While the sailors pushed down Evrane and tightened the manacles, Merik turned as if to walk away.

"You would resort to torturing a domna?" Evrane shouted. "You will harm her, Merik! You will ruin your own contract!"

Merik paused, glancing back at his aunt. "I resort to punishment, not torture. She knew the consequences for disobedience. And," he added, lethally calm now, "what sort of admiral—what sort of *prince*—would I be if I didn't uphold my own laws? The domna has survived a sea fox attack unscathed, so a few hours in the irons will cause no damage. But it *will* give her time to consider the Hell she has brought here."

"I didn't mean to," Safi said, eyes on Merik. "I never meant to hurt you or Kullen or . . . or Nubrevna. I didn't know about the Marstoks—I *swear* it, Admiral. My uncle told me no one would follow!"

Iseult's jaw slackened as she watched on. The Threads over Safi's—and Merik's heads—throbbed with a harsh, urgent need. Safi's Threads grabbed for Merik's, and his wrapped and twined into hers.

Right before Iseult's eyes, Safi's Threads were changing from those that build into those that bind.

In two long steps, Merik was back to Safi's side and crouching down. He stared hard into her eyes; she stared back.

"If not for Kullen's magic, we would all be dead right now, and it was your impulsive disobedience that almost killed us. That cannot go unpunished. There is still a contract with your family, and one way or another, I will get you to Lejna. Then I will feed my country."

For a heartbeat . . . then two, the space between Merik and Safi—the Threads burning between them—ignited into a full flaming Thread of scarlet.

But Iseult had no time to distinguish the exact shade—if it was a growing Thread of love or one of unforgiving hate—before the color was gone again and she was left wondering if she hadn't imagined the entire thing.

* * *

It was almost funny how fast Safi went from standing upright to being locked, like a battered dog, in the irons. Stuck. Trapped. Unmoving.

And she hadn't fought at all. She'd just given in, wondering why she was accepting these fetters so easily. Wondering when she'd lost her ability to attack. To *run*. If she couldn't run properly, then what did she have left from her old life? Her happy life full of taro and coffee and daydreams.

All of her hopes for freedom had scorched away. No place of her own with Iseult. No escaping Emperor Henrick's court or her uncle Eron's schemes or a life as a fugitive Truthwitch.

But Iseult would live. Her wound was healed and she would *live*. That made it all worth it, didn't it?

Safi watched her Threadsister, who was scrambling after Merik across the deck—pleading with him, her face blank despite the sailors recoiling from her path. Merik ignored her and climbed to the quarterdeck. He took his spot at the helm and ordered the wind-drum to resume.

And Iseult gave up. She stopped her chase at the companionway and twisted around to meet Safi's eyes, looking even more helpless than she had when she'd been dying.

Rain started to fall. A gentle whisper on Safi's skin that should have soothed, but felt like acid instead. Safi was falling into herself. The world was pulsing at her. She couldn't move her legs. She was trapped here, inside herself. Forever, she would be *this* person. Stuck within *this* body and *this* mind. Tied down by her own mistakes and broken promises.

This is why they all leave you. Your parents. Your uncle. Habim and Mathew. Merik.

The prince's name pounded in Safi's ears. Roared with her blood in time to the rain. In time to the drum.

He only wanted to save his homeland, yet Safi hadn't cared—not about Merik, not about all the lives depending on him.

Iseult stumbled over the deck toward Safi, her face pinched and pale. She was the only person Safi had left, the only piece from her old life. But how long before Iseult gave up too?

Iseult reached Safi and dropped to her knees. "He won't listen to me."

"You need rest," Evrane said. "Go to the cabin."

Safi flinched; her chains rattled. She'd forgotten the monk was fettered beside her. She'd been so caged in her own skin, she'd forgotten everyone else.

Like she always did.

It was Safi's selfish greed that had put a price on Iseult's head. That had forced Iseult to leave Veñaza City—and somehow earned a cursed arrow in the arm too. Then, when Safi had fought for Iseult—had done everything she could to compensate and to save her other half from the damage she'd wrought—Safi had ended up hurting someone else. Lots of someones. Her tunnel vision had led her down a broken path. Now Merik, Kullen, and his entire crew were paying for it.

With that thought, Uncle Eron's words from Veñaza City settled over Safi's heart.

When the chimes toll midnight, you can do whatever you

please and live out the same unambitious existence you've always enjoyed.

She had done just that, hadn't she? At midnight, she had dropped the act of domna. She'd resumed her old impulsive, oblivious existence.

But . . . Safi refused to accept that. She refused to be what Eron—or anyone else—expected her to be. She was stuck in this body, with this mind, but it didn't mean she couldn't reach outside. It didn't mean she couldn't change.

She met Iseult's eyes, sagging and overbright in the twilight. "Go to the cabin," she ordered. "You need to get out of the rain."

"But you . . ." Iseult scooted closer, gooseflesh on her rain-slick arms. "I can't leave you like this."

"Please, Iz. If you don't heal, then all of this will have been for nothing." Safi forced a laugh. "I'll be fine. This is nothing compared to Habim's jab drills."

Iseult didn't offer the smile Safi had hoped for, but she did nod and unsteadily push to her feet. "I'll check on you at the next chime." She looked at Evrane and lifted her wrist. "Do you want the Painstone back?"

Evrane gave a tiny shake of her head. "You'll need it to fall asleep."

"Thank you." Iseult looked once more at Safi—stared hard into Safi's eyes. "It'll be all right," she said simply. "We'll make it all right again. I promise." Then she hugged her arms to her chest and walked away, leaving Safi with the rising tide of her Truthwitchery.

Because somehow they *would* make it all right again.

TWENTY-SEVEN

In the seven hours since the Cartorran cutter had set sail from Veñaza City, the sun had set, the moon had risen, and Aeduan had not stopped puking. His only consolation was that this misery had sparked a story among the Void-fearing sailors on board: *Bloodwitches can't cross water.*

Yes, let them spread *that* rumor at every port they visited.

It was just as Aeduan had transitioned into welcome dry heaves that the cutter came upon four destroyed naval vessels—three of them Marstoki and one Nubrevnan. Despite Aeduan's most snarling protests that Safiya fon Hasstrel was not upon these ships, Prince Leopold insisted on stopping anyway.

For it would seem that the Empress of Marstok *was* onboard—and Leopold wanted Aeduan to join him on that ship. When none of the Hell-Bards opposed this madness—not even the Commander, a lazy, irreverent young man named Fitz Grieg—Aeduan soon found himself flying to the Empress's galleon via Windwitch. There, ten Adders gave him and Leopold a casual once-over. The

Adders made no move to claim any weapons, though, before leading their visitors to the Empress's cabin. Clearly they were confident that neither Leopold nor Aeduan stood any chance against their Poisonwitch darts.

Aeduan recognized some of the Adders—by blood-smell alone, though, since he could see no faces behind their headscarves. Their zigzagged swords, like flames of steel, flickered in the Firewitch lamps across the deck.

Stupid weapons. They were unwieldy and unnecessary—especially when an Adder's best advantage was his or her Poisonwitchery.

Their power over poison was such a dark subset of Waterwitchery—a corruption of Waterwitch healers, Aeduan had once heard—yet it was Aeduan's power that was considered Void magic. Aeduan was the one called demon.

It had always struck him as . . . unfair.

Then again, it also worked in his favor.

Once inside the Empress's cabin, the Adders settled evenly around the room and against the walls. A low, unadorned table and two benches were at the room's center, and beside one stood the Empress of Marstok.

She was smaller than Aeduan had realized, having only seen her from afar, yet despite her delicate bones, her blood-scent was unyielding. *Desert sage and sandstone walls. The blacksmith's anvil and gall ink.* It was the scent of an Ironwitch—a powerful one—as well as a woman of education. And despite the fact that Vaness's fleet was in shambles, she wore a fresh white gown, and her expression was coolly civil.

Aeduan settled into a wide-legged stance behind the second bench, calculating the best exits from the cabin as he did so—and the Empress smiled. It breezed over her lips—as if she and Leopold were merely meeting on the dance floor.

The Empress must have known who—and what—Aeduan was, yet she made no comment on his presence. Gave no indication that she found it odd Leopold lacked any sort of Hell-Bard escort.

Clearly, she was an expert at appearances, each expression a careful mask designed to keep the power of the room in her slender hands.

But why bother? Aeduan wondered. If she was as powerful an Ironwitch as the stories claimed, then she didn't need tricks to get her way. The older Carawen monks still spoke of the day she destroyed Kendura Pass—the day she tapped into a magic so vast and so fearless, that she toppled an entire mountain.

And she'd only been seven years old.

Aeduan took that as a sign this meeting was peacefully intended.

"I will take some Marstoki dates, if I may," said Prince Leopold. He hovered beside the table, seemingly more interested in examining his jacket cuffs than in speaking with Vaness.

Yet the mask Leopold wore was clumsy and overdone. It was like the prince played at being royalty while the Empress simply was.

Vaness motioned to the bench, the iron of her bracelets

rattling. "Have a seat, Prince Leopold. I will have candies brought in."

"Thank you, Your Holiest of Holies." Leopold flashed her a bright grin, and with the sigh of someone who has worked a long, hard day, he sank onto the bench. Its black wood creaked.

Vaness swept onto the bench opposite him. Her spine straight, she cocked her head to one side, waiting. Her pause was quickly rewarded by a serving boy, who scurried in with a plate of sugared fruit. Leopold snatched up one, moaned his pleasure, and then snapped up two more. Seconds slid into minutes, and though Aeduan had no doubt the prince meant this as some sort of insult, the Empress showed only patience—which was more than Aeduan could lay claim to.

If Leopold's point in coming was to offer petty insults, then this detour was an even greater waste of Aeduan's time than he'd first feared. At this rate, Safiya fon Hasstrel would reach the Sentries of Noden before Leopold even finished downing his candies.

On the fourth fruit, Vaness's face slid into a narrow-browed frown. "When I said that my fleet was hurt," she said politely, "I had hoped for your assistance. Perhaps I was not clear."

Leopold bared his usual flash of a grin and wiped a slow thumb over his lips. "But surely Your Most Majestic of Majesties realizes that sugar can improve even the most dire of situations." He offered her a fig.

"I am not hungry."

"One needn't be hungry to enjoy these." Leopold

shoved the candy at her once more. "Taste one. They are almost as divine as your beauty."

She bowed her head respectfully and, to Aeduan's surprise, she accepted a sugared fruit. She even went so far as to nibble off a corner.

Aeduan ran his tongue over his teeth, at a loss for how to interpret this behavior. Leopold clearly wished to anger Vaness, yet she deftly avoided taking his bait. Which meant whatever she wanted was important—and whatever she wanted, she got. So why drag this out? Why keep a veneer of serenity with a power like hers? Aeduan certainly never bothered.

Leopold seemed to think the same, for on his sixth date, he abandoned his game. With poorly veiled annoyance, he slouched back and crossed his legs.

"What happened to your fleet, Your Worshipped?"

"Sea foxes," she said simply—which earned a laugh from the prince.

"*Sea foxes,*" he repeated, eyebrows rising. "You expect me to believe that? Did shadow wyrms and flame hawks get you as well? Or let me guess: the Twelve returned with their wicked swords and bashed a hole in the hull."

Vaness showed no reaction, yet the air in the room seemed to contract. The Adders stiffened, and Aeduan's hand moved to his sword hilt.

"Flame hawks are still present in Marstok," Vaness said, her tone as smooth as before. Her mask preserved. "And it would seem that the sea foxes have returned."

Aeduan's eyes flitted to Leopold, trying to gauge the

prince's reaction. Aeduan had heard of sea foxes, yet as far as he knew, there hadn't been any sightings for decades.

For once, though, Leopold remained silent and unreadable.

So Vaness continued. "I am due in Azmir, Your Highness, but I fear it will take my men too long to repair our fleet's damage. I ask that you lend us Tidewitches from your crew. We have none left."

Then why, Aeduan mused wryly, *do I detect at least three Tidewitch scents belowdecks?* There was no mistaking them. They smelled of high-water marks and river rapids.

As Aeduan considered how best to inform Leopold of the Empress's lie, Leopold flourished his hands. "Your Imperial Perfection," he murmured, "I couldn't help but notice an intact ship in your fleet. It didn't match your other ships. In fact it looked—what did we say?" Leopold threw a pointed glance at Aeduan—one that made it clear he didn't expect a response. Then the prince snapped his fingers. "It looked Nubrevnan. That was it. I wonder, Your Imperial Perfection, how it came to be in your possession?"

"We found the warship by chance," Vaness answered smoothly. "It must have been attacked by sea foxes as well."

"Then, surely"—Leopold propped his elbows on his knees—"its dead crew will not mind if you take it ashore."

For half a breath, Vaness froze. She did not speak, blink, or even breathe. Then she shot to her feet, bracelets clattering and a new mask settling into place: anger. Or perhaps it was no mask, for when Aeduan sucked in a full breath, he sensed her pulse was faster. Hotter.

"You would deny me help?" she said softly. "I, who am

the Empress of the Flame Children, the Chosen Daughter of the Fire Well, the Most Worshipped of the Marstoks?" She stretched both her hands on the table with such poise that not a single iron link clanked. "*I*, who am the Destroyer of Kendura Pass? To deny me is to ignite your own funeral pyre, Prince Leopold. You do not want me as an enemy."

"I wasn't aware we were allies."

Vaness's body tautened like a waiting snake, and Aeduan instinctively summoned his own magic—a mere ripple that would leave his eyes clear of red. If this moment escalated, Aeduan would lock down the Empress in a heartbeat.

Leopold tipped a single finger at Vaness. "Here is the situation as I see it, Your Highest of Highs. First, I think that you are following my uncle's betrothed—because why else would you abandon a truce summit at which you are supposed to be?

"Second"—he unfurled another finger—"I think you met Safiya's kidnappers here and engaged in a battle that somehow fell between the Truce's cracks." Leopold flexed a third finger, frowning now. "I cannot sort out this third finger—which is the *reason* for it all. Safiya cannot possibly hold any value for you, Your Most Beloved."

The air in the room tightened even more. Vaness's chest expanded . . . but then Aeduan felt her blood cool, her fury back in control. "I," she murmured, "do not want your uncle's betrothed, Prince Leopold."

"And I," Leopold flowed to his feet, towering over the Empress by a full head and a half, "do not believe you, Empress Vaness."

Magic rushed out—faster than Aeduan could ever

have guessed. It stripped three knives from his baldric, launched them over the bench, and aimed them at Leopold's neck, heart, and stomach.

Aeduan's power roared to life. His blood reached for Vaness. His body tensed for action.

But in a slippery whisper, ten Adders unholstered their blowguns and aimed them at Aeduan and Leopold.

Aeduan's gaze raced back over the room, mind groping for an escape route. He could control Vaness, but he'd still end up with a chest full of poison or steel—and although Aeduan would survive, Leopold would not.

The prince lifted a cool hand, no sign of fear in his voice—or, to Aeduan's surprise, in his blood. "If you find Safiya fon Hasstrel before I do, Empress, you will return her to me immediately, or you will face the consequences."

"Do you love your uncle's plaything so much?" Vaness flipped up one palm, and the knife at Leopold's neck drew back several inches. "Do you value her life so highly that you would risk my displeasure?"

Though the prince's lips twisted up, there was no amusement in his smile. "I have known Safiya fon Hasstrel my entire life, Your Royal Perfection. She will make an incredible leader when the time comes. The kind who puts her nation before herself." His eyes flicked significantly to Vaness's bracelets. "So mark my words, Chosen Daughter of the Fire Well, if you do not give me the future empress, then I will come to Marstok and I will claim her myself. Now lower your blades before I accidentally step into one. *That* will erase your name from the Twenty Year Truce, I can assure you."

A rigid pause stretched through the room, and Aeduan kept his witchery quaking high. Ready . . . Ready . . .

The blades lazily twirled back. Then they slid away and fell.

Aeduan caught the nearest from the air, but the other two hit the table. The bench. As he snatched them up, Leopold dipped forward to pluck another candied fruit. "Thank you for the treats, Great Destroyer." He smiled blandly. "It's always such a pleasure to see you."

Without another word, and with the squared shoulders of a man in charge, Leopold the Fourth strode for the door. "Come, Monk," he called. "We have lost time, and we must now make it up."

Aeduan marched after Leopold, his eyes and his power never leaving the Empress or her Adders. Yet no one made any attempt to stop Leopold or Aeduan as they departed, and moments later, the men were rocketing off the splintered Marstoki galleon.

Once firmly on their cutter again—and with Leopold shouting for Commander Fitz Grieg to fetch him clean breeches—Aeduan watched the prince through slitted, distrustful eyes.

"The Empress," Aeduan said once the Hell-Bard Commander had vanished belowdecks, "lied about having Tidewitches onboard."

"I assumed so." Leopold scowled at an invisible mark on his cuff. "She also lied about not wanting Safiya fon Hasstrel. But"—Leopold glanced up—"I have one advantage over the Empress."

Aeduan's eyebrows lifted.

"I have you, Monk Aeduan, and trust me when I say that *that* has the Empress of Marstok now sailing scared."

TWENTY-EIGHT

"Keep the light steady!" Merik bellowed from the tiller. Two sailors aimed the *Jana*'s spotlights on the waves. The moon gave some light when the clouds bothered to part, but it wasn't enough—especially not with the lingering rain.

Without Kullen to fill the *Jana*'s sails or Merik's witches to carry her hull, Merik had to push his meager crew hard—and push himself hard too.

But he had no other choice, and time was short.

He needed to find that one jagged peak—the Lonely Bastard, as he and Kullen had always called it—before the tide swallowed it whole. Behind it was a hidden cove. A family secret that would allow Merik's crew to rest in safety.

If the *Jana* missed the tide, though, Merik would be forced to wait until tomorrow afternoon—allowing the Marstoks or the sea foxes to catch up.

Merik's gaze snapped to the domna and Evrane, still chained. Safiya's golden hair was damp and hanging, his aunt's white cloak soaked to gray. For once, Iseult was nowhere to be seen. She'd checked on Safiya and Evrane a hundred times during the first four hours of their punishment. In the last two chimes, though, the girl had stayed belowdecks. Sleeping, probably.

Merik was glad for it. Each time Iseult had come to beg for Safi's release, the muscles in his neck had hardened. His shoulders had strained toward his ears, and he'd patted his pocket—checking that the Hasstrel agreement was still tucked inside. Those pages had become his last hope for salvation, so he kept them close.

He checked the document for the thousandth time now, the pages flattened and rain-splattered . . .

The signatures were intact, so Merik would leave Safiya in her chains a bit longer. He might not be Vivia when it came to discipline, but there were consequences for disobedience. Merik's crew knew that—expected it, even—so Merik couldn't suddenly go soft. Even if there might be long-term repercussions for binding a woman who could one day be Empress of Cartorra . . . Even if Safiya and her betrothed, Henrick, could make Merik pay for this sort of treatment . . . Merik didn't care. He'd rather keep his crew's respect than worry over what some idiot emperor could do to a country that was already crippled.

Henrick. Merik had always disliked that foul old man. To think that Safiya was his betrothed. To think she would marry—would *bed*—a man three times her age . . .

Merik couldn't reconcile that thought. He'd believed Safiya was different from other nobility. Impulsive, yes, but loyal too. And perhaps as alone as Merik was in a world of cut-throat political games.

But it turned out Safiya was just like the rest of the

Cartorran doms and domnas. She lived with blinders on, attuned only to those she'd deemed worthy.

Yet even as Merik nursed his fury, even as he told himself he loathed Safiya, he couldn't keep the "buts" from churning in his stomach.

But you would have done the same for Kullen. You would have risked lives to save him.

But maybe she doesn't want to marry Henrick or be Empress. Maybe she is on the run to avoid it.

Merik shoved aside those arguments. The simple fact remained that if Safiya had only told Merik of her betrothal from the beginning, he could have returned her to Dalmotti and been done with her immediately. He never would have been on this side of Jadansi where he'd been forced to fight a sea fox, battle the Marstoks, and ultimately push Kullen too hard.

"Admiral?" Hermin hobbled onto the quarterdeck, expression bleak. "I still can't make a connection with the Lovats Voicewitches."

"Oh." Mechanically, Merik brushed rain off his coat. Hermin had been linked into the Voicewitch Threads for hours, trying to get through to Lovats. To King Serafin.

"Might be," Hermin mused, tipping his voice over the waves and rain, the squeak of ropes and the grunts of seamen, "that all the Voicewitches are busy."

"In the middle of the night?" Merik frowned.

"Or maybe," Hermin went on, "my magic is the problem. Maybe I'm too old."

Merik's frown deepened to a scowl. Age didn't diminish a witchery. Hermin knew it and Merik knew it too, so if the old man was trying to soften what was obviously going on—that the Voicewitches in Lovats were ignoring Merik's calls—then there was no point.

If Vivia's words turned out to be true and Merik's father really had ordered the Aetherwitched miniature, then Merik would deal with that later. For now, he just had to get his men ashore and away from Marstoki flames.

He glanced at the leg irons—at Safiya—only to find Ryber crouched beside her.

"Take the helm," Merik snarled, already stalking for the companionway. Then he lifted his voice in a roar. *"Ryber! Get away from there!"*

The ship's girl jerked to attention, yet Safiya kept her head bowed as Merik slammed onto the main deck and advanced on Ryber. "You," he growled, "should be swabbing." He thrust a finger at the nearby new recruit, who diligently scrubbed water off the deck. "That is your duty, Ryber, so if I catch you shirking again, you'll be whipped. Understand?"

The domna lifted her chin. "I called Ryber over here," she rasped.

"Someone needs to check on Iseult," Evrane inserted, her voice hoarse. "The girl is still healing."

Merik ignored Safiya and Evrane, his fingers reaching for his collar. "Swab the deck," he told Ryber. "Now."

Ryber saluted, and once she was out of sight, Merik wheeled toward the domna, ready to shout that she leave his sailors alone.

But her head was tipped back, her eyes closed and mouth open. Even with only lantern light to shine on her skin, there was no missing the wobble in her throat. The flick of her tongue.

She was drinking the rain.

Merik's rage vanished. Dread swallowed it whole, and he tore out the Hasstrel agreement. The signatures were still there.

Of course they are, he thought, annoyed with himself for caring. *Safiya isn't bleeding.* Yet his fingers trembled—and distantly he wondered why that might be. Perhaps this fear had nothing to do with the contract.

That thought tickled at the base of his skull—and he hastily tamped it down, buried it deep, and returned the contract to his pocket. Then he dug out the leg-iron keys. Whatever the reason for this hollow fear, Merik would dwell on it later—along with his unshakable worry over King Serafin, Vivia, and Kullen.

Right now, though, this punishment had to end.

Crouching beside Safiya, Merik unlocked the first fetter. She seemed wearily surprised. "I am free?"

"Free to stay locked in your cabin." Merik undid the remaining irons and then stood. "Get up."

She drew in her soaked legs and tried to rise. The ship rocked. She toppled forward.

Merik lunged for her.

Her skin was slick and cold, her body shivering. With a grunt, he hefted her up, cradled her close. His men watched on, and Merik didn't miss the nod of approval from Hermin as he strode toward the ladder belowdecks.

The domna had served her punishment; the men respected that.

Safiya's face was near, her eyelashes thick and wet. Her damp clothes rubbed against Merik's skin, and her breaths were shallow. Merik firmly ignored it all, focusing on getting one foot in front of the next until at last he pushed into the darkened passenger room. Iseult slept, shuddering on her pallet.

"Iz," Safiya murmured, shifting in Merik's arms and straining for her Threadsister. Merik carried her to the pallet, bent slightly, and then dropped her. She fell beside Iseult, who shook awake.

As Iseult scrambled to help Safiya, Merik whirled about and left the room, telling himself that Safiya was taken care of. That he wouldn't think of her now. That he wouldn't think of her ever again.

Yet when at last he reached the tiller of his father's ship and caught sight of the Lonely Bastard piercing the horizon ahead, his arms were still warm—his neck still humming from Safiya's grip.

Before Safi had returned, Iseult had been trapped in her nightmares again . . .

Sever, sever, twist and sever.

Fingers tore at Iseult. Yanked at her hair, her dress, her flesh.

Threads that break, Threads that die!

An arrow ripped through her arm; pain exploded through her entire being. And magic, magic—black, festering magic—

"Nasty dream you're having." The shadow's voice jolted Iseult from the nightmare.

"You tremble and quake so much today," the shadow continued, a syrup on its voice that was overly gleeful. "What upsets you? It wasn't just the dream—you have that one all the time."

Iseult tried to turn away, but every direction she shifted, the shadow followed. Every kick or mental thrust, the shadow avoided. Every desperate retreat, the shadow dug its talons in deeper.

And on and on the shadow babbled—or rather *she* babbled, for the shadow was a woman. A fellow Threadwitch, convinced that she and Iseult were somehow alike.

It was *that* talk that frightened Iseult the most. The possibility that this strange voice was like her. That maybe the shadow understood Iseult's private pains more than anyone else.

Which of course made Iseult wonder if she wasn't just imagining the entire thing. Going crazy while all of her hopes for the future trickled away between her fingers.

Or maybe Iseult was finally buckling beneath the Threads of the world—her ordinary heart pounded to dust.

"You are upset about your tribe," the shadow declared matter-of-factly, stumbling on Iseult's most recent memories. "My tribe pushed me out too, you know, because I wasn't like the other Threadwitches. I couldn't make Threadstones or control my feelings, so the tribe didn't want me. That's why you left yours, isn't it?"

The curiosity on the shadow's voice was double edged. Iseult knew she shouldn't answer . . . yet she couldn't help it when the shadow asked again: "That's why you left, *isn't it?*"

The urge to tell the truth—about her shame with Gretchya, her jealousy of Alma—tickled Iseult's throat. Why couldn't she fight this shadow? *Use that frustration,* she told herself almost frantically. *Use that to fight her.*

Iseult ripped her dream body sideways and latched on to the first mindless memory she could find: her multiplication tables. *Nine times one equals nine. Nine times two equals eighteen—*

But the shadow simply laughed.

"It's silly that we're expected to feel nothing," the shadow continued, her tone dulcet once more. "I don't believe the stories—the ones that say we don't have Heart-Threads and Thread-families. Of course we do! We just can't *see* them is all. Why would the Moon Mother give all of her children such powerful bonds, but then exclude *us?*"

"I don't know." Iseult was grateful for that easy question. If she answered it—if she seemed to cooperate—maybe the shadow would leave.

She didn't. Instead, the shadow laughed her gleeful laugh and cried, "Why, look! Talking of Thread-families upsets you, Iseult. Why? *Why?*"

Nine times four equals thirty-six. Nine times five—

"Oh, it's your mother! And her apprentice. They have left you hurt and broken. Goodness, Iseult, you are so easy to read. All your fears gather at the surface, and I can skim them off like fat from a borgsha pot. Here, I see that you couldn't make Threadstones, so your mother sent you away. And, oh—what is this?" The shadow was exultant now, and no matter how wildly Iseult fought, she couldn't keep her thoughts locked away.

"Gretchya and Alma planned their escape before you were even gone! And Iseult, look here—she tried to claim she loved you. Well, she obviously didn't love you enough to take you with her. She manipulated you quite well, Iseult, just as her job entailed. Just as *our* job entails. We must weave Threads when we can—and *break* them when we have to. It's the only way to untangle the loom."

The shadow's voice lowered to a whisper. A sound like wind through a graveyard. "Mark my words, Iseult: Your mother will never love you. And that monk you admire so much? She will never understand you. And Safiya—oh, Safiya! *She* will leave you one day. One day soon, I think. But you can change that." The shadow dragged out a pause, and Iseult imagined she was smiling as she did so. "You can change the very weave of the world. Grab hold of Safi's Threads, Iseult. *Break* them before they hurt you—"

"*No,*" Iseult hissed. "I've had enough of you. I've had . . . *enough.*" With every ounce of power in her muscles and her mind, Iseult opened her mouth—in the real world—and said, "Nine times eight equals seventy-two."

The world plowed into her, carrying pain from her arm and the sound of footsteps—of Safi's voice.

Iseult opened her eyes, and Safi toppled into her.

Safi shivered from the rain, and try as she might, she couldn't seem to analyze her terrain, to evaluate her opponents—and there was something about strategy she was supposed to consider too.

"You're freezing," Iseult said. "Get under the blanket."

"I'm fine." Safi forced a smile. "Really. It's just a bruised ego and some rain. But are you all right? How's your arm?"

"Better." Iseult's expression didn't budge—a good sign. "It hurts now that the Painstone is dead." She jiggled her wrist to show Safi the dull quartz. "But it's not as bad as before."

Nodding, Safi sank onto the mattress. Hay wuffed out the corners. "And how do you feel here?" She thumped her chest. "You were talking in your sleep. Was it . . . was it the curse?"

"Nothing so awful." Iseult settled beside her. "It was just a nightmare, Saf."

Gingerly, Safi touched the bandage on Iseult's right arm. "Tell me what happened."

The lines on Iseult's face smoothed and with her gaze fixed on some middle distance, she explained how—to escape the Bloodwitch—she'd been forced to travel home. Her voice stayed flat and hollow as she went on to describe the settlement, the Cursewitch, the mob.

Safi's gut turned harder. Harder still. Guilt stirred up her throat.

For this was *her* fault. Like everything else that had gone wrong in the past two days, Iseult's near-death was *Safi's* fault.

And somehow the lack of inflection—the fact that Safi knew Iseult didn't blame her—only made it worse.

Before Safi's lips could open and apologies scrape out a

smile flickered over Iseult's face. It was so at odds with the tale she'd just told—so startling, too.

"I almost forgot—I have a gift for you." Iseult plied a leather cord from her blouse and tugged it over her head.

Safi's forehead crinkled, her thoughts and guilt swirling away. "Is this a Threadstone?"

"Yeah." Iseult nudged her with her left elbow. "It's a ruby."

"But aren't Threadstones for finding Heart-Threads?"

"Not necessarily. They can be used to find anyone in your Thread-family." Iseult eased a second stone from her dirty blouse. "I have a match, see? Now, when either of us is in danger, the stones will light up. They'll dim the closer we get to each other."

"Wells bless me," Safi breathed. The stone suddenly felt twice as heavy on her palm. Twice as dazzling beneath the pink threads—and a thousand times more valuable. The power to find Iseult wherever she was—the power to protect Iseult from the hell like she'd experienced last night—that was a gift, indeed. "Where did you get these?"

Iseult ignored the question. "That stone," she said, "saved your life. It was how I found you north of Veñaza City."

North of Veñaza City. Where Iseult had gotten the arrow punched through her arm by her own people. No wonder she didn't want to talk about it.

Safi draped the cord around her neck. "I'm sorry," she said quietly. "You'll never have to go back to the Midenzis. Ever."

Iseult scratched her collarbone. "I know, but . . . where

will we go, Safi? I don't think we c-can go back to Veñaza City now."

"We'll go with the prince. To Lejna, so I can fulfill his contract."

"With the prince," Iseult echoed. Though her face stayed smooth, there was the slightest tic in her nose. "And after Lejna?"

Safi drummed her fingers on her knee. What could she say that would make Iseult smile? Where would her Threadsister possibly feel safe again?

"How about Saldonica?" She offered her goofiest grin. "We'd make great pirates."

Iseult didn't even ghost a smile back. Instead, her nose twitched more obviously and she glanced at her hands. "My mother is there. I-I . . . don't want to see her."

Gods thrice-*dammit*. Of course Safi would pick a place where Gretchya would be. Before she could suggest other options—ones that were *guaranteed* to make Iseult smile—the cabin door banged open.

Evrane staggered in, with two sailors prodding her from behind. The monk slammed the door in their faces before stumbling for the girls—and Safi didn't miss how Iseult's spine erected. How her shoulders rolled properly back.

"Let me examine you," Evrane croaked, sinking onto the floor beside Safi. "You're bruised, Domna."

"It's nothing." Safi tucked in her legs.

"The bruises might not hurt, but this isn't about you anymore." Evrane threw a glance at the window—a moonlit shore streamed by. "A bruise is spilled blood beneath the skin. We should not mock the contract's demands."

Safi eased out a long breath, her mind careening back to Merik. The prince. The admiral. He was never far from her thoughts, and she'd barely thought of anything else for all those hours in the irons. She'd barely *looked* at anything but his rain-slicked hair and hard gaze while he steered the *Jana* toward his home.

After Evrane seemed satisfied with Safi's health, she examined Iseult's arm and Safi moved to the window to watch the approaching shore. Her muscles burned from the movement, from the strain of simply standing. She liked it, though. It kept away the cold, the thoughts of Merik, the horrors of Iseult's tribe, and all the other things that were best ignored.

There was little for Safi to see outside, though. Rock walls and spindrift misting the glass. If she craned her neck, she could *just* glimpse pale dawn skies.

"Where are we?" she asked Evrane.

"A cove that belongs to the Nihar family," the monk answered. "It has been a secret for centuries. Until today." Her tone was icy, and when Safi glanced back, she found the monk scowling as she wound a fresh bandage around Iseult's arm.

"The cove is inaccessible from land," Evrane went on, "since cliffs surround it and there is only enough space for a single ship. But"—she tied off the clean linen with a satisfied nod—"I think you will see it for yourselves soon enough. The admiral plans to take us ashore. From here, we continue to Lejna on foot."

TWENTY-NINE

Merik stood in Kullen's cabin, staring down at his Threadbrother. Kullen's face was gray, his knuckles massaging his breastbone as he watched Merik from a low cot. Ryber had stuffed a sack of flour behind Kullen's back to prop up his head and lungs, so now white powder stuck to his hair and cheeks. With only the pale dawn to illuminate his face, he looked like a corpse.

The cabin, however, looked very much alive.

Kullen's single trunk beneath the window overflowed with his usual organized chaos, and there was no missing the clear trail of shirts and breeches that led to the bed.

"Too busy reading to fold up your uniform?" Merik asked, settling onto the edge of the cot.

"Ah, you caught me." Kullen clapped shut a red-leather book. *The True Tale of the Twelve Paladins*. "I can't resist rereading the epics. If I'm forced to stay in bed, I should be entertained." He pitched a glance at the clothes on the floor. Then winced. "I suppose I did make a mess."

Merik nodded absently and leaned onto his knees. He didn't care about the uniform; Kullen knew that.

"I shouldn't be gone more than half a week," Merik said.

"Don't rush on my account." Kullen flashed one of his frightening attempts at a smile—but it was almost instantly shattered by coughing.

Once the attack had passed, Merik went on. "I'll go north to the estate and find Yoris. I don't think he'll mind Safiya, but he might make trouble over Iseult. He never liked the 'Matsis."

"He also never liked your aunt." Kullen hissed out a careful breath and leaned onto the flour sack. "I assume she'll join your little party?"

"I doubt I can keep her away."

"Well, if Yoris gives you any trouble, tell him"—Kullen twirled a hand, and a current of cool air tickled over Merik—"I'll crush him with a hurricane."

Merik scowled at Kullen's display of power, but again, he held his silence. They'd argued for years over how often and how deeply Kullen tapped into his witchery; Merik didn't want to leave on that note today.

"Should I visit your mother while I'm inland?"

Kullen shook his head. "I'll go once I'm better. If that's all right with you."

"Of course. Take Ryber with you. Just in case."

Kullen's eyebrows sprang high.

"I'll tell Hermin I've ordered it," Merik hastened to add. "Ryber knows how to help you in case of an attack—and the crew is aware that she knows. It's only logical she join you. Besides . . ." Merik frowned at his fingernails; there was flour and dirt beneath them. "I don't think it matters anymore if the crew finds out about you. The admiralty's over, Kullen. Lovats won't answer, and it's looking more and more like Vivia spoke the truth about my father."

"I'm not surprised," Kullen said quietly.

Merik grunted and picked at his thumbnail. This was another long-hashed point of disagreement—Kullen believed that Vivia's nature was spurred on by Serafin. That the king *wanted* his children forever at odds.

But Merik considered that theory complete crap. For all of King Serafin's failings, he wouldn't waste his energy on stirring trouble—particularly when Vivia instigated plenty of it on her own.

"What I *do* know, Kullen, is that this grave is deep, and I still haven't dug us out."

"You can, though." Kullen angled forward, flour puffing from the top of the sack. Were the situation any different, it would've made Merik—and Kullen—laugh. "If you get to Lejna and you get your trade agreement, then it'll all work out. You're destined for greatness, Merik. I still believe that."

"Not much greatness. The trade will only be with one Cartorran estate out of hundreds. And the land here . . ." Merik gestured to the window, a self-deprecating laugh stuck in his throat. "It's no better than a year ago. I don't know why I keep hoping, but I do. Every cursed time we come back, I hope it'll be alive again."

Kullen exhaled, a rattling sound that made Merik sit up. "You're tired. I'll go."

"Wait." Kullen snagged Merik's jacket sleeve, and the warmth in the air vanished again. "Promise me something."

"Anything."

"Promise me you'll consider a tumble in the sheets while you're away. You're so tense"—he gulped in air—"I can't even look at you without my lungs wanting to seize."

Merik barked a laugh. "And here I was expecting something serious. I have plenty of reasons to be tense, you know."

"Still." Kullen waved wearily.

"And with whom should I tumble exactly? I don't see many women clambering for the position."

"The domna."

Now Merik *really* laughed. "I am *not* tumbling with a domna. Especially one who's betrothed to the Emperor of Cartorra. Plus, she makes my temper flare out of control. Every time I think it's smooth sailing, she'll say something offensive and the squall returns."

Kullen choked, but when Merik's eyes snapped to him with alarm, he found that Kullen was simply laughing—albeit wheezily. "That's not your temper, you big dolt. It's your magic responding to a woman like Noden intended. What the Hell do you think happens to my witchery when Ryber and I—"

"I don't want to know!" Merik flung up flat-palmed hands. "I really don't want to know."

"Fine, fine." Kullen's laughter subsided, though a crooked grin stayed on his lips.

And Merik had to smother the urge to throttle his Threadbrother. This was not the conversation he'd come for, and he didn't want to leave Kullen on the thoroughly pointless topic of sheet tumbles.

So Merik forced himself to nod and smile. "Give your

mother my best, and if you need me, pound the wind-drum. We'll stay beside the coast most of the way to Lejna."

"Hye." Kullen's fist returned to his breastbone, and he nodded tiredly. "Safe harbors, Merik."

"Safe harbors," he answered before marching from the room. Once he was topside, he shouted for Ryber to bring up the prisoners—and he made sure to call them prisoners. Not collateral, not passengers. Simply *prisoners.* It made it easier to ignore Kullen's suggestions. He wouldn't look at Safiya, he wouldn't speak to her, and he certainly wouldn't think of her in *that* way. Then, when Merik reached Lejna, he would leave her behind and he would never, ever see her again.

Iseult followed Safi—who followed Evrane who followed Ryber—through the dark hold to the ladder. Two sailors glared at Iseult as she mounted the first rung. They muttered to themselves, their Threads shivering with dislike.

Safi—in typical Safi fashion—fixed a glare on the sailors and dragged a slow thumb across her neck.

Their Threads flared with gray fear.

Iseult gritted her teeth, glancing at Evrane to see if she'd noticed. The monk hadn't, but still—Iseult would have to remind Safi (for the thousandth time) not to show that sort of aggression. Safi meant well, but her threats only brought more attention to Iseult's otherness—only made Iseult more aware of the stares and the curses and the gray, gray Threads.

Usually Safi knew better than to raise her hackles so

blatantly, but things were different now. Ever since her time in the leg irons, Safi's Threads hadn't stopped beating with rusty guilt. Golden shame. Blue regret.

Iseult had never seen anything like it from her Threadsister. Had never known Safi could care so deeply about causing someone grief—someone who wasn't Iseult, at least.

Iseult and Safi reached the *Jana*'s empty quarterdeck. Abruptly, Safi's Threads flamed with new colors. Taupe horror. Blue sadness. It all wound within the guilt and shame and regret.

At the foot of the cliffs spanning high over the *Jana* was a silent gray-pebbled beach. Only the footsteps of sailors disrupted the rhythmic waves and wind. There was no chittering from swallows or laughter from raucous gulls. No pelicans to sit elegantly on the rocks, no shearwaters to glide by.

The birds *were* there, but they weren't in any state to sing or fly. Crooked corpses and hollow skeletons covered the beach or floated on the gentle, low-tide waves. There were hundreds of dead fish too—washed ashore and crispy from the sun.

How many thousands of corpses had gathered here over the years? How many more washed in each day?

Iseult bent her gaze to Evrane, wondering how the monk felt seeing her home again. But Evrane's Threads remained calm, and only a flicker of sadness twined through them.

Iseult cleared her throat and swallowed the need to stammer. "I thought it was the water that was poisonous, Monk Evrane. Not the fish."

"But the fish," Evrane answered, moving to Iseult's other side, "travel through the poisoned water and die. Then the birds eat them and die too."

Safi swayed against the bulwark, her face and Threads a mask of horror.

Iseult, however, stayed perfectly still, wishing she knew how to sculpt her face like Safi. Wishing she could *make* Evrane understand that her lungs ached at the sight of this ruined land, that her ribs felt like ice-veined granite. Yet Iseult had no masks and no words, so she stayed locked in place.

Threads flamed at the edge of her vision, and she didn't have to turn to know who strode up the companionway. Who moved to Evrane's side and slid his spyglass from his jacket.

The Threads between Merik and Safi were stronger now, and a confusing clash of contradictions. The outer strands, like a starfish's legs, reached and grabbed with purple hunger. Burgundy passion. A hint of blue regret.

And more than a little crimson rage.

This bond could get explosive, Iseult thought, rubbing furiously at the bridge of her nose.

"What is it?" Safi asked.

Iseult flinched. She'd been so caught up in the Threads, she hadn't noticed Safi turning toward her. "It's nothing," Iseult murmured, even though she knew Safi would recognize the lie.

"She has no shoes!" Evrane cried, snapping away Safi's attention.

Merik's nostrils flared, and though Safi's lips parted—

likely to argue she was fine without shoes—Merik roared, "Ryber! Get the domna some shoes!"

The ship's girl popped up the companionway, chewing her lip. "I can get her boots, Admiral, but she'll need to come with me belowdecks. It's easier to bring her to the shoes than the other way around."

"Do it." Merik waved dismissively, already focusing his spyglass to shore again.

Safi glanced at Iseult. "Want to come?"

"I'll stay." If she joined Safi, then Safi might ply her with questions. Questions that could lead to the binding Threads . . .

Or worse—to the shadow voice in Iseult's nightmares.

"I want to be outside," Iseult added, "in the fresh air."

Safi wasn't buying it. She glanced at the nearest sailors, who scrambled up the masts. Then she dragged her skeptical gaze back to Iseult. "Are you *sure*?"

"I'll be fine, Safi. You forget that *I* taught you the art of evisceration."

Safi scoffed, but her Threads flared with amused pink. "Is that so, dear Threadsister? Have you already forgotten that it was *me* they called The Great Eviscerator back in Veñaza City?" Safi flung a dramatic hand high as she twirled toward Ryber.

Now Iseult didn't have to fake a grin. "Is that what you thought they said?" she called. "It was actually The Great *Vociferator,* Safi, because that mouth of yours is so big."

Safi paused at the companionway—just long enough to bite her thumb in Iseult's direction.

Iseult bit her thumb right back.

When she angled to the railing, she found Merik with his eyebrows high and Evrane stifling a laugh. It pleased Iseult inordinately to see the monk amused, and warmth trickled through her shoulders.

"It is good to see you feeling better," Evrane said.

"It's good to feel better," Iseult answered, ransacking her brain for something clever to add. Or *anything* to add, for that matter.

But nothing came, and an uncomfortable silence swept in with the breeze. Iseult started massaging her right elbow, just to have something to do.

It caused Evrane's Threads to flash green with concern. "Your arm hurts—and foolish me, I have left my salves belowdecks." She hurried off, leaving Iseult with Merik.

Alone with Merik.

A prince who could become part of Safi's Thread-family—or just as easily become her enemy. A prince who now dictated where—and how—Iseult and Safi traveled.

Without quite realizing what she did, a question popped from Iseult's mouth: "Are you married?" It was the first question Threadwitches asked when crafting a person's Threadstones, and Iseult had heard Gretchya ask it a thousand times growing up.

Merik's fingers tightened on the spyglass; his Threads flashed with surprise. "Uh . . . no."

"Do you have a lover?"

Merik wrenched down the glass, his Threads now pulsing with revulsion. "I have no lover. Why are you asking?"

Inwardly, Iseult sighed. "I'm not interested in you, Your

Highness, so there's no need for the disdain. I'm simply trying to decide if we should follow you to Lejna or not."

"*If* you should follow?" Merik's Threads and posture relaxed. "You have little choice."

"And if you think that, then you severely underestimate Safi and me."

Merik's cheeks—and Threads—flashed an angry red, so Iseult decided to cut short the Threadwitch interrogation. But when Merik spun on his heel to leave, Iseult *did* sidestep him. "You don't like me," she said. "And you don't have to. Just remember that if you ever hurt Safiya fon Hasstrel, then I will cut you to pieces and I will feed you to the rats."

Merik didn't reply—though he did look *thoroughly* incensed as he stamped around Iseult toward the companionway.

But the flash of cyan understanding in his Threads told Iseult that he'd not only listened, but that he'd taken that warning to heart.

Which was good, because she'd meant every word.

Safi hunkered low in the gig, water splashing over the sides as Ryber rowed Safi, Iseult, Evrane, and Merik ashore.

When Ryber had taken Safi belowdecks, Safi had apologized for getting the girl in trouble, but Ryber had shrugged it off. "Admiral's all growl and no bite. Besides, it isn't *me* he's mad at."

It was all too true. Merik had barely *looked* at Safi since reaching the cove, and whenever she attempted a question—

Are we traveling by foot? Do we have supplies?—he'd simply turned away.

Which of course made Safi all the more determined to illicit some response. She'd rather feel his growl or his bite than have him pretend she didn't exist.

In mere minutes, the gig was ashore and Ryber was hopping into knee-deep waves to drag in the boat. Merik and Evrane hopped right out. Safi and Iseult, however, were considerably less graceful.

"This is something Habim and Mathew failed to teach us," Iseult said, using Safi's and Ryber's hands to alight. "We should inform them that gig-exiting is a valuable life skill."

"It's not that valuable," Ryber said. "It's just getting in and out."

Safi coughed lightly. "That was Iseult's attempt at a joke."

"Oh." Ryber chuckled. "Sorry. I've only met one Threadwitch before, and she was ancient. I guess you can see my Threads right now?"

"Hye," Iseult answered. "They are currently green with curiosity."

A pleased smile split Ryber's face. "So . . . can you see my Heart-Thread too?"

Iseult's nose wiggled, and she shot a quick, almost nervous glance at Safi before saying, "Hye. I can see it. He's on the ship."

Ryber's grin widened—though there was no missing the haunted, empty look that filled her eyes.

"Ryber," Merik barked. The girl started—then marched earnestly toward her admiral.

Safi leaned toward Iseult. "Why did you look at me when Ryber asked about her Heart-Thread?"

"Because it has blue in it," she said flatly. "That means part of her love is grief-stricken."

"Oh," Safi breathed. The idea of a shared sadness between Ryber and Kullen made her throat tighten.

While Iseult slunk over the beach to join Evrane—who inspected a dead petrel several paces away—Safi waited for Merik.

"As the second mate," he told Ryber, whose braids bounced on the wind, "Hermin commands the ship until Kullen is better. And remember: Don't eat the fish or drink the water. This isn't like the River Timetz—our Water-witches haven't made it here. You'll die before you've even swallowed. Also, make sure Hermin doesn't push his witchery too hard. If Lovats doesn't answer, then there's nothing we can do."

Ryber saluted, fist to heart, and Merik rested his eyes on the ship. For several long moments, the seawater lapped at Safi's feet—at Ryber's boots—but she didn't skip away. She simply waited for the prince to finish his silent good-bye.

Once he had finished—as marked by his sudden straightening and sudden collar tugging—he twirled around and stomped past Safi.

"Safe harbors!" Ryber shouted after them.

"Safe harbors," Safi called back, already kicking after Merik.

Iseult moved into step beside her—Evrane walking

steadily behind and with far more poise than Safi or Iseult displayed. The beaches around Veñaza City were sand, and Safi's ankles didn't appreciate this tiny gravel. She also quickly learned that vaulting over dead birds *wasn't* the easiest.

When she turned toward Iseult to complain, though, she found her Threadsister already panting. "Are you all right? Should we slow?"

Iseult insisted she was fine. Then she lifted her voice. "Where are we going, Your Highness? Because it looks like we're walking toward a wall."

Indeed, it *did* look like they were aiming toward two high cliffs that met in a low overhang dripping with stalactites.

"A cave is hidden back there," Evrane answered once it was clear Merik had no intention of speaking—though Safi was impressed with Iseult for trying. "It is meant to be a *secret* cave, though, just as this inlet is meant to be secret."

"No one will see us," Merik muttered, aiming for the right-most edge of the overhang. He ducked beneath a stalactite.

Safi sank after him. Pinpricks of dawn shone through gaps in the craggy ceiling. The path before Safi—clearly hewn by men's hands—was so narrow she had to turn sideways.

Several steps later, Merik straightened, so Safi risked rising as well. No sharp rocks stabbed her head—though water dripped.

"Is this water poisoned?" she asked, rubbing her hair.

"Not to the touch," Evrane answered, voice muffled by

Iseult in front of her. "Most of the freshwater in this area *is* dangerous to drink, but there is some that remains pure no matter what."

Merik gave a strangled groan. "No one wants to hear about the Origin Wells."

"I want to hear about the Wells," Safi countered.

"Me too," Iseult said, her breaths audibly shallow. "I've read so much about them. Is it true that the Water Well can heal you?"

"It used to. All the Wells could heal when they were still alive—*Merik*," Evrane snapped, "slow down. Not all of us are familiar with this path and not all of us are in perfect health."

Merik slowed—though not by much. So Safi took it upon herself to shorten her stride. Once Merik realized everyone was flagging, he would have no choice but to lag as well.

Soon, Safi's thighs burned, her ankles stretching as the path rose. "There was an Origin Well on my family's lands," she offered once she felt certain Iseult was having no difficulty with the incline. "It wasn't alive, though."

"No," Evrane said. "It wouldn't have been—there are only two intact Wells left. Of the five, only the Aether Well at the Carawen Monastery and the Fire Well in Azmir still live. Their springs flow, the trees blossom year-round, and the waters can heal you. Though they say—"

"Stairs coming," Merik barked.

"—that if the Cahr Awen were to return, the other Wells would regain their powers and the springs would flow once more."

As Safi squinted to see the slick steps that Merik now vaulted up, she tried to recall the stories from her childhood. "How many Cahr Awens were there before the last pair died?"

"We estimate at least ninety," Evrane said, "but we only have Memory Records for forty pairs."

"Records," Merik inserted dismissively, "don't make them real."

"*Memory* Records," Evrane countered, "make them inarguably real. A Sightwitch Sister transferred the memories directly from the Cahr Awens' corpses."

"Unless those Memory Records were faked, Aunt Evrane. Now, if you are done lecturing, we have to be quiet from here on."

"But there's nowhere else to go," Safi said. Thirty steps ahead, lit by a weak beam of sunlight, there was nothing but flat wall. "Good job, Prince."

He didn't rise to her jab, so Safi tiptoed behind until she and Merik had both reached the wall—until Merik was finally addressing her, the sun showing only the faintest lines of his face.

"We have to push together," he whispered, leaning his shoulder against the wall, a hand pressing flat. Safi mimicked his pose with her other shoulder.

"One," Merik mouthed. "Two . . . *Three*."

Safi pushed. Merik pushed. Then they pushed harder. And then harder again and Safi hissed, "Nothing's happening!" Of course, as soon as the not-very-quiet words left her mouth, the wall lurched forward in a rush of air and sound.

And Safi toppled into a world of dead trees and pale soil. Merik fell too, but the idiot tried to catch himself—tried to grab hold of the swinging rock-door, which just swung him around so that he fell on his back.

Safi fell on top of him, chests colliding. Merik *oomphed*—as did she—and emitted a pained moan.

"What?" she demanded, trying to push off of him. Her hand was stuck beneath him and each yank jostled her body against his.

Heat flamed through her. She'd been close to Merik yesterday—during their brawl—yet this felt . . . different. She was all too aware of Merik's shape. Of the angle of his hip bones and the muscles in his back—muscles that her fingers insisted on digging into. By accident. *Completely* by accident.

Safi was also keenly aware of Evrane laughing and Iseult gawping in a most un-Threadwitch way. But before Safi could order them to help, Merik rolled up his head, and his stomach clenched against hers. "Get. Off. Me."

His growl rumbled through Safi's rib cage, yet she had no chance to snarl back, for Evrane's chuckles broke off—and the sound of creaking wood reverberated through the clearing.

Twenty arrowheads peeked out from behind the sun-bleached pines as Iseult murmured, "Oh, Safi. He *did* say to be quiet."

THIRTY

Merik had expected the soldiers with bows—he really had. What he hadn't expected was that it would take so long for their leader, Master Huntsman Yoris, to call them off.

Or that Safiya fon Hasstrel would be on top of him while he waited.

Iseult and Evrane—his aunt's hood pulled low—stood with their backs against the cave and their hands up, and Merik did everything he could to pretend he wasn't pinned beneath Safiya. That his legs were not twined in hers, that his chest was not heaving against her much softer chest, and that those were not her nails scratching at his back or her storm blue eyes mere inches away.

It was her eyes that always did it—that pulled the rage to the surface. But he wouldn't let his magic loose, no matter how much it ached for release. No matter how much he wanted to flip Safiya over and . . .

Noden save him.

A groan stirred in the back of Merik's throat, and he prayed the earth would swallow him whole.

Safiya mistook his distress for laughter. "Do you think this is funny? Because I'm not laughing, Prince."

"Nor am I," he answered. "And I told you to be quiet."

"*No*, you told me to push. Which I did—except that you *fell*. Where was your wonderful Windwitchery then?"

"I must've left it onboard the *Jana*." Abdomen tightening, he lifted his face close to hers. "Right next to my patience for your constant harping." As long as he stayed angry, he wouldn't have to think about the shape of her mouth. The weight of her hips pressing into his.

Her eyes thinned. "If you think *this* is harping, you're in for quite a treat—"

"Your Highness?" a voice boomed. "Is that the royal son of Nubrevna I see cozying up to a lady? Lower your weapons, boys." As one, the arrows in the forest dropped. Merik immediately shoved Safiya off him and scrambled to his feet.

As soon as Safiya was also upright, Iseult and Evrane moved in close, their stances defensive while Yoris's "boys" trickled out from the forest with their leader at the fore.

Yoris was a lean man with only three fingers on his left hand—supposedly he'd lost the others to a sea fox.

"'Matsi scum." Yoris sucked his teeth in Iseult's direction. Then he spat at her feet. "Go back to the Void."

Iseult barely managed to grab Safiya before she lunged. "I'll show you the Void," Safiya growled, "you hell-ruttin'—"

Six of Yoris's soldiers trained their bows on Safiya—and more arrowheads materialized from the dead pines.

Merik's hands shot up. "Call them off, Yoris." This was

not the happy reunion he'd hoped for with one of his childhood idols.

"Arrows won't save your skin," Safiya muttered. "I'll shred it with my kni—"

"Enough," Iseult snapped with more emotion than Merik had ever heard. "His Threads are harmless."

Safiya clamped her mouth shut at that—though she still moved in front of Iseult.

"Lower your bows," Merik ordered, louder now. Angrier. "I'm the Prince of Nubrevna, Yoris—not some raider."

"But who's this, then?" Yoris tipped his head toward Evrane—who still had her cloak tugged low and body poised for action. At Yoris's nod, a soldier extended his bow and flicked back her hood.

"Hello, Master Huntsman," she drawled.

"You," Yoris growled, shoving past Merik. "The Nihar traitor. You aren't welcome here."

Evrane's sword rasped free at the exact moment that Merik yanked out his cutlass—and thrust it against the old man's back.

"If you slander anyone else in my party, Master Yoris, I will run you through." Merik prodded the blade forward until Yoris's shirt wrinkled in. He'd had enough, and Yoris knew damned well how quickly the Nihar rage could escalate. "Evrane is a vizer of Nubrevna and a sister to the king, so you will show her the respect she deserves."

"She abandoned her title when she became a Car—"

Merik's boot connected with Yoris's knee. The man crumpled to the earth and all around, arrows nocked.

But Yoris only erupted with laughter—a sound like

crunching stones. His head swung up. "Now *there's* the prince I know. I just had to check you weren't bewitched by the 'Matsi girl—that's all. That's all." Another chuckle, and the Master Huntsman rolled easily to his feet.

Bows and arrows lowered in a rustle of movement, and Yoris flourished a graceful bow. "Allow your humble servant to escort you to your new home."

"New?" Merik frowned, sheathing his cutlass.

A sly grin spread over Yoris's face. "Noden smiled upon us this year, Highness, and only a fool ignores His gifts."

The morning sun beat down on Merik, sent his shadow slivering behind him or into the sun-bleached pine stumps and dusty yellow earth. Safiya stayed ten paces behind, keeping close to Iseult while Evrane bought up the rear.

Merik was relieved to find he could easily ignore the domna so long as she remained just out of earshot, just out of sight.

And so long as she wasn't on top of him.

He did glance back every few minutes, though, to make sure the women kept up. Though Iseult didn't complain and she didn't slow, she wasn't fully healed. Even with her face as blank as snow, there was no mistaking the tightness in her jaw.

Then again, she'd looked comparably severe on the *Jana* when she'd struck Merik with those strange questions. It was hard to ever tell what she felt—or if she felt at all.

Fortunately for Iseult and Evrane, Yoris's prejudiced guards had vanished into the silent woods during the first mile of their hike. And fortunately for Merik, those same soldiers crawled within this ghost forest for thousands of acres.

If Safiya decided to run, Yoris's men would be upon her in minutes.

Merik didn't expect Safiya to flee, though. Not with Iseult still healing.

The group hiked onward, and the silent landscape never changed. On and on, it was an endless graveyard of splintered trees and sun-whitened trunks, bird corpses and soil dry as bone. Whenever Merik was here, he kept his voice low and head bowed.

Yoris had no such impulse. He regaled Merik—loudly—with updates on the men and women Merik had grown up with. Men and women who'd once lived and worked on the Nihar estate. It would seem everyone had now moved to this new home with Yoris and his soldiers.

Despite all the evidence, Merik still caught himself hoping to find something alive. A flake of lichen, a scrub of moss—he would have taken anything so long as it was green. Yet it was just as he'd told Kullen: nothing had changed. Moving east or west made no difference in a world of death and poison.

When Yoris reached a fork in the path—the right road continuing along the Jadansi while the left trail veered inland—an alarmed thought occurred to Merik. "If everyone has moved, did Kullen's mother also go? He planned to visit her."

"Carill stayed at the estate," Yoris said, "so Kull will find her exactly where he left her. She was the only one who wouldn't join us. Then again, this was never her home. She's still Arithuanian at heart." He unhitched a flask from his belt, head shaking as he marched down the left fork.

Merik followed, slowing his pace just enough to ensure Safiya, Iseult, and Evrane also followed. They did.

"Water?" Yoris asked.

"Please." Merik's lips were like paper, his tongue like glue. It was as if the dryness of the world sucked the moisture from his very pores.

But he was careful not to drink too much. Who knew how much purified water Yoris had these days?

"This new place of yours," Merik began, returning the flask, "is clearly nowhere near the Nihar estate. Is it worth traveling so far?"

"Hye," Yoris said with a sideways grin. "But I won't tell you any more than that. I want you to see Noden's Gift for yourself. The first time my old eyes beheld it, I cried like a babe."

"Cried?" Merik echoed skeptically. He could no more imagine tears on the huntsman's face than he could imagine leaves on these oaks and pines.

Yoris's three-fingered hand shot up. "I swear on Noden's Coral Throne, that I cried and cried, Your Highness. Just you wait and see if you don't do the same." Yoris's smile fell as quickly as it had come. "How's the king's health? We don't get much news around these parts, but I heard a few weeks ago that he was getting worse."

"He's stable" was all Merik said in return. *He's stable and ignoring Hermin's calls and possibly rewarding Vivia for piracy.*

In a burst of movement, Merik shrugged off his coat and swiped sweat from his eyes. He was boiling. Suffocating. He wished he'd left the cursed jacket on the *Jana*. It was just a cruel joke. Each reflected beam off its gold-plated buttons—buttons he'd kept so meticulously polished and that denoted his rank as leader of the Royal Navy—was like a flash of Vivia's grin.

Yoris and Merik rounded a bend in the path, and the dead forest gave way to a barren hillside. Merik's thighs burned within the first ten steps, and his boots slipped too easily on the scree. He paused halfway up to blink sweat from his eyes and check on the women behind.

Safiya met Merik's eyes. Her lips parted, and she lifted one hand, fingers trilling with a wave.

Merik pretended not to see, and his gaze shifted to Iseult, whose jaw was set and attention fastened on the ground. Sweat poured down her face, and with her black Threadwitch gown, she looked dangerously overheated.

Merik's attention skipped at last to Evrane. Like Merik, she'd removed her cloak and held it bunched in one arm. He was pretty sure that was against the Monastery's protocol, but he hardly blamed her.

Just as Merik's mouth opened to call for a short break, Evrane's footsteps slowed. She said something inaudible and pointed east. Safiya and Iseult paused too, following Evrane's finger. Then their faces eased into smiles.

Merik snapped his gaze left—only to catch his own lips relaxing. He'd been so focused on moving forward, he hadn't bothered to look east, to see the distant black peak silhouetted against the orange morning. With two ridges on either side, it looked like a fox head.

It was the Water Well of the Witchlands—the Origin Well of Nubrevna. Centuries ago, it had been the pride of this nation, and the most powerful Waterwitches had hailed from Nubrevna. But people had moved, and the Well had died. Now, if *any* full Waterwitches were left on the Continent, they certainly weren't in Nubrevna.

"Hurry up, Highness!" Yoris called, splitting Merik's thoughts and urging him forward. His heels slid on stones, his knees cracked . . . Then he was there—at the top—with his jaw sagging and his legs turning to mud. He had to grab Yoris by the shoulder to stay upright.

Green, green, and more green.

The forest was alive—a great strand of it still breathed and burgeoned at the bottom of the hill, winding through a world of white and gray. Hugging a river until . . .

Merik's eyes hit pastures with grazing sheep.

Sheep.

A laugh burbled in his throat. He blinked and blinked again. This was the land of his childhood. The jungle and the life and the movement. *This* was home.

"The river ain't tainted." Yoris pointed to the snaking stream in the forest, where birds—actual *birds*—swooped and dove. "It goes right past our settlement there. Can you see it? It's that gap in the trees."

Merik squinted until he spotted the opening in the woods, just south of the grazing cattle. In the clearing were flat roofs and . . . a boat.

An upside-down boat.

Merik fumbled out his spyglass and pushed it to his eye. Sure enough, the curved, fat hull of some sun-bleached transport ship sat upside down at the center of the settlement. "Where did the ship come from?" he asked, incredulous.

Before Yoris could answer, footsteps gritted out behind Merik—heavy breaths too. Then Safiya was beside him, gulping in air and shouting for Iseult to wait—that she'd be right back for her.

Merik's fingers curled around the spyglass. The domna was disrupting everything, as she always did. He angled toward her, ready to demand peace.

Except Safiya was smiling. "It's your *home*," she said softly. Urgently. "Your god listened to you."

Merik's mouth went dry. The breeze, the rattle of branches, the crunch of Evrane's and Iseult's feet—it all became a dull, distant roar.

Safiya swung her face away, and her voice dropped to a whisper, almost as if she spoke to herself rather than to Merik. "I can't believe it, but there it is. Your god *actually* listened."

"That He did," Yoris said.

Merik flinched—he'd forgotten Yoris was there. Forgotten that Evrane and Iseult were climbing up. Everything inside of him had been lost in Safiya's smile. In the truth of her words. Noden *had* listened.

"That ship," Yoris continued, "fell from the sky almost a year ago, somehow carried by a storm. She hit the earth with a shudder like you wouldn't believe. Upside down, just as you see her, and with food bursting out the windows."

Merik shook his head, forced his mind back to the present. "And . . . what about the ship's sailors?"

"There was no one onboard," Yoris answered. "There were signs of cleaving, though. A few black stains that we scrubbed away, and some damage on the hull that might've been foxes. But that was it."

A cry sounded behind Merik—he jerked around. Evrane had crested the hill—had seen the forests and the life.

She crumpled to the earth, her palms hitting the dusty soil before Merik could reach her. She just waved him off, a prayer tumbling off her tongue and tears pooling in her eyes. Streaking down her dirty cheeks.

Merik's own eyes started to burn then because this was what he'd worked for—what he and Evrane and Kullen and Yoris and everyone else from Merik's childhood had *worked* for and *sweated* for and *fought* for.

"How?" Evrane murmured, hugging her rumpled cloak to her chest and shaking her head. *"How?"*

Despite Yoris's long-standing distrust for Evrane, his expression melted. Even he couldn't deny that Evrane Nihar loved this land.

"The river's clean," Yoris said, voice gruff but gentle. "We don't know why, but we only discovered that—and the start of this new forest around it—when we found the ship. Didn't take us long after to start a new settlement, and we have more families comin' in every week."

Families. For a moment, Merik wasn't sure what that word meant . . . Families. Women and children. Was such a thing possible?

A new realization hit then, punching the breath from Merik's lungs. If Yoris had created this in mere months, then what might happen with a steady supply of food? What more could be built and be grown?

Merik's fingers moved to his coat, to the agreement there. He glanced at Safiya. She met his gaze and grinned wider.

And Merik forgot how to breathe entirely.

Then Safi shifted away to help Iseult climb the rest of the hill, and Merik's lungs regained their function. His mind regained clarity, and after a sharp tug at his collar, he offered a hand to Evrane.

"Come, Aunt. We're almost there."

Evrane dabbed at her cheek, smearing the dirt and tears more than wiping them away. Then she bared a tentative grin, as if she'd forgotten how to smile.

Actually, Merik couldn't remember the last time he'd seen his aunt smile.

"We are not simply 'almost there,' Merik." She took his hand and clambered to her feet. "My dear, dear nephew, we are almost *home*."

THIRTY-ONE

Noden's Gift was easily the *happiest* village Safi had ever seen. She and Iseult followed Yoris, Merik, and Evrane over a crude bridge, the river below a choppy slice in the yellow earth. It led to an outer cluster of wooden huts with rounded thatch roofs and plank walls, as bleached as the trees from which they were hewn. The homes seemed awfully precarious to Safi—like the first big storm would bluster them all into the fast-moving river.

Then again, Nubrevnans were clearly a resilient lot. If a squall stole their homes, they would simply start over again. And again and again.

A sparrow plunged over the bridge, a raven croaked from a rooftop, and fat fern leaves shivered up from the steep riverbanks.

And everyone—*everyone* Safi passed—was smiling.

Not at Safi—she just earned curious stares. And *definitely* not at Iseult, who was hooked on Safi's arm and slouched deeply within Evrane's cloak. But Merik . . . When the people caught sight of their prince, Safi had never seen such brilliant smiles. Never felt such a burn of her witchery at the truth behind them.

These people loved him.

"You're impressed," Iseult said, her cloak's hood pulled low so that no one could see the pallor of her skin, the pitch of her hair. She was walking slowly, breathing heavily on Safi's arm, but she seemed determined to make it all the way to Yoris's base before she acknowledged any sort of pain or exhaustion.

"Your Threads are bright enough to give sight to a blind man," Iseult continued. "Do you mind reining it in? I might get the wrong idea."

"The wrong idea?" Safi snorted. "In what way? Aren't *you* impressed?" Safi jerked her chin toward a gnarled grandma in the doorway of a windowless lean-to. "That woman is actually *sobbing* at the sight of her prince."

"That baby's crying too." Iseult waved to a wide-hipped woman who held a toddler at her hip. "Clearly the youths of Nubrevna adore their prince."

"Ha-ha," Safi said dryly. "I'm serious, Iseult. Did you ever see people react like this to the Guildmasters in Dalmotti? Because I didn't. And the people in Praga certainly never fawned over their Cartorran doms and domnas." She shook her head, pushing aside thoughts of her own estate, where no one had ever—*ever*—looked at Uncle Eron in this way.

Or at Safi. Her whole life, she'd told herself she didn't care. That she didn't want the villagers or farmers to like her—or even notice her. So what if they blamed Safi for her drunken uncle, as if *she* were supposed to stop his debauchery somehow.

Yet seeing how the people of the Nihar lands felt about Merik—seeing a devotion like she'd never had . . . Perhaps there was something to be said for investing yourself in your people.

Of course, Safi had no people anymore. Returning to Cartorra would be suicide—or at least guaranteed enslavement as Henrick's personal Truthwitch.

Since Merik was lingering at the garden, a knot of admirers gathering around, Safi let her own feet slow to a stop.

Iseult wheezed a tired, grateful sigh beside her and angled toward the river. "They're building a mill over there."

Sure enough, across the rapids men shouted and towed, hammered and heaved at the frame of a new structure. They were dressed like the soldiers from earlier, and behind them, pines—*living* pines—swayed on the breeze.

"They look like more of Yoris's men," Safi said, heel drumming on the dirt. "It seems like a lot of them, doesn't it? There were at least twenty to corner us this morning—and those were just the ones stationed near the cove. There are even more here." She motioned to two soldiers now stamping across the bridge. "They can't all be men at arms from the Nihar estate. Even when my parents were alive and the Hasstrel lands were in top shape, Habim said there were never more than fifty men."

"We're right on the border with Dalmotti." Iseult scratched her chin thoughtfully. "Which makes this prime fighting territory."

Safi nodded slowly. "And since it's already crippled, then it's the perfect battleground for when the war resumes."

"Resumes?" Iseult shot a narrow-eyed glance at Safi. "Do you know for certain that the Truce won't be extended?"

"No . . . but I'm *pretty* sure." Absently, Safi watched a dog trot by the construction site. It had something small and furry in its mouth—and looked immensely pleased by its catch. "When I was in Veñaza City," she said, choosing her words carefully, "Uncle Eron said that war was coming, but that he hoped to stop it. And Mathew mentioned something about the Truce dissolving early."

"But why have the Truce Summit if no one plans to negotiate peace?"

"I'm not sure—though I do know Henrick wanted to use the Summit as a stage for announcing my . . . *betrothal*." Safi could barely choke out that word. "And that announcement threw a kink in Uncle Eron's plan."

"Hmmm." Iseult's cloak rustled as she shifted her weight. "Well, since the Marstoks know you're with Prince Merik, then Emperor Henrick must know too. I would think that means both empires might show up here at any moment."

The hair on Safi's arms sprang up. "Good point," she murmured, and there was no ignoring the sandstone grit of fear along her spine—nor the certainty in her gut that Cartorra and Marstok *would* show up here.

And that they wouldn't care at all about breaking the Truce if it meant getting their hands on a Truthwitch.

* * *

"We need to hurry," Safi told Merik as he bowed over a map of the Hundred Isles. They stood several paces apart in a windowed cabin similar to Merik's on the *Jana*—except that everything was upside down. The walls curved inward instead of out, and the door hung a foot off the floor, requiring a long-legged step to climb through.

After Safi had urged Merik and Yoris to move *faster* through Noden's Gift—Merik could greet his people later—Yoris had guided everyone to the galleon, where even Iseult had mustered a grin at the sight.

The ship rested on its quarterdeck while support had been added beneath the forecastle to allow the galleon to lay flat. An open passage ran through the ship's middle, the main deck now a ceiling. Ladders slung down to allow access to the hold, and a rough set of stairs had been built up to what had once been the captain's cabin.

While Yoris had grudgingly taken Evrane and Iseult to get food, Safi had followed Merik into the captain's cabin and over to a table of charts—also like the one on the *Jana*—at the center of the room. There was no glass in the windows now, but the open slats of the shutters let the sound of everyday bustle slide through—as well as a welcome breeze. The ship was thick-walled, the midmorning heat oppressive, and Safi found herself wiping away more sweat indoors than she had outside. Even fussy Merik had his jacket off and shirtsleeves rolled up.

"The Cartorrans likely follow me," Safi said, when Merik refused to look up from his careful scrutiny of the map. She planted her hands on the table. "We need to leave for Lejna as soon as possible, Prince. How far is it?"

"A full day if we stop for the night."

"Then let's not stop."

Merik's jaw clenched, and he finally fixed his gaze on Safi. "We have no choice, Domna. Yoris can only spare two horses, which means if Iseult joins—"

"Which she absolutely will."

"—and Evrane joins us too, which I'm certain she'll do, then we'll have to ride two people per horse. And *that* means we'll need to stop for the night so our steeds can rest. Besides, no one can find the Nihar cove, so no one will be able to go ashore anywhere near us." Merik snagged his jacket off a nearby stool and rummaged inside before pulling out a familiar document—now flattened and creased.

With infuriating slowness, he unfolded the document beside the map. Then he snagged a piece of dry bread from a bowl at the center of the table and took off a fat, mocking bite.

Safi bristled. "I suppose you're still mad at me."

Merik's only response was to chew faster and stare harder at the map and contract.

"I deserve it," she added, dragging a step closer and thrusting away her temper's desire for ignition. Now was her chance to talk to Merik alone—to finally apologize for . . . for *everything*. He couldn't flee and there was no one to interrupt. "I made a mistake," she added, hoping her expression looked as sincere as it felt.

Merik gulped back a glass of water and wiped his mouth in a most un-Merik-like way. Then he finally hauled his gaze to Safi. "A 'mistake' makes it sound like it was an accident, Domna. What you did to my crew and my first mate was calculated malice."

"Calculated *what?*" Indignation towed at Safi's jaw. "That's not true, Prince. I never meant to endanger Kullen or your men—and my power says that *you* don't even believe what you're saying."

That shut him up—although his nostrils did stay flared and Safi thought he might choke if he guzzled his water any faster.

She scooted around the stool that held his jacket.

He immediately stepped away two feet. The chart and agreement rustled over the wood.

Safi thrust out her chin, and this time she advanced three more steps—right up to his side.

And with a harsh exhale, he stomped all the way around to the opposite side of the table.

"Really?" she cried. "Am I *that* awful to be around?"

"You are."

"I just want to look at the agreement!" She tossed her hands high. "Shouldn't I know what my uncle expects from you? Expects from *me?*"

Merik's posture turned stony, but at last he offered a resigned sigh—and when Safi strode around the table, he stayed firmly in place. Though his shoulders did rise to his ears, and Safi didn't think she imagined how quickly his breaths came.

"Relax," she muttered, bowing over the contract. "I'm not going to bite."

"Has the feral lion been tamed, then?"

"Look at that," Safi purred, sharing her most feline sideways grin. "It has a sense of humor."

"Look at that," he retorted, "it's trying to change the subject." He dug a pointed finger into the agreement. "Read the cursed contract, Domna, and go away."

Her smile sank into a glare and she bent down, resting her elbows on the table and pretending as if this was the very first time she'd ever read the agreement.

Except, it *was* a different read-through this time. The language of the contract was unchanged, yet the way Safi felt about it, the way it gnawed at her stomach . . .

All negotiations on page two of this contract will terminate should Merik Nihar fail to bring the passenger to Lejna, should the passenger spill any blood, or should the passenger die.

Her knee started juddering. She had been so close to spilling blood—or dying—when she'd fought the sea fox. And though she'd do it all again for Iseult, she could have done it *differently*. Safi could have considered the risks first and thought outside of herself.

But what Safi *really* hated—what made her itch to draw knives and eviscerate something—was that Uncle Eron had put this requirement in the contract at all.

She swallowed, rage scalding the back of her throat. "My uncle is a real horse's ass. Spilling blood is ridiculous and could happen from a paper cut. He knows that, and I'm sure he added this on purpose. I'm sorry."

The room's sweltering air burned hotter. It practically

shimmered with Safi's apology, and for several long heartbeats, Merik regarded her.

Then a smile brushed over his lips. "I don't think you're apologizing for your uncle right now. At least not entirely."

Safi bit her lip and held his gaze. She wanted him to see what she felt. She needed him to read the regret in her eyes.

His smile crooked higher and with a nod that could *almost* be interpreted as an acceptance of her apology, he turned back to the contract. "Your uncle simply wants you unharmed. He was quite emphatic on that point, and it's only natural that he'd be particular about his niece's health."

"My uncle," she said, twirling a careless hand, "would deem me in perfect health even if I'd been stabbed four times and pegged with a hundred arrows. You could probably maim me, Prince, and my uncle wouldn't bat an eye."

Merik snorted. "Let's not try it, all right?" With a sigh, he slanted inward until his left arm rested *almost* against Safi's. Until the smell of him expanded in her nose. *Saltwater, sweat, and sandalwood.*

It wasn't terribly unpleasant. Not to mention she found she couldn't look away from his exposed wrists—easily twice the size of hers—or the fine hairs on his forearms.

"What about," Merik asked softly, carefully, "your betrothed? How would Emperor Henrick feel if you were pegged with a hundred arrows?"

In less than a blink, Safi's blood hit a boil in her ears. Why was Merik asking her about Henrick? And why did she feel like the fate of the world rested on the answer?

When at last she attempted to speak, her voice was taut

as a bowstring. "Henrick isn't my betrothed. I can't accept that. I *won't*. One moment, I was dancing with you at the ball, and the next . . ." She gave a harsh laugh. "The next moment, Emperor Henrick was declaring me his future bride."

Merik's breath expelled roughly. "You mean you didn't know before then?"

She shook her head, avoiding Merik's eyes—though she felt them sear into her. "I didn't know my uncle would stage this wild escape either. He had mentioned big plans, but never in a million years could I have guessed that I'd be stolen from Veñaza City, hunted by a Bloodwitch, and forced onto your ship. It has been a huge, endless cascade of surprises. At least, though, it keeps me out of Henrick's clutches." She gave another tense laugh and tried to lean forward, to pretend to examine the map. But seconds slid past without her absorbing a single river or road. It was as if the power in the room was shifting—tumbling out of her hands and into Merik's.

Then Merik reached across the map to tap at a snaking line of blue. His arm brushed hers.

It was a seemingly accidental touch, yet Safi knew—*knew*—from the way Merik moved, confident and determined, that it wasn't accidental at all.

"We'll set up camp here," he said. "Yoris said this stream is clean."

Safi nodded—or tried to. Her heart was stuck somewhere in her throat, and it made her movements jerky. Frantic, even, and she couldn't seem to meet his stare. In fact, she stared at every part of his face *but* his eyes.

He had stubble on his chin, on his jaw, and around the curve of his lips. The triangle between his brows was creased in, but not with a frown. With concentration. It was the hollow of Merik's throat, though, that grabbed her attention—the pulse that she thought she saw fluttering there.

Finally, she risked flicking her gaze upward—and found Merik's eyes roving across her face. To her lips. To her neck.

The door flew wide. Safi and Merik jerked apart.

Evrane strode in . . . then instantly reared back. "Am I . . . am I interrupting something?"

"*No,*" Safi and Merik intoned, stepping apart two paces. Then a third, for good measure.

Iseult tottered into the room behind Evrane, her face pale and the Carawen hood pulled back. She looked like she might vomit or pass out—or both.

Safi lurched for Iseult and grabbed her arm, guiding her to a stool. Then Safi unfastened the Carawen cloak from Iseult's neck and shoved it toward Evrane. "You're sweating too much. Are you sick?"

"I just need rest," Iseult answered. Then, she nodded gratefully as Merik handed her a glass of water. "Thank you."

"She needs more than rest," Evrane insisted. "She needs healing."

Cold terror caught Safi's breath. "Firewitch healing?"

"Not Firewitch healing," Evrane rushed to assure her, "but more than I can offer right now. I am drained from days of tapping into my power . . ." She trailed off, her gaze moving to Merik. "If we could go to the Well, then I could help her."

Merik stiffened, the triangle on his brow deepening. "The Well hasn't healed anyone for centuries."

"It might augment my witchery, though," Evrane countered. "At the very least, we can wash Iseult's wound there, where the water is completely pure."

"It ain't far," said a new voice. Yoris. He stepped over the knee-high threshold and mopped his sleeve on his brow. "There's a path along the river. Shouldn't take more than ten minutes to reach."

"What about your men," Merik asked, brow still folded. "Do they patrol that area?"

"Of course. All the way to the edge of the Nihar lands."

A pause. Then Merik nodded, and his expression melted into something almost calm. "Aunt," he said, twisting toward Evrane, "you can take Iseult to the Well. Heal her, if you're able, and I'll come for you at the next chime."

Evrane's breath sighed out. "Thank you, Merik." She slid a hand behind Iseult's back. "Come. We'll go slowly." Iseult rose, and Safi moved to follow . . . but then paused.

She turned to Merik, who stared at her. "I would like to join," she said. "But I won't go if you think it's a risk to the contract."

He straightened slightly, as if startled she'd considered the contract. Considered *him*. "The contract should be fine. Although . . ." He stepped in close, and with aching slowness, he reached out to slide his fingers around Safi's left wrist. When she didn't resist, he lifted her hand, palm up.

"If you run, Domna," his voice was a low thrum that shivered into Safi's chest, "I will hunt you down."

"Oh?" She arched an eyebrow, pretending Merik *wasn't* touching her. That his voice *wasn't* making her abdomen gutter and spark. "Is that a promise, Prince?"

He laughed softly, and his fingers slipped behind her wrist. His thumb trailed fire over her palm . . . Then he dropped her hand, leaving no indication of why he'd picked it up in the first place.

"It's a promise, Domna Safiya."

"Safi," she said, pleased to note her voice was steady—and that Merik was actually smiling now. "You can call me Safi."

Then she bowed her head once and left the room to follow Iseult and Evrane to the Origin Well of Nubrevna.

The path to the Water Well was no easy walk, and Iseult was bone-tired before Noden's Gift was even out of sight. In fact, she wasn't even convinced that Evrane followed a real path. It was steep, overgrown by stinging nettle (that Safi stepped in and proceeded to howl over), and the insects and birds chattered so loudly, Iseult thought her ribs might shatter from the vibration of it all.

The hardest part, though, was the steep climb to the double-ridged peak on which the Origin Well stood. With Safi's and Evrane's help, though, Iseult finally reached the top of the black-rocked hill, and promptly gasped.

For she was at an Origin Well. *The* Water Well of the

Witchlands. There had been an illustration of it in her Carawen book, yet this, the reality . . .

It was so much *more* in person. No painting could ever capture all the angles and shades and movement of the place.

The narrow basin, with its six cypress trees (albeit skeletal and leafless) spaced evenly around the sides, held water clear enough to reveal a sharp, rocky bottom. The flagstone path circling the Well had always looked gray in the book, but now Iseult saw it was actually a million shades of ancient white. Beyond the Well's ridge of stone was the Jadansi, blue and endless—yet strangely calm. Only the lightest salty breeze swirled up to ripple tenderly at the Well's surface.

"It looks nothing like the Earth Well," Safi said, her expression and Threads as reverent as Iseult knew hers must be.

Evrane hummed an acknowledgment. "Each Well is different. The one at the Carawen Monastery is on a high peak in the Sirmayans and covered permanently in snow. We have pine trees, not dead cypresses." She raised questioning eyebrows at Safi. "What did the Earth Well look like?"

"It was beneath an overhang." Safi's gaze turned distant as she rummaged through her past. "There were six beech trees, and there was a waterfall that fed into the Well. But it only flowed when it rained."

Evrane nodded knowingly. "The same happens here." She pointed to a stone dam splitting the eastern ridge in half. "That used to feed into the river, but now it only flows during a storm."

"Can we look?" Iseult asked, curious as to what the canyon looked like. There'd been no mention of that in the book.

"Don't you want to rest first?" Safi asked, brow furrowing and Threads concerned. "Or try to heal?"

"Yes," Evrane chimed. She swooped an arm behind Iseult and led her to a ramp descending beneath the water. "Let's get you undressed and into the Well."

"Undressed?" Iseult felt the heat drain from her face. She braced her heels against the flagstones.

"You need to clean more than just your wound," Evrane insisted, heaving Iseult onward. "Plus, if there is any magic to be had in this Well, you need as much skin exposed as possible." Then, almost as an afterthought, she added, "You can keep on your underclothes, if that will help."

"I'll strip with you," Safi offered, grabbing for her shirttails. "If anyone shows up"—the shirt slid over her face, muffled her words—"I'll dance around and distract them."

Iseult forced a shrill chuckle. "Fine. You win—as always."

By the time Safi had flung her shirt to the flagstones, Iseult started undoing her own buttons. Soon, both girls were stripped to their small clothes, their Threadstones glittering at their necks. As Safi helped Iseult sit on the ramp—oh, it was shockingly *cold* water—Evrane also undressed.

The monk glided into the Well, barely a wave around

her chill-bumped skin. "Give me your arm, Iseult. I will dull your pain so you can swim."

"Swim?" Safi squeaked. "Why does Iseult need to swim?"

"The healing properties are strongest at the center of the Well. If she can touch the spring's source, it could heal her completely."

Safi took Iseult's left hand. "I'll help you reach the bottom. I didn't fight sea foxes just to have a simple swim stop me."

Even though Iseult wasn't particularly excited at the prospect of swimming, she offered her arm to Evrane. Soon, the familiar warmth rushed through Iseult's biceps, shoulders, fingers, and she felt the lines of her face smooth away. Felt her lungs inhale fuller than they had in hours.

Iseult rolled her shoulder. Straightened her arm. Then she heaved an overly forlorn sigh. "If only they made stones that could dull pain this easily."

Evrane's forehead puckered. "They do. You used one on the . . . oh. *Oh*. That was a joke."

Iseult's lips tugged up—Evrane was starting to understand her humor—and Safi laughed. Then she shoved out into the well, lugging Iseult with her.

Together, they awkwardly frog-legged toward the center, spraying up a storm. "Just hold on," Safi called, "and I'll pull you down to the bottom."

"I can manage alone."

"And I don't care. Just because you don't feel pain doesn't mean it isn't there. Now hold your breath."

Iseult sucked in, chest expanding . . .

Safi ducked under, hauling Iseult in a roar of exhaled bubbles. Iseult's eyes snapped open. Then she heaved a clumsy kick and aimed down.

Iseult wasn't sure how she or Safi knew where the spring's source was. The world of the Well was rock, rock, and more rock. Yet something stirred inside her. A string winding tighter and tighter—but only as long as she swam in this one, true direction.

Pressure built in Iseult's ears, pounded behind her eyes. Each stroke brushed colder and colder water against her flesh, making it harder to hold fast to Safi. Before they were halfway down, Iseult's lungs started to burn.

Then they were to the bottom, and Safi was reaching for the rocks. Iseult reached too . . .

Her fingers hit something. Something she couldn't see but that sent power—*static*—rushing over her body.

A red light flashed. Then flashed again—brighter. Safi's and Iseult's Threadstones were blinking.

That was when it happened. A *boom!* that slammed into Iseult. It yanked her sideways, wringing the air from her lungs. But she didn't release Safi, and Safi didn't release her as they churned toward the surface, pushed by water. By the charging roar that still quaked around them.

They broke the surface. Waves kicked and swept toward shore. Iseult sputtered and spun, completely disoriented by the Well's roughness. By the power shivering through her.

Suddenly a gray head splashed up beside her. "Come on!" Evrane hooked her arm in Iseult's and towed her toward the ramp.

"What's happening?" Safi shouted, straggling behind.

"Earthquake," Evrane called, her strokes sure. Then Iseult's feet scraped stone, and she shoved to her feet. Evrane and Safi did the same, and all around them, the Well's waters kept reaching and spraying, twirling and trembling.

"I should have warned you," Evrane panted, "we have tremors from time to time." Already, the water was calming, the earth stilling once more. But Iseult barely noticed, her gaze caught on Evrane's Threads. They were the wrong color for fear of an earthquake or even for concern over the girls' safety.

Evrane's Threads burned with a blinding sunset-pink awe.

And now that Iseult was staggering from the water beside the monk, she thought she saw tears falling from Evrane's dark eyes.

"Are you all right?" Safi asked, clutching Iseult's shoulder and distracting her from Evrane.

"Oh. Um . . ." Iseult stretched her arm and honed in on the feel of the muscle, the roll of her joints. "Yes. It does feel better." Her whole body felt better, in fact. Like she could run for miles or endure the worst of Habim's drills.

And now that she was focused on it, she found a strange, boundless joy rushing through her—almost in time to the waves against her calves. The wind gusting over the Well. The twirling happiness in Evrane's Threads.

"I think," Iseult said, meeting Safi's bright eyes and grinning, "it's all better now."

THIRTY-TWO

"She has gone to shore," Aeduan said. He stood at the door to Leopold's cabin—which was, surprisingly, no larger than his own. It was made smaller, though, by the prince's trunks against the walls and by the dozens of colorfully bound epics strewn everywhere.

Sunlight beamed over a single cot, on which Leopold groggily propped himself up. "Who has done what, Monk?"

"The girl called Safiya has gone to shore, and now your ship sails too far east—"

Leopold burst out of bed, blankets flying. "Why are you telling *me* this? Tell the captain! No . . . I'll tell the captain." Leopold stopped, gaze dropping to his night robe. "Actually, I shall dress and *then* tell the captain."

"I'll tell him," Aeduan snarled. Why the prince was sleeping at midmorning Aeduan couldn't fathom anyway. Much less why the man had bothered to don special attire for it.

Soon, Aeduan found himself at the tiller, speaking in broken Cartorran while sailors backed away, fingers flying into the sign against evil. Aeduan ignored them all. The domna's scent had moved due north, and due north meant land.

Land meant that time was running out.

"You want me to go ashore *where?*" the bearded captain asked, his voice rising in volume as if Aeduan were deaf. He held a spyglass to his eye and scanned the craggy shore. "There is nowhere to moor here."

"Ahead." Aeduan pointed at a single sharp rock rising up from the waves. "The Nubrevnans went behind that, so we must follow."

"Impossible." The captain frowned. "We'll be smashed and sunk in moments."

Aeduan snatched the spyglass from the captain, then honed in on the lone rock surrounded by wild waves. Their Cartorran cutter was hauling past and would soon leave this spot entirely. Yet the captain seemed correct that landing here was impossible.

Except . . . that it *wasn't.*

Now that the ship was lurching by, Aeduan could see behind the single rock. There was a gap in the cliffside. An inlet.

Aeduan shoved the spyglass back to the captain—who didn't take it. The brass fell to the deck. The captain swore.

Aeduan ignored the stupid man and tipped up his nose. Breathed in until his chest bowed out and his magic had hooked onto the snow-swept truth of Safiya's blood.

She had gone in that inlet and then set foot on land—moved east. Yet she was not far. Her scent was strong ahead.

Excitement roiled through Aeduan. Sparked in his

blood, his lungs. If he moved fast enough, he could catch the Truthwitch today.

And the Nomatsi girl too.

"I need a Windwitch," Aeduan said, turning to the captain—and making sure to keep his witchery alight. He wanted red in his eyes as he made his demands. "A Windwitch or several of them. However many it takes to fly me to the cliffs along with my things." *Along with my money.*

The captain stiffened, eyes dropping. But then a voice rose from behind.

"Do as the monk orders, Captain. We will be going to shore immediately."

Ever so slowly, he turned to face Prince Leopold, who was now dressed in a thoroughly impractical tan suit.

"We?" Aeduan asked. "I cannot accommodate eight Hell-Bards—"

"No Hell-Bards, Monk." Leopold ran his hands through his hair and stared at the Nubrevnan hills. "Safiya is my uncle's betrothed, so *I* will join you. Alone."

Aeduan's neck stiffened with frustration. "You will only slow me," he said at last, no longer bothering with formalities.

But Leopold simply glanced at him with a smile that didn't quite reach his eyes. "Or perhaps, Monk Aeduan, I will surprise you."

Aeduan lost several hours of precious time because of the prince. To start, Leopold took forever to pack a single satchel and to strap on his useless rapier. Next, Leopold and the Hell-Bard Commander slunk off to speak in hushed, emphatic voices about only the Wells knew what.

All the while, Aeduan stood on the quarterdeck, stretching his wrists and fingers, fuming at the prince's slowness.

Once the Windwitches finally blasted everyone off the cutter, Aeduan thought surely the pace would pick up. It didn't. As soon as they touched down on the nearest cliff, Leopold wasted even more time by informing the Windwitches of all the same orders he had just given the captain. Something about a Wordwitched scroll that would alert the Hell-Bards to when and where Leopold and his uncle's bride would need retrieval.

So, Aeduan abandoned the prince for several minutes and set off into a world of bleached pine trunks. The weight of the silver talers and its iron case was too much for Aeduan to carry at maximum speed, so he might as well use this wasted time to hide the lockbox.

There were no smells or sounds here. It was like being at sea, alone, with only salt to fill the nose and a breeze to tickle the ears. There were scents, as if humans had passed, but no one was near right now.

The emptiness made Aeduan . . . uncomfortable. Exposed, like a man on the chopping block. Even at the Monastery, high atop its mountain, there were still birds dotting the skies. Still signs of life.

Unbidden, a story from Aeduan's old mentor rose to the surface. A story of poison and magic and war. This was not the image Aeduan had conjured, though. He'd imagined a crispy wasteland, like the ones of his childhood. The ones left by Marstoki flames.

Somehow this silent desert was worse than smoldering homes. At least with charred earth and village ruins, there was a sign of man's hand at work. Nubrevna, however, looked liked the gods had simply given up. Decided the land wasn't worth their time and abandoned it.

At least in a godless world, though, there was no one to see Aeduan hide his talers.

He found a hollowed tree stump and laid his iron box inside. Unless someone happened to pass close enough to peer within the trunk, the lock box was invisible.

Flicking his knife against his wrist, Aeduan sliced open his left hand. Blood welled, dripped down his palm, and finally splattered to the iron.

Now the money was marked. Now Aeduan could find it, even if he forgot where he'd hidden it. Or worse, even if someone tried to take it.

Wind exploded. The Windwitches shot above the trees.

"Monk Aeduan?" Leopold shouted over the gusting air. "Where are you?"

For half a breath, a chaotic rage swept up from Aeduan's toes. Burned in his veins. It was Leopold's empire that had desolated this place. Who had ended the lives of not just the people but the earth itself. And now the prince stomped around with no respect, no remorse.

Aeduan reached the prince in seconds, teeth grinding. "Silence," he hissed. "No speaking for the rest of our journey."

The prince bowed his head. A slouch to his posture. A layer of sluggish cold in Leopold's blood.

Leopold *did* know what his people had done here, and

he was ashamed. More importantly, he felt no need to hide that from Aeduan.

But Aeduan had no time to dwell on that. "Men approach," he said in a low growl as he yanked up Leopold's bag. "They smell like soldiers, so stay close and stay quiet."

For a time, they covered decent ground. The farther they traveled, the more the landscape came alive. Insects hummed, birds called, and small patches of green foliage rustled in the Jadansi breeze. The seaside cliffs grew taller and eventually Safiya's smell moved inland—toward a dip in the land.

Soldiers patrolled, but Aeduan had no trouble avoiding them. He could sniff them out long before he and Leopold reached them. The detours slowed their progress, though, and the sun was descending into midafternoon before signs of civilization grew frequent.

First came distant smoke and footpaths. Then came voices—women and children mostly. Since Aeduan and Leopold were approaching a river and the path seemed well traveled, it was time for greater stealth. Aeduan would need to scout ahead—*alone*—and leave the prince briefly behind.

In moments, Aeduan had found a fallen oak that was well hidden from the path and carried no scents of a passing patrol. The tree was recently toppled, so decomposition and undergrowth were almost nonexistent—though Aeduan felt certain that Leopold would still complain.

However, when Aeduan ordered the young man below, Leopold neither complained nor resisted. In fact, he crawled beneath the oak's trunk with unexpected grace.

Dread scraped down Aeduan's spine as he watched. The

prince had been far too compliant and surprisingly cautious on this inland trek.

But once the prince was invisible, Aeduan thrust aside thoughts of Leopold. Safiya was all that mattered now.

As Aeduan crept toward the thunderous river, his magic latched on to many scents—too many. This place was crowded, and there was no way he or Leopold could sneak by. The river was also a problem. Aeduan could easily cross it on his own, but he couldn't tow the prince over too.

They would have to find another route and try to regain Safiya's trail at some later point.

Stealing back to the prince, Aeduan debated the best direction for travel—and also how quickly he could move the prince, even at a willing top speed.

He knelt beside the fallen log, ready to offer a hand to the prince.

Leopold wasn't there.

Instantly, Aeduan sniffed for the prince's blood—grappled for the new leather and the smoky hearths.

But it wasn't there either. There was nothing but the faintest lingering of Leopold's scent. Aeduan fell to all fours and scrabbled under the fallen oak, just in case a Glamourwitch deceived him or there was some hidden escape below.

Neither was the case; Prince Leopold was gone.

Aeduan crawled back out and rolled to his feet, his pulse ratcheting up and a violent sort of fear winding through him. Should Aeduan search for the prince or should he leave him?

A burst of wind lashed through the trees, breaking Aeduan's thoughts—and then smashing them completely.

There was a second blood-scent here. One that he had smelled before.

Clear lakes and frozen winters.

Aeduan's hand instantly moved to his sword hilt. He scanned the forest, his witchery racing to pin down that scent. To identify and remember.

When the recognition hit, Aeduan almost rocked back. He'd smelled this blood in Veñaza City at the pier.

Which meant someone had followed him to Nubrevna—and now that someone had kidnapped Prince Leopold fon Cartorra.

THIRTY-THREE

Merik never knew riding a horse could be such a contradicting experience of misery and pleasure.

The afternoon sun cut through dead oak branches and speckled the dusty path in a lace of shadows. Thirty leagues east of Noden's Gift and life was gone again. A silent graveyard reigned, and the only sound was the crunching hooves of Merik's chestnut mare, the jingle of her tack, and the clomp of Evrane's and Iseult's roan twenty paces behind.

Yoris had given Merik the best steeds he could spare, and he'd outfitted Merik's party with food, water, bedrolls, and an alert-stone—an Aetherwitched chunk of crystal that would flare to life if danger reached the camp. It would let them sleep that night without the need for watch duties.

Merik welcomed sleep. It had been so long since he'd had any.

The tang of salt filled Merik's nose—carried on a fresh burst of wind. Though the Jadansi was hidden behind the sun-faded forest, the path never veered too far from its breeze.

Not that the breeze did anything to cool Merik. Not with Safiya fon Hasstrel sharing his saddle.

Though Merik had every excuse to be flush against the curves of her body, to have his arms around her and holding the reins, it also meant his knees rubbed all the more and his legs kept turning to pins and needles. He had a feeling, when they stopped to make camp, he'd be hobbling like Hermin.

Still, his muscles were the furthest thing from his mind as the mare ambled easily down the barren trail. Each of the horse's steps jostled his thighs, his hips, his abdomen against Safi's lower back, and though he tried to think of Noden's Gift—to replay the welcome he'd received and to hold tight to that heady pride—Merik's brain had other topics in mind.

The shape of Safi's thighs. The slope where her shoulder met her neck. The way she'd challenged him in the captain's cabin—a four-step with eyes and words and casual touch.

Since then, the pressure of Merik's magic—of a rage that might not be rage at all—writhed beneath his skin. Too hot. Too hard.

At least, though, he and Safi were on better terms, and she was easier to talk to now. A thousand questions rolled off her tongue. *How many people live in Lovats? Is Noden the god of everything or just water? How many languages do you speak?*

Merik answered each question as it came. *Around 150,000 people are in Lovats, though that number can quadruple during war; He's God of everything; I speak bad Cartorran, decent Marstok, and excellent Dalmotti.* Eventually, though, he had a question of his own.

"Are the Cartorrans or the Marstoks close? Can your power tell me that?"

She gave a tiny headshake. "I know when people tell the truth or lie. And if I look at a man, I can see his true heart—his intentions. But I can't verify facts or claims."

"Hmmm. A man's true heart?" Merik offered water to Safi. As she sipped carefully, he added, "So what do you see when you look at me?"

She stiffened in his arms, and the slightest hum of static trilled into his chest. Then she relaxed, laughing. "You confuse my witchery." She handed back the water bag. "It says right now that I can trust you."

He grunted lightly and tipped back the water. It was hot from the sun. Two gulps and he stopped.

"*Can* I trust you?" She peered at him over her shoulder.

He smiled. "As long as you follow orders."

He was pleased—inordinately so—when this earned him a haughty sniff.

"That's a dangerous power you have," he said, once she'd turned forward once more. "I see why men might kill for it."

"It *is* powerful," she acknowledged. "But it's not as powerful as people think—and lately, I'm learning that it's not as powerful as *I* think. I'm easily confused by strong faith. If people believe what they say, then my magic can't tell the difference. I know when someone outright lies, but when people *think* they speak the truth, my witchery accepts it." She trailed off, then almost grudgingly added, "That was why I didn't believe you when you told me Nubrevna needed a trade agreement. My witchery told me it was true. Yet it also believed the lies in my history books."

"Ah," Merik breathed, unable to ignore the sorrow in Safi's voice—or how that made his witchery skitter beneath his breastbone. His grip tightened on the reins. His Witchmark rippled over the tendons in his hand.

For half a heartbeat, Merik caught himself pretending that Safi wasn't a domna and that he wasn't a prince. That they were simply two travelers on a barren road, where the only sounds were the gentle clunking of the horses' hooves, the scampering breeze, and the murmur of Evrane and Iseult behind.

But the bleakness of the land soon wedged into Merik's thoughts—alongside the same rotation of worries he couldn't control. Kullen. Vivia. King Serafin.

As if sensing the direction of his thoughts, Safi said, "You carry too much weight, Prince." She nestled back until she rested against his chest. "More than anyone I've ever met."

"I was born to my title," he said roughly, pulling her slightly closer. Accepting the steadiness she offered in conversation. In touch. "I take it seriously—even if no one wants me to."

"That's just it, though, isn't it?" A challenge shivered up her spine. "You love feeling needed. It gives you purpose."

"Perhaps," he murmured, distracted by her nearness. By the way his breath and the wind twirled through the unruly strands of her hair. "You speak Nubrevnan like a native," he said at last, forcing his brain to change subjects. To concentrate on Safi's *words* instead of her proximity. "Your accent is almost imperceptible."

"Years of tutors," she admitted. "I mostly learned from my mentor, though. He's a Wordwitch, so his magic smooths away his accent. He used to make Iz and me practice for hours."

"All that education." Merik shook his head. "All that physical training plus a witchery men would kill for. Think of all you could do, Safi. Think of all you could *be*."

A soft shudder moved through her, and a bounce shivered in her leg. "I suppose," she said eventually, "I could be powerful or make changes or do whatever it is that you seem to be so good at, Prince, but I'd be fighting a losing battle. I don't have what it takes to lead people. To *guide* them. I'm too . . . restless. I *hate* standing still, and except for Iseult, there has been nothing constant in my life."

"So you will never stop running? Even if someone wanted you . . ." He didn't finish. He couldn't quite get those last words—*to stay*—over his lips.

But it sparkled in the air between them, and when Safi angled toward him, her brows were drawn. Then her gaze clicked into place, an inch below Merik's and far too blue.

Suddenly, the space between them was too small. This river was out of Merik's control, careening over the banks, and he could think of nothing but stopping the mare, heaving Safi off, and—

No. Merik couldn't let his brain go there. He *wouldn't.* Flirting was one thing, but touching . . . He couldn't risk what that might lead to. What it might end in. Not with a Domna of Cartorra. Not with an Emperor's betrothed.

So Merik sent up a desperate prayer to Noden that this day would end soon, before he—or his magic—lost control entirely.

THIRTY-FOUR

By the time Iseult and the group reached their chosen campsite, the pink sun was dropping behind the Jadansi—and Iseult was convinced her inner thighs were permanently deformed.

As Yoris had promised, the stream was a clean one, and as such, a miniature jungle had burst forth. The stream had grown too, and if a rain came, it would overrun its narrow banks. So, after letting the horses drink, Merik ordered they make camp on a nearby hill shaded by oaks and boulders.

Of course, it took Merik a long while to actually give that order. He and Evrane spent at least a quarter hour simply staring at the fern trees and listening to the night frogs sing. Their Threads were so euphoric, so triumphant, that Iseult told Safi to simply leave them be.

At last, though, the chestnut mare had had enough waiting. She lipped Merik's shoulder, startling him back to the present. While Iseult and Evrane gathered wood for a cooking fire, Safi and Merik rubbed down the horses.

Swifts chittered overhead, seeming as pleased for the

company as Iseult was glad for their noise. She was glad for anything that distracted her from the Threads throbbing over Safi and Merik. While they'd shared a horse, their Threads had been so bright as to give Iseult a headache.

Evrane's Threads were blinding too, and they hadn't stopped pulsing with giddy pink or green certainty since leaving Noden's Gift.

How three people could feel *so* much amazed—and exhausted—Iseult.

Swooping down, she flicked a cicada skeleton off a fallen branch and then added it to her growing pile of kindling. Merik had insisted the fire be kept small and Iseult had more than enough wood, but she wasn't ready to return to the group. She needed the time to regain control of her mind. Of her Threadwitch calm.

Eventually, though, she dragged herself back and helped Evrane lay out the bedrolls beneath an enormous, overhanging rock. An alert-stone sat atop it, searing magenta in the sunset.

When at last everything was situated and a meal of hot porridge gulped back, Iseult wiggled into her bedroll and closed her stinging eyes, grappling for that perfect sense of belonging she'd felt in the Origin Well's cool, kicking waters. Yet, for all that Iseult could remember what she'd felt, she couldn't actually summon back the feeling.

As she lay there, thinking and reaching and analyzing, she drifted off.

And the shadow was waiting.

"You're here! And you're all *healed*." The shadow seemed genuinely pleased by this, and Iseult imagined she clapped in the real world—a real world that Iseult was certain existed. This voice wasn't just some mad extension of her deepest fears.

"You're right," the shadow crooned. "I'm as real as you are. But look—I'll let you see through my eyes for a moment, just to convince you."

It was like coming up from a deep dive. Light swam across Iseult's vision followed by colors—gray and green—and distorted shapes . . . until finally a shuttering of black, as if the shadow blinked long and slow, and the world materialized. Gray stones, worn and crumbling, met Iseult's eyes. No, the *shadow's* eyes, through which Iseult now saw.

It was like the ruined lighthouse by Veñaza City but rather than sea-soaked beach, this land was covered in rich shades of green. Ivy wound and broke through the walls. Grass tufted at the building's base.

"Follow me, follow me," the shadow sang—though it wasn't as if Iseult could truly follow or move at all. Just as she saw through the shadow's eyes, she moved in the shadow's body.

"Where are we?" Iseult asked, wishing she could swivel the shadow's head and see more than just an arched entry into a round room.

An evening sun—brighter than the one in Nubrevna—beamed in through windows with broken glass, and the shadow aimed for a winding staircase at the back. She moved with a strange, bouncing gait, as if she stayed on the balls of her feet when she moved. As if she might start skipping at any moment.

She *did* start skipping when she reached the worn stairs. Up, up, up she spun, her gaze on the steps and thoughts silent. When she reached the second floor, she traipsed toward a window with shards still dangling from the iron lattice.

"We're in Poznin," the shadow finally answered. "Do you know it? It's the capital of the once great Republic of Arithuania. But every nation rises and falls, Iseult. Then, eventually, they all rise again. Soon these ruins will flourish into cities, and it will be the *other* nations that die this time." As the shadow spoke, she leaned onto the windowsill and a wide avenue slid into view—along with hundreds . . . No, hundreds upon *hundreds* of people.

Iseult gasped. The men and women stood in rows, and even in the amber sunset, there was no missing the charred color of their skin. The pure blackness of their eyes.

Or the three Severed Threads drifting over each of their heads.

"Puppeteer," Iseult breathed.

The shadow girl became very still. As if she held her breath. Then she gave a curt nod that sent the view lurching. "They call me the Puppeteer, yes, but I don't like it. Would *you*, Iseult? It sounds so . . . oh, I don't know. So frivolous. Like what I do is a game for children. But it *isn't*." She hissed that word. "It's an art. A masterpiece of weaving. Yet no one will call me Weaverwitch. Not even the King! He was the one who told me I was a Weaverwitch in the first place, yet now he refuses to call me by my true title."

"Hmmm," Iseult said, barely listening to the girl's rambling. She needed to evaluate as much as she could with each flick of the Puppeteer's eyes toward the Cleaved. Plus, it seemed that the girl couldn't read Iseult's thoughts so long as she was too absorbed in her own.

Each row had ten across. Men, women . . . even the occasional small figure, like an older child. But the Puppeteer's gaze never lingered on individuals, and Iseult was too busy estimating the army's size to focus on the few details she could grab.

Iseult had counted up to fifty rows—and was not even halfway down the avenue—when the Puppeteer's words cut into her awareness: "You're a Weaverwitch too, Iseult, and once you learn to weave, we'll change our title together."

"To . . . gether?"

"You're not like other Threadwitches," the Puppeteer elaborated. "You have a need to change things, and the *hate* to do it. The *rage* to break the world. Soon, you'll see that. You'll accept what you really are, and when you do, you'll come to me. In Poznin."

Hot sickness rose in Iseult's chest—vile and almost impossible to hide. So she blurted the best lie she could craft. "You s-seem tired. I am so sorry. Is weaving exhausting?"

The Puppeteer seemed to smile. "You know," she said softly, "you are the first person to ask me that. Breaking Threads wears me out, but it is talking to you that drains me the most. Yet . . ." She trailed off, her eyes falling shut, and her weariness was palpable as she dipped forward—pressed her forehead against an eye-level iron bar. She sighed, as if the metal soothed. "It is worth the exhaustion to talk to you. The king has been so angry with me lately, though I do everything he demands. Talking to you is the only bright spot in my day. I have never had a friend before."

Iseult didn't respond. Any thought or movement would betray what pulsed deep inside her: horror.

And worse, a slight digging of pity.

Fortunately, the shadow girl didn't notice Iseult's reticence, for her talking never slowed.

"I will be gone for the next few days, Iseult. My King has given me a task that will drain my power. I imagine I'll be too tired to find you after that. But," she said with a promising sort of emphasis, "when I am fully restored, I'll come to you again."

She paused for a jaw-cracking yawn. "I must thank you before I go. All those plans and places tucked away in your brain have made the Raider King very happy. That's why he gave me this grand mission for tomorrow. So thank you—you made all of this possible. Now, I need my rest if I am to cleave all these men as ordered."

What men? And what plans and places? Iseult tried to ask. *What did you take from my brain?*

But the words wouldn't come. Nothing but frantic, skittering fire came to her now—in her brain, on her tongue, across her lungs like veins of lightning.

Then, as abruptly as it had appeared, the view of Poznin spluttered out like a lantern, leaving Iseult back in her own skin. Back in her own dreams and stuck with her own horror.

* * *

Never in Aeduan's life had it taken this much focus or power to track someone. Safiya had been easy—her blood took no effort to hold—but *this* person's blood, with its crisp lake water and snow-filled winters, was elusive. One moment Aeduan would have it, then twenty paces later he would lose it—only to stumble on it farther into the forest.

It made no sense, and by the time Aeduan lost the scent for the hundredth time, he had all but given up on the prince. He was supposed to betray the man anyway and keep the Truthwitch for his father's use. Yet each time Aeduan considered leaving the prince to some invisible foe, a strange nagging dug into his shoulders. Scraped along his neck. It was as if . . .

As if he owed the prince a life-debt and felt obligated to repay it.

By the time the trail went completely cold, the sun was already lowering on the horizon. Aeduan stood before a black, shadowed cliff with steep stairs ascending to the top. The river was almost deafening here, and fat bats swooped overhead.

The Truthwitch had been here earlier—Aeduan caught traces of her scent—but she hadn't stayed. Which meant Aeduan shouldn't stay either. Prince Leopold was not his concern; Safiya was. It was time to give up on the prince.

However, just as Aeduan swiveled around to resume the only hunt that actually mattered, a breeze gusted off the cliffs and carried a smell into Aeduan's nose—into his blood.

Leopold.

Aeduan launched himself up the worn steps. Two, then

three at a time, he flew upward until at last he reached the top. A pink sun glittered over rippling water. Wind rustled through the green-filled branches of six cypress trees, and a thunderstorm rumbled in the distance.

Aeduan was at an Origin Well. *The* Water Well of the Witchlands. He should have known it was here, should've guessed this would be it. His old mentor had spoken of it endlessly when Aeduan was a child.

Yet this place didn't look like what his mentor had described. There was life here. Green on the trees, a ripple in the water. It was almost as if the Well were alive—except that that was impossible.

Aeduan dismissed it. He didn't have time to inspect the area, nor did he care to.

Nose high, he stalked to the right of the Well. He made it twelve steps before the blood-scent switched back to the enemy's—and a slow applause broke out.

Leopold stepped out from behind the nearest cypress, clapping. "You found me, Monk." The prince offered a humorless smile. "Faster than I'd hoped."

Aeduan's nostrils twitched. He reached for a throwing knife. "You planned this."

Leopold sighed. "I did. Before you impale me, though, I would like to point out that I was supposed to kill you and chose not to."

"Kill me," Aeduan repeated. In a heartbeat, he had his knife out and arm reared back. "On whose command?"

Leopold only smiled again. That inane, vapid smile that Aeduan hated.

So Aeduan raised his left hand . . .

And took control of Leopold's blood.

He halted the new leather, the smoky hearths. "I can force the answer from your throat," he said flatly. "So tell me who commands you."

A salty breeze swept through Leopold's hair while lightning sparkled on the horizon, looking—at this angle—like a crown atop the frozen prince's head.

"No one commands me," Leopold finally answered, "and no one is with me." Aeduan tightened his grip on Leopold's blood. The prince's pupils shuddered wider, wider . . . Not wide enough. Leopold was unsettled, but he wasn't terrified.

That was when Aeduan realized, *He wants this.* Leopold wanted Aeduan to torture the truth from him . . .

Because it will take time.

The prince had intentionally wasted as much of the day as possible. His aim since Veñaza City had been to delay Aeduan.

"You've figured it out," Leopold said. "I can see it in your eyes, Monk."

"Call me demon like everyone else." Aeduan squeezed the prince's blood even tighter—enough to hurt.

But Leopold only stared at him steadily before saying in a hoarse voice, "I can't . . . let you find Safiya before she reaches Lejna. She is almost there now, and soon she will be out of your reach entirely."

"How do you know that? Who commands you?" As soon as the question left Aeduan's throat, he knew the answer—and by the Wells, he'd been an *idiot* for not seeing it sooner.

Leopold was a part of the scheme to kidnap Safiya.

Fury—scalding and complete—surged into Aeduan's skull. His neck and shoulders. He hated Leopold for tricking him. He hated *himself* for not spotting the deception.

Though there seemed to be no logic to it, it was clear now that the prince was working with the Nubrevnans, the Marstoki Firewitch, the Glamourwitch . . . and who else? This web to steal away the Truthwitch was widespread, and Aeduan was half-tempted to torture out the answers he needed.

But if Safiya was indeed almost to Lejna, and if that would indeed—as Leopold had said—put her out of reach entirely, then Aeduan couldn't waste any more time.

He released Leopold's lungs and throat, but nothing more. Aeduan would hold the prince until he was too far away for Leopold to catch up.

Yet as soon as Aeduan spun around to launch into a magic-fueled sprint, Leopold whispered, "You aren't the demon your father wants you to be."

That stopped Aeduan dead in his path. With methodical slowness, he twisted back. "What did you say?"

"You aren't the demon—"

"After that!" Aeduan stalked to Leopold and dipped his face in close. "I have no father."

"You do," the prince rasped. "The one who calls himself—"

Aeduan latched on to all of Leopold's blood then. He stopped every single function in the prince's body—breath, pulse, vision.

But not the prince's hearing. Not the prince's thoughts.

"I," Aeduan whispered, "*am* the demon they think I am. And you, Your Highness, should have killed me when you had the chance."

He tightened his grip. Tighter, tighter . . . until he sensed the blood in Leopold's brain grow too weak to sustain thought. To sustain consciousness.

Aeduan released the prince. Leopold collapsed to the flagstones, still as stone. Still as death. Even the stormy breeze did not reach the prince now.

For several long, salt-filled breaths, Aeduan stared at the prince's body. He'd found Leopold, but not the second scent. That blood was gone. Whoever it was, though, was undoubtedly working with Leopold—and perhaps knew about Aeduan's father as well.

Aeduan should kill the prince. His father would say to kill him. Yet if Aeduan did that, then he would never learn whose blood smelled like clear lakes and frozen winters. He would never learn who had ordered Leopold to kill him—or why.

Aeduan supposed he could always lie to his father and then investigate on his own.

Aeudan nodded, satisfied with that. He would leave Leopold alive and hunt down the prince again later. For answers.

So without a second glance, Aeduan left behind the Imperial Prince of Cartorra and the Origin Well and as he ran, the setting sun warmed his back and a wind picked up speed behind him.

THIRTY-FIVE

Merik jerked awake to the sound of distant thunder—and the touch of fingers against his collarbone. Were he not so deeply asleep, he might've guessed the only three people who could've put their hands this close.

But Merik was too submerged in slumber, and his brain didn't kick in until long after his instincts had.

He snatched the fingers at his chest, swung up a single leg, and flipped the perpetrator over . . . His eyelids snapped wide, breath ragged yet every piece of his being alert.

His gaze met blue eyes, made almost black in the cloudy moonlight. "Domna." One of his hands hit the dirt beside her head. His other squeezed her wrist.

Her fingers furled in, making her wrist flex wider in Merik's grip, and he thought he felt her heartbeat against his chest. That he heard it pounding over the storm-carried breeze and endless song of the forest—though that might have been his own heartbeat.

Safi wet her lips. "What are you doing?" Her whisper tickled against Merik's chin. Sent a chill down his neck.

"What are *you* doing?" he whispered back. "Pickpocketing me?"

"You were snoring."

"You were drooling," he retorted—a bit too quickly. He *had* been known to snore.

Merik slid his free hand behind her head and lowered his own until he blocked all moonlight from her face. Until all he saw were her glittering eyes.

"Tell me," he said slowly, "the truth, Domna. What were you doing with your hand in my shirt? Taking advantage of me in my sleep?"

"No," she growled, jutting out her chin. "I was only trying to *wake you*. To make you stop snoring." She wiggled again, her body tensing beneath Merik's—a sign her temper was rising. If Merik didn't move soon, her legs would weave between his, her fingers would claw, and her eyes would burn in a way that would make resistance of his rage—of his magic—impossible.

Merik relaxed his grip on Safi's wrist, eased his hand from behind her head, and used his knees—palms flat against the earth—to lift his chest from hers.

Her back arched.

Merik froze.

Halfway to his elbows, a rawness opened in his rib cage. Spiraled through him—and spiraled through her as well. It was as if a string connected their chests, and any movement he made would be matched by her.

His eyes ran the length of her. She was vastly different from the women of his homeland. Her hair was the color of the sand, her eyes the color of the sea. Merik exhaled harshly. No matter how his fingers and lips ached for it, he couldn't give into this . . . hunger.

He slid off of her and onto his back, draping a hand over his eyes to block out the sky. To block out the hot awareness of Safi beside him. Every drop of his witchery and every inch of his flesh responded to her.

"I can't do this," he finally admitted—to her. To himself. Then he was on his feet, yanking his coat off the bedroll and striding toward the forest. Toward the sea.

He towed on his jacket as he marched. Somehow, wearing it made him feel calmer. In charge . . . Except, of course—of *course*—Safi followed.

"Why are you here?" he demanded, once he'd rounded the overhang into a buzzing, breezy forest. She padded several steps behind.

"I can't go back to sleep."

"You haven't tried."

"I don't need to."

Merik sighed. Why argue with that? He had enough wrinkles without adding Safi into that mix. So on Merik marched, his fingers drifting over fern leaves or trailing through pine needles. So cool to the touch. So alive.

When he reached the sea—when the distant, glittering storm and white-capped waves hit his eyes, something inside him unfurled. Relaxed. Safi scuffed left toward a huge outcropping of limestone, and Merik followed—though he kept two long steps between them. Then, they both leaned against the rock, and for a time, stared silently at the sea, the moon, the lightning.

It was peaceful, and Merik found himself relaxing. Slipping into the rhythm of the waves and the humming insects.

Until it wasn't peaceful anymore. At some point, the night's pulse had gathered inside him—a pressure needing release. A violent heat like the storm on the horizon. Safi shifted, drawing Merik's eyes. The light off the limestone cast her in a muted, moon-like glow.

Her lips sank into a scowl. "Stop staring like that, Prince."

"Like . . . what?"

"Like you're going to attack me."

Merik laughed, a warm, genuine sound. Yet still, his gaze was trapped by Safi. By her throat in particular. Its curve was silhouetted against the limestone, and he couldn't recall ever seeing a neck so elegantly shaped. "My apologies," he said at last. "Attacking you is the farthest thing from my mind."

She flushed a moonlit pink, but then, as if annoyed with herself, she popped her chin high. "If you are imagining a more . . . *intimate* sort of attack, Prince, then I should inform you I'm not that sort of girl." She looked—and sounded—every inch a domna.

"I never thought you were." It was Merik's turn to flush now—not with embarrassment. With annoyance. A hint of fury. "And you shouldn't assume that I even desire you, Domna. If I were looking for a casual tumble, then you are easily the last person I would choose."

"Good," she retorted, "because you're the last person *I* would choose."

"Which is your loss, I promise."

"As if you're so talented, Prince."

"You know that I am."

Her gaze snapped to Merik. Her chest expanded. Froze.

And Merik took a step closer. Then another until he was right beside her. "If you *were* that sort of girl, then . . ." Merik lifted a hand to her jaw—tentative at first, then more confident when she didn't pull away. "Then I would start here and move down your throat." His fingers whispered over her neck, to her collarbone—and Merik was pleased by how punctuated her breaths grew. How much her lips trembled.

"Then," he continued, voice rumbling from somewhere low in his throat, "I'd circle back. Move behind you." He pushed away her braid—

"Stop," she breathed.

Merik stopped—though, Noden's breath, he didn't want to.

But then came a twist of Safi's body, and suddenly her lips were to Merik's. No, her lips were *above* his. Pausing. Waiting, as if she'd surprised herself and now didn't know what to do.

A breath stirred in Merik's chest—snagged there along with his thoughts. Yet, the inches between their bodies could have been miles and the gap between their lips felt uncrossable.

Safi's breath scraped over his chin. Or maybe that was the breeze. Or maybe it was his own breath. He couldn't tell anymore. It was getting hard to do anything but stare at her eyes, sparkling and close.

Her gaze moved down, her brow furrowing—like she

wanted to do more. Then her hands lifted to rest over Merik's hip bones. Her fingers curled in.

Merik's witchery ignited.

Wind thrashed upward, spraying Safi's hair from her face and almost pushing her away—except that Merik moved in. He pressed Safi to the rock and, in a roar of wind and heat, he kissed her.

The hunger of the day scorched through him and, to his vast pleasure, Safi took it in. She *grabbed* it from Merik with digging fingers and a rhythm in her hips that went beyond any four-step.

She was savage now—unabashedly so—and Merik found himself biting, tugging, and pushing. All talons and teeth and brutal, charged winds.

But he couldn't get her close enough. No matter how hard his lips crushed hers or her hands clutched beneath his jacket . . . beneath his shirt . . .

Hell, her fingers were on his bare skin now.

Fresh heat slashed through him. His knees almost buckled, and his winds tore outward. Upward. He hefted Safi onto a low outcropping, his fingers tugging at the hem of her shirt. His mouth tasting in all the places he'd promised. Her ear—where she moaned. Her neck—where she writhed. Her collarbone . . .

Her hands shot between them. Pushed him away.

Merik staggered back, gaping. Lost. Safi's chest heaved, and her eyes were huge—but Merik couldn't see why she'd stopped this storm between them. Had he crossed some line?

"Do you," she finally rasped, "hear that?"

Merik shook his head—still lost—and sucked in a tattered breath.

Then he heard it too. A steady beat thumping over the sea. *A wind-drum.*

Merik lurched around.

The Jana's *wind-drum.*

In an instant, he was hurtling back the way they'd come, Safi right behind. Scrub and gravel twisted underfoot, but Merik barely noticed. The wind-drum was getting louder. The *Jana* would sail into view at any moment, and Merik had to know why—had to see how far his ship was from shore. He could fly to his men, but only if he had a visual . . .

Safi grabbed Merik's shoulder, yanked him to a stop. "There." She pointed south, to where Merik could barely discern gray waves from gray clouds.

He rooted out his spyglass, scanned the water . . . until he caught sight of the lights—he'd thought them part of the storm, but no. The image sharpened into a Nubrevnan warship. The *Jana,* with her lanterns and mirrors illuminating the water ahead. The white sails ballooned—Windwitched by Kullen.

The wind-drum pounded on and on, far too loud for such a distance, meaning Ryber used the magicked mallet and had the drum aimed for shore. For Merik.

Kullen was calling him.

So Merik inhaled deeply and gathered his wind. It charged up his skin, burned into his body. "Step back," he warned Safi. He would need to aim this wind-flourish perfectly—need to hit that tiny speck on the horizon so his crew would know where he was.

He reared back both arms . . . Then Merik loosed his air. A great funnel of wind erupted outward across the waves.

And Merik waited. Waited and watched with Safi at his side. He was grateful she was there. Her squared shoulders and fearless gaze kept him from thinking too hard. From leaping off the cliff and flying straightaway to his Threadbrother . . .

The wind-drum stopped, and Merik readied himself for whatever message Kullen would send. When it finally came though—when the combination of beats and pauses finally thrummed into Merik's ears—he found his teeth grinding and fury rising.

"What is it?" Safi asked, clutching his arm.

"The Bloodwitch follows," he croaked.

Safi's grip tightened on his arm. "We'll go back to Noden's Gift—"

"Except he follows us from behind. And the Marstoks sail to Lejna—*ahead* of us." At those words, Merik's rage flamed into being—real anger, that sent him stalking away two steps.

He had to keep this fury contained, though, for it wasn't with Safi that he was angry. It was these thrice-damned circumstances that were out of his thrice-damned control. How did the Marstoks even know where Merik was headed?

"I'll fly to the *Jana*," he said at last, his chest boiling.

"You, Iseult, and Evrane can ride east. To Lejna. As fast as the horses will go."

"Why not fly us to the *Jana* and sail to Lejna?"

"Because the Marstoks will reach Lejna first, and Kullen isn't strong enough to fight them. He shouldn't even be sailing." Merik threw a terrified glance to sea. To the *Jana*.

Cursed fool of a Threadbrother.

"Our best chance is to catch up to the Marstoks," he continued. "If Kullen and I can at least distract them, then you might still be able to reach Lejna by land. Go to the seventh pier, and then get the *Hell* out of there."

"How will you find us? After . . . after that?"

"The alert-stone. Evrane can ignite it, and I'll see its light from sea." In two long steps, Merik was to Safi. "Ride east, and I'll find you. Soon."

Safi shook her head, a sluggish side to side. "I don't like this."

"Please," Merik said. "Please don't argue. This is the best plan—"

"It's not that," she cut in. "I just . . . I have a feeling I'll never see you again."

Merik's chest split open, and for half a second, he was at a loss for words. Then Merik cupped her face and kissed her. Soft. Short. Simple.

She broke the kiss first, biting her lip as she reached for Merik's shirttails. She tucked in the edges, smoothed the cotton front. "I lied to you, you know. You aren't the *last* person I'd choose."

"No?"

"No." She grinned, a mischievous flash of teeth. "You're the second to last. Maybe third."

Laughter swelled in Merik's stomach. Up his throat. But before he could summon a worthy retort, Safi glided back and said, "Safe harbors, Merik."

So he simply replied, "Safe harbors," before walking to the cliff. Then Merik Nihar stepped off the edge and *flew*.

Safi did not watch Merik go. The need for haste spurred her to action—as did the all-too-fresh memory of the Bloodwitch. The way he'd locked her in place . . . The way his eyes had swirled with red.

It lifted the hairs on Safi's arms. Sent fingers walking down her spine.

Safi wove through the forest, accelerating . . . accelerating until she jogged, until she *sprinted*. Fern tendrils lashed her arms, spores tumbled down. To think she and Merik had only just rushed through this same jungle.

Safi stumbled into camp to find it already struck and the horses saddled. Evrane was roping the bedrolls to the saddlebags and Iseult was adjusting the girdle on the roan. The horses tossed their heads—ready to ride, despite their long journey from the day before.

At the crunch of Safi's boots, Iseult's attention whipped to Safi.

"Leaving . . . without me?" Safi panted.

"We heard the drums," Iseult explained, tack jingling as she tugged the girdle tighter. "Evrane told me what the message said."

"But where is Merik?" Evrane asked, moving away from the mare's saddlebag. Her cloak was in her hand, her baldric cinched tight to her chest.

"He flew to the *Jana*," Safi said. "He'll try to head off the Marstoks."

Iseult gave the slightest frown. "We aren't riding north, then? We aren't going to flee?"

With a quick headshake, Safi shuffled to the campfire. "We can still reach Lejna before the Marstoks." She kicked dust and ash over any remaining embers. "*Then* we can flee north."

"Mount up, then," Evrane ordered.

"Safi, you can ride with me—"

"No. You each get a horse." Evrane shrugged on her cloak, fastening the buckle with efficient, mechanical movements. "I will wait here and stop Aeduan."

A taut pause. Then Iseult: "Please don't do that, Monk Evrane."

"Please," Safi agreed. "We'll outrun him—"

"Except you cannot," Evrane interrupted, cutting her voice over Safi's. "Aeduan is as fast as any horse, and he will catch up to you no matter where you go. I can find a defensible point in the path, though, and do my best to slow him."

"Slow," Iseult repeated. "Not stop?"

"Aeduan cannot be stopped, yet he *can* be reasoned with. Or, if necessary, these"—she patted her only two remaining knives; the buckles clanked—"are not just for show."

"You'll get yourself killed," Safi argued. The demand for speed *breathed* down her neck, yet she couldn't let Evrane do something so profoundly stupid. "Please, just do as Merik ordered and come with us."

Evrane's face stilled, and when she spoke, her tone was knifed with impatience. With offense. "Merik forgets that I am a monk trained for battle. I will face Aeduan myself and you two will ride to Lejna. Now, mount up." She offered a stiff hand to Safi, and though Safi hardly needed it, she accepted.

After helping Iseult mount as well, Evrane stepped purposefully to the gelding's saddlebag and rifled out the quartz alert-stone. It glimmered gray, like the predawn sky above, and as she murmured "Alert," a brilliant blue light flared within.

"Now Merik will find you." She offered the stone to Safi. "Keep it out whenever your path goes by the sea."

Safi stared at Evrane, her silver hair rippled in the dawn breeze and flickered with sapphire from the stone. Safi unfurled her fingers to accept the heavy quartz.

Evrane gave a mollified nod. Then she removed her sword belt. "Iseult, take Merik's cutlass. It's strapped to the roan's saddle. And Safi, you take this." She laid her sheathed blade over Safi's lap. "Carawen steel is the best, after all."

Safi gulped. That small attempt at a joke had reeled her back to the moment—back to the heavy truth that many people were risking their lives to ensure Safi got to Lejna and that Merik got his trade agreement.

Safi would *not* let them down.

"Iseult," she said, drawing the words from her core—

from the very center of her witchery, "we're going to Lejna now. We won't stop, and we won't slow."

Iseult met Safi's gaze, her hazel eyes a vivid green in the alert-stone's flare. The fierceness was there—the one that always made Safi feel stronger—as she lifted her chin and said, "Lead the way, Safi. You know I'll always follow."

At those words, Evrane's lips twisted up. "You have no idea how long I have waited to hear those words. To see the two of you, astride. *Alive.*" There was an odd gleam in her eyes. "I know my words mean nothing to you now, but they will soon.

"After I face Aeduan—after I show him what he stands for—I will find both of you in Lejna. Thank . . ." Evrane choked on the word, and more laughter sputtered in her chest. "Thank you for giving me hope, girls. After all these centuries, Eridysi's Lament is finally coming true; I have found the Cahr Awen and you have awoken the Water Well. So now, as my vow demands, I will protect you with everything I have." She bowed, a somber movement that set Safi's magic to singing with the truth behind it.

Then Evrane Nihar turned and marched away.

"Moon Mother protect us," Iseult whispered. "Wh-wh . . . what *was* that?"

Safi swung her gaze to Iseult, who had regained her Threadwitch mask, though not complete control of her tongue. "I don't know, Iz. Does she think we're the . . ."

"Cahr Awen," Iseult finished. "I . . . I think she does."

"Gods below, I can't handle anymore surprises today." Safi reined the horse toward the sunrise, punching down her confusion and doubt—deep, deep, out of reach.

And, as she guided her horse to the trail, she was pleased to see the mare drag at the bit. The horses were ready for speed, Iseult was ready for speed, and Safi was ready to *end* this.

Digging her heels into the mare's ribs, Safi launched into a scudding gallop and set off for Lejna of the Hundred Isles.

THIRTY-SIX

The *Jana* was in an uproar when Merik finally touched down on the main deck. They sailed west now, the rising sun an angry thing behind the ship.

When Merik squinted at the tiller—right into the sun—he found Kullen. A hunched, wheezing shape who somehow kept a wind hauling in the sails. *Kullen.* Merik pushed off across the deck, thunder rolling over the wind-drum's boom.

An entourage streamed behind.

"Admiral," Ryber called.

Merik waved her off. "Hermin," he panted, trying to jog, speak, and catch his breath. If he was already tired, he could only imagine Kullen's exhaustion. "What's happening?"

Hermin hobbled alongside Merik. "Yoris found Prince Leopold unconscious by the Origin Well. Apparently the Bloodwitch attacked and betrayed him."

Merik's footsteps stumbled. Leopold was here now too? What the Hell was he going to do with a blighted prince?

He mentally swatted that aside for later.

"Admiral!" Ryber shouted again. "S'important, sir!"

"Not *now*." Merik hopped the steps to the quarterdeck, where the wind whipped louder, harder. As he approached Kullen, slumped at the tiller, he wondered why Ryber had allowed her Heart-Thread to push himself this hard.

"Stop this boat!" Merik roared. "Stop your wind!" He grabbed hold of Kullen's coat and yanked the man upright.

Kullen's face was gray, but his eyes were sharp behind his wind-spectacles. "Can't . . . stop," he panted. "We've got to catch up . . . to the . . . Marstoks."

"And we will, but we don't need so much speed—"

"But that's just it!" Ryber shouted, shoving up to Merik. "We *do* need speed because the Bloodwitch is here."

For half a breath, Merik could only stare at Ryber. Bewitched air stung his eyes, screamed in his ears. Then he bolted for the bulwark and yanked his spyglass free.

"Where?" he breathed, heart lodged in his throat.

"More east." Ryber gently aimed the spyglass right, until Merik saw it: a lone blur of white streaming down the sea-side road.

Merik slid the glass farther east until . . . There. Two figures, one in white and one in black, on horseback. They coursed down the same road, and the Bloodwitch was no more than a league behind them. He would be upon Safi and Iseult before Merik could even fly back to shore.

Merik snapped down the glass and forced himself to inhale—in through his nose. *The heavy scent of oncoming rain*. Then out through grinding teeth.

It helped nothing. "How the *Hell*," he ground out, "did that monster get here so fast?"

"By all that's holy," Hermin swore, peering through his own spyglass. "Is that white speck *him*?"

"His powers are straight from the Void," Ryber said gravely. Then she cried, "Kullen!" and lurched from the bulwark.

Merik bolted after, and with Ryber's help, he peeled Kullen's white-knuckled hand off the tiller. Then he slid his arm beneath his Threadbrother's.

Kullen was too cold to the touch, his clothes too damp with sweat. "You have to stop this!" Merik shouted. "Stop your winds, Kullen!"

"If I stop," Kullen answered with surprising strength, "then we lose your contract."

"Your life is worth more than a contract," Merik said, but Kullen started laughing then—a hacking, gulping sound—and he lifted a weak arm to gesture south.

"I have an idea."

Merik followed Kullen's finger, but all he saw there were dark skies and the flickers of distant lightning.

But then Ryber breathed "No," and Merik's stomach bottomed out.

"No." He towed Kullen around to face him. The first mate's hair was so plastered by sweat, it didn't even move in the wind. "That is *not* an option, Kullen. Ever."

"But it's the only option. Nubrevna needs this . . . trade agreement."

"You can barely stand."

"I don't need to stand," Kullen said, "if I'm riding a storm."

Merik shook his head, frantic now. Panicking, while

Ryber whispered over and over, "Please don't do it, please don't do it, please don't do it."

"Have you forgotten what happened last time you summoned a storm?" Merik looked at Ryber for support, but she was crying now—and Merik realized, with a sickening certainty, that she had already resigned herself to this course.

How, though? How could she give up so easily and so fast?

"We don't need the trade agreement," Merik insisted. "The Nihar lands are growing again. *Growing*, Kullen. So as your Admiral and your Prince, I command you not to do this."

Kullen's coughing subsided. He sucked in a long, vicious breath that sounded like knives and fire.

Then the man smiled. A full, frightening smile. "And as your Threadbrother, I choose not to listen." In a clap of heat and power, magic sizzled to life and Kullen's eyes shivered. Twitched. His pupils were shrinking . . . vanishing . . .

A wind ripped over the deck—collided into Merik and Ryber, almost knocking them flat. It left Merik with no choice.

He ripped off his coat, and Ryber moved to take it. The wind battered them, but they both bent into it—she aiming belowdecks with his jacket and he staggering for the tiller.

As he moved into position at the helm of his father's warship, Merik prayed once more to Noden—but this time he prayed that Kullen and everyone else in his crew survived the night.

Because the storm was on its way now, and Merik could do nothing to stop it.

Safi had never pushed a horse so hard. Sweat streaked her mare's sides, foamed on Iseult's roan. At any moment, they might throw a shoe or twist a leg, but until that happened—until the creatures gave out from exhaustion—Safi had little choice but to keep galloping down this cliff-lined road.

The girls' long shadows galloped beside them, the dawn sun a pale flame over the Jadansi that lit up a bay so wide, Safi couldn't see its end. Bare rock islands of all shapes and sizes speckled the glowing tide waters.

The Hundred Isles.

The road followed a descending curve, eventually reaching sea level—and Lejna too. After green for half a mile, they'd suddenly galloped back into a wasteland. It was all too quiet. Too dead. Safi didn't like how the alert-stone pierced the sky from its spot tied to her saddlebag. They were *literally* asking to be noticed.

"Anyone here?" Safi shouted over the four-beat hammer of hooves.

Iseult's eyes squeezed briefly shut. Then burst wide again. "No one. Not yet."

Safi's grip tightened on her reins. One hand moved to her sword hilt. *Just get to the pier.* That was all she had to do.

"Sign!" Iseult barked.

Safi squinted ahead. What had once been an ornately stamped sign now dangled atop an iron column. It was the fourth like it they'd seen.

One league—that was minutes away. Despite the tears in Safi's eyes from the wind and the dirt, despite the fact that her heart might rip from her throat with fear, and despite the fact that she and Iseult could be cut down by a Bloodwitch at any moment, Safi grinned.

She had her Threadsister beside her. That was all that mattered—all that had ever mattered.

Her horse rounded a bend. The ghost forest opened up to reveal a city ahead. Lejna's crescent shape hugged the shore, and the row-buildings that lined its streets might have once been colorful and crisp. Now they crumbled and their roofs caved in. Only three docks still stood, the rest reduced to abandoned posts jutting up from the waves.

Safi spurred the mare faster. Harder. She would get Merik his thrice-damned trade agreement.

"Is that Merik?" Iseult asked, blasting apart Safi's thoughts.

Safi searched the sea, hope soaring into her skull . . . until she spotted the Nubrevnan warship coasting into Lejna's crescent bay. It moved at a breakneck speed, sails glowing orange in the sun.

And with green-clad sailors crawling the decks.

Safi's hope plummeted to her toes. She shouted for Iseult to break, and she reined her own mare to a stop.

Iseult's roan pulled up short, dust pluming, and both girls walked their horses alongside the cliff, squinting into the sun. The horses huffed their exhaustion, but their ears were still high.

"I think that's the ship we left to the Marstoks," Safi said at last. "Princess Vivia's ship."

"It certainly looks like their uniforms. Which means we could be dealing with Firewitches."

Safi swore and ran a hot hand over her face. It was gritty with dust. Everything was gritty—her throat, her eyes, her brain—and more dust kept gusting in. "Why are there so many soldiers on a single ship? Surely they're not all *me*."

Thunder boomed from the south, brief and all-consuming. Safi twisted her head toward it . . . and a fresh slew of oaths fell off her tongue.

Storm clouds were rumbling in *fast*, and at the mouth of the bay were more ships. Marstoki naval galleons, waiting in a row as if to guard the Hundred Isles.

Or to keep the *Jana* out.

"Merik won't be able to sail in." Safi pushed the mare into a slow trot. The path veered inland; maybe the dead pine forest would offer some protection from the quickening gales and the eyes of Marstoki sailors.

"That's the least of our worries," Iseult said, increasing her roan's pace. "That first ship is almost to the Lejna piers. This is clearly an ambush—" She broke off as a fresh burst of wind pounded into her—and into Safi.

They both turned their faces away, blocked their eyes and mouths. The air tangled in their clothes and hair, clattered at the horses' tack, and then rattled through bone-dry branches ahead. The only thing that didn't bend to the wind's will was the alert-stone's light—which, Safi realized, she should probably put away. No need to *attract* the Marstoks.

As she untied the stone from her saddlebag, Iseult called, "Which pier do you need to get to?"

Good question. Safi had no rutting idea which dock was Pier Seven. There were too many empty posts to sort it out. "I'll have to try all three." She patted the mare, who was still dark with sweat but seemed better for the walking. Then she led the horse into the dead pines. "Got any ideas for a plan?"

"Actually," Iseult answered slowly, "I might. Do you remember that time outside of Veñaza City? When we wore each other's clothes?"

"You mean when we almost got killed by those Nommie-hating bastards at the tavern?"

"That's the time!" Iseult veered her roan closer to Safi, clearly hoping not to have to shout her way through this plan. Her hair flipped and flayed across her face. "We gave those men what they wanted to see, remember? But then the Nomatsi girl they *thought* they'd cornered turned out to be you."

"One of our finer tricks." Safi smiled tightly, swatting her own wayward hair from her eyes.

"Why wouldn't that same plan work now?" Iseult asked. "We can still try to reach Lejna before that ship, but if that doesn't work out—"

"Doesn't look like it will."

"—then we can ditch the horses, hide the alert-stone, and split up. I'll be the decoy and draw them into the city. You can go to the piers. Once you've reached all three, go back to the alert-stone. Light it up, and I'll find you."

"Absolutely rutting *not*." Safi glowered at Iseult.

"That's the worst idea you've ever had. Why would you put yourself in danger—"

"That's just it," Iseult interrupted. "The Truce says they can't kill anyone on foreign soil, right?"

"It also says they can't land here, but they clearly don't care about that."

"Actually, the Truce says no *foreign* vessels can land here," Iseult countered. "Their vessel isn't foreign."

"And that's exactly my point, Iz! They're tricking that clause, so why couldn't they trick other clauses too? For all we know, they don't even care if they break the Truce."

That gave Iseult pause—thank the gods—but when Safi lifted her reins to set off once more, Iseult's hand shot up.

"Threadstones," she said flatly. "You'll know if I'm in danger from your Threadstone. If it lights up, then you can come to my rescue."

"No—"

"Yes." A smile lifted the corner of Iseult's lips as she towed out her Threadstone and gripped it tight. "You know this plan could work and it's the only worthwhile strategy I can think of. Let's just be glad that Lejna is a ghost town. There's no one around to get hurt."

"Except for *us*, you mean."

"Stop arguing and start undressing." Iseult slid from the saddle and looped her reins over a low branch. Then she began unbuttoning her blouse. "A storm's coming, Saf, and you're at its eye. I can be the right hand and you can be the left."

The left hand trusts the right, Mathew always said. *The left hand never looks back until after the purse is grabbed.*

Iseult had always been the left hand—she'd always trusted Safi to distract until the end. Which meant it was Safi's turn to do the same.

Charged air burst through the forest. It lashed into Safi, around her . . . and then gathered itself *behind* her. She flung a glance back, eyes watering. Storm clouds, dark as pitch, swirled above the treetops.

"I don't like this," Safi said, *really* having to yell now. "In fact, I *hate* this—the storm and the plan. Why does it have to be 'we'? Why not just *me*?"

"Because 'just me' isn't who we are," Iseult hollered back. "I'll always follow you, Safi, and you'll always follow me. Threadsisters to the end."

A fierce, burning need rose in Safi's lungs at those words. She wanted to tell Iseult everything she felt—her gratitude, her love, her terror, her faith, but she didn't. Instead, she smiled grimly. "Threadsisters to the end."

Then she did as Iseult had ordered: she clambered from her mare and began peeling off her clothes.

Aeduan smelled his old mentor a mile away. Her scent—crisp spring water and salt-lined cliffs—was unmistakable. As familiar to Aeduan as his pulse.

And as unavoidable as death unless Aeduan was willing to leave the path—which he wasn't—or slay her where she stood.

Which he also wasn't.

The mile leading to her passed in a smear of green forest and yellow stone, predawn light and a rumbling sea storm. When he reached the narrowest point in the path—a place bordered by overhanging rocks to one side and wave-pounded cliffs on the other—Aeduan relinquished control of his blood. He gave the power of pulse and muscle back to his body and slowed to a stop.

Monk Evrane stood still as a statue before him. The only movement was the hot wind in her hair, through her Carawen cloak. Her baldric lacked all of her blades save two. Her sword was nowhere to be seen.

The older monk had not changed in the two years since Aeduan had left the Monastery. A bit browner in the face, perhaps. And tired—she looked as if she hadn't slept in days. Weeks even. Yet her hair was as silver as it had always been.

And her expression as gentle and concerned as Aeduan remembered.

It angered him. She'd never had a right to care about him—and she most certainly didn't have that right now.

"It has been too long," she said in that throaty voice of hers. "You have grown."

Aeduan felt his jaw clench. Felt his eyes twitch. "Stand aside."

"You know I cannot do that, Aeduan."

He unsheathed his sword. It was a bare whisper over the crash of waves below. "I will cut you down."

"Not easily." Evrane flicked up her wrist. A vicious blade dropped into her hand. With a smooth dip of her back foot, she sank into a defensive stance. "You have forgotten who trained you."

"And you have forgotten my witchery, Monk Evrane." He

eased his parrying knife from his hip and matched Evrane's knee-bent stance.

She moved—a spin that sent her white cloak flying. Distracting—certainly, but Aeduan had his eyes on her hand. After all, she was the one who'd taught him that the key to any knife fight was controlling the knife hand.

Evrane whirled in close. He ducked low to meet her.

But it was not her blade that he met. It was her feet—a boot heel in his neck. *Then* the dagger at his chest.

He tottered back, not as fast as he should have. As he could have if he were fighting anyone but her.

With a burst of magic, he shot back ten steps—too fast and too far for her to easily catch. Then he glanced down.

Her knife had cut him. Four shallow slices that his witchery would heal whether he wanted it to or not. He would waste power on harmless surface wounds.

"You know who they are," Evrane called. She stalked steadily toward Aeduan. "It is your sworn duty to protect them."

Aeduan watched her from the tops of his eyes. "Have you heard the rumors, then? I can promise you, Monk Evrane, they are not the Cahr Awen. They're both Aetherwitches."

"It doesn't matter." She smiled, a terrifying smile of rapture and heady violence combined. "We must have misinterpreted the Records, and no Voidwitch is needed. For I saw it, Aeduan: those girls woke the Nubrevnan Origin Well—"

Aeduan attacked then, sword out, yet for some reason, he did not lunge as hard as he should have. He did not veer his course at the last second or toss out knives in quick succession. He simply thrust out his sword, and, as he expected, Evrane swirled left and parried easily.

"The girls swam to the spring's center," Evrane said.

"Impossible." Aeduan spun left.

"I saw them do it. I saw the magic ignite and the earth tremble." She jabbed at Aeduan with her knives—and then snap-kicked her toe into his knee.

A toe that had a blade upon it.

Pain exploded in Aeduan's leg—as did blood. He bit back a roar, and twirled aside before more blades could reach him.

She was trying to wear him down. Small wounds to slow him.

But she was breathing heavily now—something that would never have happened two years ago. She *was* tired, and she would never outlast Aeduan. Even with her quick, relentless attacks. Even with him going easy.

"What you saw," Aeduan said, skipping back, "was what you wanted to see. The Well would never let them reach its center."

"Yet it *did*." Evrane paused, hands and blades at the ready and an exultant gaze fastened on Aeduan. "Those girls touched the spring's source and it awoke. Then the waters healed Iseult."

Iseult. The Nomatsi girl with no blood-scent.

She was *not* one of the holy Cahr Awen—Aeduan refused to believe that. She was too plain. Too dark.

As for the Truthwitch, if she were indeed the other half of the Cahr Awen, then giving her to his father would mean breaking his Carawen vow. The mere thought of that ignited ire in Aeduan's veins. He would *not* lose all his fortunes because Monk Evrane was a gullible, desperate old fool.

So in a burst of speed, Aeduan let a throwing knife fly.

Evrane swatted it from the air and used the momentum of her spin to loose a knife of her own.

Aeduan jerked left. Caught the knife—volleyed it back.

But Evrane was already dancing up the overhang, using the terrain to her advantage. She scrabbled easily up the stones, unsheathing her stiletto—her final weapon—and then sprang out at Aeduan.

He dove forward, rolling beneath her. Then he was on his feet, sword slashing out—

It clashed against Evrane's stiletto, locking in place on a parrying prong. Her arm trembled. Her small blade would never stand up to a sword; her strength would never stand up to Aeduan's.

"Remember . . . who you are," she ground out. The steel of Aeduan's sword slid . . . slid ever closer to her. At any moment, her elbow would give. Aeduan's blade would slice through her neck. "The Cahr Awen have come to save us, Aeduan. Remember your duty to them."

Her stiletto slipped.

Aeduan's blade arced down. Bit into her neck—

But he stopped it. Halted the blade at the last fraction of a second. Blood pooled on the steel. Evrane gasped for air, eyes huge.

"We are done here," Aeduan said. He wrenched back his sword. Drops of blood sprayed. Splattered on Evrane's face and Aeduan's uniform.

Evrane's whole face fell. She became a tired, old woman before his eyes.

It was more than he could bear so, without another word, he sheathed his sword and launched himself down the path.

Yet as he rounded a bend into the woods—and as thunder clapped much closer than it should've—steel thunked into Aeduan's back. Grated against his ribs. Pierced his right lung.

He recognized the feel of it. A Carawen throwing knife—the very one he'd thrown at Evrane only moments before.

It hurt—not to mention all the blood that bubbled up in his throat made breathing tricky. Yet Aeduan couldn't help but smile, for Evrane was as ruthless as ever. At least *that* hadn't changed.

THIRTY-SEVEN

This might have been the dumbest plan Iseult had ever enacted and, by the Moon Mother, Merik and his contract had *better* be worth it.

Eighty paces, Iseult thought as she watched the seventeen sailors approach her at full-speed down Lejna's main seaside avenue. Twelve more thumped down the first pier at which their ship was now anchored.

Because, of course, Marstoks had reached town right as Iseult and Safi had. Now soldiers—some of them no doubt Firewitches . . . or worse—were pelting toward her with terrifying grace.

Iseult didn't move. Didn't flinch. She stood at the very edge of the city. When the sailors reached twenty paces away, she would move. That would be enough distance to stay ahead—or at least stay ahead long enough for Safi to get into town.

Iseult had gotten a good glimpse of the terrain on the ride in, but most of her planning was based on guesswork. A lot of what she *thought* she knew about the cobblestoned streets and byways of Lejna could be wrong, and if those gaps in rooftops weren't streets and that big square hole wasn't a central courtyard, then she was, quite simply, screwed.

There were other holes in her plan too—like how the white kerchief cut from Safi's shirt (meant to hide Iseult's hair) might not stay put in all this wind. Or how her choice of an alleyway between row houses—with its shadowy darkness and steep incline—was a terrible one.

Or how standing here with her arms high and cutlass still sheathed might be a bit too vulnerable.

Sixty paces. The sailors' eyes were now visible, the gleam of their outthrust sabers impossible to ignore—as were their Threads of purple eagerness.

They won't kill you, she reminded herself for the hundredth time. *Stasis. Stasis in your fingers and in your toes.*

Iseult sensed Safi's Threads behind her—burning with dark green readiness as she crept through the shadows of the forest. If Safi was ready, then Iseult would be ready too. Initiate, complete—just in reverse this time.

Thirty paces.

Iseult braced her heels, sucked in a breath . . .

Twenty paces.

She ran.

Shadows swallowed her whole, but gray light shone ahead. Cobblestones and storefronts.

Footsteps followed behind. Even in their soft boots and with lightning crashing closer every second, there was no missing the drum-roll of Marstoki feet.

Iseult skidded to the end of the alley, turning hard and aiming right. *Street—a wide one.* It was exactly what she'd hoped for, and it headed diagonally up the hill, toward some distant place that might be a courtyard.

That had better be a courtyard.

Broken doors and shattered windows coursed along the sides of her vision. The wind was still at her back, pushing her forward. Rain fell now too. It splattered on the street—made the cobblestones slick.

In the back of her mind, Iseult considered how to account for the rain when she reached the courtyard. It would affect her defenses . . .

Or not, since there were definitely more men pouring out of the street ahead. The ones on the pier must have moved up the hill to cut her off.

Iseult had run herself directly into a corner and her plan was ruined before it had even begun.

No, no. She could *not* let panic claim her. All she needed was a moment—just a brief second without Marstoks breathing down her neck.

Iseult twisted sharply left; her feet slipped; she tumbled forward . . . and caught herself on a signpost. She lost precious time doing it, but no time to regret. Gulping in air, she punched her legs back into full speed. Surely this alleyway would lead her to another main road. Surely she could find a moment to think.

Iseult honed in on individual cobblestones. On slamming one heel in front of the other and sucking down one more breath . . . Then one more after that. *Stasis. Stasis.* She could do this.

She wheeled onto another wide lane.

Where there were *more* Marstoks—barreling from

another alleyway ahead. One after another, they sprinted at her. She was trapped. Or . . .

Iseult skidded left—right through a broken door.

Her shoulder shrieked at the impact. She bit through her tongue, filling her mouth and her mind with the bark of pain and the taste of blood. It was exactly the distraction she needed. Calm briefly swept in and allowed her to scan her terrain: a shop with a counter and a doorway beyond.

Iseult launched herself over the counter. The window exploded, and the storm bawled through.

Soldiers too, but Iseult was already uncoiling and hammering out the back door into an alleyway. She skirted right—sharp and fast. Lightning flashed and wind gusted overhead, but the buildings protected her.

Iseult hit a corner, swooped around . . . and poison darts skittered into the wall behind her. Which meant there were Poisonwitches in the mix now. Marstoki Adders.

Suddenly the buildings opened up. Light and wind sprayed down, and Iseult found herself in a courtyard. *The* courtyard she'd hoped for. A stained, ancient fountain stood at the center. It was the Nubrevnan god Noden—all carved muscles and coiling hair—waiting on His coral throne.

Iseult hopped onto the knee-high fountain rim, slick with wet algae and bird crap. It made spinning toward the Marstoks easier, but didn't offer much stability.

All the while, the sailors tumbled toward Iseult, a swarm of rain-soaked uniforms and focused Threads. Small and lithe to enormously broad-chested, decidedly female to could-be-anything-really.

With the wind and the rain thrashing down and with black clouds churning overhead, Iseult's ears were useless, her skin hammered to wet numbness.

Then the first soldiers reached the courtyard . . . and slowed. They eased to careful stops, and a female voice bellowed over the tempest's howl, "She isn't the one!"

Iseult's gut cracked. Her left hand flew to her head. No kerchief. Her black hair was soaked through and fully visible.

"Find the real domna!" the woman ordered. "Back to shore!"

The ice in Iseult's stomach spread upward. Choked off her air. They were going to leave—just like that?

"Wait!" she shrieked, springing off the fountain. If she could engage a few of them and keep them here, then maybe Safi could still make it.

Iseult hurtled after the retreating soldiers. Several had paused and were swiveling back. Slowly, so slowly. Iseult reached for her cutlass, ready to attack.

Until a *crack!* of heat slashed through her. Then a coiling in of Threads, so violent that Iseult's knees almost caved.

In the space of a single breath, countless Threads had simply snapped. Broken.

Cleaved.

The nearest soldier twisted all the way toward Iseult, his eyes black. His skin boiling.

Then he started shredding at his sleeves—at his skin—while behind him, more and more soldiers were lurching back around toward Iseult.

And all of them were cleaving.

THIRTY-EIGHT

From behind a bleached alder, Safi watched the ramshackle wharfside street. Her toes tapped, her fingernails dug into rough bark, and the urge to help Iseult was practically shredding her spine.

But she stuck to the plan, and she waited until every single Marstok had followed Iseult down the alley. Then she scooted toward Lejna.

She kept her eyes on the ship, rocking wildly at the first pier. Several sailors scurried about, but they were too busy with the growing thunderstorm to look Safi's way. Still, Safi unsheathed her Carawen sword just in case.

Her eyes skipped between the approaching road and the nearest pier. Empty, empty . . . all of them were empty of life. One of those docks had to be Pier Seven that Uncle Eron had specified in his contract.

Although, at this point, Safi wouldn't have been surprised to learn there was no Pier Seven at all—that Uncle Eron had never had any intention of fulfilling his end of the deal.

Well, the joke was on him, then, because come hell-flames or Hagfishes, Safi was getting Merik that contract.

A fat raindrop smacked Safi's head right as she stepped onto the first cobblestones. She glanced at the sky—and then promptly started swearing. The storm was almost to Lejna, and it was definitely *not* a natural one—not with all those black clouds.

What are you doing, Prince?

The rain picked up speed. A sudden wave crashed over the high-water mark, submerging the first dock and swathing the cobblestones in slime.

So much for stealth, then. Safi kicked into a jog . . . then into a full sprint. At the storm's current rate, all three piers would be swallowed entirely in minutes.

Safi reached the first expanse of wood. It was coated in algae and creaked dangerously beneath her heels. She took four steps out, her eyes never leaving the tipping warship at the end, and then turned back, ready to barrel for the next pier.

But the dock was slick, the waves too rough and the wind far too strong. Safi was so focused on where to put her feet, on when to hop over the next surge of waves, that she didn't notice the dark figure slinking nearby.

Not until Safi was on the street again did she finally catch sight of the Marstoki Adder thirty paces away and *right* between her and the next pier.

"If you come with me," the Adder shouted, her voice—and shape—decidedly feminine, "then no one gets hurt!"

No thank you, Safi thought, flinging up her sword. This

woman was weaponless, and Safi was not. She flung up her sword.

"I'm giving you one chance, Truthwitch! You can either join the Marstoks as an ally or you can die as our enemy!"

Safi almost laughed at that. A dark, angry laugh, for *here* was the moment she'd spent her whole life waiting for: the moment when her witchery put a target on her forehead and soldiers came to claim her.

Admittedly she'd expected Hell-Bards all these years, but Adders would more than suffice.

Safi sank into her stance, ready to attack. Lightning burst. She blinked—she couldn't help it—and, by the time she got her eyes wide, wind was slashing into her. Rain piercing her. And, of *course,* the woman was no longer weaponless. Where heartbeats before her hands had been empty, there was now a flail, its iron ball the size of Safi's skull.

"Where the rut did that come from?" Safi muttered. "And are those *spikes* on that ball?" She skipped back—though the wind would hardly let her move—and briefly considered if Carawen steel was strong enough to slice through iron.

She decided it wasn't—right as the spiky mass of death flew at her head.

Safi ducked sideways. The flail zoomed past her forehead. A single barb slashed across her skin. Blood gushed into her eyes, and for the smallest fraction of a moment, the contract's words blazed behind her eyeballs: *All negotiations will terminate should the passenger spill any blood.*

Then the Adder's boot was kicking at Safi's face and she had no more space to think.

Safi smacked the foot with her elbow, successfully tipping the Adder's balance—and also successfully bringing down the flail.

Safi met the iron chain with her blade. Yet where she thought the ball's momentum would carry the chain around her sword—and allow her to *yank* the flail from the Adder's grip—the iron seemed to melt apart . . . to slide over the steel . . . and to re-form on the other side.

Safi blinked blood and rain from her eyes, thinking *surely* she had mis-seen. But no. The woman was shifting chain link after chain link down to the iron ball—making the flail even bigger, the spikes even larger.

Oh, shit. Safi was facing an Ironwitch. *Oh, shit, shit, shit.* She had *severely* misjudged her opponent. She couldn't fight this woman alone. Carawen steel was still iron, so her only chance would be to lose the sword, get past the Adder, and then run like the Void was at her heels.

So that was exactly what Safi did. She flung her sword sideways—silently apologizing to Evrane—and when the Adder snapped out her flail, aiming for Safi's thighs, she jumped as high as she could.

Not high enough, though. The flail zoomed for her ankle, spikes and iron to crush her bone.

Instinct took over. Midair, Safi twirled and punched out her right heel. It crunched into the Adder's throat.

She didn't get a chance to see what happened next. A charged wind exploded behind her, and the next thing she knew, she was flipping over the Adder, *carried* by the cycloning storm. Then cobblestones were careening toward her face—

much too fast—and Safi crashed down. Pain jarred through her.

Rain fell now. Lightning crackled and hissed, carried on this raging wind.

Safi scrambled up, blinking away water and teeth-shattering aches. Then she set off, stride determined, for the second pier. As before, she took four steps onto the slick wood before racing back to the quay.

To where the Adder had caught up to her.

So Safi did the only thing she could conjure: she tossed up her hands and shouted, "You can have me!"

But the Adder didn't lower her flail. "Allow me to shackle you, Truthwitch, and I will believe you!"

"Truthwitch?" Safi called, shrugging innocently. "I think you have the wrong girl!" *False,* her magic scraped. "I'm only a domna, and not even from a good estate!"

"You can't trick me," the woman roared. Her uniform rippled in the wind. Her scarf was unwinding, a black flag that flipped and flew.

For some reason, Safi couldn't stop staring at that black flap of fabric . . . and she couldn't push past her witchery. *False, false, false!* it shrieked over and over. *Wrong, wrong, wrong!* It was far too great a reaction for a simple lie.

Then Safi understood. Then she recognized.

Cleaving.

As soon as that word sifted through her consciousness, the sky exploded.

A blast of heat and light erupted from the clouds. It blanketed all sight, swallowed all sound, masked all feeling.

Safi's knees gave out. She toppled forward, blinking and

reaching and *straining* for some sense of where she was, where the Adder was . . .

And above all, who was cleaving.

A fuzzy image coalesced—the Adder. On her knees. Staring at her arms in horror—arms that Safi noticed hazily had the sleeves ripped back.

Was *this* woman cleaving?

Safi pushed all her strength into sitting upright, into fighting the wind and the static so she could search the woman for signs of black or oil . . .

Then she realized the Adder's scarf was missing. It had unwound completely and now the woman's black hair sprayed in all directions, framing a bronze, sharp, *beautiful* face.

Safi was staring at the Empress of Marstok.

The Airwitched storm had disrupted Aeduan's magic—blocked Safiya's scent from his blood. Or maybe she wore more salamander fibers. Either way, he'd had no choice but to push his power aside and simply follow the Marstoks by sight through Lejna, hoping they led him to Safiya. When he'd realized the sailors were converging in a courtyard, he ascended to the rooftops, for a better view—and hopefully better speed.

Yet by the time Aeduan had reached the courtyard, he'd spotted the sailors sprinting back toward the sea . . . And the Nomatsi girl with no blood-scent standing beside a statue of the Nubrevnan god. She had duped them all. A decoy.

Aeduan cursed, instantly flinging out his magic to search for the Truthwitch. He would deal with the Nomatsi girl later. But then Aeduan caught the scent of something familiar: *Black wounds and broken death. Pain and filth and endless hunger.*

Cleaving.

Aeduan's witchery fell into the background, briefly dulled by surprise. By revulsion as the Marstoks ripped at their uniforms. As black oil bubbled beneath their skin. As the Nomatsi girl squared off to fight them.

Aeduan knew he should leave—*now.* Yet he didn't. He waited. He watched . . . Then he decided.

A snarl broke through his lips. This was the Puppeteer's doing. Aeduan recognized her work by now. She must have figured out where the Truthwitch was—and now she tried to help Aeduan in her own twisted, cleaving way.

Which meant that if Iseult died here, Aeduan would be to blame—the exact opposite of a life-debt repaid.

So Aeduan ran to the roof's edge and jumped. He flew three stories toward the fountain. Air rushed into his ears. Loud, fast. His right foot touched down. He pushed the power into a roll and tumbled to his feet—with barely enough time to keep from careening into the Threadwitch.

Who was swinging her cutlass at Aeduan's head. He dove low and steel whistled through the air.

"*No!*" was all he could shout before he unsheathed his sword and rounded on the nearest Cleaved. The man was an Adder, his black hood scratched off and his skin oily and writhing. He chomped at the air, searching for someone worth devouring.

Aeduan drove his blade through the Adder's shoulder . . . then ripped it back out. Hot acid sprayed harmlessly onto Aeduan's cloak. Yet a drop landed on his exposed face, searing into his cheek.

So their blood really is *poison.*

There was no time to dwell on that revelation. The cleaved man was already dragging himself onward. His acid blood eating through his uniform, revealing chest and arms fit to erupt from the roiling pustules.

"The head!" the girl shouted before spinning her blade wide.

Steel bit through flesh. Through nerve and bone. The Adder's head went flying, his body wobbling uncertainly while acid spurted like a fountain into the courtyard. It splattered the girl's clothes, eating through the fabric. She stumbled back . . . then front-kicked the headless body. It collapsed.

The girl gaped at her sleeves, as if shocked by the holes. *Fool.* Hadn't she seen the acid at work? It was her fault she'd stepped into it like that. Yet Aeduan still found his mouth opening and the words "Stay behind me" coming out.

Then he angled toward four more Marstoks and set to work. They lurched at Aeduan . . . and, of course, the stupid Threadwitch did not stay behind him as ordered. Instead, she swooped out, blade arching at neck height.

She missed; the nearest Cleaved hopped back with unnatural speed. *Windwitch,* Aeduan realized as he lanced out with his own blade. Again, the man leaped backward, skin brewing with black.

Air blasted into Aeduan; he staggered toward the fountain. The Threadwitch listed too, though she held her stance better.

A deafening crack sounded behind Aeduan. He had just enough time to twirl around—to see a rift splintering the fountain—before the Threadwitch grabbed his cloak and *yanked.*

The fountain exploded in a blur of ancient stone and water—but Aeduan and the girl named Iseult were already soaring for the nearest alley. Clearly one of these Marstoks was a Tidewitch, and now that he had a source, Aeduan would be no match.

A magicked wind battered into Aeduan's back, knife-like and meant to flay apart his skin. Yet Aeduan's cloak protected him, and he protected the girl.

Aeduan pumped his legs faster, pushed Iseult on. "Right!" he bellowed, and she skittered down the new passage.

Rain fell hard now. Biting. It only added to the cleaving Tidewitch's power. A bloodthirsty screech lifted over the streets. Several screams—tens of them, even.

"Left!" Aeduan barked at the next shadowy intersection. He had no idea where he was going, only that he needed a larger gap between him and the Cleaved. He could hide the Nomatsi girl until this ended.

Yes, Aeduan would repay his life-debt to Iseult, and then he would never think of her again. She wasn't the Cahr Awen; she wasn't his problem.

Aeduan spotted a recessed doorway at the end of the road. The door was loose on its hinges. "Ahead!" he shouted. "Inside!"

The Threadwitch's sprint faltered. She flung a look back, eyes wide.

"*Do it.*" He grabbed her arm, grip vicious, and *pumped* his witchery through his blood. His speed doubled, the alleyway blurred, and the girl cried out. She wasn't running as fast, and he couldn't push her blood faster.

But then they were to the doorway and he was shoving her in, yanking her toward the back of the house, pushing her through a kitchen—their gasps for air almost as loud as the howling wind and beating water outside.

Pantry. Aeduan saw the tall cupboard at the back corner of the room, dangerously close to a shattered window . . . but the only hiding place he could spot. He shoved the girl toward it. "Get inside."

"No." She spun around to face him. "What are you trying to do?"

"Repay a life-debt. You spared me; now I spare you." With a flick of his wrist, he unfastened his salamander cloak. "Hide beneath this. They won't smell you." He offered it to her.

"No."

"Are you deaf or just stupid? Those Cleaved are seconds away. Trust me."

"No." Her hazel eyes shook—but not with fear. With stubborn refusal.

"Trust. Me." Aeduan spoke more softly now, ears and magic straining for signs of the Cleaved. They would be here at any moment and this Nomatsi girl still wasn't budging.

And if she didn't budge, then Aeduan's life-debt would remain unpaid.

So he summoned the only words he could find that would make her go: "*Mhe varujta,*" he said. "*Mhe varujta.*"

Her eyebrows shot high. "How . . . how do you know those words?"

"The same way you do. Now get inside." Aeduan shoved her into the cupboard—hard. His patience was spent, and he smelled the approaching Cleaved. *Bloodstained secrets and filth-encrusted lies.*

The girl did as she was told. She stepped into the pantry, staring back at Aeduan with that odd face of hers. He tossed her the cloak. She caught it easily.

"How long should I wait?" she asked. Then her gaze raked over his body. "You're bleeding."

Aeduan glanced down at bloodstains from the old wounds and new patches from Evrane. "They're nothing," he muttered before easing shut the door. A shadow fell over the girl's face, but Aeduan paused before he shut her out entirely. "My life-debt is paid, Threadwitch. If our paths cross again, make no mistake: I *will* kill you."

"No, you won't," she whispered as the door clicked shut.

Aeduan forced himself to stay silent. She deserved no response—it would be her mistake if she thought he would spare her.

So, lifting his nose and pushing his Bloodwitchery high, Aeduan whirled away and strode into a world of rain, wind, and death.

* * *

Merik flew in a blind terror. Kullen was almost to Lejna, hurtling down to the first pier. But something was wrong. He had torn away from Merik quicker than Merik could fly—and with an uncontrolled violence that Merik had never seen before. It had sent him spinning wildly behind, grappling for any sort of control he could find.

When Merik finally reached the city, he slammed onto the splintered first pier—to where he'd seen Kullen go down. Yet he saw nothing in the cycloning storm. Even more frightening, his magic pulsed against his insides. Scratched wildly beneath his skin—as if people were cleaving nearby. As if they would soon send Merik teetering over the edge.

In leaping bounds, Merik crossed the pier toward shore. Lightning cracked beside a storefront, and Merik caught sight of Kullen. He knelt at the mouth of an alley, and fat, blinding veins of electricity ran the length of him. Then the lightning faded, and Kullen was hidden by air and seawater, kelp and sand.

Merik reached the street. He flew headfirst toward the spinning wall of lightning and wind.

No—there was more now. Glass and splintered wood. Kullen was felling entire buildings.

Merik crashed against it all in a roar of light, sound, and static. Then it swept him in. The wind bent him. The water beat him. The magic engulfed him.

And Merik couldn't fight it. He wasn't half the witch Kullen was, and with his own powers feeling as if they might cleave at any second, Merik could do nothing but let himself go.

The cyclone funneled him upward, so fast he left his stomach somewhere far below. Up, up, up he flew. His eyes clenched shut. Debris pelted him. Glass peeled off his exposed skin.

But then, as quickly as he'd been sucked into the storm, Merik was released. The spinning stopped; the wind let go. Yet the storm raged on—Merik heard it, felt it . . .

Below.

He forced his eyes open, forced his witchery to keep him aloft just long enough to gauge what had happened.

Merik was in the clouds above Kullen's storm. Yet the cyclone was climbing, sucking in the clouds around Merik and, soon enough, sucking at him too.

But there, hundreds of feet below, was a dark speck amidst the storm. Kullen.

Without thought, Merik threw himself forward in a painful thrust of his own wind. Then he released his hold on the magic, and he fell. Faster than he had risen through this storm, he now plummeted back to the street. As he flew through a world of hell and witch-storm, he never let his streaming eyes lose sight of his Threadbrother.

Kullen saw him. Crouched on the cobblestones beside a torn-apart . . . no, a *still* tearing-apart building. Kullen clutched his chest with his head tipped back, and Merik knew that Kullen saw him.

Kullen's hands thrust up. A blast of wind knocked into Merik, catching him as he fell. Easing him onto the street. Into the eye of Kullen's storm.

As soon as Merik's boots were on the ground, he lurched for his Threadbrother. Kullen was kneeling, facedown now.

"Kullen!" Merik yelled, his throat ripping to produce any sounds over the storm's endless thunder, the crack of building frames, and the shattering of windows. He dropped to the street. Glass shards bit into his knees. "Kullen! Stop the storm! You have to relax and *stop this storm!*"

Kullen's only response was a shuddering in his back—a shudder Merik knew too well. Had seen too many times in his life.

Merik yanked his Threadbrother upright. "Breathe!" he roared. "*Breathe!*"

Kullen angled his face toward Merik, his lips moving ineffectually, his face gray and bubbling . . .

And his eyes as black as Noden's watery Hell.

Breathing could not save Kullen—not from this sort of attack. Merik's Threadbrother was cleaving.

For a single, aching moment, Merik stared at his best friend. He searched Kullen's face for some sign of the man he knew.

Kullen's mouth opened wide, the cyclone *screaming* with his fury, and the corrupt magic charged through Merik, threatening to cleave him too.

But Merik didn't cower back or push Kullen away. The storm outside was nothing compared to what raged within.

Kullen's fingers, black blood oozing from burst pustules, latched on to Merik's shirt. "Kill . . . me," he croaked.

"No." It was the only thing Merik could say. The only word that could possibly contain everything he felt.

Kullen released him and, for the briefest flicker of a heartbeat, the black in Kullen's eyes shrank inward. He gave

Merik a sad, broken smile. "Good-bye, my King. Good-bye, my friend."

Then, in a blur of speed and power, Kullen sprang upward and rocketed off the pier. Wind and wreckage crashed down on Merik, slammed him against the street and blanketed all his senses. For an eternity, all that Merik felt and all that Merik *was* was Kullen's cyclone.

Until a great *crack!* split the chaos, and wood and pain thundered down.

Merik's world went black.

THIRTY-NINE

Iseult sat in the cupboard, her eyes squeezed shut and her senses extending outward, her witchery reaching for some sign of life. Of the Cleaved.

As for the Bloodwitch named Aeduan, she was as blind to his Threads as she had been. Only by looking at his face had she had any idea of what he'd felt—which was nothing at all as far as she could tell. And though Iseult had trusted Aeduan not to kill her—and to probably not feed her to the Cleaved—there had been no *verujta* there.

Mhe verujta. It was the most sacred of Nomatsi phrases—a phrase that meant *trust me as if my soul were yours.*

It was what the Moon Mother had told the Nomatsi people when she guided them out of the war-filled far east. It was what parents said to their children when they kissed them good night. It was what Heart-Threads said in their marriage vows.

For Aeduan to know such a phrase could only mean he'd lived with a Nomatsi tribe . . . Or that he *was* Nomatsi.

Whatever the source of his knowledge, though, it didn't matter. He had helped Iseult; now he was gone.

Iseult's magic pricked up—she sensed a cleaved Marstok stalking by the broken window. Three wriggling strands of death moved with it, just like the ones she'd seen over the corpse in Veñaza City. Just like the ones she'd seen through the Puppeteer's eyes.

These Threads were bigger, though. Fatter and strangely long. Stretching into wispy tendrils that vanished into the sky, like a marionette on a stage . . .

Iseult's breath punched out. *Puppeteer.* She was looking at the Puppeteer's work right now. These Severed Threads stretched all the way to Poznin—Iseult was sure of it—which meant the Puppeteer had somehow cleaved all these men from afar.

No, not somehow. She'd done it with Iseult's help.

All those plans and places tucked away in your brain, the Puppeteer had said, *have made the Raider King very happy. That's why he gave me this grand mission for tomorrow. So, thank you—you made all of this possible.*

The Puppeteer had realized Iseult and Safi aimed for Lejna, and she had cleaved whomever she could grab hold of.

Iseult was suddenly boiling beneath her cloak. Suffocating inside this cupboard. Burning inside her own head. She should have fought the Puppeteer harder. She should have avoided sleep and stayed *away* from that woman's shadowy grasp.

Iseult was going to retch . . .

No, she *was* retching. Dry heaving and hacking because

these Cleaved were on her soul now. She had killed them by being weak.

A new set of Threads flickered into Iseult's awareness. A bright, living set that shoveled through Iseult's sickness. She knew these Threads—that particular shade of determined green and worried beige.

Evrane. The monk was right outside the window.

In a heartbeat, Iseult was out of the cupboard. She couldn't let Evrane die too. She leapt through the shattered window. Glass grabbed at her cloak, but its buckle held fast. Then she was pounding down the narrow street—aiming right, in the direction she sensed Evrane's Threads.

Rain cut her, burning the wound on her face. The storm was getting worse—the sky had come alive. It all roiled and tossed in a single direction: toward the wharf.

Through the rain, Iseult glimpsed white. She pushed her legs faster, screaming, *"Evrane!"*

The white paused. Materialized into Evrane's shape and silver head. She glanced back, her face a mask of surprise but her Threads blue with relief.

Black moved along a rooftop. Streaked from a shadowy storefront.

The Cleaved.

"Behind you!" Iseult shrieked, heaving out her cutlass.

She was too late. The Cleaved converged on Evrane, and the monk vanished beneath a horde of death.

Iseult burned up the road as fast as she could, screaming and slashing the entire way. Her blades severed necks, sliced through legs. Pustules burst and acid hissed on the walls. On Iseult's cloak.

Yet she swung and heaved and chopped, screaming Evrane's name all the while.

Soon enough, there was no one left to kill. The Cleaved were running . . . and where Evrane had fallen, there was nothing but a wide stain of red.

Iseult spun, frantically searching doorways and shadows.

But the monk was as gone as the Cleaved.

So Iseult squeezed her eyes against the storm and reached for Threads. *There.* On the other side of the nearest alley was a set of frightened white Threads, swirling with gray pain. A *lot* of gray pain.

Iseult pushed into the wind and hugged Aeduan's cloak tight. He had told her the truth: the Cleaved didn't seem to smell her.

She reached an intersection of narrow row houses. Blood dragged along the ground, already splashing away with the rain.

Iseult picked up her pace and followed Evrane's trail as long as she could, but the downpour quickly washed away the blood. Even straining to sense the monk's Threads, she soon lost sight of them too. They moved so fast. Much faster than Iseult could travel in this storm.

When Iseult shoved onto a familiar narrow street, she caught sight of the wave-beaten harbor several blocks ahead. She was on the western edge of town where she'd first come in. Sand and sea-spray bore down on her, and the storm surged out. Wood cracked; buildings crumbled.

With an arm thrust up to protect her face, Iseult frantically searched for signs of Evrane. A flash of white in the storm or a flicker of the monk's Threads. But Iseult saw nothing. The storm devoured everything. Iseult could barely sense the Cleaved anymore—in fact, they seemed to be fleeing the city and racing north.

Lightning exploded. Iseult's eyes shuttered against the light, the heat. Magic crashed over her, shivered on her skin and in her lungs. She tumbled against the nearest wall and shrank within the cloak.

For half of a seemingly endless breath, Iseult was crippled by her guilt. By how much she hated herself and her magic and the Puppeteer.

But then the storm withdrew. The noise and the pressure and the mauling rain pulled back . . .

And Threads scissored into Iseult's awareness. *Living* Threads nearby. She lurched upright, tossing back the cloak to find the cyclone leaving. It spiraled over the sea like a writhing black snake.

Iseult limped into a demolished alley, searching for the living Threads. Her feet crunched through glass until at last she found the Prince of Nubrevna, bruised, bleeding, and trapped beneath a fallen building.

Yet he was still alive, and Iseult was still alive to save him.

A laugh writhed in Safi's throat as she stared blearily at Vaness. Of *course*, it would be the Empress of Marstok. Who else would have the balls to fight with a flail? Or be insane enough to come after Safi herself?

Rain fell. Wind charged—strong as an ox and growing

stronger—and waves threatened to cover the entire street. A hurricane roared at the other end of the city, but Safi never looked away from Empress Vaness. If the woman cleaved . . .

But gods below, could she kill an Empress?

Safi's eyes flicked to the flail, an arm's length from Vaness and all but forgotten. *If* the Empress was cleaving, that weapon was Safi's only option . . .

Vaness stilled. She stopped scratching her arms, stopped moving at all. Her gaze was pinned behind Safi.

"Twelve protect me," she said.

If she's speaking, then she isn't cleaving, Safi thought. Whatever corrupt magic had surged through Vaness, the Empress hadn't succumbed.

But then Safi made the mistake of following Vaness's gaze. The storm was leaving, a single figure at its center. Lightning sizzled down its black form as it curved and twisted and charged out to sea.

Kullen.

Oh gods. Safi swayed, but forced her head to stay up so she could search the street. She saw no sign of Merik. Surely he had not been killed. Yet before Safi could propel herself that way, Vaness shouted, "Give up, Truthwitch."

Shit. Ever so slowly, Safi turned back to Vaness, who stood with her flail ready.

Safi wet her lips. They tasted like blood and salt. Maybe if she could distract Vaness, she could bolt away. "Why you?" she asked. "Why not send your soldiers to kill me? Why risk yourself?"

"Because, I am a servant to my people. If I must dirty someone's hands, then I will always dirty my own."

Safi blinked. Then she laughed—a broken, shocked sound. It would seem Vaness was just like Merik in that regard. Still . . . "This is much more than just . . . *dirtying* your hands, Empress. You were almost killed by a hurricane—and you almost cleaved too."

"If my enemies had claimed you first, then you could topple me. Yet in my hands, you will save a kingdom. My kingdom. To me, that is worth dying for."

Ah. Safi sighed at those words, and something deep and ancient flickered awake at the base of her spine. *One for the sake of many.* She understood that now.

"Surrender." Vaness flicked her hand, and the spiked flail pendulumed. "There is nothing you can do."

False, Safi's magic breathed, and with that prickle of power, *everything* from the past few days washed over her. A deluge of words and lies that people believed about her.

. . . live out the same unambitious existence you've always enjoyed . . . This isn't about you anymore . . . Only you would be so reckless . . . There is nothing you can do . . .

Then a single bright thought rose to the surface: *If you wanted to, Safiya, you could bend and shape the world.*

Uncle Eron had said that, and Safi realized—almost laughing as she did—that he was right. She wasn't trapped inside her skin or her mistakes, and she didn't need to change who she was. Everything she needed was inside of her: the tools from Mathew and Habim—even Uncle Eron—and the solid, unwavering love of her Threadsister.

Safi *could* bend and shape the world.

And it was time to do so.

In a single, fluid burst, Safi hooked a heel behind Vaness's ankle and punched the Empress in the nose. Vaness fell backward to the street.

And Safi *ran*—flat out for the third pier. No looking back, no thinking. *This* was who Safi was and who she wanted to be. She thought with the soles of her feet, sensed with the palms of her hands. A bundle of muscles and power honed to fight for the people she loved and the causes she believed in. Her life hadn't been leading up to Veñaza City or the flight from the ball. It had been leading up to this race to the final pier.

It wasn't freedom she wanted. It was belief in something—a prize big enough to run for and to fight for and to keep on *reaching* toward no matter what.

She had a prize now. She ran for Nubrevna. She ran for Merik. She ran for Iseult. She ran for Kullen and Ryber and Mathew and Habim, and above all, she ran for *herself*.

Soldiers bloomed in the corners of her vision. A blur of green uniforms pouring from Lejna's side streets. But they were too slow to catch up—at least not before Safi got to where she needed to be.

She felt it to the very core of her witchery, and with each explosive cry of *true-true-true* in her chest, Safi drove her legs faster.

She was ten paces from the pier now.

Five.

Something small and *strong*—like the handle of a flail—punched into Safi's knee. She fell, but instinct took over. She swiveled into a graceless roll . . . and unfurled back into her sprint.

Then she hit the first plank of the pier, and pain shattered through her.

So furious, it masked all sight.

So explosive, it swallowed all sound.

Safi screamed. She crashed forward. Her arms crumpled beneath her.

Her left foot. She'd been hit by the flail's spiky head. Her bones were smashed. Blood gushed.

But she was on the pier, and spilled blood or not, that contract had to be fulfilled. It *had* to be.

Black boots swarmed into Safi's vision from all directions. In seconds, two Adders had hauled Safi upright and locked her in manacles.

As the Empress approached, shouting orders in Marstok that Safi found *far* too difficult to understand, she was pleased to spot a black eye blossoming on the Empress's face. And ah, that was a lot of blood coming from her nose.

The two Adders clamped their hands on Safi's shoulders despite the fact that she couldn't have run—or even have *walked*—no matter how hard she tried. In fact, were it not for those hands on her shoulders, she wasn't sure she could keep standing as Vaness leaned in close.

And though Safi wanted nothing more than to blink, to cry, to *beg* for someone to heal her foot, she met Vaness's gaze and did not look away.

At last, Vaness smiled. It was a *terrifying* smile with all the blood dripping between her teeth. "You cannot escape me now."

"I . . . wasn't trying to," Safi croaked—even though she really just wanted to scream. She forced herself to raggedly laugh. "If it's my magic you want, Empress . . . if you think I'm so powerful . . . then you're mistaken. I know truth from lie, but that's it. And even when I know the truth . . . that doesn't mean I always *tell* it."

Vaness's jaw tightened. She leaned in close, as if trying to read the secrets in Safi's eyes. "What would it take to earn your loyalty, then? To ensure you tell me the truths that I need and help me save my kingdom? Name your price."

Safi stared at the Empress's swelling, purple face, and she nudged at her Truthwitchery for some sign of the woman's sincerity. It seemed impossible that Vaness would offer something so vast . . . Yet beneath all of Safi's blazing pain, her witchery shimmered its confirmation.

A triumphant smile curled on the edge of her lips—although that *might've* been a pained grimace. It was hard to tell at this point.

"I want trade with Nubrevna," she said. "I want you to send an envoy to Lovats, and I want you to negotiate the export of food in exchange for . . . for whatever it is Nubrevnans have to offer."

Vaness arched a bloodied eyebrow, and a breeze sent her wet hair flying across her face. "Why would you want that?"

"Same as you." Safi tipped her head back toward the city—then wished she hadn't. She was losing too much blood for quick movements. Or for *any* movements, really. "I'll dirty my hands for the people that matter to me. I'll run as far as I have to and fight as hard as I can. If that's what it takes to help them, then that's what I'll do."

To Safi's surprise, Vaness offered a small—*genuine*—grin in return. "You have a deal then, Truthwitch."

"And you have the use of my magic." Relief shuddered through Safi—or maybe that was a warning jolt from blood loss.

Safi swung her fuzzy gaze toward the street she thought Merik had vanished down—it was near where she'd last seen Iseult. For a long moment, all Safi heard was the slosh of water against the dock. All she felt was the soft, cleansing rain on her cheeks. All she thought of was her family.

She nodded in her friend's direction, wishing them a silent good-bye. Praying they were all right . . . and knowing they'd come for her.

Then the hollow *thwack* of more feet cut through Safi's thoughts and brought on *excruciating* pain.

"We will fly now," Vaness said, beckoning to the shortest sailor in the crowd. He bore the tattoo of a Windwitch. "Our fleet is not far. Can you do that, Truthwitch?"

"Yes," Safi breathed, swaying into one of the men holding her up. She flashed a grin at him and said, "I'm Safiya fon Hasstrel, and I can do *anything*."

As those words fell from her tongue, her magic perked up . . . and then purred like a lion in a sunbeam.

True, it said. *Always and forever true.*

FORTY

When Aeduan had seen the Cleaved attack his mentor, he had acted without thought—diving in to retrieve her bloodied form. Hacking, slashing, disemboweling *anyone* in his way.

Once he was to her—once he had her limp form in his arms—Aeduan had latched on to Evrane's blood to keep the hole in her neck from bleeding out.

Then Aeduan had sprinted from Lejna as fast as he could, his witchery fueling him on. He would take Evrane to the Origin Well, for that was the only place he could think of. If its waters were indeed flowing once more, then it might just save Evrane from the hole in her neck.

When he couldn't sprint anymore, Aeduan jogged.

When he couldn't jog anymore, he walked, his magic never releasing Evrane's blood. Distantly, he knew he had lost his chance to claim the Truthwitch, but he didn't care. Not right now.

Aeduan carried Evrane league after league, cliff after cliff, step after staggering step and, for the first time in years, he was afraid.

It took him half the day to recognize what he felt. The emptiness in his chest, the endless loop of his thoughts—*Don't die. Don't die.*

He knew this went beyond life-debts. Against everything Aeduan wanted to be—against everything he *believed* himself to be—he was afraid.

Before he saw the river, he heard its rumble over the buzz of afternoon insects and screeching birds. He felt the mist off its rapids, mingling with the day's humidity. He also smelled the eight soldiers waiting by the Origin Well's stairs. Someone must have found Prince Leopold and thought Aeduan might return.

So Aeduan used what little power he had left to choke off the soldiers' breaths. It took forever. Aeduan was weakened; the eight men were not. Aeduan swayed in the wind, listing as wildly as the trees. He would drop Evrane if he had to stand much longer.

The soldiers finally thumped to the earth, and Aeduan stumbled by. Then he climbed, slowly but purposefully, up the worn steps to the Origin Well. Over the flagstones to the ramp. Into the water to float Evrane on her back.

She began to heal.

Aeduan sensed it more than he saw it. Whatever power was at work here moved so gradually that it would take days for her body to fully repair. Yet Aeduan felt her blood start to flow on its own. He felt the new flesh grow where her throat was cut.

Still, he kept a firm hold on her blood until enough of her throat had mended for her to breathe. For her heart to pump unhindered.

Then Aeduan carefully floated Evrane to the Well's ramp and eased her onto the stones. He kept part of her legs submerged—so the healing would continue—before he clambered out of the Well, spraying water on the flagstones. Despite the extra weight of saturated clothes, he was surprised to find his spine erect. His witchery fully restored . . .

And his mind unable to ignore what was clearly before him: the Origin Well was alive again. Even if he hadn't seen the magic at work, when he'd stood in that water, he had felt sentience.

Oneness.

Completion.

This Well was opening a single, sleepy eye, and it wouldn't be long before it awoke entirely.

Which meant—as impossible as it was for Aeduan to accept—the Truthwitch was half of the Cahr Awen and Iseult . . .

That Nomatsi Threadwitch with no blood-scent—and another Aetherwitch too . . .

She was the other half. They were the pair that Aeduan had pledged his life to protect. The vow he'd sworn when he was thirteen—before his father had reentered his life—was now being called upon, yet Aeduan couldn't decide if he should answer.

He'd never thought this day would actually come—a day when all his training and his future would be given up to the mythical, ancient Cahr Awen.

It was easy for Evrane. She'd spent her entire life a believer. It *completed* her to have the Cahr Awen return.

But for Aeduan it was a hindrance. He'd been forced

into the Monastery by circumstance, and he had stayed there because he'd had nowhere better to go—nowhere else that wouldn't kill a Bloodwitch on sight. Now, though, he had plans. Plans for himself. Plans for his father.

Aeduan didn't know to whom he owed his loyalty—his vows or his family—yet he was at least certain of one thing: he was grateful the Well had saved Monk Evrane.

Perhaps that was why Aeduan found his feet carrying him to the nearest cypress tree. Its trunk glowed red in the brilliant dawn sun, its green, vibrant branches rustled on the humid breeze.

More leaves had grown since yesterday.

Aeduan knelt on the flagstones. Water dripped, dripped, dripped—from his clothes, from his hair, and even from his baldric, which he'd forgotten to remove. He barely noticed and simply curled over, flat against his knees and with his palms resting on the cypress trunk. Then he recited the prayer of the Cahr Awen.

Exactly as Evrane had taught him.

I guard the light-bringer,
And protect the dark-giver.
I live for the world-starte,
And die for the shadow-ender.
My blood, I offer freely.
My Threads, I offer wholly.
My eternal soul belongs to no one else.
Claim my Aether.
Guide my blade.
From now until the end.

When he'd finished the memorized words, he was glad to find them as tasteless as they'd always been—and he was also glad to find a mental list already scrolling through his brain. *My blades are wet; I'll need to oil them. I need a new salamander cloak—and a horse too. A fast one.*

It was liberating to know he could ignore his Carawen vow so easily, even with the Origin Well right beside him. For the time being, he had a box of silver talers to give his father, and that was all that mattered.

Aeduan gave a final glance to his old mentor, the monk called Evrane. She had color in her cheeks now.

Good. Aeduan had finally repaid one of his life-debts to her.

So with his fingers flexing and wrists rolling, the Bloodwitch named Aeduan set off to join his father, the raider king of Arithuania.

With great effort and *all* the strength left inside her, Iseult heaved and rolled and shoved wooden beams off Merik Nihar. Shafts of morning light broke through gray clouds. The first pier and an entire block of buildings had been leveled. Reduced to splintered timbers by Kullen's storm—a storm that must have claimed the first mate as well. No souls or Threads moved alongside the now gentle waves. No birds winged, no insects sang, no life existed . . .

Except for a swarm of green, flying into the horizon. At the very center, Iseult sensed the faintest hint of dazzling Threads.

Safi.

She was gone. Gone. Iseult had lost her, and it was just one more mistake to add to her soul.

But she muscled past those thoughts and continued her back-bending fight against the building frame. All the noise and movement roused Merik from unconsciousness, his Threads abruptly raging into life. Iron pain and blue grief.

He lay on his back, hunks of skin gone and glass shards burrowed deep.

"What hurts?" Iseult asked, dropping beside him. No stutter held her tongue. No emotions held sway.

"Everything," Merik rasped, eyes cracking open.

"I'm going to check you for broken bones," Iseult said. *Or for worse.* When Merik didn't argue, she set to gently kneading his body, from the top of his head to the tips of his boot-clad toes. She had done this a hundred times with Safi over the years—Habim had taught her how—and she sank into the forgiveness of a cold, methodical movement.

Stasis. The breeze skipped through someone else's wet clothes and kissed someone else's skin. Merik's wounds—they all bled on someone else—and Iseult wouldn't think of the Puppeteer. Of the Cleaved. Of Evrane or Kullen or Safi. *Stasis.*

Throughout the inspection, Iseult's eyes darted to Merik's Threads, checking for any flash of brighter pain. Each plucking out of glass sent them flashing, but only when Iseult hit his ribs did they erupt with agony. A groan rolled off his tongue. His ribs were broken; it could be worse.

Next, Iseult turned her attention to Merik's skin, checking that none of the removed glass or wood had opened any dangerous cuts. Blood stained the street, and as she wrapped his own torn shirtsleeve around a gash on his forearm, Merik asked, "Where . . . is Safi?"

"The Marstoks took her."

"Will you . . . get her back?"

Iseult loosed a tight breath, surprised by how much her lungs ached with that movement. *Would* she get Safi back?

In a panicked rush, she finished the makeshift bandage and wrenched out her Threadstone. No light flickered, which meant Safi was safe. Unhurt.

It also meant Iseult had no way to follow her Threadsister. But what had Safi told her? One of Eron's men would be coming here—to a coffee shop. Iseult could wait—would *have* to wait—for that person. He would help Iseult reach Safi, whoever he was.

She dropped the Threadstone. It thunked against her breastbone. Then she returned her attention to Merik and said, "You need a healer." As soon as the words were out, she wished she could swallow them back, for, of course, Merik raggedly asked, "My . . . aunt?"

The urge to lie was overwhelming—and not just a lie for Merik, but a story that Iseult could cling to as well.

It wasn't my fault, she wanted to say. *The Cleaved got to her, and* that *wasn't my fault either.*

But it was Iseult's fault, and she knew it.

"Evrane was attacked by the Cleaved." Iseult's tone was colorless. Deliberate. A thousand leagues away and coming from a different person's mouth. "I don't know if she survived. I followed her, but she left the city."

Merik's Threads gave out then. The blue grief took hold

completely, and he blinked back tears, his breaths choking in a way that must have sent pain shattering through his broken ribs.

That was when the glacier finally cracked, and Iseult gave up her control. She curled onto her knees beside Merik and, for the second time in her life, Iseult det Midenzi cried.

She had killed so many people today. Not on purpose, and not directly, yet the burden seemed no less vast. No less complete.

She almost . . . she almost wished Corlant's curse had killed her in the end. At least then all of these lost souls might still be alive.

Eventually, Merik was too ill for her to ignore. He was pale, shaking, and his Threads were fading too fast.

So Iseult shoved aside everything she felt—every Thread that was never meant to hold sway—and she scooted closer to Merik. "Where is the *Jana*?" she asked, thinking his crew could get him to a healer. She and Safi had left the horses, and Iseult had no idea where the nearest living city might be. "Highness, I need to know where the *Jana* is." She cupped his face. "How can I reach it?"

Merik was shivering now, his arms clutched to his chest, yet his skin roasting to the touch. His Threads were growing paler and paler . . .

But Iseult would be damned if she was going to let him die. She leaned in close. Made him meet her eyes. "How can I contact the *Jana*, Highness?"

"Lejna's wind . . . drum," he croaked. "Hit it."

Iseult released his face, her gaze flying over the street . . .

There. At the eastern corner of town, only a few blocks away, was a drum identical to the one on the *Jana*.

Iseult scrabbled upright. The salty morning spun, and her muscles felt like shredded glass. But she put one foot in front of the other . . . until at last she reached the drum.

She hefted up the mallet—there was only one, and she prayed it was a bewitched one, able to blast wind far and true. Then Iseult pounded the drum. Over and over and over again.

As she hammered—as she *slammed* her soul and her mistakes into the hide drumhead—she strategized. Because she still had that. She still had the skills to analyze her terrain and her opponents. She still had the instincts to pick the best battlegrounds.

Safi had initiated something a bit larger this time—getting kidnapped by Marstoks was definitely a new high—but no matter what it took, Iseult would figure it out.

She would get Merik to a healer.

She would find a way to stop the Puppeteer—to keep that shadow girl from *ever* cleaving anyone again.

She would get answers about Corlant's curse—and perhaps find Gretchya and Alma again too.

And, above all, Iseult would go after Safi. Just as she beat this wind-drum, just as she ignored the screaming in her arms and the exhaustion in her legs, she would follow Safi and she would *get her back*.

Threadsisters to the end.

Mhe verujta.

* * *

Merik was unconscious when the *Jana* arrived. By the time he reached Noden's Gift and the Origin Well, he was almost dead. There was saltwater in his wounds, his witchery had been pushed too far, and his three broken ribs didn't want to heal.

When he finally awoke on a low bed in an upside-down cabin in Noden's Gift, he found his aunt beside him, her silver hair as radiant as always. Her tender smile shaking with relief.

"I have good news," she told him, her grin quickly shifting to a concentrated frown as she dabbed salve onto Merik's arms, his face, his hands. "The Voicewitches in Lovats have been calling Hermin nonstop all day. It would seem that, despite their attack on Lejna, the Marstoks want to open trade. Yet they will only negotiate with *you*, Merik—and I imagine that has Vivia frothing at the mouth."

"Ah." Merik sighed, knowing he should be happy. Trade was all he'd ever wanted, and now he had proven that he could bring it back to Nubrevna.

Yet the triumph tasted like ash, and he couldn't convince himself it had been worth the cost.

"Where is . . . Iseult?" he asked, voice reedy and weak.

Evrane's expression soured. "Your crew left her in Lejna. Apparently, she convinced Hermin that she was fine by herself—that she had someone coming to meet her at a coffee shop."

As Merik tried to puzzle through whom Iseult could possibly meet, Evrane went on to describe how Prince Leopold had vanished from Noden's Gift. "One moment, he was in the brig, under heavy guard, and the next, his cell was completely empty. All I can guess is that a Glamourwitch somehow helped him escape."

It was too much for Merik's grief-addled, pain-stricken brain. He shook his head, mumbled something about dealing with it all later, and then settled into a magically induced, healing sleep.

Two days later—and three days after losing Kullen—Merik finally trekked from Noden's Gift to the Nihar cove. Evrane parted ways with him, claiming she had to go to the Carawen Monastery immediately, and Merik couldn't push past his pride long enough to ask her to stay.

She had been coming and going since he was boy, and why should that change now?

So, with Hermin limping at his side, Merik hiked past trunks and branches—all of them spindly with *new* bursts of life. Lichen, insects, green, green, green—Merik couldn't explain it . . . and he couldn't help wishing that Kullen were here to see it.

In fact, Merik couldn't seem to move past Kullen. Memories burned behind his eyeballs, and loss throbbed at the base of his skull. Even as he watched living birds swoop over the cove, even as Hermin rowed him to the warship and fish inexplicably splashed in the waves—all of it tasted of ash.

Merik's crew was lined up on the main deck when he finally dragged himself onto the *Jana*. Each man wore strips of iris-blue linen around his biceps to mourn their fallen comrade, and they all gave a crisp salute as Merik walked past.

He barely noticed, though. There was only one person he wanted to see—the one person who would understand how Merik felt.

He glanced at Hermin. "Bring Ryber to me, please."

Hermin cringed. "She's . . . gone, sir."

"Gone?" Merik frowned, that word incomprehensible. "Gone where?"

"We don't know, sir. She was on the ship when we came to you in Lejna, and we thought she was on it when we reached the Nihar cove again. But . . . we aren't sure. All we know is she ain't on the ship now."

Still, Merik frowned—for where would Ryber go? *Why* would Ryber go?

"She did leave a note, although it doesn't say a thing about where she went. It's on your bed, sir."

So Merik heaved into his captain's cabin, ribs shrieking their protest at that burst of movement. He took long, almost jogging steps to cross the room, where he found his wrinkled coat draped across the mattress. Resting atop it was a slip of paper.

Merik snatched it up, eyes flying over Ryber's almost illegible scrawl.

My Admiral, my Prince,

I'm sorry to go, but I'll find you again one day. While I'm gone, you have to become the king that Kullen always believed you to be.

Please. Nubrevna needs you.

Ryber

(Also, check your jacket pocket.)

Merik's forehead tightened at those final words. His jacket pocket? *The trade agreement.*

Merik grabbed for his coat, hands shaking, and gently towed out the contract. On the last page, ashy fingerprints were everywhere—along with a fat scribbling.

Uncle:

Don't be such a horse's ass about this trade agreement. Prince Merik Nihar has done everything he could to get me to Lejna unharmed, so

Merik flipped over the page.

if I get hurt on the way or I don't even reach this pier that you've arbitrarily chosen, you can't blame him. Prince Merik and Nubrevna deserve a trade agreement with the Hasstrels. I promise you this, Uncle: if you don't fulfill this contract and open up trade with Nubrevna, then I will simply write an agreement of my own. It will be a terrible one that gives Nubrevna all the advantage and all the money.
Remember: my name carries power, and contrary to your beliefs about me, I don't lack initiative entirely.

Then, in hideously uncoordinated script, was a signature:

Safiya fon Hasstrel
Domna of Cartorra

Something hot scratched up Merik's throat. He whipped the contract back over and saw that his signature and Dom Eron's were still there—while any reference to "spilled blood" had been removed entirely.

Merik didn't believe it. His mind was numb; his heart had stopped pounding. That night when he'd awoken to Safi's hand on his chest—it was because of this. She'd stolen the document and written on it with ash from the fire.

And now Merik had trade with the Hasstrels. With Marstok too.

A silent, hysterical laugh rose in his throat. He had lost more than he'd ever thought he could lose, yet there was an aching certainty welling in his lungs.

Slowly, almost dizzily, Merik sat on the edge of the bed. He smoothed out the trade agreement, his fingers smudged black, and set it aside.

Then Merik Nihar, Prince of Nubrevna, rolled back his head and prayed.

For all that he had loved, for all that he had lost, and for all that he—and his country—might still regain.

Safiya fon Hasstrel leaned against the bulwark on the Empress of Marstok's personal galleon, crutch in hand. The verdant coastline of Dalmotti-claimed lands drifted by, and Safi tried to pretend she *wasn't* boiling in this midday sun.

This was a land of palm trees and jungle, frequent fishing villages and humidity thick enough to swim in. She wanted to enjoy the beauty of it all, not melt into the miserable heat.

Hundreds of years ago, this land had belonged to some

nation called Biljana. Or that was what Safi remembered from her tutoring sessions. She knew better than to believe history books now.

At least, despite the heat, her gown of white cotton was relatively cool—though the uncomfortable iron belt that cinched her waist wasn't. Iron was all the fashion in Azmir—no doubt because Vaness had *made* it the fashion. She could, after all, control anyone wearing it.

Yet, even with the belt, Vaness had still insisted Safi don a steel necklace as well. It was a chain, delicate and thin, but with no end and no beginning. The empress had fused it around Safi's neck, and despite grunting and straining as hard as she could, Safi hadn't been able to snap it off.

Thank the gods, though, that Vaness had deemed Safi's Threadstone harmless.

With a crooked smile at the landscape, Safi angled her weight onto her crutch. Her left foot was bandaged and healing, thanks to the concerted effort of six healer witches from Vaness's navy. Apparently—as the Empress had continually insisted—she hadn't intended to hurt Safi as badly as she had. Safi was simply too valuable (as Vaness put it) for any "rough handling," and Safi's life had never been at any risk back in Lejna.

Safi's Truthwitchery had told her that *that* wasn't true, but she'd let the lies slide.

Footsteps clipped out behind Safi, and the Empress of Marstok glided to her side. Her dress of black cotton flipped in the wind—a tribute to the eighteen Adders and sailors that had cleaved in Lejna. Vaness would hold a memorial once they reached her palace in Azmir.

"I have news for you," she said, speaking in Marstok. "The Twenty Year Truce has ended." Vaness showed no reaction as she added, "Cartorra already prepares for its first attack to try to reclaim you. So let us hope"—she raised a single, cool eyebrow—"that you were worth it, Truthwitch."

She offered an emotionless, inscrutable smile. Then, without another word, the Empress of Marstok strode back the way she'd come.

And Safi sank onto her crutch, dazed. Lost. She didn't know if she should laugh out loud or sob hysterically, for this was exactly what Uncle Eron—and everyone else in his scheme—had tried to prevent, wasn't it? The Truce had dissolved early; now there could be no peace.

And Safi certainly wasn't helping Uncle Eron's plans by allying with Vaness—and therefore the entire Empire of Marstok. Yet she refused to feel guilt or regret to her recent choices. For once in her life, Safi had carved her own path. She had played her own cards and there'd been no one to guide her hand but herself.

A hand that includes the Empress and the Witch, she thought whimsically—even though thinking of taro made her think of the Chiseled Cheater . . . and *that* just pissed her off. She'd get her money back from him one day.

Forehead puckering, Safi brought out her Threadstone. The ruby glinted in the sun, and seeing the coral fibers wrapped around the rock made her feel less alone. She liked to pretend that Iseult—wherever she was—held her Threadstone too.

Safi might not be with her Threadsister, she might not

be buying a home in Veñaza City, and she might *technically* be a prisoner, yet she felt no fear over what lay ahead.

All that physical training, Merik had said, *plus a witchery men would kill for. Think of all you could do. Think of all you could* be.

Safi sighed, a full exhale that loosed something tight from within her chest and sent her heart uncoiling in a way she'd never felt before—in a way that slowed her bouncing legs. Stopped them completely.

Because now she knew what she could do—what she could *be*. She had gotten Merik his contract and won negotiations with Marstok too. She had bent the world and shaped it into something better.

Safi's magic hummed, happy and warm with that truth, and after dropping her Threadstone behind her dress, she opened her arms. Let her head loll back.

Then Safiya fon Hasstrel reveled in the sun on her cheeks. In the spindrift on her arms. And in the future that awaited her in Marstok.

ACKNOWLEDGMENTS

First and foremost, I want to thank my Threadsister, Sarah J. Maas. *Mhe Verujta,* braj. You're the soul twin I can't live without; the best friend who reads draft after draft; the cheerleader who always hauls me out of my cookie-eating, video-gaming binges; and basically the inspiration behind this entire series. Friendships can be just as epic as romances—maybe even more so—and I wanted the world to see that. Plus, if we lived in the Witchlands, we would *totally* be the Cahr Awen, right? At the very least, we'd be sea foxes chomping up anyone who dared oppose us ("Get out of the way!").

To Amity Thompson: You read so many iterations of this book—and you did so with babies and books of your own to deal with. You were always there when I needed to work through a broken plot point, vent my endless frustrations, or gush about Dragon Age. So, thank you.

Enormous thanks to Erin Bowman, for being a Hero Squad sister for life, for listening when I needed listening, for critiquing when I needed critiquing, and for just being there. Always.

To Ashley Hubert: You're amazing. You read *Truthwitch* and gave me feedback (plus an ego boost) *right* when I desperately needed it. I'm so glad we became friends.

To Nicola Wilkinson, the brains behind the Witchlanders street team: Merik is yours. Or Special Baby K. Or any of the characters, really, since you have gone above and beyond for this book and this series. There are no words to express how grateful I am for all you do and all you have done.

To Maddie Meylor: You've been with me since the start, and for some reason, you're not sick of me yet. Thank you for all the reading, the gushing, and the simple fact that you're you.

To my fellow slayer of darkspawn, Rosanna Silverlight: You singlehandedly saved my muse with your pep talks. Plus, your feedback was exactly what I needed *when* I needed it.

To the rest of my Thread-family, Dan Krokos, Derek Molata, Biljana Likic, Alexandra Bracken, Vanessa Campbell, Sarah Jae-Jones, Jodi Meadows, and Amie Kaufman: Thank you. For the support, the shoulders to cry on, the much-needed beta reads, and the many, many giggles.

Thanks to Lori Tincher, for answering my horse questions, and to Cindy Vallar, for all the help with nautical shenanigans.

A giant thanks to Jacqueline Carey, for putting up with my naïve, star-struck self. *Thank you.*

To the teams at Tor and New Leaf that have worked tirelessly to sell my books and turn my drivel into something worth reading, as well as package and design the entire *Truthwitch* world: I would be lost without you. Thank you from the bottom of my three Link hearts (that one's for you, Jo). And Whitney, you "have a whole relationship with dairy products I don't understand."

To the Misfits & Daydreamers (and every other reader, blogger, and aspiring author out there): I have no words to express my gratitude. You guys listen, support, and remind me every day of *why* I do this.

To my family—Mom, Dad, David, and Jen—thank you for enduring (and often nurturing) my distracted daydreaming for all these years . . . And also thank you for bragging about me at the grocery store. That makes me feel truly special.

And last—but not least—I have to thank my husband, Sébastien. I couldn't have written this book (or any other) were it not for you and your endless, unconditional support. I love you forever and then some.

AND FOR THE TRUTHWITCH STREET TEAM . . .

I want to give a huge thank you to the #Witchlanders, a fabulous group of international readers that helped spread the word about *Truthwitch* and became my dear friends along the way. Below are the members divided by their various elemental clans! Thank you so, so much!

AETHER CLAN

Melissa Lee
Julia Espejo
Karina Romano
Jen Stasi
Lizzie Shillington
Jillian
Hannah Hudson
Cassie Frye
Mishma Nixon
Jessica Sun
Jocelyn Beck
Nicole Brake
Kaye Thornbrugh

AIR CLAN

Kelly Tse
Meg McGorry
Roxanne Stouffs
Brian Gould
Jordan Bishop
Casey Marie Sennett
Ryan Bada
Theresa Snyder
Katie Steele
Tanvi Berwah
Becca Fowler
Cristian Gallego Dominguez

EARTH CLAN

Kelly Peterson
Melanie R.
Adriana Marachlian
Hannah Martian
Adriyanna Zimmermann
Sana
Hedvig Solveig
Samantha Smith
Tiffany Jyang
Hannah Mae Astorga
Isabel C.
Meredith Anderson Coffman

FIRE CLAN

Jana Lenart
Sondra Boyes
Faith Y.
Aneli Aguillon
Emily Louie
Megan Miklusicak
Lindsey Y.
Rachel C.
Brittany Todd
Nancy López

VOID CLAN

Danielle Fineza
Michaela Gustafsson
Jennifer Laird
Nori Horvitz
C.J. Listro
Elena M-ski
Laura Ashforth
Karen Bultiauw
Sarah Kershaw
Olivia Walther
Lauren Johnstone
Claudia Victoria

WATER CLAN

Louisse Ang
Stephanie Kaye
Katrina Tinnon
Alejandra Garcia
Olivia Whetstone
Carine Verbeke
Cat Moll
Alyssa Susanna
Charlene Cruz
Kim Lüneburg
Kim Lisibach
Madeleine Rose
Gabi Mohrer